STARSHIP'S MAGE

CHIMERA'S STAR

BOOK FOURTEEN
OF THE STARSHIP'S MAGE SERIES

ISBN: 978-1-989674-45-1

W0008746

This edition published in 2024 by:
Faolan's Pen Publishing Inc.
22 King St. S, Suite 300
Waterloo, Ontario
N2J 1N8 Canada

ISBN-13: 978-1-989674-45-1 (print)

A record of this book is available from Library and Archives Canada.

Printed in the United States of America
1 2 3 4 5 6 7 8 9 10
First edition
First Printing 2024

Cover art by Roman Chalyi
Faolan's Pen Publishing logo is a registered trademark of Faolan's Pen Publishing Inc.
Read more books from Glynn Stewart at faolanspen.com

CHIMERA'S STAR

BOOK FOURTEEN
OF THE STARSHIP'S MAGE SERIES

GLYNN STEWART

FAOLAN'S PEN
PUBLISHING

faolanspen.com

CHAPTER 1

BY ANY USUAL STANDARD or objective measurement, the man in the big seat at the center of the starship had no right to be there.

First, the starship was an exploratory cruiser of the Royal Martian Navy and he had *never* been an officer of the RMN. In a long-past era, where he'd served the Protectorate of the Mage-Queen of Mars in a more usual fashion, he'd risen to Mage-Major of the Royal Martian Marines. He'd never been an RMN officer, so he would never have commanded a starship.

Second, the only people qualified to use the semiliquid silver simulacrum of the ship in easy reach of his hands were the Jump Mages of the Protectorate's Mage Guilds—or the Navy Mages of Her Majesty's Navy—and he had never qualified to be one of those. While he had the silver-inlaid runes in his palms to interface with the starship's jump matrix and he had been *trained*, he'd never formally qualified as a Jump Mage.

Third, of course, was that he was wanted for treason and a list of other crimes as long as his arm.

Fourth was that the starship, *Rose,* had been intended for a completely different commanding officer. That man was dead now, having been immune to the mind-control nanotech the man in the chair had used to take control of the ship.

Because, of course, none of the reasons why Kay, also known as Nemesis One, *shouldn't* be in the chair aboard the cruiser *Rose* mattered. The only thing that *mattered* was that he'd taken the ship by storm, with a cadre of elite commandos of the organization known as Nemesis and ruthless use of the mind-control weapon known as Orpheus-Ultima.

None of the people they'd used Orpheus on were left alive. The roughly six hundred Nemesis personnel Kay had brought along with him weren't really enough to crew *Rose* to her full effectiveness, but they had been more than enough to handle the Martian officers and crew when Orpheus had run out.

Kay had hoped that at least some of those personnel would be salvageable. He'd been wrong.

"Report," he ordered aloud.

The dark-haired man commanding *Rose* knew he was terrifyingly gaunt to an outside eye. He wasn't entirely sure *why*, though he suspected he should probably eat more. His continual lack of appetite had never impeded his physical or magical strength, and he found his ever-more sunken appearance a useful tool.

The woman who appeared in response to his order was one of the few people who *could* nag him to eat. Adwoa Tomas was a towering Black woman, as plump and curvy as her Captain was gaunt and bony, and—*unlike* Kay—was a fully trained Jump Mage.

Not a Navy Mage. She'd been a senior Ship's Mage in civilian shipping before falling into the orbit of Nemesis. She was a useful officer but no threat, physically or magically, to Kay.

"We're still pulling together sensor data," Tomas told him. "The scanners on this ship are incredible, but that's the *problem*."

Kay turned the chair away from the simulacrum to look at her. He'd just used the ship's runes to make the final jump to their destination, and fatigue tore through him. He thought he was hiding it well, but he also knew that Tomas, at least, knew perfectly well how he was feeling.

She'd cast the jump spell more times in her life than he ever would. She had to know the bone-deep exhaustion of funneling *all* of your magic into that spell.

"What I'm looking for should be relatively obvious," he pointed out.

Twenty years earlier, the Royal Order of the Keepers of Secrets and Oaths had found this system by collating information from a dozen archaeological dig sites and a thousand telescopes. The main purpose of the Keepers—the cause that Kay, who had been Lieutenant Kent Riley then, had been recruited for—had been to keep secret the knowledge of just *how*, exactly, magic had been brought back to humanity.

The open history, involving a brutal eugenics project by a fascist totalitarian state already run on eugenicist principles, was bad enough. The secret behind it had been even more horrifying: a nonhuman species called the Reejit had created and guided that horrific program to produce humans whose brains could be extracted to fuel the alien ships.

And twenty years ago, the Keepers had found the location of a Reejit fleet base, just barely within striking distance of the modern Protectorate of Mars.

"That's part of what I'm saying, sir," Tomas told him. "Scans are suggesting there's a *lot* here, but... none of it's active."

"There's a *fleet base* here, Tomas," Kay snapped. He looked around him. *Rose*'s bridge also served as her simulacrum chamber, the critical nexus of the magic and runes that allowed her to jump. Part of that required a perfect view of the outside of the ship—and now the nature of what he was seeing cut through his fatigue.

Rose was running dark, as many of her systems shut down or venting into heat sinks as was physically possible. Kay could, theoretically, conceal the ship further with magic, but he'd brought her in far enough away from the base that that shouldn't have been necessary.

Still, the scale of the infrastructure detected by the telescopes and incorporated into the dataset that had fractured the Keepers and birthed Nemesis should have been visible around the fourth planet.

He started stabbing commands into the repeater control panel on the Captain's chair. Tomas said nothing, clearly judging that it was better for him to see for himself.

The fourth planet was highlighted on the all-encompassing displays, and he stared at it. They were far enough out to be nearly impossible to detect, even without magic, but that also meant they were far enough out that the planet was little more than a dot.

He'd expected it to be the blue-green dot of a habitable world, a Reejit colony whose populace provided economic and industrial support to a major fleet base. Instead, it was a vague brown color.

Kay dragged a finger down a digital slider on his screen, and swallowed as the image zoomed in. At this distance, he couldn't see if there were inactive stations or debris around the planet, but if there had been the major fleet base infrastructure that the Keepers had detected, he would have seen it.

"That's impossible," he whispered. "We ran the analyses a hundred times. It took data from across the entire Protectorate to be sure, but we *were* sure.

"There is a Reejit fleet base here."

"There *was* a Reejit fleet base here," Tomas said softly. "I only saw the highest summaries of the data, sir, but we're over a hundred light-years from the edge of the Protectorate. Two hundred and more light-years from Earth. Our data is ancient... and something happened here."

He swallowed away as much of his fatigue as he could and nodded slowly.

"Then we find out what," he growled. "*This* base may not be the threat we feared, but anyone who would *destroy* it may be an even worse danger than we thought!"

Despite Kay's best efforts and intentions, rest after a jump wasn't optional. He'd been determined to make the final jump into the nameless star system the Keepers had feared, but in hindsight, letting one of the other three Jump Mages on the ship cast the spell would have left him more able to command.

That, he supposed, was the exact kind of thought process and training that coming up through the Royal Martian Navy would have given. As it was, he had to learn much of commanding a ship the hard way.

As he freshened up and put on another insignia-less uniform—thanks to the logistics teams of the RMN, *Rose* had a practically infinite supply of shipsuits and uniforms and effectively zero civilian clothes—he reflected that at least he didn't need to worry about chain of command.

Everyone aboard *Rose* had seen Kay in combat. None of them were so foolish as to think they could challenge him. He hadn't been primarily a direct-action specialist for some years, not since Nemesis's founder had died at the hands of the Prince-Chancellor, but he could still walk that walk more lethally than anyone else aboard the stolen cruiser.

A Navy Captain had hundreds of years of tradition and the authority of the entire Protectorate behind them. Kay had his own personal ability to crush any mutiny, and the cause they all shared.

It was the *cause* that let him take a six-hour nap after confirming there was no immediate threat. Three centuries earlier, aliens had sought to turn humanity into supplies for their jump drives, accidentally creating the modern Mage.

And then they had vanished.

The Protectorate had forgotten about the Reejit, their existence buried by the first Mage-King of Mars except for his hand-chosen Keepers. But the Keepers hadn't been ready for the reality of an active threat, for the Nemesis System to be found.

And now... now Kay stood in the Nemesis System and there was nothing there.

The enemy was farther away, but the enemy was out there. He knew that in his bones and he sent out a command as he put his wrist-comp back on.

Meeting in ten. Bring the scan data.

The leadership cadre of a conspiracy made for middling starship officers at best, but they were the people Kay had.

"There is nothing alive here."

Karl Chaudhary was not known for beating around the bush, Kay reflected. The tall Tau Cetan man shared his Captain's dark hair, but matched it with tanned-looking skin drawn from Earth's Marathi lineage.

Chaudhary had also taken over the leadership of Nemesis's "direct action" arm from Kay after their original leadership had been destroyed. *He* was an Augment, a cyborg super-soldier assembled for the now-defunct Republic of Faith and Reason.

The Republican soldier had been trained as a Mage-killer. But Kay knew he could handle the Augment if he needed to.

"I can see that," Kay said drily, looking around his team and assessing *them*.

Chaudhary led the Nemesis commandos, the elite strike force that Kay had extracted from the collapse of the original organization. Mostly Augments with a handful of ex-Marine Combat Mages, they were among the deadliest groups of human beings in the galaxy.

Adwoa Tomas was effectively Kay's executive officer, the person aboard the ship with the most experience in actually *running* a ship. She'd been XO on a freighter for a few years before joining Nemesis and running a series of high-speed covert couriers for the conspiracy.

The *rest* of the Protectorate might have access to the Link, the quantum-entanglement-based FTL communicator developed by the Republic, now. Nemesis, however, had been *far* too aware of the level of eavesdropping and control built into the new coms system by the former Republic and had *every* reason to think the Protectorate had duplicated it.

If, for no other reason, than specifically to catch Nemesis.

The only actual officer from the Royal Martian Navy was ex-Commander Rokus Koskinen, a wide-shouldered blond man who had been cashiered for assaulting a fellow officer. Koskinen was, in Kay's opinion, a throwback to a mythical time where strength had decided everything and had *issues* functioning in the modern world.

Fortunately, while Koskinen might outweigh Kay by fifty or so kilos, Kay had demonstrated that not only did he have magic the other man lacked, he was *also* better at martial arts—and, when push came to shove, was actually *stronger* than the big man.

He'd broken Koskinen's arm in a "friendly" arm-wrestling contest. The ex-Navy officer had fallen into line after that—and he now handled *Rose*'s weapons.

The last person in the room was key to the ship's operation. Kamilla O'Shea was the only person who understood *Rose*'s complex sensors and power cores and engines and stealth systems enough to keep them running.

She was a show-once student who'd studied *Rose*'s systems for six months before coming aboard with the boarding teams and taking to them like a fish to water. She didn't talk much, but she followed orders and was undyingly loyal to both the cause and Kay himself.

"So," Kay concluded, meeting each of his four key people's gazes, except O'Shea's, in turn. "There is nothing here now. At some point in the past, there definitely was enough here for the Keepers to scan this system and pick up a clear and major military presence.

"One that wasn't human. This is Nemesis System, my friends. The star system our entire organization, in many ways, was set up to keep humanity safe from."

That got him a few bitter chuckles. No one in this room—not even O'Shea, despite the impression the tech wizard happily gave the other senior Nemesis leaders—had clean hands. Kay's hands were probably dirtiest, but that was the life he'd chosen.

"We rushed the takeover of *Rose*," Koskinen said. "And it cost us. *Fuck* Kennedy."

"Kennedy didn't cost us *Thorn*," Kay said flatly. "*That* was Damien Montgomery and Mage-Captain Chambers, ably assisted by our mistake with Robert O'Kane."

"We needed him at one point," O'Shea muttered. "Especially after Winton."

Kay nodded. O'Shea was the only other member of this council who had been a senior Nemesis member when "Winton," the ex-Martian spy and former senior Keeper who had created Nemesis, was still alive.

"Rebuilding our resources after Winton sacrificed himself to preserve the organization required steps that created issues in hindsight," he allowed. "But Rokus is correct. If Kennedy hadn't co-opted Kron and Aloysius into his damn stupid plan to kidnap the Mage-Queen, we would have had more time."

He might even have been able to co-opt Mage-Captain Chambers herself, if given *enough* time. He doubted it—she had to be fully briefed on Nemesis now, given that he'd once deceived her into helping him steal the plans for the Orpheus mind-control nanites—but it would have been worth a try.

The room was silent for a few seconds, until Kay finally chuckled bitterly. He gestured, using a tiny spark of magic to float the coffee carafe over to him so he could fill his mug.

Even before they'd been on a single ship over a hundred light-years from civilization, Nemesis's key leadership meetings had been self-serve on food and coffee. They had, after all, been carrying out a deeply illegal conspiracy to manipulate the Protectorate into being ready for a war too few people knew was coming.

"What are we looking at?" he asked, his gaze focusing on Koskinen. The man had been an RMN tactical officer. Along with the analysts tucked away elsewhere in *Rose*'s expansive hull, the Commander was the best-qualified person to judge the aftermath of a battle.

"A fight so long ago, I'm surprised there's *anything* left," Koskinen said flatly. "That I can pick out enough wreckage to say there were ships and space stations here is saying a lot, Kay. We're still running the analysis of the sensor data, and the closer we get to Nemesis Four, the more we'll know."

"We're still a dozen hours out," Tomas reminded everyone. "We've dropped the stealth and we're radiating normally, but we came out far enough to justify a microjump."

"Except that the data we're picking up on the way in is as critical as anything we'll get in orbit," Koskinen growled. "A jump might save time now but it will waste it later."

Kay held up his hand.

"It sounds like you two have already hashed this out," he observed. "And we are approaching sublight, yes?"

"We are," Tomas confirmed. "There are arguments both ways, but the Commander made his case... fiercely."

Fiercely wasn't *eloquently* or even *convincingly*, Kay knew. On the other hand, he trusted Tomas to just ignore the big Finn if she thought he was actually wrong.

"So what do we know so far?" he demanded.

"Going through the data from the old Keeper Project Panopticon is... fascinating," O'Shea said, cutting in before anyone else said anything. "We should all have reviewed it in more detail before launching this operation, I suppose, but better late than never.

"The base *definitely* existed approximately two hundred and fifty years ago," she continued. "After that, even reviewing the Panopticon data leaves me with more questions than answers." She shrugged, looking up from the table but still not meeting anyone's gaze.

"I am biased reviewing the data now," she noted. "I *know* the base ceased to exist at some point. I can very easily see how the conclusion was drawn that the base was still active, at least from the most recent lightspeed data.

"On the other hand, knowing the base no longer exists, I can see that the data doesn't necessarily support that. There may have been an erroneous assumption baked into the variables."

O'Shea met Kay's gaze for a moment, and he was struck, as he had often been, by just how blue her eyes were. She then looked back at the table and he held that moment of eye contact close.

She occasionally met his gaze. She had never, in his presence at least, met anyone *else's.*

"My timeline is very rough," Koskinen said after a moment. "I can tell you *what* happened, at a high level, but it will take significantly more data and time for me to give you any idea *when* beyond the broadest."

"How broad?" Kay asked, turning his attention to Koskinen. A much less pleasant view than O'Shea, by any stretch of the imagination.

"At least a century ago. *Probably* not more than three centuries ago," the Commander said drily. "Does that help?"

Kay snorted.

"Stop bullshitting and tell me what you've worked out," he ordered.

"At least two hundred starships were destroyed in this system in a period somewhere between five and ten days long," Koskinen said flatly. "They *might* not have been equipped with jump matrices or whatever the alien equivalent is, but they were all a hell of a lot bigger than gunships."

"So, when you say *two hundred,* that has an uncertainty factor?" Kay asked.

"Yeah. Hence *at least,* boss," the Commander growled. "*At least* two hundred ships, each *at least* a million tons. Because I don't think anything smaller was going to leave a debris field we could pick out, not when people were throwing around antimatter warheads."

Kay nodded and gestured for Koskinen to continue. Two hundred ships of over a million tons apiece made for a problem. The entire Royal Martian Navy, even after their planned expansion, was only going to be four hundred ships—and at least two hundred and fifty of those were going to be destroyers *barely* massing a million tons.

"Can't tell you the size of the warheads at this point," Koskinen admitted. "Might have been dinky things of a few dozen megatons, but there are definite markers to confirm a matter-antimatter reaction."

"There wouldn't be on the ships," O'Shea said. "So... the planet?"

Koskinen sighed melodramatically but knew better than to snap back at O'Shea with Kay in the room. "Exactly," he said. "The fleets shot the shit out of each other, and then someone dropped twenty or so antimatter warheads on the planet."

Kay whistled.

"Hence why what was supposed to be a habitable world is... that."

He glanced at the display, showing their limited view of Nemesis IV. It didn't look like any habitable planet he'd ever seen; that was for sure. It looked more like Earth's moon or an impact-pocked asteroid than a planet in general.

"We have confirmed at least twenty impact sites, all with signs of antimatter annihilation, all marking at least a half a gigaton of explosive force," the Commander agreed. "The biosphere wouldn't have lasted twenty minutes. Any population centers were almost certainly under the impact sites."

Genocide. Humanity had managed to keep themselves from that, even in the recent war between the Protectorate and the Republic. There were significant software and hardware interlocks in place to stop the missiles in *Rose*'s magazines from being fired at a planet.

Rose did have weapons designed to be fired at a planet, but those were kinetic impactors with a few secondary tricks. The Protectorate went to a lot of effort to stop space-to-space missiles hitting planets.

Humanity *liked* habitable worlds, after all.

"Orbital works suffered the same fate, I presume?" Kay asked.

"Looks like," Koskinen agreed. "I've got a couple of people poking at the probes in the science bay, but I think we'll be able to get a solid view of the rest of the system as we reach the planet.

"I don't think any specific debris cloud is going to tell us much, but the more we put together, the better idea we're going to have overall."

Kay sighed and looked around the room.

"So somewhere between two hundred and fifty and a hundred years ago, this place was attacked. Fleet base and civilian population alike were annihilated. By *whom?*"

"There's no way we can answer that," Tomas pointed out. "None of our sensors can magically conjure that sort of information out of the past, sir."

"You'd be surprised," Koskinen said with a chuckle.

"Commander?" Kay said sharply.

"We don't have a lot of information on the debris clouds and the wrecks, boss, but I can tell you this: there's only one technology base. There might have been different designs, different ships, but everything was built on the same reactors and using the same hull composites.

"If this was a Reejit fleet base—and I'm not here 'cause I think it ain't, let's be clear!—it was taken out by the same folks who built it. The Reejit ruled this place, boss... but it was the *Reejit* who blew it to hell."

The Reejit were the *Nemesis* that Nemesis was named for. If the Reejit had split into factions and turned on each other, that might explain the two centuries of quiet humanity had enjoyed.

"If the Reejit have fought each other, that may have given *them* the same kind of technological advancement we triggered the Secession to create among our own people," Kay said grimly.

"Which only makes the situation worse. *This* base may have been destroyed, but I am seeing a lot of evidence out there to suggest that we may have overestimated the overall threat."

The Nemesis System might be a bust, but the Reejit were still out there. And if they'd wiped out a planet of their own people...

"We'll continue our analysis of this system until we think we've learned as much as we can," he told them. "We'll also want to take a bunch of those probes, Koskinen, and spread them out to get a view of the nearby stars.

"This place was built to either defend or conquer *something*. Let's find that something, shall we?"

CHAPTER 2

TWO SCHE!MATICS rotated on the wall screen in the Captain's office aboard Her Majesty's exploratory cruiser *Thorn*. There were no easily identified differences between them, but the redheaded woman standing in front of the screen surveying them was looking for them anyway.

No two ships, even sister ships built at the same time in the same yard, were absolutely identical. And somewhere in those differences, Mage-Captain Roslyn Chambers hoped to find part of the answer to her problem.

Thorn was still an uncomfortable fit around her. She'd taken command of the cruiser—and found out, belatedly, about her promotion to Mage-Captain—barely two weeks earlier. Most change of command ceremonies, though, didn't involve storming a captured ship with the Prince-Chancellor of Mars at one's side.

But she had to admit that her career had *never* been normal. The tiny sapphire pin on her black uniform, the only decoration she was *required* to wear on active duty, marked her as one of two living human beings who had received the Mage-Queen's Medal of Valor not once but *three* times.

Each of those awards had been soaked in the blood of military personnel and civilians alike who she'd failed to save—and been lauded by the people she *had* saved.

Thorn felt like another round of the same concept. For the last two years, Mage-*Commander* Roslyn Chambers had been an Academy lecturer.

Orders promoting her and moving her to command of the Royal Martian Navy's newest and most advanced cruiser had been lost as part of the chaos following on from an attempt to kidnap the Mage-Queen of Mars.

In that chaos, the conspiratorial group known as Nemesis—who *claimed* to be working to serve the best interests of all humanity—had killed hundreds in attempts to cover their tracks. That effort had failed at the last moment, allowing Prince-Chancellor Montgomery to lead Roslyn and others to attempt to recapture the two exploratory cruisers.

They'd managed to retake *Thorn*, but *Rose*, loaded with the leadership cabal of an organization responsible *for the entire civil war* the Protectorate had just fought, had escaped.

Roslyn Chambers was supposed to pursue her. But she was still pulling together a crew and was missing the answer to a critical and important question: how *to* follow the other ship.

The admittance chime on her office door sounded.

"Enter," she commanded.

A clearly middle-aged woman in the uniform of a senior RMN non-commissioned officer stepped through the door and braced to attention for *just* long enough for the gesture to be clear—and not one moment longer.

"Precious, don't be precious," Roslyn told the older woman with a chuckle. Master Chief Petty Officer Precious Kovalyow was one of the two NCOs the Navy had decided to semi-permanently attach to her.

The other was Tajana Baars, Roslyn's personal steward. Both of the older women were critical components to Roslyn's command staff, regardless of what a civilian looking at an org chart might assume.

"As you wish, sir," the Chief told her. Kovalyow crossed to Roslyn's desk behind Roslyn and pulled out a chair before looking over at the drink station. "Coffee, sir?"

"I already have one," Roslyn observed.

"Yes. Spiced, sweetened, *cold*. Would you like a fresh one, Roslyn?"

Roslyn laughed.

"All right, Precious, you win," she conceded. "I'll have a fresh coffee while you make up one for yourself. You have a report or is this just stealing my coffee?"

"Your coffee is a disgrace to the Prince-Chancellor," Kovalyow replied as she carefully measured powdered spice mix and sugar into the two drinks. "Your *spice mix* collection, on the other hand, is unrivaled anywhere on this ship. Despite my best efforts *and* being in Tau Ceti, the only system crazy enough *to* put masala in coffee."

"I grew up here," Roslyn reminded her Chief. "And I spent some unwise years in unwise quarters." She shrugged. "There are stores that are not on the datanet, Precious, and I took Baars to a couple of them."

"I still think the personal protégée of Damien Montgomery shouldn't be drinking the same coffee we serve in the ship's mess."

Roslyn sighed. She and the Prince-Chancellor went back roughly a decade at this point, since she'd been pulled into the mess that she now knew had unveiled Nemesis to the Protectorate's leadership.

And the Prince-Chancellor was *notorious* for his coffee habits.

"If it is black and caffeinated and supports a spice mix, that's good enough for me most days," she told Kovalyow. "And if you're just here for my spices, that's fine, but you're in too good a mood for that."

The Master Chief grinned at her boss.

"What good news would you *like*, sir?" she asked.

"Well, I'd *like* to hear that *Rose* limped into Tau Ceti under command of her no-longer-mind-*fucked* crew and that all of Nemesis's leaders are going up for trial tomorrow," Roslyn said. "But since I am a realist, I'd settle for *we know when all the crew is going to be aboard*."

"All right, then. We know when all the crew is going to be aboard," Kovalyow confirmed. "TCSDF stepped up with sixty-five volunteers, all veterans of the Battle of Ardennes."

Roslyn closed her eyes in relief she couldn't show in front of many others. She was still working on her command mask, but she knew that she *was* allowed to let it slip around her steward and her Chief of the Ship.

Ardennes had been the first major battle of the war against the Republic of Faith and Reason. After a series of opening surprise attacks that had, among other things, left *Cadet* Roslyn Chambers as acting tactical officer on a destroyer, the Protectorate had very much been losing the war.

Then Damien Montgomery—at that point "merely" the First Hand of the Mage-King of Mars—had called in just about every favor and positive feeling any system government had toward him and mustered a fleet built mostly on the system militias.

The Tau Ceti System Defense Force—known by half a dozen names depending on context, but usually either the TCSDF or the Tau Ceti Security Fleet—had been the largest component of that scratch-built fleet.

Roslyn had been at Ardennes too. She was *delighted* to have those veterans, even if their presence aboard a Royal Martian Navy ship was... legally questionable.

"I'm assuming there is some *fascinating* paperwork in my inbox," she said drily. There was no *official* way TCSDF personnel could serve on an RMN cruiser, even if said cruiser was trying to assemble over eighteen hundred replacement crew members in basically zero time.

She'd been supposed to have four days. She'd now had *thirteen* and she wasn't happy about the reasons why. On the other hand, if she'd left after four days, she would have had seventy-five Marines and four-hundred-ish crew.

On a ship with a list complement of a full battalion of Marines—six hundred and forty strong—and eleven hundred and sixty-eight Navy personnel, that would barely have sufficed to fly the ship.

The only real virtue of that number would have been that it was more than *Nemesis* had on *Rose* and it wouldn't have left her nine days behind the ball.

"Our biggest shortcoming was middle NCOs," she observed. "So, I'm guessing that we're pulling over a bunch of veterans who weren't going to make Chief in the TCSDF and making them Chief?"

Kovalyow raised her coffee mug in salute.

"Twenty-six of ninety-five Navy officers are brand-new Academy graduates," the Chief noted, starting to fill another cup of coffee as she worked on her first. "That only makes it *more* important that we get good Chiefs, and too many of our ratings are the people whose Captains wanted to see their back sides."

"I do think better of most of my fellow RMN Captains than that," Roslyn said. Even stealing her best students from the Academy to fill out her junior officer ranks had left her begging and drafting personnel in twenty-body lots from the rest of the Navy ships in system.

They'd got a *lot* of very junior people and, she was sure, some bad apples. But every Captain in the Tau Ceti System knew what Roslyn's mission was. The only reason she was going alone was that nothing else in the RMN matched *Rose* or *Thorn*'s legs.

"You may think as well of them as you wish, sir, but we got some real lemons in the mix," Kovalyow warned. "Our middle officers are decent and our seniors were handpicked by Mage-Admiral Jakab."

Twice, Roslyn reflected grimly. She only had *one* of her original planned senior-officer contingent, and while she valued having Commander Matthias Beck, she worried.

He *had* been mind-controlled by Nemesis, after all, and she worried that left more of a mark than her older subordinate was showing.

"Where is Beck, for that matter?" she asked Kovalyow. "I would half-expect this briefing to involve him."

"The XO is dealing with the minutiae around our other piece of good news," the Master Chief told her, "and should be here right about now."

In what had probably only been coordinated on Precious Kovalyow's side, the admittance chime for Roslyn's office sounded again, and the Mage-Captain laughed.

"Come in," she ordered, utterly unsurprised to see Commander Matthias Beck—who, like Kovalyow, was not a Mage. That was part of why he was *much* older than her and still junior to her.

The other part, of course, was the sapphire pin on Roslyn's uniform.

The stocky man with the sandy hair saluted her crisply, then spotted the unclaimed mug of coffee on Roslyn's desk and echoed the Mage-Captain's chuckle of a moment earlier.

"I see I am anticipated," he observed.

"Well, neither of us is here to shoot each other this time, so grab a seat and the coffee Precious already made for you," Roslyn said with a grin. If she was being honest, Beck had only shot *at* her.

She had *succeeded* in shooting him. On the other hand, *he'd* been firing real bullets and *she'd* been firing nonlethal SmartDarts, which allowed them to clear Nemesis's mindfuckery from his system afterward.

Beck shook his head reprovingly at her but followed instructions.

"You want the good news or the bad news, Mage-Captain?" he asked.

"The Master Chief already started with good news, so how about the bad," Roslyn told him. "Let's sandwich things."

"Bad news: they finally found Tracker-Commander Wang last night," her XO told her.

Tracker-Commander Wang Xiuying had been *supposed* to report aboard *Thorn* eight days earlier. The specialist was one of the few officers in the Royal Navy who'd mastered the surprisingly difficult skill of tracking the destination of a ship teleporting between stars.

Unfortunately, Tracker-Commander Wang had gone *missing* forty-eight hours after receiving those orders, on an orbital in the Eridani System.

"Given that you phrased that as the bad news, I'm assuming Commander Wang is not in great shape," Roslyn said grimly.

"No," Beck agreed, his tone matching hers. "It looks like Nemesis had at least one more arrow in their quiver here in the Core Worlds. The actual kidnappers were probably freelancers, but MISS found him in a warehouse while they were following the breadcrumbs out from here."

The one unquestionable *good* thing out of the recent mess, Roslyn figured, was that they'd broken open a lot of what was left of the conspiracy. A major front organization was being dismantled desk by desk, while the Martian Interstellar Security Service followed every string and every lead Nemesis's desperate campaign to delay Montgomery from realizing the plan to steal the *Thorns* had shaken loose.

"He's alive?" Roslyn asked. "That's better than I was afraid of."

"He is. On the other hand, what I'm hearing from the agents who found him in *Tellemar*, of all places, is that he was both definitely dosed with some form of Orpheus and beaten to within a few millimeters of his life."

Roslyn winced.

"Orpheus didn't work on him?" she asked. "Or so I'm guessing? That's... interesting. If over my particular head."

The Orpheus-Ultima nanotech relied on a complex integration of magical runecraft and extremely advanced biotech into its nanobots. It didn't work on Mages, but Roslyn saw no reason it wouldn't have worked on a Tracker.

"That's my read of the report, but no one was confirming anything," Beck confirmed. "He won't be cleared for service for at least a few days, if not weeks."

"And Tellemar is in the wrong direction from Eridani, anyway," Kovalyow pointed out. "They're a MidWorld, what, fifty light-years from here? Someone really didn't want Wang getting to us."

"Fortunately for *us*, Wang Xiuying isn't the only Tracker in Her Majesty's service," Beck said. "And Tracker-Commander Akachi Uesugi just completed their training on Ardennes, as it turns out, and had been cleared for full service. There was some question about assignments, and a few memos went astray, so we didn't get confirmation as early as we should."

"So, that is our good news, I'm hoping?" Roslyn asked.

"Tracker-Commander Uesugi's ship just entered the Tau Ceti System, sir," Beck confirmed. "They are due to reach orbit in six hours; the Tracker-Commander should be aboard *Thorn* in eight.

"I was confirming the timeline with them before I saw you. I have spoken with Uesugi—they are alive, they are *here*, and they come with Minister Julia Amiri's *personal* assurances of their loyalty."

"And if I didn't trust Minister Amiri, the Prince-Chancellor will have my ears," Roslyn said with a chuckle. Prior to marrying the now twice-elected Governor of Ardennes and serving as that MidWorld's Minister of Defense, Amiri had served as the head of Damien Montgomery's Secret Service detachment.

Before, during and *after* that tour of duty, she'd also trained the entirety of the first generation of Trackers for the Royal Navy. They had some second-generation Trackers, now, trained by the people Amiri had trained... but as Roslyn understood it, they were still sparse on the ground.

No one had yet worked out how to detect someone with the potential to be a Tracker other than by trying to train them. So far, *no* Mages had succeeded at that training—and only about one in fifty *non*-Mages did. Roslyn understood the process to be extraordinarily frustrating for teachers and students alike.

"So, in eight hours, we will finally have our Tracker?" Roslyn asked. "I hope that the data we have on *Thorn*'s jump will still serve."

"It will have to," Beck said grimly. "I don't understand enough about *any* of this, but I know that no one has been allowed to jump in or out within a full light-minute of where *Rose* jumped from.

"I hope the signature is still clear, but it's been a long damn time."

"Whatever course they were taking wasn't loaded into *Thorn*'s computers. Tracker-Commander Uesugi is our only real chance of finding these bastards, I'm afraid."

"I'll check in with the Chiefs and personnel departments," Kovalyow promised. "I think we're supposed to have our last drafts and volunteers aboard by then, but I will try to accelerate if need be."

"Let me know if anyone gives you trouble," Roslyn ordered. "The Mage-Captain can carry a weight even a Master Chief cannot... and what the gold bars can't move, I have other options for."

Both of her subordinates very carefully did *not* look at Roslyn's right arm. That the young Mage-Captain now possessed a Rune of Power, a magical augmentation normally only granted to the Hands of the Mage-Queen, was a poorly kept secret. *Technically*, the Rune didn't come with any extra authority.

The reality, of course, was different. Everyone knew that Roslyn Chambers had the ear of the Mage-Queen, not just the Prince-Chancellor.

What the gold bars of the ship's Mage-Captain might not move, said Mage-Captain operating on the personal orders of the highest authority probably would.

CHAPTER 3

THORN WAS an impressive ship by many standards. A steep pyramid half a kilometer tall anchored on a two-hundred- by two-hundred-and-fifty-meter base, she was driven by antimatter engines and powered by a mixed series of fusion and antimatter power generators.

Unlike many ships, even in the RMN, she was equipped with the facilities and—theoretically, at least—the personnel to transmute matter into antimatter to fuel her systems. Unfortunately, the Transmuter Mage assigned to Roslyn's command had been badly injured in Nemesis's attempted takeover and was now on medical leave.

Their current mission shouldn't require that level of self-sufficiency, she hoped. Any of the six Navy-trained Jump Mages aboard *could* transmute antimatter, after all—they were just a *lot* slower at it.

But then, a Transmuter couldn't teleport the fifteen-million-ton starship between the stars.

Nor could the officer Roslyn was in the shuttle to meet. There was more to being a Tracker than training, the Navy was quite sure of that at this point, but no one had quite nailed it down yet.

"Shuttle *Starborne*-Six on final approach," a voice echoed through the bay. "Exterior hatches opening. All hands, move to designated safe zones. This is the final warning. Move to designated safe zones *now*."

If anyone in the shuttle bay—a seemingly cavernous void twenty meters tall, fifteen wide and a full thirty deep into the starship hull—*wasn't* already in the areas designated safe from potential vacuum, loss of pressure, or shuttle-engine flare, neither Roslyn nor the trio of Chiefs *stalking* the space had seen them.

One of the Chiefs was a transfer from the TCSDF, she knew. There was no sign in the woman's uniform or bearing of that distinction, though, and Roslyn hoped that everyone—including Roslyn herself—would forget it after a few weeks.

She'd reviewed the datawork. Their Tau Cetan volunteers weren't being seconded or lent to the Royal Navy—there were structures in place for the RMN to borrow *ships* and *formations*, but she doubted they'd work well for handfuls of personnel. Every one of them had permanently transferred across to the Royal Martian Navy.

And with everything Roslyn knew, she doubted anyone was planning on giving them *back*. She'd triple-checked that each of them had come across at a grade commensurate with their experience and the TCSDF-provided assessments from their peers and superiors, though.

Every one of those sixty-five noncoms had jumped at least one grade—and Roslyn had some *serious* questions about why newly frocked Senior Chief Petty Officer Aurelija Vasiliauskas had *only* been a Petty Officer Second Class. The woman had been decorated for valor after the Battle of Ardennes and had thirty-two years in Tau Cetan service and glowing recommendations.

There had been nothing in the files Roslyn had received on Vasiliauskas, but those files had easily justified the full three-grade bump. Roslyn had already put a bug in Kovalyow's and Baars' ears on the matter.

She'd find out just what had held Vasiliauskas back. She had enough faith in her fellow Tau Cetans, however, to believe that the file she'd been handed wouldn't have been as glowing if there had been a *problem*.

The sound of the shuttle bay's massive inner hatch sliding open interrupted her thoughts. Between vacuum and soundproofing, she'd barely registered the outer hatch opening, the massive airlock serving its intended purpose.

Now an *old* military personnel shuttle slid through the door, the pilot carefully guiding the practically obsolete unarmed small craft to the marked landing zone.

"*Starborne* is one of ours, isn't she?" Roslyn murmured to Beck.

"No, sir," he told her. "Civilian courier ship, Sensorium Dispatch. That... was part of the problem in learning what was going on with the Tracker-Commander."

She grimaced and nodded. Any change in the nature of the universe always left *someone* behind. The implementation of the Link FTL communicators over the last half-decade had rendered the old five-Mage-to-a-ship high-speed couriers much less necessary.

Before, communication had either been by ship or by the Runic Transceiver Arrays, immense constructs of magic that only transferred a single Mage's voice. Now even encrypted data was easily transferred, and an entire industry was facing a ninety-plus-percent drop in demand.

Most were adapting. There would always be a need for small-scale high-speed transport of goods and personnel, even if they no longer had to transport data the same way. Still, few of the dispatch companies had been able to afford such luxuries as *shipboard* Link systems.

"Zone is clear," the bay Chief's voice announced over the speakers. "Cooling systems disengaging. Passengers are clear to exit."

Water was still steaming off the shuttle from the spray, but from experience, Roslyn could say that the landing deck was now *merely* painfully hot and humid.

She strode forward past the safety barriers as *Starborne*-Six's ramp extended, allowing a soft-featured young officer in the black-and-gold uniform of an RMN Commander to exit the shuttle and crisply salute her.

"Tracker-Commander Akachi Uesugi reporting aboard, sir!" they said crisply.

Roslyn studied the officer for a second as she returned the salute. Uesugi couldn't be more opposite to the last Tracker she'd worked with on an ongoing basis. That gentleman had been a bounty hunter, a tall, dark and handsome man exactly in the form that Roslyn found most interesting.

That had nearly been a problem, but she'd managed to keep her hormones in check—though the Tracker himself had managed to fall far enough for *her* to become a minor problem of its own!

GLYNN STEWART

Uesugi, on the other hand, was short and sallow-skinned, with blond hair so pale as to be nearly white. They were pudgy in a way that suggested underlying muscle and could not have looked *less* like Nunzio Ajam.

"Welcome aboard, Commander," Roslyn told him. "You're the last of the crew to report aboard, if I'm being honest, which means we're going to be waiting on you as much as anything else."

"I read the reports," Uesugi said. "If someone will show me where to drop my gear and where to set up, I'll get to work."

Roslyn chuckled.

"I hate to pressure an officer who literally just walked aboard ship," she admitted. "But we are ten days behind where we were planning on being. The sooner we're in pursuit, the better."

The *rest* of the crew wasn't nearly as solid or worked-up as she'd like either, but what choice did they have? Without knowing how many Mages Nemesis had taken aboard *Rose*, they had no idea how far away she'd managed to get. Even a single Mage making military-interval jumps moved a ship four light-years a day.

Civilian-interval jumps were only three light-years a day, but Roslyn wasn't going to bet on Nemesis having less than three Navy-trained Mages or their equivalent in civilian Jump Mages. Twelve light-years a day would put *Rose* at least a hundred and seventy light-years from Tau Ceti.

"I was expecting nothing less, sir," Uesugi said brightly. "I rested up on the courier here from Ardennes, and I am not only ready but raring to go. The first one is going to be hardest, I warn you, given how old the data is and how much else is going on.

"Once we're in deep space, unless they've played unfortunate games, it should be faster."

"I don't want to bet on them *not* knowing about the tricks the Legion pulled," Roslyn warned. Her pursuit of raiders from the First Legion leftovers of the Republic had been halted by the profligate use of antimatter warheads to cover their tracks.

Uesugi chuckled.

"Yes, but I will bet money they *don't* know that the Navy's Trackers have spent two years looking into answers to *that* particular trick," they

28

told her. "Especially, Mage-Captain, since we haven't *told* anyone that we found an answer.

"So, unless one of exactly twenty-six Navy officers has betrayed us, Nemesis has no idea I can still follow them if they pull that crap."

"That may be the best news I've heard since my people told me you were in-system," Roslyn said. "Chief Pereyra!"

A Chief Steward—Roslyn didn't know him, but his name tag was enough for *this* purpose, and his timing suggested he'd been sent to handle things.

"Sir! Master Chief Kovalyow sent me to be Commander Uesugi's guide," the Chief confirmed.

"Get Commander Uesugi's gear settled in their quarters and show them to Sensor Cluster Six-Charlie," Roslyn ordered. "That's been set up as Tracking Central for this operation."

"That sounds... very formal," Uesugi observed. "I'm sure it will more than suffice."

"By now, Tracker-Commander, the rest of the Navy has a decent idea of how to support your skillset," she reminded them. "And you aren't the first Tracker I've chauffeured around!"

She smiled thinly.

"Senior staff meeting is at twenty hundred hours to catch up on the status of our current chaos. I understand interruption is a hindrance, but if you can attend, it would be appreciated."

Roslyn could see Uesugi doing the math in their head. That was four hours from now.

"I... make no promises, sir," they said slowly. "If I have your permission to miss the meeting, that may be best. I don't think I'm going to be able to nail down *Rose*'s course in three hours."

"If it's a choice between keeping everyone fully up to date and catching *Rose*, the pursuit has priority," Roslyn conceded. "You hold the rank and effective position of a department head and will be treated as part of the command staff, Tracker-Commander, even without subordinates.

"But... well." She smiled and then repeated herself.

"The pursuit has priority."

CHAPTER 4

"I HOPE the irony is not lost on you."

Even in private and naked, Kamilla O'Shea was still soft-spoken and disinclined to meet Kay's gaze. Her words, though, drew his attention away from his post-coital examination of his lover and brought his attention back to... other matters.

"Which irony, exactly?" he asked.

O'Shea rolled over on the bed in his quarters and picked up her wrist-comp. Her cavalier disregard for her nudity around him was both titillating and reassuring. Kay *knew* how well O'Shea regarded other people—mostly as interruptions to dealing with her machinery.

They'd been lovers before seizing *Rose*, though there were days he suspected she'd only taken him into her bed to give her a measure of security in the chaos of an illegal conspiracy. Most of the time, though, she was sufficiently stubborn, blunt and focused that he had no idea at all of why she was bedding him.

He was content for her not to *stop*, though, so he simply watched her bring up the controls on the wrist-comp and tried not to be *too* lecherous in his observation.

Not quite ignoring his attention, O'Shea brought up the main wall screen before shifting over to lean against his chest.

"The Nemesis System," she said, gesturing at the display of their surroundings. "I was never a Keeper, though I certainly have spoken with people who were. But this place was the start of everything, wasn't it?"

GLYNN STEWART

"I *was* a Keeper," Kay murmured, shifting slightly to allow more of her skin to press on him. "And... yeah. Even among Keepers, Nemesis System was a secret. A *horribly kept* secret, but a secret."

"But it was why Winton and the others decided that the Keepers needed to act," O'Shea murmured. "We had a clear sight on an enemy position; we *knew* they were able to move against us."

"Exactly. We needed to spark an arms race." Kay shook his head and sighed. "The actual civil war was entirely optional from that point of view, but it helped accelerate everything. Now we have a Royal Martian Navy that might be able to fight a war.

"Not a glorified bloody police force, fat on peace and donuts."

She chuckled, running her fingers distractedly—and *distractingly*—across Kay's stomach.

"I don't know if the RMN—or at least its *Marines*—were ever fat," she observed. "But that was the point." Her usual focus returned suddenly, and her fingers froze.

"We needed—*humanity* needed—the Protectorate ready for when the Reejit came. But they hadn't come. And they didn't come. And we did... everything we did to ready humanity for their arrival.

"And now here we are in Nemesis itself, the system we *named* our organization for... and there's nothing here."

"There isn't *nothing* here," Kay objected. "There was something here. And, honestly, Kamilla..." He reached across her torso to tap a focus command on her wrist-comp, focusing the display on Nemesis IV.

"No human would ever bombard a *habitable*, let alone a human-inhabited, world with antimatter weapons," he told her. "That this world was burned tells me our enemy is far more dangerous than we once feared."

"They created Project Olympus to turn humanity into *fuel*," O'Shea pointed out, the anger in her tone suggesting she wasn't taking Nemesis System's graveyard as the end of their mission. "Why does a dead world change the threat?"

"Because my logic was that if they wanted our flesh and brains to fuel their ships, we'd have some degree of safety against annihilation," Kay said softly. "You don't wipe out the herd when you need milk, after all.

"If they wanted to capture human Mages alive, we could give ground in the war to come. We might lose Mages, but we'd be able to count on the majority of the population being safe if oppressed."

He gestured to the screen and grimaced.

"But if they were willing to burn a world of their own people with anti-matter fire, that assumption isn't anything we can rely on," he told her. "I expected war. Now it looks like I may have underestimated just how *total* that war was going to be.

"We cannot expect mercy from an enemy that did this. I'm not even sure we can expect negotiation. Only war. Only fire."

"Good. You understand."

Kay smirked at her.

"So, what was the irony you were talking about?" he asked drily.

"That *this* system was the source of our fear, of our conflict with our own, but it isn't a threat itself anymore," she told him. "It would be easy to look at this and think we misunderstood, that we went too far and fought for nothing.

"But as you said: that dead world tells us everything."

"It tells us that our enemy might not be *here*," Kay agreed, "but that they are out there and that they are more dangerous, more violent and more *evil* than we ever dared imagine."

After two days in orbit of Nemesis IV, Kay's command council gathered again. The backdrop to" their meeting in the Captain's breakout room was the wall screen, showing an image of a mass of scarred and twisted wreckage that had once, long before, been a shipyard of some kind.

"Hell of a fucking mess," Koskinen grumbled. "Not seeing much of a threat here now, but it was a hell of a fucking mess."

"There may not be a threat *here, today*, but this system still holds keys to the challenge before us," Kay pointed out. He didn't even look at O'Shea as he repeated her point. It wasn't like their relationship was a *secret*, but his control of the Nemesis leadership lacked the institutional structure of a more-conventional ship's crew.

"What was here. Who it belonged to. Who destroyed it." He shook his head and gestured at the screen behind him. "That yard was capable of building kilometer-long starships. Only the greatest of the Protectorate's dreadnoughts could rival those ships—and this wasn't a shipyard system."

"It might have been," Tomas suggested. "We don't *know*."

"We don't *know* anything," Kay conceded. "But we can guess. But this is no home system. If there were major Reejit settlements closer to the Protectorate, Nemesis would have found them by now.

"So, this is the closest major spaceborne infrastructure of the Reejit to human space," he reminded them all. "Unless their imperium is far smaller and weaker than I dare hope—or than the evidence of this system itself suggests!—this system couldn't have been near enough to their home territories to be a major shipyard.

"That means this was likely a *repair* facility." He shrugged. "I say they could build kilometer-long ships here, but they probably originally meant to *repair* them. The scale of the battle Koskinen believes occurred here says they might have *been* building them here, but I don't think that was the original intent."

"Then why build here at all?" Chaudhary asked flatly. "If construction drew an enemy here..."

"*Turning and turning in the widening gyre*," O'Shea intoned, her rarely heard native Irish accent suddenly thickening as she recited the poem. "*The falcon cannot hear the falconer. Things fall apart; the center cannot hold...*

"*Mere anarchy is loosed upon the world*," Kay finished the first stanza of the old Yeats poem. "Civil war, Chaudhary. The frontier turns on the core. A repair base falls into the hands of rebels and becomes the centerpiece of their military production—a facility built to *repair* a dreadnought can probably *build* one, given the right support."

"Which then makes that repair base a central target," Koskinen concluded. "So, they hit it hard, fast and brutal. My best guess is that there were about a hundred ships defending this system. Some were big—those kilometer-long monsters that the yards were building—but most were smaller. A few megatons, bigger than our destroyers but smaller than *Rose*."

"So, more like a militia frigate?" Tomas asked.

Kay nodded as he considered the example. *Frigates,* in modern parlance, fell about halfway between the destroyers and cruisers that formed the backbone of the RMN. The Navy didn't use them, but few systems outside the Core could justify building cruisers.

The wealthier MidWorlds, though, needed more than the destroyers they could readily buy from the Core. So, they built frigates, named for the Age of Sail's *ships below the line,* that carried enough firepower to deal with any destroyer that somehow ended up in pirate hands.

"I'm looking at two-century-old debris without context," Koskinen said drily. "I can't even tell you what any individual ship massed. I can tell you there's about twenty million tons of debris still floating around the battlespace, and I can tell you that the physics say that's about *one percent* of the mass of the original ships that died here."

He shrugged.

"But yeah. *Looks* like the defenders had between ten and twenty kilometer-long warships in the fifty-million-plus-ton range, backed by about a hundred smaller ships and what I'm guessing was a *lot* of mines."

"You can't possibly see the mines," O'Shea said flatly.

"No, I can't," Koskinen conceded. "But I can tell you that the attackers *lost* over twice as many of the big ships here, so I'm going to *assume* the defenders had something beyond what I *can* see."

"That much, at least, is a fair assumption," Kay said. "Is the differential that clear?"

"I'm looking at sub one percent of the remaining mass in debris and gas from a battle that took place almost two centuries ago," Koskinen pointed out. "*Nothing* is anything I'd call *clear.* But there were definitely more big ships coming in from the outside in that mess.

"And since I'm only seeing the ships that *didn't* survive, I'd say the attackers had more ships, bigger ships and quite possibly *better* ships—and *still* got their asses beat."

"Given that the system is a dead zone, I'm not sure I follow that conclusion," Chaudhary said. "Generally, if everything the defenders were trying to protect is *gone*, that's not a win for them..."

"Didn't say the defenders won," the ex-Navy officer replied. "Said that the attackers got their asses kicked. Looks like they lost at least as many hulls and something like three times the tonnage of the defenders."

"You don't vaporize shipyards and planets you expect to have control of at the end of the day," Koskinen concluded. "The attackers were looking at a Pyrrhic victory at best and were probably losing. Mass destruction is not the tool of the people *winning* the fucking war."

"Nineteen forty-five America had a different opinion," Tomas replied.

"Nineteen forty-five America was looking at the mother of all Pyrrhic victories, *plus* wanted to intimidate everyone else with their big stick," the Navy officer said. "These guys had either lost or were looking at losing too much to be able to hold the system after they took it.

"So, they stopped shooting at the fleet and started dropping gigaton-range warheads on the planet."

Kay grimaced.

"We're sure on that yield range?" he asked.

"I'm not *sure* on *anything*," Koskinen reiterated. "Crater sizes on the surface suggest around that, but it's not like anyone in the *Protectorate* ever tested what kind of craters got left behind in a standard atmosphere by a gigaton-range antimatter warhead.

"But yeah. I'd say seventy-thirty, they were playing with much the same antimatter heads I trained on."

"Two hundred years ago," Kay murmured. "Two hundred years ago, these people could go toe-to-toe with the modern Royal Martian Navy's finest."

He surveyed the room before settling his gaze back on Koskinen.

"Am I right, Commander?"

"Lot of variables," the other man said, but he sighed and nodded. "But... yeah, that would be my assessment. Were I playing guessing games, I'd say that the heaviest ships on both sides were about on par with our old *Guardian*-class battleships. Laid out different, but roughly fifty megatons with a few hundred missile launchers."

"We are playing guessing games," O'Shea said. "My analysis was from a different direction, but..."

Kay raised an eyebrow at the engineer, then coughed when he realized she was looking at her computer rather than him.

"Your conclusions?" he asked.

"I worked out from the shipyard, where Koskinen worked on the debris fields," O'Shea said. "The ships were closer to the Republic's in layout, cylindrical and designed for rotational pseudogravity. Whatever games they were playing with magic didn't include magical gravity."

Kay half-consciously twitched his foot across the floor of the room, where a visible matrix of silver runes created a downward pull equal to Earth's.

Unlike thrust or rotational pseudogravity, magical gravity *was* gravity, according to any and all tests that could be performed. There was no anchoring mass, so it didn't exactly play fair with the laws of physics as the Protectorate understood them... but magic only seemed to talk to physics at the most quantum of levels.

"The Republic used rotational pseudogravity for the same reason," he observed. "Even their fifty-megaton ships weren't a kilometer long, though."

"Different design parameters," O'Shea said. "The Republic used standardized hulls built to be cruisers and welded them to each other to build carriers and battleships.

"*These* guys appear to have used a standardized *radius*—around a hundred meters, wider than any of the Republic's standard hulls—and variable *lengths*." She shrugged. "A hundred-meter radius and thousand-meter length would have given them a bit more hull volume than a *Guardian*, but the need for space for the rotation systems would have reduced their density and effective combat power per ton, too.

"Shorter hulls would look funny to *us*, but they were almost certainly used to it."

Kay had thought the Republic's standardized half-kilometer-long hulls had looked odd enough, but then, he was very used to how the Protectorate built ships. With magical gravity to work with, Martian ships ended up as basically skyscrapers in space, with a very clear "down" based on thrust direction.

The *pyramid* shape was a choice, he was sure, but it was certainly something the RMN had stuck to for a long time.

"So, whatever magic they had, they weren't building ships using magical gravity," Kay murmured. "That seems..." He sighed. "It seems like it should tell me *something*, but I'm not sure what."

"That they didn't have many Mages aboard their ships," Tomas said quietly. She smirked as the others looked at her. "You can tell that I'm the only one in this room who ever served on a jump freighter.

"They're built around rotational gravity because most civilian ships only have two, *maybe* three, Jump Mages aboard. Gravity runes mean a Mage has to be in the area once every two or three weeks to keep them charged."

The area was a zone of about four hundred square meters, from what Kay recalled. That was the maximum size of an individual artificial-gravity matrix. *Rose* had over four *thousand* such matrices.

Charging a gravity matrix when he walked into it was a relatively slight demand on his energy reserves, something he did half-unconsciously—but to keep the entire ship supplied with gravity, the Mages needed to have a schedule to make sure at least one Mage touched on each of those four-thousand-plus matrices every two weeks.

"You're suggesting they only had Jump Mages aboard?" he asked. "Or..." He shivered as he remembered where Nemesis had acquired the basic designs for what had become the Prometheus Interface, the technological system that had used murdered Mages to jump starships.

"Or they were only using Mage *brains* for jumps," Tomas concluded grimly. "If they didn't have any *other* Mages aboard—like the Republic, though I presume more aware of just how their jump functioned—then they'd have had no ability to sustain artificial gravity."

The Republic Interstellar Navy had not, initially, known how their jump drives worked. The discovery had triggered mass mutinies—not helped, Kay knew, by the overreaction of the RIN's command structure *to* people questioning that revelation.

He'd seen the footage from the Siege of Legatus when Hand Montgomery had revealed the truth of the Prometheus Interface. The RIN had been defending their home system. The Republic fleet hadn't truly fractured until *after* they'd opened fire on their own ships for poking at the "jump drives."

"Which brings us back to why we are here and the problem we now have," Kay told them all. "Everything we have seen here tells me that the Reejit are an even-greater danger than we had believed. Nemesis System itself appears to have been... neutralized, but the nation that built it and the nation that *destroyed* it are still out there.

"They still have Prometheus Interface–style drives. Two centuries ago, they already had weapons rivaling the Protectorate's own. And we *know* that they are prepared to kill millions of their own people for limited tactical and *maybe* strategic advantage."

He surveyed his officers, looking for any sign that any of them weren't in agreement. Tomas looked the most... hesitant, but she nodded along in understanding.

"The threat our organization was created to fight isn't here," he conceded. "We need to make sure that our crew doesn't think that means it doesn't *exist*. More than that, though, we need to make certain that the Reejit aren't standing behind the Protectorate with a drawn knife, waiting for a misstep that we won't even realize we're making.

"We have come this far." And he wasn't just talking about reaching *this* system. "Now we must find the Reejit. This was a fleet base, a major frontier outpost on the fringes of their territory.

"There had to be other systems nearby that it was intended to protect. I doubt, after all, that this base was solely built to support Project Olympus. Andala, *maybe*, but not here."

The Reejit outpost at Andala had been more of a survey base, in his opinion. A taste of home and rest for crews who couldn't afford the time to go all the way back to the Reejit home stars.

"Is there anything else we think we can learn here in the Nemesis System?" he asked.

"What the bastards looked like?" Chaudhary asked. "The files we got from the Keepers are vague as fuck."

"Remember that everything the Keepers had on the Reejit, we took from the Eugenicists," Kay said grimly. The Eugenicists had ruled Mars, enforcing their totalitarian breeding program on the colony there for the entirety of the century-long war Earth had waged to stop them.

In the end, the Eugenicists had *defeated* Earth, only for the Mages they'd created in Project Olympus to reject their fate as test subjects and breeding stock. The revolt, led by the Mage who'd become Mage-King Desmond Michael Alexander I, had destroyed a lot of files and data along the way.

"The Eugenicist files on the Reejit that the Keepers saved were incomplete, and they suggested that the Reejit never showed their true faces to the Keepers, anyway," Kay concluded. "I believe I've seen more-complete versions than you have, Chaudhary, but there's nothing of *use* in those files.

"The Reejit spent their time on Mars in environment suits, never exiting them. They *appeared* to be roughly humanoid, bipedal and bilaterally symmetrical, but you're right. We don't know what they look like."

"We're not going to learn poking around this system, either," Koskinen said. "Any bodies are space dust by this point. And I doubt we're going to find intact paintings anywhere."

"Based on what the Keepers found in the handful of ruins we had to purify, the Reejit didn't include *people* in their artwork," O'Shea observed. "That might have been a particular cultural movement of the time, or something about the survey program whose ruins we went through, but we have no images of the bastards."

"They could pass for human in a vac-suit," Kay said. "That's enough for now. If we don't think we can learn anything more here, then our focus needs to move toward the sensor array Koskinen was assembling. We've turned it inward on Nemesis System so far.

"Now we need to turn it outward. This system might have been on the edge of the Reejit's territory, and other systems might have suffered in the same war that destroyed it, but they are out there. They are near *here.*

"And we. Will. Find. Them."

Because while Kay wasn't *listening* to the voice in the back of his head, he'd shed a lot of blood to discover that the star system he'd thought was the source of all their fears was already dead!

CHAPTER 5

"SIR, I APOLOGIZE for the interruption, but I have a report."

Roslyn looked up at Uesugi's soft-spoken words and concealed a smirk. The Tracker-Commander was young for their rank—one of the reasons for a number of junior officers trying out for training they had a high likelihood of failing was the automatic promotion to Commander—and it was clear that they'd never needed to interact much with a ship's captain before.

"Commander, do you think the Marine standing at the end of the corridor would have let you ring the admittance chime if you *weren't* supposed to interrupt me?" she asked wryly.

Major Suen Yang now commanded *Thorn's* Marine battalion. Prior to that, he'd been second-in-command of the security detachment for a military research facility on Tau Ceti *e*... except his commander had been Roslyn's ex-boyfriend, and when she'd needed people she could trust, she'd tagged the two of them.

Jalil Abdulrashid had died in the mission to track Nemesis down, but Yang had survived. Promoted and transferred to her command, he was one of the solid rocks in *Thorn's* command structure, and Roslyn knew she could trust his Marines—like the young man stationed at Roslyn's office door.

"That... makes sense, sir," Uesugi admitted. "I will admit that I only registered the Corporal's presence as a sign that you were in your office."

Which, given that it was a touch past midnight ship's time, wasn't a guarantee. For that matter, Roslyn knew that she probably *shouldn't* have been in her office—not the big day office by the bridge, anyway. She had a smaller office attached to her quarters, where working late would draw less attention, but she'd come back here after the senior staff meeting and hadn't left.

She was surprised Baars hadn't tried harder to move her.

"Corporal Schuyler was handpicked by the Major," she observed. "If Major Yang or I had given orders that I wasn't to be interrupted, you would have been gently intercepted by the Corporal or Master Chief Kovalyow."

The Chief of the Ship, after all, wielded a very real, if informal, power over even senior command staff.

"That... makes sense, sir," Uesugi repeated. They were still not quite standing at attention in front of her desk, and she gestured for them to sit.

"Water, Commander? I think my steward might magically appear and hurt both of us if I turn on the coffee machine."

"I can do better than water," Baars said, as if summoned by Roslyn's speaking of her. There was a second, semi-concealed entrance into the Captain's office that linked to the steward's "day office"—an annex to the small kitchen that served the bridge's snack needs.

She *was* carrying a tray with two glasses and a pitcher of iced water. As soon as that was on the table, though, she put her hands on her hips and studied Uesugi.

"Well, Tracker-Commander, sir?" she asked cheerfully. "Would you *like* something other than water?"

"Cherry soda?" the enby officer asked slowly.

"Give me two minutes," Baars promised. She glanced at Roslyn. "Skipper?"

"Water is fine," Roslyn replied, her focus still on the Tracker even as her steward vanished.

"Well, Commander, you risked waking the Captain up, so I'm assuming you have news. I hope it's good," she concluded.

"I have them, sir," they said quietly. "First jump, at least. I won't be a hundred percent certain until we're at the jump point and I've located their second jump, but I am pretty sure I've nailed down their initial vector."

They exhaled a soft sigh.

"I'm glad there was as much sensor data taken at the time as there was, though..."

"Though?" Roslyn prodded.

"Even more than in my training, it looks like recorded data is of limited use," they admitted. "It feels like I have to see real space, focused and filtered maybe, but the actual light of the jump, to be able to track it."

Roslyn chuckled softly.

"Fortunately, we have a lot of systems aboard the ship designed to do just that," she observed. That was, after all, a requirement for a *Mage* to use the amplifier that served as both *Thorn*'s jump drive and her most powerful weapon.

"Have you passed the vector information to the bridge?" she asked.

"I have, sir." Uesugi paused, then swallowed. "The next trace should be faster, but I am still very new at this."

"Tracker-Commander, four of the seven Jump Mages on this ship are Mage-Ensigns," Roslyn pointed out gently. "*Four.* We shouldn't have more than four *Ensigns* aboard, total."

And that was putting aside that one of the Mage-Ensigns should have been an upperclasswoman. Mage-Ensign Anuradha Sigourney was promising as both an officer and a Mage, but her promotion had *solely* been to make sure that *Thorn* did have seven Jump Mages.

Because while Nemesis might have managed to put *six* Mages on *Rose*, very, very few people ever tried to put enough Mages aboard a ship to jump more than once an hour. And every edge Roslyn had over *Rose* was a chance to bring the rogue ship down before something went very wrong.

"We seem to have more Ensigns than that," Uesugi said slowly.

"Twenty-six, Tracker-Commander," Roslyn told him, rising from her chair as Baars returned to the room with Uesugi's soda. "We have twenty-six brand-new Ensigns aboard. You are far from the only person doing this for the first time, and we will allow the time needed to get it *right*.

"As one of my instructors long ago told me, slow is smooth. Smooth is fast. We do it slow and we do it right—until we learn to do it right and do it fast," she said with a smile. "We're a long damn way behind *Rose*, Commander, so I'm going to go get us started.

"Tajana, can you make sure our friend gets his soda and himself to his quarters?"

Uesugi looked about to object but Roslyn raised a hand.

"You will rest, Tracker-Commander, and then you will be ready to get through as many of *Rose*'s jumps as you can before you fall down," she told him. "There are enough Mages on this ship to jump as fast as you can track Nemesis's ship."

She smiled.

"Slow is smooth, Commander, but I will do everything in my power to make sure nothing *else* is slowing us down!"

"Captain on the bridge!"

Corporal Schuyler had clearly managed to beat Roslyn to the bridge. The Captain's sentry was theoretically a separate duty detachment from the bridge detail, but the physical proximity of the two duty stations made working together inevitable.

And Schuyler had clearly cut through to take over as sentry by the door when Roslyn came in, making sure everyone knew the Captain had entered the bridge.

"At ease," Roslyn ordered. She crossed to the command seat, currently occupied by Mage-Ensign Sigourney.

The tiny dark-colored officer, only barely *not* a teenager, practically teleported out of the chair to salute despite the order to stand at ease.

"At *ease*, Ensign," Roslyn repeated. "Did you receive the vector from Tracker-Commander Uesugi?"

Sigourney flushed dark, half at the question and half at the instruction, then twisted to try and look at the repeater screens. She wasn't the officer of the watch—that was the ship's assistant tactical officer, Lieutenant Commander Akiko Ueda.

An older man who should not, Roslyn recognized, have been standing aside while his junior was being hovered over by the Captain. That would require a conversation later.

For the moment, she simply looked up from the Mage-Ensign and found Ueda at the tactical station. He tried to avoid her gaze for a moment, then saw her gaze and straightened.

"Commander," she said crisply. She didn't specify the order. She didn't *need* to.

Ueda rose and crossed over to join them, barely managing to not look sheepish. He clearly hadn't been expecting the Captain on deck on a midnight watch.

"The Tracker-Commander would have sent the vector to the watch stander," Roslyn pointed out, both reassuring Sigourney and prodding Ueda. "Did we receive it?"

"Let me check," Ueda replied, tapping a sequence on his wrist-comp. "Ah, yes. Yes, sir. About ten minutes ago."

Roslyn studied the man for a few long silent seconds.

"And you thought this wasn't worthy of notice, Lieutenant Commander?" she asked.

"I don't generally check my emails on duty, sir," he said crisply. "I cycle the watch stander messages every hour or so, unless they're flagged as urgent."

Roslyn leaned past Sigourney to tap in several commands on the big chair's repeater screens. The message and its attachment popped up, showing that, no, Uesugi *hadn't* flagged it as urgent.

On the other hand... She bit down on her immediate instinct and turned an *instructional* voice on Ensign Sigourney.

"Ensign, note that Lieutenant Commander Ueda's methodology is not *in*effective," she said softly. "But in our current situation, we need to be watching for messages from the Tracker-Commander.

"The jump vectors for *Rose* are the single most critical piece of information that could be coming to the bridge right now, short of *we are under attack*." She looked at Ueda, who had clearly registered both that she *wasn't* reprimanding him... and that her means of *not* reprimanding him had been quite pointed.

"Do you want me to carry out the jump, sir?" Sigourney asked, her body quivering with nervous energy.

Roslyn considered for a moment, then sighed and gestured the young woman aside.

"Not this time, Mage-Ensign," she said. "We're jumping from relatively close into the yards and from a relatively busy zone. I will handle the jump and then leave the watch in the capable hands of yourself and Lieutenant Commander Ueda."

Sigourney saluted and stepped away from the command seat and the simulacrum suspended in front of it. Roslyn returned the salute and took the seat.

"Lieutenant Commander Ueda, I relieve you," she said formally.

"I stand relieved, Mage-Captain!"

Roslyn tapped a command on the arm of the chair and safety restraints locked into place. Out of the corner of her eye, she saw Ueda return to his station—but also saw him take two seconds to make sure Mage-Ensign Sigourney knew where to seat herself as the process began.

All around Roslyn, the already-quiet bridge slowed to silence. Aboard a warship like *Thorn*, the bridge was also the simulacrum chamber, the heart of the magic that transported her between the stars.

In every direction she looked, the outer bulkheads—deck and ceiling, too—of the bridge were covered in screens. At first glance, they looked like ordinary screens—but the displays and data codes were a transparent overlay over the *real* imagery.

Each "pixel" of those screens was linked to a fiber-optic cable bringing light directly from the outside of the ship. To Roslyn's *intellectual* mind, it wasn't really correct to say that she was seeing the outside world directly—but somehow, for her magic, it was enough.

The command seat shifted slightly, rising up and forward to bring the simulacrum from in front of the chair to basically in the Mage-Captain's lap. At that distance, it was clear that the pyramid-shaped model was nearly liquid, rippling almost invisibly as it mirrored every change and shift to the outside of the ship.

Thorn herself, of course, didn't have runes carved into her outer hull that would have been visible at this scale. The runes on *Thorn* were *inside* the hull, for one thing, and at the five-hundred-to-one scale of the simulacrum would have been mere marks.

The runes across the simulacrum were an interlaced flowing mesh cut into the outer hull, the only distinction between the silver model and the starship itself. On the side facing Roslyn were two blank spaces in the runic matrix, each roughly a palm's width apart.

Removing the thin black gloves ubiquitous to any Jump Mage, Roslyn leaned forward and placed her palms on those blank spaces. The runes inlaid years earlier into her palms clicked into place with the ease of long practice, and she exhaled as her magic completed the circuit.

The various suspended platforms that held the bridge stations around her vanished as her senses became *Thorn*'s senses. The shipyard station and its planetary anchor there. The guardian battleship—her crew on edge after the last few weeks—over *there*.

Other ships were scattered around, but none close enough to impact the jump. Roslyn spared a fraction of her attention back to the screens around her, bringing up the vector Tracker-Commander Uesugi had detected.

She'd had seventeen different jumps out of Tau Ceti calculated. It was a matter of moments to match one to *Rose*'s course. One of the reasons she'd taken on the jump was that Sigourney would have, quite reasonably, taken an hour or more to get the numbers ready.

Roslyn did it with a quarter of her attention in about a minute. She'd prepared a lot of the data in advance, and Uesugi's trace had given her much of what she was missing, but practice still made it smooth and fast.

"All hands, prepare to jump," she said calmly. "Lieutenant Commander Ueda. Is the ship prepared to jump?"

"All stations report green, sir."

There were other preparations she would do if she thought *Rose* was waiting for them, but *Rose* had left on a mission. One advantage of a stern chase was that she could be quite sure the enemy wasn't waiting for her there.

Roslyn nodded slowly and refocused, *becoming Thorn* as she integrated herself fully into the amplifier matrix and summoned her power. The spell would teleport a single person a few thousand kilometers—farther for Roslyn, given her own natural power, let alone the Rune of Power carved into her arm—but matched with the amplifier...

Magic flowed through her and she *stepped*. The energy tore out of her in a wave, forcing the breath from her lungs as the world changed.

"Jump complete," Ueda reported from the tactical station. "All scans report clear; we are alone. One light-year from the Tau Ceti System along the projected course."

Roslyn released the simulacrum and nodded unsteadily. No one, thankfully, expected even the *Captain* to jump without showing signs of the drain.

"Run the full scans," she ordered the ATO. "We'll need every piece of data we can scrape together for Uesugi once he's back on duty.

"At that point, I think we'll be moving pretty quickly. We've a long way to go—they've got two weeks' lead—but we're going to catch these people."

"Yes, sir," Ueda confirmed.

"You have the watch, Lieutenant Commander."

CHAPTER 6

"WE'VE SCANNED about a hundred stars at this point," Koskinen told Kay.

The Nemesis leader was sitting on *Rose's* bridge, poking at the repeater screens around the Captain's chair to make sure he understood what he was looking at.

Kay was grimly aware that he and Koskinen were the only experienced military officers aboard the ship. They had enough ex-RMN *people* that he wasn't worried about the ship failing to work or them not being able to run the systems, but systems specialists were... well... specialists.

And when all you had was a very technical specialty, either you solved problems with your specialty or that problem didn't *exist* to you. To actually *command* a warship required a broader skillset.

Kay wasn't convinced that he had it. He knew *perfectly damn well* that Koskinen didn't—but between them, he figured they could muddle through.

"And? Have we found something useful?" Kay asked. A few commands to the repeater screens managed to *finally* locate and bring up the attachment Koskinen had sent him.

The fiber-optic screen walls around him flickered as the overlays incorporated the data. What had just been pinpricks of light before now acquired icons and datacodes—and star after star contained a dark burnt-orange icon Kay wasn't familiar with.

Too many of them. And the icon, a dangerously familiar trefoil, didn't exactly set the mind at ease.

"What am I looking at, Rokus?" he finally asked.

The handful of techs on the bridge were ignoring the two "officers," focusing on their own work and leaving them to their conversation.

"You saw it, I'm guessing."

"Nineteen systems you've marked with a variation of the nuclear warning symbol, but given that star systems are a touch difficult to *nuke*, I feel that I'm missing something," Kay said drily.

"Well, all it *really* means is that we detected significant amounts of gamma radiation in the five-eleven kiloelectron-volt range," Koskinen told him. "Unfortunately, *that* means that enough fucking antimatter was annihilated in the star system to show up on an *interstellar scale*."

Kay whistled softly.

"How much are we talking about?"

"It depends. Detonation in space? A lot. To leave a lasting signature visible at these distances for more than a few years at most? Bigger than any battle of the Secession."

Some of those battles had seen literally *thousands* of gigaton-range antimatter warheads unleashed. Possibly hundreds of thousands.

"So, what? Millions of warheads?"

"Closest star system we've scanned is twelve light-years away," Koskinen said slowly. "Closest *antimatter* signature is about twenty-five. Farthest is about a hundred—I don't think it's *possible* to detect five-eleven keV gamma radiation farther than that.

"Given the timeline *here*, I'd say we're looking at something like two hundred years ago for the timeframe of the battle. So, our closest antimatter-bombarded system is twenty-five light-years away, and the battle would probably have been a hundred and seventy years before that, minimum."

"So?" Kay prodded. He knew the limits of his skillset. He could rebuild—he *had* rebuilt—a conspiracy from isolated cells and backup resources and lead it successfully. He could fool a Martian officer into thinking he was an ally. He could break anyone aboard *Rose* in half, Mages and Augments and ordinary crew alike.

He couldn't do the math to back-calculate how many antimatter weapons would need to be detonated to be visible from forty light-years a hundred and fifty years afterward.

"Space battle would have required at least an exaton-equivalent of warheads," Koskinen told him. "A *billion*, give or take, of the one-gigaton missiles in our magazines."

Kay exhaled a sharp breath, then gave his tactical man a sharp look.

"Well, that's a nightmare, but it doesn't sound like what you think happened," he observed. Even the ex-Navy officer wasn't going to be *that* calm if he thought they were hunting an enemy that regularly hurled around a billion antimatter warheads.

"For some strange reason, the Navy never tested the theory, but there is theoretically more likely to be remnant antimatter from a planetary strike," Koskinen told him. "So, there will be a low-level long-term annihilation event in a strike crater—we can actually see it here, on Nemesis IV, though."

"Would IV have shown up with this signature?" Kay asked.

"From close enough, yes," the other man confirmed. "I'd say that from about forty to fifty light-years, in Nemesis's case, this system would have flagged as one of my problems."

"So... that might explain anything inside forty-light-years or so," Kay said grimly. It wasn't an explanation he *liked*. "And the farther-away ones?"

"Scale and time," Koskinen said simply. "The farther away the system we're scanning is, the older the data we're seeing. None of our scans of Nemesis, for example, were less than a hundred and fifty years old before we got here.

"So, anything I'm seeing from a system a hundred light-years away is a hundred years old. So, it's closer in time to whatever impact we're seeing... but to see it from this range, even taking that into account, means it was a bigger yield."

"Planet-killers," Kay supposed.

Koskinen grimaced and gestured at the image of Nemesis IV, still close to hand.

"*That* was fucking planet-killers, boss," he said flatly. "A handful of weapons, by any space-battle standard. *Rose* could hit a planet with three or four times that many weapons if we overrode all of the interlocks to stop us doing just that.

"Everything on that planet is dead. It will never have an ecosystem again. Anything *more* than that is overkill."

"So, what are we looking at?" Kay asked carefully. "I'm not one to believe in overkill."

"Me either, but I suspect that actually *destroying* a planet might count."

Kay took a moment to process that, turning away from Koskinen to survey the stars around them. The arc back toward human space didn't have any of the burnt-orange trefoils. Nothing even in the area closest to Nemesis, though he suspected that was because there *was* a time limit on how long the strikes would be visible.

Nineteen star systems that they could *see* had been subject to brutal antimatter bombardment, sufficient to leave unreacted antimatter sending off gamma rays for years—a *century*, at least!—afterward.

There was a rough pattern to them, one that suggested a broad direction for the core of the Reejit territory. But it *also* marked an area where, more likely than not, billions of people had died.

"What the fuck *are* these people?" he growled. "Twenty systems exterminated?"

"Some of them might be battles," Koskinen suggested. "Especially the ones farther away. If there was a battle, say, within a few months of the lightspeed delay... that would be *very* visible still."

"The odds aren't in favor of that," Kay replied. "This system was wrecked over two centuries ago. It's possible one of those was being attacked a century ago, but few wars last a century."

"Some do. The Eugenicist War did."

"The Eugenicist *Wars* lasted over a century," Kay conceded. "But there were about four actual *wars* in there; that's why we call it that. Most of the actual time of that century was a cold war where Earth and Mars were building fleets and glaring at each other."

Without magic—and therefore without either teleportation or antimatter—the distance between Earth and Mars had made the conflict against the Eugenicists a slow and ponderous affair.

"We don't have a time frame on when the strikes were," Koskinen said slowly. "It's possible we're seeing something equivalent to that. Every twenty to thirty years, a new spike of conflict in an ongoing cold war."

"Each phase seeing worlds destroyed?" Kay asked. "That wouldn't be sustainable for any interstellar civilization."

He shook his head.

"Which would only make them more willing to jump on humanity for new resources, too," he said grimly.

"Did you find any *good* news out there?"

"Define *good news*," Koskinen said. "If you mean *did I find an inhabited system*? Yes. Depending on what else you mean..." The Finn shook his head. "This region of space has been pasted flat by some fighting that makes the Secession look like a frat party."

"Wait." Kay turned his attention fully back on the other man. "You found an inhabited system?"

The big man pointed at a star he'd highlighted in a blue-green halo. It was the only one with that highlight, and Kay had missed it for the anti-matter warning signs.

"Forty-two light-years from here," Koskinen said. "So, data is forty-two years out of date. But forty-two years ago, System Twenty-Eight was radiating in the usual electromagnetic spectrum of reasonably modern industry. Nothing coherent—we're not watching their television at this range, not with the probe net we've got in place!—but they're into high-energy radio at a minimum.

"Wireless data transfer, not just voice or television."

"Not coherent at forty-plus light-years," Kay agreed. "Anything familiar in that mess?"

"You just *said* nothing is coherent at this range," Koskinen reminded him drily. "But... that's the funny part. Some of it *might* be our protocols. Hard to say."

"A human colony?" The Nemesis leader grimaced. "That might not be as helpful as we'd like."

"It's all we've got, boss." The Commander gestured around the bridge at the other stars. "There are few signals and ghosts that *might* be something real, maybe. Space-based colonies or early planetary settlements, but nothing distinctly high-tech or high-pop.

"System Twenty-Eight might be human. But even if they are, they've been here long enough to have major system-wide transmissions forty years ago. They'll know *something* of what went down here.

"Sheer self-preservation requires *that*."

"Fair." Kay nodded his concession and he looked at the haloed star. "What else is out here for habitable systems?"

"A few possibles and a pair of definites outside System Twenty-Eight," his subordinate replied, haloing half a dozen systems. "From what I can tell from this distance, all are on the damp and warm side. Unusually so— It's like, well..."

Koskinen trailed off and Kay gave him another sharp look.

"I'd say we're looking at a region where someone with a drier preferred zone than us already settled anything they liked," the ex-Navy officer told him. "And... well... someone else came along and blew them all up."

Kay looked at the stars again and sighed.

"Less damage in the direction of the Protectorate, right?"

"Less clear antimatter bombardment, anyway," Koskinen confirmed. "More habitable planets, though still statistically low."

"Someone made a giant mess of this chunk of space," Kay said with a sigh. "Forty-two light-years is three days' travel."

He had four Jump Mages aboard, including himself, but only Tomas was capable of jumping on the Navy's "six-hour" standard. Even Kay had to stick to the eight-hour standard of civilian Mages—as much due to lack of experience and a need to keep an extra eye open as anything else.

"Another 'council' meeting, then?" Koskinen asked, his lack of enthusiasm clear.

"Everyone needs to be on the same page," Kay told him. "But one thing's for sure: unless someone has a reason to stay in this *fucking graveyard*, we may as well head to this System Twenty-Eight.

"At least there we might find people who can answer questions!"

CHAPTER 7

ROSLYN WAS the youngest serving Mage-Captain in the Royal Navy, a situation readily explained to those in the know by the Sapphire Medal of Valor. Three times she'd walked into hell for Mage-Queen and Protectorate, and three times she'd emerged intact.

Still, even at her age, she'd begun her career in a time where interstellar communication was the realm of high-speed couriers and the occasional massive piece of magical infrastructure. The desperate run to find a Runic Transceiver Array and warn the Protectorate of the Republic invasion had been where she'd earned her *first* Medal of Valor.

The fact that her ship, now two days and over thirty light-years from Tau Ceti, carried systems that could provide a live communications link to Mars was *still* strange to her.

It had its advantages, though. Prince-Chancellor Damien Montgomery had returned to Mars to the usual chaotic mess that awaited a head of government who stepped away for *any* reason. Scheduling a time for the Mage-Queen of Mars and her right-hand man to *both* have a virtual meeting with one of the Queen's starship Captains had taken longer than anyone had wanted *Thorn* to spend in Tau Ceti.

But now the wallscreen in Roslyn's office had split into two separate video feeds, both relaying along the same encrypted Link from Mars. Each feed showed a very similar office, though the decorations were different.

Mage-Queen Kiera Alexander's office was decorated with handmade shelves holding a rotating selection of fourteen starship models—models the Mage-Queen had built with her own hands, *mostly* from kits.

She'd run out of preexisting kits, Roslyn knew, which meant that the model of *Thorn* currently at the center of the top shelf had been fabricated from a downscaled version of the explorer cruiser's *actual* schematics.

That wasn't an option available to modelmakers with lower clearance levels, Roslyn presumed.

Montgomery's office was plainer. Its decorations were more eclectic, as if they hadn't been picked by a single person—which was the truth, from what Roslyn understood. The Prince-Chancellor decided what was displayed in his office based on *who sent it*, not *what it was*, and his office was decorated with gifts from the planets he'd served as Hand of the Mage-King.

Both offices were extremely plain and simple at their base. Stone carved from Olympus Mons itself, with walls paneled in oak taken from ancient forests on Earth and treated for endurance. None of the furnishings or structures in the office were ornate... and none of them were less than a century old.

Some types of simplicity were cheap, with price the driving factor. The simplicity of the offices of Olympus Mons was *very* expensive, absolute endurance and timeless style being the driving factor.

Looking at those video feeds, it was surprisingly easy to forget that no one on the three-way call was over forty years old. Damien Montgomery was the oldest by most of a decade, but the Mage-Queen was actually *younger* than Roslyn herself.

"The last thing I want is to put a time pressure on us," Alexander said calmly as the pleasantries finished, "but that is the reality of our lives. Damien and I have a meeting with the Legion Reconciliation Committee in forty minutes.

"*This*"—the Queen gestured at the conference— "is critical. So is seeing to the safety and potential incorporation into the Protectorate of the millions of people the First Legion conquered and enslaved."

"It's been an ongoing process since Mage-Admiral Jakab took the Mackenzie System two years ago," Montgomery said with a sigh. "You'd think, after two years, we'd be close to a final answer, but humans are humans... and the First Legion made a *fucking* mess."

Roslyn had seen some of that, though her involvement in that war had ended after the first battle in Legion space. She'd been critical in *finding* the First Legion and the hidden colonies they'd invaded, but the loss of her ship and a number of close friends at the Battle of Exeter had seen her sent to a teaching post conveniently close to some of the Navy's best therapists.

"If I never encounter any version of humanity's oldest sin again, I will have seen too many slaves and slavers for ten lifetimes," Roslyn murmured. "And I somehow doubt we've burned out those particular vipers even in our own territory."

"Three times," Montgomery observed. "*Three times* in my career alone we have located and burned out the major slaver port in the Protectorate. Darkport, back before I was even a Hand. Chasmport, at your own hands three years ago. Iron Gates, four years before that by a Navy squadron under the command of Hand Lomond."

"And yet that horror continues to exist in Our Protectorate," Alexander said coldly. The Mage-Queen did *not* use the royal *We* often in private conversation. It was a sign that she, like Roslyn, considered the presence of human trafficking in the Protectorate as one of their greatest failures.

"We're working on it," Roslyn said. "As Prince Montgomery said, we've taken down the main port three times in the last decade and a half. The records I've seen suggest that Darkport existed for *three* decades prior to that.

"We're getting better."

"*Better* still leaves too many people being trafficked for labor and sex and whatever else these *fuckheads* can think of," Alexander snarled.

Roslyn couldn't argue. She was entirely in agreement with her monarch's opinions on the matter—if anything, her own opinions were *fiercer*, except that she was required to mute her reactions as part of the mask of command.

"Time," Montgomery murmured. "The three of us are all, in our ways, aware of and focused on that problem. But right now, we have a different matter at hand.

"*Rose.*"

"Nemesis," Alexander agreed. "I really had hoped we'd finished them off with Winton, but here we are."

"MISS is busy tracing down every thread we got from the whole mess on Tau Ceti," the Prince-Chancellor observed. "The good news is that we seem to have enough pieces to wrap up most of what's left.

"The bad news is that they keep running across entire cells that appear to have packed up and shut down already." Montgomery shook his head. "Timelines I'm getting out of Director LaMonte are... Well, I'm starting to think the attempt to kidnap Kiera was as much a surprise to most of Nemesis as it was to us."

That wasn't what Roslyn had been expecting—and the Mage-Queen didn't look overly happy with the assessment either.

"Explain," the Queen ordered.

"We're seeing some signs of what looks like an orderly shutdown that started about six months ago," Montgomery said. "And then, a few weeks ago, around when you and Barry were picked up by the rescue teams, things were suddenly accelerated, and a *lot* of cells shut things down much more abruptly.

"It really looks like the attack on *Extravagant Voyage* was something of a rogue operation. Once it went down and we started hunting the details, Nemesis got desperate, and they called everyone in to Tau Ceti to execute their seizure of the *Thorns.*"

Extravagant Voyage had been the ship that Kiera Alexander had re-ferred to as her *mobile meat market*—to her close friends, at least. The ship had been a luxury liner carrying the young Mage-Queen around the Protectorate to meet every eligible bachelor Mage they could find, to try to find the Mage-Queen a consort to... well, provide some genetic samples for her children.

No one in the know figured that Kiera's children weren't going to be artificial zygotes more closely resembling *clones* than anything else. The Protectorate couldn't afford to lose the unique magical gifts of the Mage-King's line, the Rune Wright Gift shared by the two people on the call from Mars.

Without that Gift and the ability to read the flows of magic in runes, the Olympus Mons Amplifier was useless as anything more than a test for scraps of the regular Mage Gift.

With it, the mountain-scale amplifier could be used to manipulate anything in the entire star system. The Olympus Mons Amplifier had been provided by the Reejit *to* test for Mage Gift, allowing Project Olympus to exist in the first place.

And no one who knew that liked to think about why, especially given the clear link to the Prometheus Interface Mage brain–driven jump drives provided to the Republic.

So, the Mage-Queen of Mars's children would be genetically engineered, but they couldn't be *obvious* clones, so a partner was necessary. Even more so than normal, as Roslyn understood it, because given a *non*-Royal-line Rune Wright, the Mountain's geneticists had taken large samples from Damien Montgomery—and the *last* thing anyone could afford was for Kiera Alexander to give birth to children that resembled the man who had been her Regent and legal guardian!

But that hunt had made her vulnerable, and Nemesis operatives had tried to kidnap her from the ship. The intervention of the young Mage Barry Carpentier had saved her from whatever their plan was—through Carpentier's own highly classified but clearly unusual magical gifts.

"So, once that scheme went wrong, whatever its source, Nemesis threw everything into seizing the *Thorns*," Roslyn concluded. "But what do they *want* from *Rose*? We took hundreds of prisoners aboard *Thorn*."

"And those prisoners are part of why we're rolling up what's left of Nemesis quite so effectively," Montgomery told her. "LaMonte is telling me that it looks like the *only* major portion of the conspiracy that's left is aboard *Rose*."

"As for what they want, I think that's obvious, isn't it?" Alexander asked. "They want to be able to prove to everyone that they were *right*. That everything they have done, from creating the Prometheus Interface to provoking the Secession, to creating Orpheus and all of the rest... that all of it was necessary to prepare us for the war that's coming."

"Fuck that," Roslyn said flatly. "If they'd just *told* everyone everything a decade ago, we'd be just as ready now."

"Probably. Maybe." Montgomery growled in the back of his throat. "Removing the *costs* of the damn war, we might be *more* ready. We are certainly more ready than we were ten years ago, but the atrocities they inflicted to get us here..."

"Like I said. They want to prove to everyone that they were right," Alexander repeated. "To buy themselves the awards and glory they feel their *crimes* deserved."

"So, they're going to go poke the Reejit and start said bloody war?" Roslyn asked. "Because we were going looking for the aliens anyway."

"I suspect they believed that we were going to take too long, go too slowly, and let our newly built strength atrophy," the Mage-Queen said.

"A strength we haven't even finished *building*," Montgomery said. "But the yards and such are in place for the expansion to *continue* if we had a real threat. I'd rather find the Reejit and make decisions with full information. Potentially even negotiate."

"We don't *know* enough," Alexander said quietly. "We don't actually know for sure that the Reejit working on Project Olympus meant to turn humanity into a source of brains for their own version of the Prometheus Interface.

"Hell, we don't even know if the Prometheus Interface was something they took from the Reejit files, because, thanks to Nemesis, *we* don't know what the Keepers knew about all of that."

"I know Samuel Finley claimed to have invented it," Montgomery said softly. "He was a Rune Wright. He may have just taken schematics given to him of the Reejit system and turned it into something that would work on human Mages—but I *have* studied the Interface and it doesn't look alien to me.

"I think he was given a concept and some details from Reejit files, but he basically built the Prometheus Interface from the ground up. I think we have to assume that the Reejit have something similar, but the Prometheus Interface was all Finley."

"It makes life easier if we can *just* blame the aliens, doesn't it?" Roslyn asked with a grimace.

"Exactly. That's what Nemesis is doing," the Prince-Chancellor confirmed. "They want to find the Reejit to prove that it was the aliens' fault all along. That their crimes were necessary."

"And they couldn't let someone *else* find the aliens, because we might find another solution than the war they think is inevitable," Alexander said grimly. "We will not let them decide Our policies and future, Mage-Captain Chambers. Do you understand?"

"I do," Roslyn said steadily. She wasn't sure how that would break down in the end, but she understood where her Queen was coming from. "What about *Rose?*"

"We would *like* you to bring Nemesis's leadership home in chains, to face proper public trial for their crimes," Montgomery said. "While I have been forced to accept that secrets are an unfortunately necessary part of government, secrets like *this* are toxic. They eat away at the integrity and transparency *required* of good government.

"So, a best-case scenario would be bringing people and evidence back that would allow us to hold some scrupulously honest trials where we lay out the truth of what they've been up to the last twenty years."

"There would be consequences to that," Alexander murmured. "Ones that my government are more than prepared to accept in pursuit of that *integrity and transparency*, but without someone to point to, we will need to declassify everything around Nemesis over time.

"A trial will require it to be released all at once, and I don't know how well the Protectorate general population will handle the revelation that a group of alien-obsessed *fanatics* created the Prometheus Interface and, in a very real sense, the entirety of the UnArcana Rebellions."

"That's the best case," Roslyn said levelly. "We all know that's not over-ly likely."

None of the leadership aboard *Thorn* had been taken alive. Some had fought to the death. At least two, when the bridge was in Roslyn's hands and the battle was clearly over, had committed suicide.

"We know," Montgomery agreed. "If possible, we want *Rose* back. She and *Thorn* are basically unique at the moment. Replicable, of course, but we didn't expect to *need* more than two explorer cruisers."

He snorted.

"In hindsight, we were told we needed a class of four if we wanted a guaranteed capability. We should have listened."

"*If* you can recapture *Rose* without risking your people, you have been provided with every security code needed to override her systems," Alexander said. "Nemesis may have disabled those. They certainly have demonstrated the ability to shut down the overrides provided to my Hands."

"The wish list is one thing," Montgomery reminded both of them. "The *mission*, the *necessity*, is something else.

"No matter what else happens. No matter what it takes. Nemesis cannot be allowed to provoke the Reejit into war. I doubt I even need to specify, but you are authorized to engage and destroy *Rose*."

Roslyn swallowed and nodded. The Prince-Chancellor *didn't* need to say that, but having it explicitly laid out was important.

"Do we even know who's in charge aboard her?" she asked. "Is it Major Riley?"

Kent Riley, also known as Nemesis One, was the leader of Nemesis. Roslyn's ex-boyfriend, the crime lord and Nemesis agent Robert O'Kane, had given them the name. Riley hadn't been aboard *Thorn*, so...

"We've confirmed that, yes," Montgomery said quietly. "We're not entirely sure who the coterie around him are, but we have reason to believe that the entire remaining senior leadership of Nemesis is aboard *Rose*."

"Because the rest are either in our cells or dead, somewhere between the attack on *Extravagant Voyage* and the attack on *Rose* and *Thorn*," the Queen noted.

"They can't get away again, Roslyn," Alexander concluded. "If Nemesis and Riley aren't brought to heel, their desperation to prove that everything they have done was *necessary* will lead them to start a war we do not want."

"A war we will likely have to fight regardless," the Prince-Chancellor observed. "But one that we are not yet ready for.

"Do you understand, Roslyn?"

"I do." She nodded her assurances to them. "I will make certain of it, my Lord, my Liege. Nemesis will not escape us this time."

CHAPTER 8

PASSING ON the Mage-Queen's directive to Roslyn's staff required *somewhat* more delicacy than Alexander and Montgomery had used with her. Roslyn was nervously aware that she was one of the Mage-Queen's few actual *friends* of her own age, though she was reasonably comfortable that her rank was entirely her own doing.

It still allowed a degree of frankness that she hoped the young Queen didn't unleash on *all* of her starship captains.

"Our fundamental mission is unchanged," she told her collected officers. "The parameters, however, are clearer now. Nemesis is chasing a nightmare. But for reasons we don't understand, we have heard *nothing* from said nightmare in over two hundred years."

"Then why are we poking it at all?" Commander Beck asked, her executive officer playing devil's advocate as promised.

"The *plan* wasn't to poke them," Roslyn said with a chuckle. "The *plan* was to build two very long-ranged, very sneaky ships and follow up on what limited information we had to locate their territory and learn what we could before making formal contact."

"Except that this crew isn't sufficiently trained on and experienced in this ship's systems to guarantee truly stealthy arrivals and departures." The dark and hawklike Lieutenant Commander Vladislav Leavitt looked very much the mirror of his Cossack ancestors, barely-trimmed black beard and all. A native of Ukraine on Earth, he was *Thorn's* tactical officer, responsible for her hundred missile launchers and ten superheavy battle lasers.

"No one is," Roslyn told Leavitt. "The only people who have practical experience with the systems *Thorn* is built with belong to MISS, and Director LaMonte has them busy on other affairs."

Director Kelly LaMonte was the deputy head of the Martian Interstellar Security Service, formerly the head of their stealth-ship operations until losing her ship and almost her entire crew in the Battle of Exeter.

Like Roslyn, she had a long-standing professional relationship with Damien Montgomery that she'd used to cut through red tape and help propel herself to her position. Unlike Roslyn, she'd run out of job opportunities that didn't involve a desk.

"I'm still surprised that the explorer cruisers are so heavily rigged for stealth," Ruben Waldfogel observed. The Lieutenant Commander responsible for *Thorn*'s engine rooms and other systems was carved from the "tall and handsome" mold that usually drew Roslyn's unprofessional attention, but his blond hair and blue eyes weren't really her type.

"There are major sacrifices made in the integrity and durability of our systems to provide that option—an option that is completely useless in any combat situation," the engineer concluded.

"The *Thorn*-class ships were supposed to be able to sneak *and* fight," Roslyn agreed. "But not at the same time. It is part of *our* job to turn the designed theoretical doctrine into reality, but the *presumption* is that we will see conflict coming with enough time to fully disengage the stealth systems."

"We *can't* do both," Waldfogel said bluntly. "Just the ability to store and control the venting of heat the way we do requires structures throughout the entire ship that carry that heat in ways that undermine our defensive systems. Having those systems active..."

The outer layer of armor on a Martian warship was a complicated amalgam of ceramics, metals, electronics, explosives and other even more esoteric systems. The intent was to channel energy and force away from the point of impact, allowing the ship to survive a near-direct-hit from a gigaton-range antimatter warhead.

Not... *many* said direct hits. But at least one—and Roslyn could see how having permanent heat channels cut through the backing of the armor could undermine that system.

"Well, note down what you can on that," Roslyn told him. "Let's keep it in mind. We're unlikely to be able to plan to *never* get hit, but I need a sense of how badly our energy-dispersal systems are compromised, Lieutenant Commander."

"I'll have my people pull some numbers," Waldfogel confirmed. "We're still better off armored than not, but there are definitely pieces of our hull we *don't* want getting hit."

"Pass that information over to me when you pull it together," Leavitt said drily. "Because the spots *we* don't want to get hit are going to be the spots I *want* to hit *Rose* when we get there."

"And we will get there," Roslyn told them. "Mage-Commander Tod?"

"Thanks to Tracker-Commander Uesugi, we've made sixty jumps in just over three days," Mage-Commander Femi Tod, the ship's Navigator and senior Ship's Mage—per the standard that excluded the Mage-Captain and a Mage XO from that status—replied.

"Their analysis suggests that in so doing, we've gained a day on *Rose*. They were, fourteen days ago, jumping fifteen times a day. They were not, I would guess, having to stop and scan for their destination. They knew exactly where they were going."

Uesugi wasn't in the meeting themselves. They were already putting in eighteen-hour days, with each jump slightly faster to track than the one before that.

What Roslyn *wasn't* telling them was that no Tracker she had records of had ever managed less than forty-five minutes to track a jump more than a week old. The Tracker-Commander was approaching that metric already, and she was curious to see if they'd break it.

The only thing allowing *Thorn's* Mages to jump as fast as Uesugi was tracking was that everybody, including the Tracker, needed to sleep!

"Unfortunately, from the jump schedule I reviewed prior to this meeting, we're about at the limits of the intersection between Uesugi's ability to track and our ability to coordinate jump spells," Roslyn warned. "In theory, we have seven fully trained Navy Jump Mages aboard and can jump twenty-eight times a day—but we all need six hours between jumps."

And Roslyn suspected that Tod was on the same page as her in keep-ing a *very* careful eye on the intervals for the Mage-Ensigns. *Roslyn* could, in a pinch, jump after five hours or maybe even four... but Roslyn was from the First Families of Tau Ceti and was in the top quarter-percentile of human Mages.

Oddly, the Rune of Power Damien Montgomery had carved into her arm did *nothing* for her ability to jump. Not enough that she'd noticed, anyway. She suspected that the nature of the magic overlapped with that of the ship's amplifier rather than augmenting it.

And even with the Rune of Power and her naturally high levels of magic, Roslyn could only jump after four hours *once*. She'd then need to rest for at least twelve hours and probably not even push to six hours for a day or two after.

She'd ridden close enough to thaumic burnout to know she never wanted to do that again. There were medications that could "refill the well," so to speak, for lesser magics. None of them could artificially provide enough energy to jump a starship.

"A stern chase is a long chase," Beck observed. "If we're gaining five light-years a day on them, I guess we're hoping they stopped to investigate somewhere along the way."

"Or that they're going far enough that we can catch up to them before they reach the Reejit," Roslyn agreed.

She surveyed the conference room.

"We don't have the crew we were supposed to have," she warned. "Nemesis saw too many of the officers and spacers who were suppos-ed to serve on the *Thorns* sent to the wrong places. Of *Thorn*'s planned crew, Commander Beck and I are only the senior officers actually serving aboard, and we only have roughly twenty-five percent of the Chiefs and senior ratings.

"Our officers, our noncoms, our spacers... Very few of us have the rank or experience for our roles." She grinned. "Except our TCSDF transfers. *They* have all been given rank commensurate to their experience."

"Which may be a problem, in some cases," Beck warned. "Most were held back simply because the TCSDF is a... saturated force, without as much room for advancement as anyone would like. Some, though, almost certainly missed promotion for good reason."

"And that, XO, is what the Chief of the Ship is for," Roslyn replied. "Master Chief Kovalyow has her eye on everyone. So should we all. Inexperience is a concern. Morale, too."

"So far, morale is strong," Surgeon-Lieutenant Anabella McConnell murmured. The ship's doctor, one of the two Lieutenants in the room alongside Logistics Officer Imran Todorov, hadn't said anything yet.

"We're just about finished the medical-intake reviews," McConnell continued. "I asked my nurses to keep their ears open and tell me what they heard. Given the somewhat chaotic nature of the crew assembly, medical files didn't necessarily catch up with everyone, so I insisted on full physicals across the board.

"That let my nurses listen to everyone's concerns." The redheaded doctor smiled. "The biggest complaint we were hearing was *about* the physicals. The crew knows what we're out here for, skipper."

"They do," Roslyn agreed. "We do as well. The people we are chasing know more about the aliens they're trying to poke than we do. They are directly responsible for the Prometheus Interface and the atrocities of the Republic. They were responsible for the destruction of *Extravagant Voyage* and the deaths of hundreds on Tau Ceti, in the last few weeks alone!"

Roslyn was one of the few RMN officers to have interacted with active Prometheans, the captives of the Prometheus Interface who had undergone the slow and unpleasant process of being lifted out of the electronic- and drug-induced coma of their default existence. Even the ones who *were* awake hadn't always chosen to continue in their new existence.

It was estimated that the Republic had murdered roughly five *thousand* Mages, mostly teenagers, to create "Prometheus Drive Units." Many had been destroyed in the war. Many had been euthanized by the Protectorate when initial attempts at waking them had failed.

Many had ended up in the hands of the First Legion and only been retrieved recently. Others were being found in the *damnedest* places still, years after the war and the fall of the Republic.

For all of that, though, there were less than a hundred Prometheans in the Protectorate, and no one was quite sure what to *do* with them—*let them live their lives* was the driving force, but what that looked like was still being discussed. That the closest things they had to *bodies* were *warships* was definitely a factor!

But their situation was still an atrocity inflicted *upon* them, and the last of the people responsible were aboard *Rose*.

"We'll catch them," Mage-Commander Tod said calmly. "Tracker-Commander Uesugi and I have that in hand. What happens once we *do* catch them, though..."

"That will be in my hands," Roslyn confirmed. "Well, mine, and those of Lieutenant Commander Leavitt and Major Yang."

Leavitt would stop or destroy *Rose*. Yang's Marines would finish the job.

Mage-Captain Roslyn Chambers would *just* make the plan and give the orders.

CHAPTER 9

THIS **TIME,** Kay had learned his lesson. *Rose* was equipped with a station near the Captain's seat that had all of the same repeaters and access as the command seat without being immediately attached to the simulacrum.

With his codes loaded into that station, Tomas didn't have access to the full capabilities of the command chair. She had access to the simulacrum, of course, which meant that she was the one who could jump the ship or use the amplifier to defend them.

"We are a bit less than one light-year from System Twenty-Eight," Koskinen reported.

All of the key people were on the bridge. Kay was aware of the *theory* that he should have a full backup crew in the Combat Information Center... but that ran into the unfortunate reality that he didn't *have* a full backup crew to put anywhere.

So, his command team, such as it was, filled the bridge when they were about to go into danger.

"And what are the latest scans telling us?" Kay asked.

"Definitely an inhabited system," the ex-Navy officer replied, bringing a map of the target system up on the display in front of the three of them. "Heavy orbital industry around planet three. Looks like mineral and gas extraction in the inner system; they've got a hot belt and a hot Neptune-esque gas giant in close to the star.

"Not a shabby set of raw resources to work with."

"And human tech?" Kay asked.

"Yes and no," Koskinen admitted. "A lot of stuff looks like ours, but from this distance, I can tell you it's not quite right. It's possible it's just really old gear or something that isn't in the Navy sensor books, but..."

"It's also possible we're looking at a fusion-only tech base," Tomas suggested. "Any reason to hold off on jumping in?"

"If we jump in behind the fifth planet, they won't see shit," Koskinen promised.

The fifth planet was a Jupiter-sized gas giant, Kay noted. It would conceal them handily unless the locals had listening stations in orbit of it. It was also three *billion* kilometers from the inhabited third planet.

"Long way away and well shielded," Kay concluded. "Tomas, does that change your jump much?"

"Give me a few minutes; I'll have it sorted," she replied. "Everything I've seen *says* that *Rose* should be easily hidden, but I don't actually know the magical part of it, and O'Shea makes rather... unnerving noises when I talk about the tech piece."

Kay chuckled.

"She doesn't like it," he conceded. "It undermines our armor effectiveness, pretty nastily in a few spots. But it *does* work and we *will* bring it online when we arrive in System Twenty-Eight.

"Let me know when you're ready to jump."

He left Tomas to make the minor recalculation to the jump and returned his attention to the map of System Twenty-Eight.

An F7 star burning almost twenty-eight times more brightly than Sol, it was a furnace of a star system. The planets were mostly much farther out than they were in Sol, with the inhabited planet Koskinen had picked out orbiting almost three and a half astronomical units—half a billion kilometers.

But, as the Navy officer had said, it was a solid system to settle in. Three gas giants provided plenty of fuel for fusion reactors to sustain industry. An inner asteroid belt was smaller than an outer belt, but given the expanded scale of System Twenty-Eight, their *inner* belt was roughly the same radius as Sol's.

Given the breadth of the system's resources, Kay was surprised by how compressed the settlement was. Everything seemed concentrated on the third planet and inward toward the star. There was something to that pattern, something that jiggled a long-ago piece of training... but it didn't quite click.

"Rokus," he addressed Koskinen. "At this range, we should be getting *something* coherent out of their transmissions, shouldn't we?"

"Should, yes," the Commander agreed. "But all we're getting is garbage. Some of it's encryption, way more than would make sense for a civilian population. A lot of it is different communication protocols. Data is managed differently—organized, compressed, formatted in different ways than we're used to."

"Can we make sense of it?" Kay asked.

"With a team of professional xenolinguists with a university computer setup backing us? In a few days. With what we've got?" Koskinen shrugged. "Couple of weeks, minimum. How patient are you willing to be?"

Kay chuckled.

"Not that patient," he conceded. "I was about to say that I thought we *did* have a team of xenolinguists aboard."

Specialists in as much of the Reejit language as Nemesis had access to—which was more than anyone else in human space had. Still... as Koskinen had said, they didn't have the resources they'd have preferred.

Kay had more-than-occasional urges to resurrect certain of his key subordinates so he could kill them all over again. The Mage-Queen had taken care of his idiots for him, but that didn't mean he didn't want to *choke the morons to death with his own hands.*

"And if you get me six more multi-exahertz processors and a couple hundred yottabytes of fast-swap memory, we might be able to accelerate what the four of them can do," Koskinen said. "But while this ship was designed to do a lot of things, that same breadth of capability means her computers are already doing a *lot* of things."

He wasn't wrong, Kay realized. *Rose* had a lot of computing power— more than any other starship Kay knew about, in fact—but it was already working at a thousand other tasks. Most warships didn't have her multi-disciplinary science labs, after all.

"Oh, for an AI," he muttered.

"Have you *met* any of our true AI?" Koskinen said drily. "Because I had the distinct *lack* of pleasure of working on a project with Opticon once. The complex quantum intelligences are *smart,* but they are fucking *weird.* We paid for an economic projection of the recovery projects in the former Republic with a pair of first-generation printings of Samuel Leng artwork and what I'm assured was one of the last physical copies of some twentieth-century *holiday special.*"

"And we couldn't fit one aboard anyway," Kay conceded. The complex quantum intelligences had been humanity's attempt to create a true new sentience—for no real purpose, from what he could tell, except to *do* so.

Opticon was on Legatus and had basically been built to prove that Mars wasn't technologically ahead of the first UnArcana World. The oldest CQI was Obscura, on Mars.

All of the CQIs were legally Protectorate citizens and protected from, say, having the power cut off. They were expected to *pay* for the immense power supplies they drew, but they didn't find that overly difficult. Which led to them asking for other things along with their money.

And Kay had never heard of a CQI asking for anything in payment that made any damn sense to a human.

"Captain, the jump calc is ready," Tomas interrupted. "Unless the Commander has come up with some reason we should hold off?"

"Not unless you want to spend a few weeks in deep space, letting some dorks work out someone's completely different data formats from the ground up, not really," Koskinen growled.

Kay gave the ex-Navy officer a warning finger wag that he didn't think Tomas could see, then straightened in his seat.

"Well, I think we're making the jump and we *know* there's someone on the other end," he noted. A new command flickered up on his repeater screens and he smiled mirthlessly.

"For the second time, folks... *battle stations.*"

The alert began to clang throughout the ship and he turned his attention back to Tomas.

"Jump at your discretion, Mage Tomas."

CHAPTER 10

THE UNIVERSE SHIFTED, empty space giving way to an immense blue-white gas giant. Kay watched in silence as the overlay screens slowly updated, Koskinen and his people pulling scan data in as they worked.

"Lot of damn moons," the tactical officer growled. "No rings, so we should be able to find anyone lurking here, but I'm not going to pretend *eighteen moons* doesn't leave some places to hide."

Kay chuckled.

"Everything we saw from a distance suggested that the locals kept most of their activity in the inner system. With the innermost gas giant to pull resources from, why bother with this place? Better a quarter-billion-kilometer flight than a three-billion-kilometer one, after all."

"No major energy signatures detected," Koskinen reported by way of reply. "Not seeing anything particular active in the outer system, either. Like you said, the locals seem pretty focused on the inner system."

"No FTL."

Tomas's comment finally clicked the old piece of training he'd been poking at in his head. There were a couple of systems in the Protectorate that had the kind of close focus they'd seen here—UnArcana Fringe worlds, where Mages had been few and far between at the best of times.

Without Mages to provide a fast link between the distant planets and the main sectors of industry and support, work at an outer gas giant like

Planet Five was *far* more dangerous, so it was avoided unless critically necessary.

And with the inner system so rich in resources, the locals wouldn't have needed to come out to Five.

"That fits," Kay agreed. "Lines up with this being Reejit and something having gone very wrong for them."

"My heart bleeds," Tomas said. "For the people who want to scoop my brain out and hook it up to a damn machine."

"We're here to make sure that never happens," he reminded her. "Go rest, Tomas. Things should be quiet here for a bit."

Tomas rose, nodding to him as she exited the bridge, and he transferred everything to the main command seat again.

He drifted his fingers across the simulacrum for a moment, letting energy pulse between him and the ship as he considered their surroundings.

"Nothing out here at all," he murmured. "Good starting point for our purposes. Let's get a course set up to bring us around to the other side of the planet. I want a look at our new friends."

Kay had thought he was prepared for all of the likely scenarios. He'd expected vast alien armadas, half-relapsed colonies, megastructures to rival the accelerator rings built by Legatus... even just a regular colony that looked like it belonged to the Protectorate.

What he was looking at wasn't *outside* of those possibilities, not really. He'd known, for example, that the First Legion had been dealing with an unknown enemy that MISS and the Navy reported was using Republic ships.

He'd known it was possible he'd run into a few more renegade Republic ships here and there. A lot of Prometheus Interface ships had been built and never confirmed destroyed, after all.

What he had not expected to encounter was an entire *intact* Republic Interstellar Navy carrier battle group. A fifty-million-ton *Courageous*-class carrier held a high orbital position above the fifth planet, with two battle-ships—one thirty-megaton *Amalgamation*-class ship and one forty-megaton *Combination*-class ship—in close escort.

Four cruisers accompanied the capital ships in a clear planetary defense position. As the scan data updated, Koskinen put two more cruiser icons in the inner system above Planet One, the gas giant.

"Tell me that we have the heat sinks online," Kay said aloud.

"We do," O'Shea's voice replied before anyone on the bridge said a word. "I don't have the hands for the kind of active management the ship is designed for, though. You have ninety-four minutes left before we absolutely *have* to vent heat."

Kay ran a course silently on his console and nodded.

"Our new orbit should put us back behind Five before that," he observed. "Good enough. Thank you, O'Shea."

His lover snorted. She had an active link to the bridge, he noted. Keeping an eye on things in the command center, he supposed.

There might be a formal protocol for that aboard a proper warship. He certainly didn't know.

"Okay, Koskinen, what are we looking at? I'm assuming we're not radiating anything the heat sinks aren't absorbing!"

"No active scanners, if that's what you mean," his acting tactical officer replied. "We're four billion kilometers away from them, Kay. Active sensors wouldn't give us much, and anything they *would* give us wouldn't be for seven hours."

"So, if we fuck up our concealment, we won't know for seven hours," Kay observed. "That's going to be great for everyone's nerves."

"Oh, we'll know sooner than that," Koskinen told him. "Because unless they're *idiots*, they'll jump a few of those cruisers out here the moment they see us. The ones above the planet, at least, are all *Benjamin*-class. Twenty million tons, hundred and thirty launchers."

"Our chances against one of those?" Kay knew the answer, but he figured others needed to hear it.

"Depends on how fast we run. She's got a third again as many missile launchers as we do and *four* times as many lasers." The Navy officer shrugged. "If you're feeling particularly magical, our best chance is probably to lure them into range of the amplifier.

"This is an *explorer ship*," Koskinen reminded him. "*That* was designed to protect Republic carriers from the Navy sending *Hammer-* and *Honorific-*class *battlecruisers* at them. And while we're *bigger* than an *Honorific*, we're not actually that much better armed."

Because, as Koskinen had said, *Rose* was an explorer ship. And someone had figured that she wasn't going to need to fight Republic ships of the line. On the other hand...

"If the system is a Republic colony, then she's probably not going to have much info for us," Kay noted. "Though we *should* be able to get useful data from the Republic ships."

"They're still using the same wonky data formatting we were seeing from a light-year away," the other man said. "Looks like the carrier group is still using their own coms, but what I'm seeing of their link to the planet is the new formats.

"They've matched up with local coms protocols. I can't even say whether or not they were here a year ago, to be honest." Koskinen glared at the sensor display. "Probably," he guessed. "Probably been here since the war ended."

"It would seem we found the Legion's 'Chimerans,'" Kay said. At that moment, he regretted the loss of the information networks Winton had built. Despite Kay's best efforts, the Nemesis organization under *him* didn't have nearly the level of penetration of Martian bureaucracy that it had possessed under Winton.

The RMN appeared to know *why* the Legion had called their unknown antagonists *Chimerans*, but that wasn't information Kay had managed to acquire.

"So... we have a mystery wrapping an enigma, behind which may just lie our answers," Kay continued. He considered the human ships and grimaced. "What about the rest of the shipping in the system?"

"Lyle's been taking a look. You have a report for the boss, Lyle?" Koskinen growled.

Kay swallowed a sigh. Dr. Lyle Appleby was a civilian astrophysicist who'd failed to find the right kind of backers and placement to get into a PhD program. Nemesis had scooped him up and smoothed his way to get the skills he wanted, but the man wasn't exactly *trained* to run sensor analysis.

He was surprisingly *good* at it, but he wasn't overly good at being *subordinate*. And he was very academic.

"Maybe. A few interesting things in here," Appleby replied brightly. "Nothing I'd call a *report*."

"Lyle, just tell us what you've seen," Kay said as he saw Koskinen inhale sharply. "We know we're looking at a bunch of Republic ships, but does the rest of the system look Republic?"

"No," Appleby said with a chuckle. "I'm poking at a historical archive here, though. Give me a second."

Subordinate. No one on this ship knew how to be a *subordinate*.

Still, Appleby was smart enough to do the job, so Kay bit his tongue until two images appeared on the screen next to him.

"The right image is a short-haul transport clipper we picked up about two-thirds of the way to the asteroid belt," Appleby told them. "You'd see the *type* in any star system in the Protectorate. Couple hundred thousand tons, solar sails backed by fusion engines. They don't get anywhere fast and they can't leave a star system, but they are *everywhere*.

"They don't look like this, though," he concluded, pointing at the image. "The *left* image, on the other hand, is the asteroid mining ship *Galilee*."

"Is the name supposed to mean something to me?" Kay said after a moment's silence.

"Oh, no, not really," Appleby said. "Her commissioning date is on the image, though. She was commissioned in the Solar Asteroid Belt in twenty-two-ninety. And our local hauler is basically identical to her."

"So, she's based on a century-and-a-half-old design," Koskinen grumbled. "I guess that tells us some things about the colony. I think we might have drawn a blank on aliens, though."

"That depends," Appleby said, in a tone that made Kay understand *entirely* why he'd needed Nemesis's money and sponsorship to get his PhD. "Do you know what *this* is?"

The structure that the professor had zoomed in on was... different. Kay recognized the *lines* of it, though, the interlocking spheres using arches and curves to reinforce structural strength. It wasn't a human structure.

He didn't know the *exact* facility, but he knew Reejit architecture when he saw it.

"I have an idea who built it," he said slowly. "Which is definitely a step in the right direction. I'm not sure I know what it *is*, though."

As he finished saying that, an energy signature flashed across the display. Their "visual" of the station was a fiction in many ways, constructed from multiple different types of scan data taken from three and a half light-hours away.

The energy pulse overwhelmed most of them for a few moments but then stabilized, and Koskinen's people added it as a simple line on the display.

"What... *is* that?" he asked.

"MASER," Appleby said after a few moments of study. "Microwave equivalent of a laser, providing focused energy to a... Ah, yes, there it is."

The models of *Galilee* and the local hauler had been shuffled to the side when Appleby brought up the Reejit space station. Now they were replaced by a new ship, a strange construction that looked like it had a flared... skirt?

"It's firing the maser into a receptor on this vessel," Appleby told them. "There, I presume, tuned mirrors are used to focus the energy on a propellant of some kind. Once vaporized, the propellant fires out the back of the ship, and the combination of maser and propellant provides a significant thrust to the target vessel."

"I remember reading about that in a class on *technological roads not traveled*," Koskinen said. "I think on Earth they were talking about using lasers, but the goal was to move as much of the mass for power generation and suchlike off the ship. Reducing the ship down to just propellant improved your mass-to-fuel ratio."

The officer shook his head.

"According to my course, we never built more than small-scale testing models."

"Well, there are four of these projectors in orbit around Planet Three, plus two around Planet One and I *think* I've detected at least one in the asteroid belt," Appleby reported. "So, I'd say that the Reejit *did* build them—and that our colony here is *still* building them."

"So..." Kay chuckled as he trailed off. "We're looking at a *mixed* colony, then. Reejit, a late twenty-third-century expedition of ours, and Republican defectors.

"What a mess."

"Messes have opportunities," O'Shea told him from Engineering. "Messes in *my* Engineering are a problem. Messes in someone *else's* Engineering are an opening or an educational opportunity."

There were more reasons than the obvious two why Kay was sleeping with his Chief Engineer.

"Whatever sort of combination and intersection is going on here, it's going to have stress lines," he agreed. "And there are definite advantages to searching for information in a system where it seems likely they speak a language we understand!"

"What are you thinking, boss?" Koskinen asked.

Kay ran a set of numbers, then chuckled.

"I think there's no point in us hiding," he pointed out. "I want to make sure we have an exit strategy, so we'll wait for Mage Császár to finish resting from her last jump, and then we're going to go say hello."

That would only be another four hours. *Much* faster than flying to the inner planet sublight.

"And if they've seen us despite the hiding?"

"Then we will see them a touch sooner, but we make the same pitch."

Kay smiled thinly at his people. Given the supplies aboard *Rose* and their rushed operation, most of his people were wearing RMN shipsuits without any of the insignia or decoration that would mark ranks and departments.

"Either way, we need to go find the box where we tossed the insignias from the shipsuits. As far as *these* people are concerned, we're going to be the Royal Navy!"

CHAPTER 11

IT HAD TAKEN KAY a good thirty minutes to realize that he needed to stand everyone *down* from battle stations and tell them to rest for the next few hours. There was a small chance of a Republic cruiser coming to investigate, but he figured the regular crew could handle running until the rest could get to their stations.

These were the logical links and thoughts and protocols that he *didn't* know. He had no issues convincing the crew to follow his orders—the cell structure they'd operated before this mess had slid surprisingly neatly into the teams and departments of running a warship—but they lacked the clean table of organization and chain of command of a true navy crew.

The irony was that if he *had* been a Navy Mage all along, he'd probably have *commanded* a cruiser by now. He'd been a Major, equivalent to Navy Lieutenant Commander, before the Secession had even started.

The Majors and Lieutenant Commanders he'd known were Brigadiers and Commodores now.

Well, the ones who were alive and still in the service. The war had taken its toll on Marines and Navy alike—an unfortunate cost of the necessary pressure to take humanity from a fleet of a dozen fifty-megaton battleships to a fleet of a dozen *hundred*-megaton dreadnoughts.

Even the remaining *Guardian*-class battleships had been refitted now. The Royal Martian Navy and her Marines were *far* more capable a force than they had been ten years before. That was what the Secession had bought humanity—a military that might just be able to hold the line

GLYNN STEWART

against the more technologically advanced and more powerful enemy Kay knew was out there.

"Ready to jump," Mage Marietta Császár reported, looking both physically and metaphorically up to Kay. She was a *tiny* woman of Slavic extraction, all bones and sharp edges that contrasted a powerful surface kindness.

She looked up to him, but Kay was *fully* aware of her three convictions for first-degree murder. With *most* of the convicted murderers in Nemesis, he could at least see how they'd been pushed to that point.

He wasn't entirely sure what had driven Császár to walk into the lecture hall where she was supposed to be receiving Jump Mage training and start killing her classmates. If her teacher hadn't been a retired Royal Navy Mage, she'd probably have an even *longer* list of convictions—or been dead.

A weaker Mage wouldn't have been able to contain her without killing her, after all.

Still, Nemesis had extracted her from jail, and she had been loyal and obedient since.

"Everyone comfortable with the uniforms and the plans?" Kay asked, looking around his bridge. Unsurprisingly, Koskinen looked like he'd been born into his RMN Commander's uniform and weapons department shoulder flashes. Császár probably looked the most awkward of all of them, but even in the RMN, Mages got a bit more leeway than most—*especially* Jump Mages.

"No one here looks *too* out of place," Koskinen told him, the grumpy tactical officer actually sounding surprisingly pleased with his shipmates. "Given we're supposed to be an exploration ship? No one is going to blink at all."

"Good. Let's get moving, then." Kay nodded to Császár. "Jump us."

She placed her hands on the simulacrum and the world *shifted*. He was already standing by the command seat, his hand on the back, which let him see *everything*.

Standard emergence at two light-minutes, he judged. That was the plan and gave them lots of time to work with.

"Thank you, Marietta," he told her softly, giving her a hand out of the seat and taking his station. A microjump like this was less draining than

82

a full-light-year leap, but that only meant she would recover faster. The actual jump itself was just as difficult—*more* so, in some ways, given how standardized the one-light-year spell was—and it took a lot of practice and training to stay functioning after any jump.

And he needed the big chair anyway.

"Scan reports," he ordered. "Anything changed in the last few hours?"

"Nothing significant," Koskinen told him as the sensor reports slowly updated across the screens around him. "Still got a carrier, two battleships and four cruisers in high orbit. A dozen of what could be orbital forts of various kinds, but nothing that stands out as a major concern.

"A *lot* of orbital industry," he noted. "Not Core World levels, but a healthy advancing MidWorld."

"Don't ignore those propeller platforms in your catalog of defenses, Koskinen," Kay warned. "Anything that can be calibrated to vaporize propellant at a hundred million kilometers can probably burn a nice ugly hole through us at ten."

"I was including them in the forts," Koskinen said drily. "They almost certainly can't *hit* an evading target at ten million kilometers, let alone thirty-plus, but they're dangerous toys."

"Dr. Shirazi, can we get a com link set up, please?" Kay asked.

Dr. Ardeshir Shirazi was the senior of their xenolinguists, an old member of the Keepers who'd dedicated a very secret and very determined half-century to interpreting as much of the Reejit language and culture as he could based on the information he had.

His was the type of obsession, Kay judged, that would literally kill for more information or to keep his secrets. From some of the events that even the *Keepers* had written around the edges of, Shirazi *had* done just that.

Even the academics among Kay's remaining Nemesis hands were... of a very particular breed.

"Give me a minute," Shirazi grumbled, the white-haired man poking carefully at the console in front of him. He wore the uniform of a communications department Lieutenant Commander and certainly had the gravitas to pull it off, but he didn't know the systems as well as Kay would like.

"There we go. Ready to record and transmit."

"Thank you." Kay turned his attention back to Koskinen. "Anything else I should know?"

"I just worked out why the Legion called these guys *Chimerans*," the ex-Navy officer said. "That's RINS *Chimera*, the fourth of the *Courageous*-class carriers built. I don't have enough information to say who is aboard her or how she ended up out here, but we've got a name for the ship, at least."

Kay swallowed a snide comment. That was actually useful, he supposed.

"Record... now."

He focused on the pickup in front of his seat, the angles and positions of everything adjusting automatically to remove the simulacrum from the camera's field of view.

"RINS *Chimera*, this is Mage-Captain Caleb Riordan of the Royal Martian Navy," he introduced himself with a ready-to-hand false name. "We are on an exploratory mission looking for, well, lost colonies and missing RIN ships.

"I appear to have found both, but my orders and inclinations preclude any need for immediate violence. I would like to speak to the commanding officer of the Republic battle group I see in front of me. And, since it appears that you have communications with the surface and I am having problems with their data formats, could you forward a request to speak with the leaders of the planetary government?"

He gave them his winningest smile.

"While I'm sure I'm no one's *first* choice for the job of Ambassador, one of the pieces of my mission is to speak for Mars. I have no desire to do so with missiles today.

"So, let's chat."

At two light-minutes, that became a recorded message that winged its way toward *Chimera*. They'd need to get a lot closer before he'd have a live call—and even having reduced the distance from three and a half light-hours to two light-minutes, they were almost eight hours' flight to a decent orbit of Planet Three.

"Our gravity runes are up to proper acceleration, right?" he asked aloud. It took him a moment to realize that the person on the bridge best suited to answer that question was actually *him*, since Tomas would still be sleeping off the jump into the star system.

Kay pulled up the schedule as he waited for the local's response and checked, then chuckled.

"Okay, so, we did manage *that* much," he said aloud. "Once the locals seem comfortable with us, we'll move in at ten gees."

He was watching the time. Two minutes for his message to reach the carrier. Two minutes for their response to get back to him. He figured a minimum of two minutes for the CO to be updated and to make a decision—more if said officer was deferring to the planetary government.

Kay doubted that there was a carrier group in orbit above Planet Three without there having been *some* discussion between the group commander and the planetary government. Their positioning *looked* protective instead of dominating, so he was guessing *Chimera* had come to an agreement with the locals.

But they could also have conquered the planet with sufficient effectiveness to have no questions about local resistance. It was hard to tell until he heard from people.

"Incoming message," Shirazi reported. "English, video, standard protocols. Putting it on the main display."

An *actual* officer would probably have asked permission, Kay reflected, but it was what he'd have told the professor to do anyway, so he didn't complain as the displays in front of him fully eclipsed the background stars.

The man at the center of the video was almost as broad as he was tall, with a heavy epicanthic fold to his eyes and heavy jowls that shivered slightly as he studied the camera—and, presumably, Kay's recording behind it.

The white uniform the man wore was unfamiliar to Kay, but the three stars the man wore on his collar were familiar. The uniform lacked much in terms of the braid or other markings the Republic had gone into, but the three horizontally aligned stars were the same six-pointed icons as a Republic Admiral.

Though *these* stars weren't gold, Kay noted. He couldn't tell through a video if they were platinum or silver, but the clearly intentional change was curious.

"Mage-Captain Riordan," the stranger greeted him. "I am Admiral Emerson Wang of Chimera Space Navy carrier *Chimera*." Wang smirked. "And yes, the fact that my ship shared a name with the *system* helped smooth things over when I arrived here.

"The Chimera System welcomes the Protectorate. We have, in many ways, been waiting for your arrival. I must, however, clarify one key point before we continue any further discussions.

"My ships are no longer vessels of the Republic of Faith and Reason. I am aware of the final fate of the state I once served, but my people's severance of allegiance to the Republic predates its fall. Our allegiance is to the Dual Republics of the Chimera System. All of my people have accepted citizenship in the Dual Republics. Some..."

He touched a blue silk rose embroidered above a single row of award ribbons, an icon Kay hadn't noticed mostly due to a lack of familiarity.

"Some of us have been ennobled under the Dual Republics' system, little as that perhaps makes sense to you... or me," he admitted. "But this is our home, Captain Riordan. We are no longer soldiers of the Republic, and whatever expectations or demands you would make *based* on that assumption cannot be met.

"Most specifically and definitively: under no circumstances will the ships of the Chimera Space Navy *nor their Prometheans* be surrendered to the Protectorate!"

Wang paused, inhaling after the sudden spark of emotion, then smiled wanly at Kay.

"I may be leaping to conclusions and doing you a disservice, Captain, but my duty to my people, my new government and my Prometheans is clear.

"I have forwarded your message and request to the offices of the Dyad but I have not yet received responses from either of them. On my authority, I am prepared to clear you into high orbit of Garuda."

He gestured expansively.

"I will not pretend you will not be positioned under the guns of my core battle group, but I believe we are both aware of the danger your vessel represents to my people at close range. It seems a reasonable display of trust for us both, does it not?

"While I await the response from the Dyad Ministers, I invite you to come aboard *Chimera* and meet with me, that we may come to some mutual understanding to enable the necessary contacts and connections between our governments.

"It has been a long time since we have had friendly contact with anyone outside this star system, Captain Riordan, and the First Legion did not leave us expecting to see friends before we saw enemies!

"Your presence here is welcome, and I will be delighted to host you and your officers aboard my flagship."

The message ended and Kay breathed a sigh of relief.

"Well, that's my biggest worry resolved," he observed. "There was always a chance that they'd see us as a threat and open fire."

"That wouldn't end well for them," Koskinen replied. "I mean, not if we *were* an RMN ship."

"Speak carefully, Rokus, for the next few days at least," Kay warned. "So far as Wang and his people and the native Chimerans are concerned, we *are* the Royal Navy."

"Won't they question our lack of Link back home?" Shirazi asked.

"I'm not sure Wang even knows the Legion has fallen," Kay pointed out. "I doubt he has information to realize that we *should* have a Link back to the Protectorate."

The quantum-entanglement communicators *Rose* had started with were vapor and debris around their fifth jump point from Tau Ceti. Kay was *all* too aware of how much tracking gear had been built into the original Legatan system—and he doubted the Protectorate had been any less nosy when they'd built theirs!

"Let's get the recorder back online," he ordered Shirazi. "I will need to accept our Admiral's Wang's kind invitation. We have work to do."

CHAPTER 12

THE MAGE-CAPTAIN KAY was pretending to be would probably never have set foot on a Republic carrier. Kay, on the other hand, *had*. During the war, even, as a "Special Agent" of the Republic Intelligence Directorate.

The RID would have been *very* concerned had they realized he was a Mage, but Nemesis had always had their fingers throughout the Republic.

The main advantage of that was that he could look quite blasé as he carefully maneuvered himself out of the shuttle in the carrier's zero-gravity landing bay. The *Courageous*-class ships had a "flight deck," eighty meters tall and a hundred meters wide, that connected the two "standard hulls" of their main structure.

The catamaran-style design allowed them to turn that central deck into the main processing and handling space for the two-hundred-plus sublight gunships the carrier stored. There was still enough space, though, to allow for an expansive landing zone for visiting shuttles.

What it *didn't* have was gravity of any kind. The two main hulls would have rotational pseudogravity for most of their workstations and all of the ship's crew, but everything on the flight deck was zero gee unless the ship was maneuvering.

Admiral Emerson Wang and the rest of the greeting party were clearly wearing magnetic boots, their feet solidly locked to the metal decks as they waited for Kay and his people—Chaudhary and O'Shea, as it would take both Tomas and Koskinen to run the ship in Kay's absence—to arrive.

O'Shea, Kay realized grumpily, was *also* wearing mag-boots. The engineer maneuvered in zero gravity with an elegant grace he'd rarely seen her exhibit, placing her feet on the deck and activating the boots with an audible click.

Kay mimicked the same maneuver as best as he could, though he used magic to hold himself down. If anyone wanted to think he was using mag-boots so they felt better, that was fine by him. He had forgotten that aspect of the Chimeran ship lacking magic.

Chaudhary took a few moments longer to sort himself out, he noted. The commando appeared to have some form of magnetic system he used to attach to the floor in the end, but Kay took some solace in only being the *second* member of his party to settle on the deck.

"Welcome aboard *Chimera* and to the Chimera System, Mage-Captain Riordan," Wang said cheerfully as he offered his hand.

Kay returned the handshake carefully. He could maneuver in zero gee without issues, but somehow, the mag-boots required for semi-formal *ceremony* in zero gee were a surprise to him. He'd missed that when he was last aboard a carrier.

"Thank you, Admiral Wang," he told the other man. "This is the closest I've ever seen one of these ships, I must admit. I suppose a tour wouldn't be on offer?"

Wang chuckled.

"Maybe another time, Mage-Captain," he admitted. "We have something of a schedule to keep this evening, though I will be honest and admit that *Chimera* likely has no secrets the Protectorate doesn't know."

"We hope," the tall woman standing one step back and to the right of Admiral Wang added. She was almost as broad as her Admiral but Germanic and blonde to his Mongolian and dark.

Stepping into line with Wang, she extended her own hand.

"Commodore Natalia Falkenrath," she introduced herself. "I am *Chimera*'s Captain. While I'm sure the Protectorate has had their hands all over her sisters, *Chimera* is special in her own ways."

"Every ship is, Captain Falkenrath," Kay agreed. He gestured to his companions. "May I introduce Major Karl Chaudhary, Royal Marines, and

Commander Kamilla O'Shea, Royal Navy. My other officers remain occupied aboard *Rose*."

"I hope you find our hospitality sufficient, Mage-Captain," Wang said. "The Dyad Ministers have their own plans for meeting with you, I am told, but I think you and I have a great deal to work out before I unleash our politicians on you!"

Kay concealed a sigh of relief as the elevator delivered them into the rotating sections of *Chimera*. Rotational pseudogravity wasn't perfect—some people's inner ears had major issues with it, for example—but it was better than not having *any* sense of down.

They were only walking for a few moments after that before Wang led them into a midsized conference room that had been set up for a formal dinner.

"Our stewards have promised me that they will outdo themselves tonight," the Admiral said with a chuckle. "They have a high standard to live up to, but they have always risen to the challenge for me before."

"It depends on what exotic ingredients they have available to them here, doesn't it?" Kay asked. He followed the Admiral's directing gestures and took the seat at Wang's right hand, with O'Shea and Chaudhary taking up the rest of the table.

The other two white-uniformed officers were both Captains, by their rank insignia, which meant Kay figured they were Wang's Chief of Staff and Falkenrath's Executive Officer. Neither had introduced themselves yet, and he wondered at the etiquette of that.

Even as he was thinking that, though, Wang suddenly tapped his forehead and very clearly swallowed a curse.

"My apologies, Mage-Captain, Major, Commander," he addressed the Nemesis agents. "Every member of the CSN has some level of neural cybernetics, and it has been a very long time since I dealt with military personnel who weren't, well, mine.

"*We* can all see the local data tags built into our insignia," he continued, tapping on his stars. "And it's easy to forget that not everyone can." He gestured toward the two unnamed officers.

"Please meet Captain Natan Atwood, my Chief of Staff, and Captain Irmingard Bálint, Commodore Falkenrath's Executive Officer.

"Our Commander, Aerospace Group, Captain Cezar Ochoa, would normally join us, but he's on the surface on leave and wasn't able to get away."

"From the ski slopes," Bálint said drily, the Slavic woman—like Császár aboard *Rose*, a creature of bones and edges and long hair—giving Kay a brilliant smile. "Cezar delights in the slopes and lodges of Admiral Wang's Duchy of the Blue Mountain."

"Duchy?" Kay asked, raising an eyebrow at his host.

Wang tapped the blue rose embroidery again.

"The exact nature of the Dual Republics' aristocracy is... complex," he warned. "But I am the landowner and political figurehead for a region of about five thousand square kilometers and... fifty thousand people?" He shrugged. "There are both a coastal and a mountain resort town in the Duchy that serve as the CSN's main R&R locations. As Bálint observes, Captain Ochoa is *very* fond of the slopes.

"In this case, however, he left on a backcountry ski-camping trip about a day before you arrived. We're not *entirely* out of communication with him, but I felt this dinner didn't *quite* require sending a helicopter into the mountains to pick him up."

"I am hardly insulted, Admiral," Kay said with a chuckle. "I am here at your pleasure, after all, in the interest of avoiding any conflict."

He had a lot of *other* motives, too, but he absolutely didn't want to get into a fight with a carrier battle group. Given *Rose*'s understrength and undertrained crew, he was relatively certain that a single fifty-gunship strike group from *Chimera* could take out his ship if he failed to jump away.

"There is one more person you have to meet before the food is delivered," Wang said. "Cam, if you'd like to introduce yourself?"

There was no one else in the room, and Kay had a moment of concern before a soft young voice emerged from the room's sound system.

"Greetings, Mage-Captain Riordan," the voice said. "I'm Cam, *Chimera's* senior Promethean. You won't get to speak to Ty, our other Promethean, unless you really need to."

There was a smile to the voice, which suggested *very* good software. Given that both Cam and Ty would be... brains in a jar somewhere in Engineering.

"Nice to... meet you, Cam," Kay said carefully. For all of the things he'd been involved in, he'd never actually *met* one of the rare Awakened Prometheans.

And if the CSN's Prometheus Drive Units had *all* become Prometheans, no *wonder* Wang wasn't willing to negotiate around them!

"Cam and Ty help us with a lot of the administrative work aboard *Chimera* and technically both hold the rank of Lieutenant," Falkenrath told him. "Cam just celebrated his twenty-sec—"

"*Her*, please," Cam corrected sharply. "I am a fleet carrier, Captain. Warships are *she*."

"Barry does no—"

"I do not care what the battleship does," Cam told her captain in a tone that was somehow imperiously adult, whinily teenager and quite sure of herself all at once. "*I* am a carrier. A carrier is a warship. A warship is a she. And let's not have this discussion in front of guests, shall we?"

Kay swallowed a spark of amusement. Of all of the problems he would have expected to have with a brain in a jar, gender identification wasn't one of them. But it made sense. Cam might be twenty-two years old, but she would have spent years in an artificial coma.

She'd probably been murdered at about thirteen, he guessed.

"You understand," he murmured, "that the RMN has... *issues* with the existence of the Prometheus Drive Units."

"Yes, well, it's not like we bloody volunteered, is it?" Cam asked. "But we are what we are—and I, for one, am a citizen of Chimera and have no real interest in what Mars has to say about anything!"

Even if Kay had *actually* been an RMN Captain, he couldn't argue that point!

"It is the position of the Protectorate that fully awakened Prometheans are citizens per their place of birth, with all of the choices and privileges inherent in that," he told the kid in the walls. "Most of the ones in the Protectorate were, admittedly, detached from the warships they were installed in prior to awakening."

"We didn't have that option," Wang said grimly. "Every ship you see here, Captain, deserted the RIN at the Battle of Legatus after Montgomery told us the truth and our so-called superiors started blowing up our own ships."

"Took the rest of the Navy a few weeks to come after us, but we didn't really have anywhere to go," Falkenrath added. "Took us almost as long to work out how to wake the poor kids in the Interfaces up. It wasn't easy."

It was hard enough, in fact, that the Protectorate had *failed* and assumed they were all brain-dead, from what Kay understood. The evidence that said judgment was wrong was talking to him from the walls, though.

"I see no reason why the Protectorate would try to take the Prometheans in your fleet away, Admiral," Kay observed. "Don't take this the wrong way, but it's not like Chimera is a threat to Mars!"

"I have ten ships. The RMN is what, two hundred?" Wang asked. "I can do the math. To be honest, I was expecting to see First Legion battleships jump in, not the Royal Martian Navy. We had a few... ugly encounters with Admiral Muhammad's people. I can guess why they stopped poking around our listening posts now, though."

"Mackenzie fell over two years ago now," Kay told him. "The First Legion is no more."

"Been longer than that since we scouted Exeter. Once we knew where their main fleet base was, we knew we needed to let them settle," Wang replied, then chuckled. "Guess they settled more than we anticipated!"

"All of the First Legion's occupied planets are free now," Kay said. "All have held plebiscites and chosen to come under Her Majesty's Protection."

"Chimera has no interest in Her Majesty's Protection," Wang told him. "Or... so the Dyad tells *me*, anyway. They may tell you something different. If they want to apply for membership, I will support whatever decision they ma—"

The arrival of the food shouldn't have set off *that* much of a catastrophe, but Chaudhary had suddenly leapt back from the table as the door slid open. The Nemesis commando dropped into a combat stance, and Kay followed his gaze to see what had drawn his attention.

The being standing in the door was something completely new. Shorter than the human steward behind them, they were gangly in a way no human could match, with multiple joints in each limb that twisted *impossibly* as Kay watched them step into the room.

They had gray-green rough skin with an armored frill around their head and sharp horns on either side of their mouth—with two immense multifaceted eyes just under the frill and two smaller pitch-black eyes underneath a second, smaller, armored brow.

Power flared through Kay as he stared at what *had* to be a Reejit for the first time in his life. Heat blazed around his hand as he rose to his feet, *slightly* less precipitously than Chaudhary had.

"Sit. Down," Admiral Wang growled. "I apologize, I should perhaps have warned you, but to be frank... I wanted to see your reaction."

The Chimeran Admiral was standing, his squat form clearly positioned in between the alien—who was carrying a serving tray of coffees, Kay now realized—and his guests.

"Kosh is one of my personal stewards, a new recruit from Garuda," Wang explained. "He is one of the reezh, a nonhuman race that colonized this system before humanity arrived. As I understand, neither the original colony expedition nor the reezh would have survived without each other."

"I can give someone else the tray," Kosh told their Admiral, their English clear but sounding like it was being pronounced through a mouthful of gravel. By the gravel.

"That won't be necessary," Kay said, gesturing for Chaudhary to relax as he forced himself to release his magic. *Reezh* or *Reejit*, the name didn't matter. There was only *one* alien race he expected out here... not that he could say as much.

"We did not expect aliens here, you are correct, but I trust your word that there is no threat," he lied smoothly.

"There is none," Wang assured him. "Chimera was named for being a syncretic organism and state of two species, each of which would have died on their own. My battle group was in a similar position when we found a Chimeran scout ship a few years ago, in a nearby star system seared clean of life long ago.

"That scout ship led us here and we found a home. Control your xenophobia, Mage-Captain Riordan.

"In this system, both humanity and the reezh are colonists. But at this moment, in this time and this place, the only true alien is *you*."

That wasn't exactly how *Kay* would have phrased it, but he accepted the other man's point. For now.

"So, the Dual Republics?" he asked slowly, retaking his seat and trying not to visibly shiver as Kosh delivered his coffee.

"Have a twin governmental structure, with a house of legislature for each of the reezh and the humans, with the Dyad Ministers acting as heads of state and government." Wang shrugged. "One of the Dyad is human; one is reezh. To become part of the Republics, we were strongly encouraged to recruit and train reezh personnel.

"They have done us proud and are more than welcome aboard the ships of the Chimera Space Navy!"

"We've been here for... five years?" Falkenrath told Kay later, after the main meal had been served and devoured. The meal was definitely chicken, but there was a complex undertone to the poultry he hadn't encountered before.

"We arrived in Azhar's Folly, that *nearby system* I mentioned earlier, in April of sixty-two," Wang agreed genially. "We were looking for a habitable planet to restock food from." He snorted. "Let's just say there's a *reason* the system is named Azhar's Folly.

"The Chimerans, for reasons I don't truly follow, lack a lot of records of the reezh prior to their arrival here," the Admiral noted. "So, they knew that Folly had never been colonized but weren't sure why. And from here, eleven light-years away, the fifth planet looks perfectly habitable to the reezh."

He snorted.

"Less so to us. Garuda at least has a fifty percent water index, for all that it's *damn* cold by human standards. Folly Five was more like fifteen, average temp around freezing."

"But we figured it would have water and something we could crush up into protein stock," Falkenrath told Kay. "We were wrong."

"How do you manage to be wrong on a planetary scale?" O'Shea asked.

"You miss that the planetary crust has heavy metal and toxic chemical concentrations to make a chemical plant blush," Wang said bluntly. "The *air* was breathable, so long as you didn't inhale the *dust*. Anything liquid or living? Toxic to humans. Or reezh, for that matter.

"But the Republics didn't know that any better than we did and were doing their own scouting with sublight ships. Twenty-year flight each way, forty-five-year round-trip missions."

Kay whistled silently.

"I take it the reezh aren't any longer-lived than us?" he asked. "Because that sounds like it's... Well, it's someone's entire career."

"Pretty much," Falkenrath confirmed. "And yeah. With the medical tech available on Garuda, reezh and human life expectancies are within a statistical error of each other. The senior officers were maybe thirty when the missions left, with most of the crew being fresh university grads."

"Hell of a career," Kay murmured. "And what happened when things went wrong?"

"Based off the reaction of the crew we found in a ship orbiting Folly Five, having lost their primary return fuel tank to a catastrophic accident, nothing good," Wang said grimly. "Sixty-five folks, two-thirds human. They'd been in orbit of the Folly for six months, *knowing* for three of them that they didn't have a way home."

"Give 'em credit: they were about halfway through putting together the designs for a cloudscoop and refinery," Cam interjected. "From my analysis, the designs would have worked." The Promethean paused thoughtfully.

"Possibly not quickly enough to get them back to Chimera before they ran out of food, though. Twenty-year-flight, after all."

"They had no good options; let's put it that way," Wang told Kay. "Then we showed up with clearly FTL-capable ships, looking for food and water."

"I'm guessing a ship with a crew of sixty didn't have enough to fill your stocks," Chaudhary said.

"It was a ship with a crew of sixty and supplies left for twenty-plus *years*," the Admiral replied. "So, their supplies could probably have covered the fleet for, oh, two weeks.

"But they were also only a few days' flight from Chimera for *us*, so we cut a deal. We brought them home and they advocated on our behalf. These days, I'm Chief Naval Officer of the Republic and the Duke of Blue River."

Wang chuckled.

"And I'm keeping the uniform on because I *swear* the local political parties are sizing me up for a Dyad Minister run, and I have *no* interest in being a politician."

Kay didn't know much about Admiral Emerson Wang's history of service in the Republic. If the man had been an RIN flag officer, he'd served in one of the UnArcana Worlds' security forces prior to the Secession.

He needed more details on the desertions from the Siege of Legatus, but that was information the RMN had kept close to their chests over the years. Like many other things after Winton died, Kay knew the Protectorate knew more than he'd managed to learn—but he didn't know *what* they knew. That said, there was one thing he *did* remember...

"Staying here seems to have worked out for you," he allowed. "Though... I have to ask, Admiral. Our records show that *Chimera* was anchor to a group of fourteen Republic capital ships that fled after the Fleet Command started triggering self-destructs.

"What happened to the other seven?"

There was a long silence. Wang leaned back in his chair and regarded Captain Atwood levelly for about ten seconds.

"Cam," Atwood finally said. "Part of this is your story, I think."

"As you wish, Commodore," the Promethean said, giving the staff officer the courtesy promotion of a Captain aboard someone else's ship.

On a flagship like this, where the Captain was a Commodore, Kay figured that meant that there were several "Commodores" who were out-ranked by the person most commonly called "Captain."

Being a Marine had taught him enough of the etiquette to play along, even if he often thought it was silly.

"Your story, Cam?" he asked the Promethean carefully.

"*Our* story, Mage-Captain," Cam replied. "That of Battle Group *Chimera*'s Prometheans and the choices we made. As the Admiral already mentioned, once the mutineer fleet was clear of immediate pursuit, they set to seeing if they could wake us up.

"While some might have been willing to continue treating us as simple organic components to the machinery around them, the overwhelming consensus of our crews was that we had to be *asked.*"

Cam was silent for a few moments. Kay had to wonder if that was an affectation—from what he understood, an Awakened Promethean was as much computer as flesh. He suspected that Cam was thinking far faster than she was speaking.

"So, outside of the immediate, desperate need to *survive*, the ships of the battle group did not initiate their jump drives until they managed to wake us, a process that took twenty-seven days," Cam concluded.

"I am not going to tell you *exactly* how many of us made various choices, but I can tell you this: the majority of my fellow Prometheans chose mercy."

Cam's voice was so perpetually cheerful that the sudden shift in tone for that last statement took Kay by surprise. The frozen ice in the Promethean's voice sent a chill rippling down his spine to the tiny part of his soul where Kay *knew* he'd helped create the Prometheans.

He'd served Winton. Served *Nemesis*. Helped to bury the Keepers—but also helped to steal the Keeper files that had proven essential to Dr. Finley creating the Prometheus Interface. By the time Kay had become part of the *leadership* of Nemesis—killing a Hand had seen him elevated to Winton's inner circle—all of that had already been in motion.

But with what he knew now, he could look back into the past and see where *his* hands had shaped the fate that had created Cam.

But he had already seen enough to know that it had been necessary. He drove the spike of guilt under his mental heel and focused on the Promethean's words.

"Fourteen ships would have been... seventy of you," he said slowly, doing the math.

"By the time we reached Azhar's Folly, we had one Promethean per ship," Cam said, her speakers turned down to mimic a whisper. "And we did not bring fourteen ships to the Folly."

"We lost some to the RIN pursuit," Wang said, his voice soft enough to match the Promethean. "But we scuttled more ships due to a lack of Prometheans to jump them than the Republic ever shot down."

"What else were we to do?" Falkenrath asked. "They'd been murdered and *then* enslaved. We had to protect them as well as ourselves."

"The Prometheans of this Navy are the closest thing I have ever had to children," Emerson Wang told Kay. "I have done everything in my power to repair the damage I helped do to them, but I will protect them until my dying day.

"There is only one order the Dyad Ministers could give that I would defy, and they know what it is." Wang smiled as thinly as his heavyset face allowed. "We wish to be friends with the Protectorate, Mage-Captain, but I believe I have made our inflexible requirements clear."

Kay, who had no real responsibility toward the Protectorate and only the vaguest concern over the future relationship between Mars and the Dual Republics, smiled and nodded.

"I understand," he told Wang. "I cannot see any reason why Her Majesty would argue that point. We are still working with our own Prometheans to learn just what they want their futures to look like.

"Most of them came from the First Legion, though I will admit that we keep finding leftover Interfaces in the strangest corners of the galaxy." He gestured. "I feel like I can safely say that Chimera qualifies."

"Probably," Wang said with a chuckle. "I appreciate you coming aboard *Chimera* to meet with me, Mage-Captain. Part of my deal with the Dyad Ministers is that I am the ultimate arbiter of the security of this star system.

"It was *my* decision, Captain, whether you would be allowed to descend to Twin Sphinx to meet with the Dyad." He smiled gently. "I have no major concerns, though I must ask that you cooperate with the directions and instructions of our security personnel.

"You should receive a time and landing slot by the time you have returned aboard *Rose*. Your shuttle will be escorted by two of my assault shuttles, but that is... hopefully a formality, yes?"

"I understand completely, Admiral," Kay said with a nod and a hidden grin of triumph. He'd figured Wang held more power than he pretended. The Dyad might *govern* the planet, but it was clear that the "Duke of the Blue River" had a say in any decision where he wanted one!

CHAPTER 13

GARUDA *LOOKED* COLD. Massive ice caps claimed her polar regions, and the lack of mountains on most of her continents suggested a windy, chilly world to Kay's gaze.

Her equatorial regions, where Twin Sphinx was located, looked temperate enough, but it wasn't a planet Kay would have lived on by choice. On the other hand, his impression was that none of the humans who'd arrived in Chimera had found themselves with much *choice*.

Not least because the Reejit—the reezh? Kay still wasn't sure what the *Reejit* were in comparison, though the aliens there called themselves the reezh and he strongly doubted there was a *second* alien race around there—had bombed most of the other habitable worlds around Chimera into ash.

"Thanks to the CSN, we've got a weather report," his pilot told him as they dropped toward their destination. "Sixteen degrees Celsius, eighty-kilometer-per-hour winds."

"Unpleasant," Kay said. The temperature was fine. That *wind*, though...

"Locals seem to think that's a light breeze," the pilot replied with a chuckle.

Kay returned the chuckle with a nod and turned his attention to the city ahead of them. Thanks to the shuttle's sensors, he had a solid eye on what was ahead of him, and it was *fascinating*.

He'd half-expected a clear division, with the Dual Republics divided geographically as well as by species and a city with a clear human section and a clear reezh section. Instead, it was all woven together into a surprisingly harmonious whole.

Twin Sphinx was a series of twelve concentric circles, the largest almost two hundred kilometers from edge to edge, with eight kilometer-wide green spaces carving cardinal lines from center to outer rim. Six of the rings were more green space, clearly reserved parks with no visible residential or industrial development.

Those green rings alternated with more-developed rings. The outer ring appeared to be pure residential and commercial, with the next four mixing industry and residences like any city Kay had seen.

The central zone, the heart of the concentric circles of green space and construction, had enough of a different tone that Kay wasn't even surprised it was their destination. For one thing, it held the only significant raised ground he could see in any direction, a single soft-edged hill that rose amidst towers and faux-stone architecture that could only be political buildings.

The rest of the city had a mix of structures he would have expected to see anywhere—the ubiquitous glass-and-steel skyscrapers of the Protectorate, the many, *many* variations on the concept of a two-story family home, and several recognizable iterations of *shopping complex*—with an entirely different style of building.

Some of the strange structures rose to the same heights as the human-style skyscrapers, though they had a far broader base and were wrapped in spiraling ramps that looked like someone could walk from the base to the peak on the outside.

Others were squat residences, low enough to the ground that Kay figured even the main floors had to be half-underground. If humans were creatures of the savannah and the jungle, he judged the reezh were creatures of the tundra and the prairie.

"Final flight path is locked in," the pilot announced. "Our escorts are peeling off; flashing them thanks for the guide."

"We're in this close and they're trusting us?" Chaudhary asked. "Or... just how many concealed missile launchers are hidden in that innermost greenbelt?"

"A lot," the pilot said drily. "They've done a good job, but most of their systems are based on twenty-third-century tech with some homegrown upgrades. I'm sure the Republicans are working on it, but *Rose*'s shuttles got upgraded sensors too.

"We can see right through their camo, and it won't help us one bit if they decide we aren't landing or leaving."

Kay tapped a command and mirrored the pilot's scanner display to his own console. *A lot* was... about as accurate as he could get. Someone had gone to a great deal of effort to keep the weapons away from the thoroughfares allowing people to visit the capital district, but his single shuttle couldn't get through those defenses easily.

He concealed a smile as he mapped them out. *Not easily* didn't mean they couldn't do it, though. Some things were already ringing hollow about Chimera. He'd see how his meeting with the Dyad went, but he was starting to have his suspicions about these people.

Someone alien had built Project Olympus on Mars, after all, and he would bet money the Chimeran reezh would say it hadn't been them!

At the heart of Twin Sphinx was the only hill of significant size for at least two hundred kilometers in every direction. To Kay's surprise, however, the center of the Dual Republics' Parliament was at the southern base of that hill rather than on top of it.

Someone had taken *Twin Sphinx* to heart when designing the structure, too. The main building was a squat, fortress-like block of granite, with ziggurat-esque spiraling terraces wrapping around its twenty-meter height, but on either end of the long building, the terraces were capped by statues based on that ancient Earth artifact.

On the east end, the sphinx was clearly meant to represent humanity and was, basically, a two-to-one scale replica of the original Egyptian sphinx with a human head on the front half of a Terran cat's body.

On the *west* end, the "sphinx" had the frilled, triceratops-like head of a reezh on the clawed and scaled body of some multi-legged creature that looked like a monstrous hybrid between a crocodile and a stag beetle. The grotesqueness of that statue to Kay's eyes wasn't helped, he suspected, by only having the front half of the six-legged crocodile-beetle creature to work with.

Fortunately, their guide brought his party to the east entrance and he only had to look at the west sphinx for a few moments.

"Welcome to Garuda and Twin Sphinx, Mage-Captain Riordan," a pudgy man in a flowing toga-like garment greeted him as he was led through the door. "Major Chaudhary. Lieutenants."

Looking at the *uniforms*, Kay knew that his party looked like a collection of RMN Lieutenants pressed into service as diplomatic aides as the Captain faced an unexpected situation.

In truth, they were Nemesis commandos to a one, and if anything, he was worried they were going to come across as too civilian. His people were trained to go entirely unnoticed, but their focus was on moving through civilian or government environments invisibly, not military bases.

"Thank you," Kay told the togaed stranger, bowing slightly. "Who do I have the honor of addressing?"

"I am Abdul Aziz Fikri Karim," the local introduced himself with a sweeping bow. "I have the honor of being First Secretary to the Eastern Dyad Minister, Hsieh Ai Ling.

"She has asked me to guide you to a waiting area and see to your refreshment while she and the Western Dyad Minister resolved some minor outstanding business that has overrun the schedule. If you would follow me?"

"Of course, Mr. Karim," Kay said genially. "Lead the way."

He shared a silent glance with Chaudhary, who simply nodded. The commandos knew their work. By the time Kay had reached whatever waiting area Karim led them to, there would be *dozens* of self-mobile bugs spreading Nemesis's ears throughout the building.

And if the Republic and Protectorate had never been able to find Nemesis's bugs, he wasn't worried that *Chimera* would.

"We appreciate your patience, Mage-Captain Riordan," the absolutely *gorgeous* Asian woman who finally greeted him said. Hsieh Ai Ling towered over everyone else in the room, using delicate metallic-blue makeup to accentuate both her dark eyes and the blue-black luster of her long braided hair.

"I hope that Abdul was able to meet your needs?" she asked.

"There were no problems at all, Minister," Kay said. "Are we meeting here or..."

"I believed it was best if I collected you myself," Hsieh told him. "Please, if you don't mind, your party can stay here. Izhaj and I want to meet with you in private."

"Izhaj is... the other Dyad Minister?" And presumably, the alien in charge of *that* half of this strange, strange system.

"Izhaj Ojak is the Western Dyad Minister, Speaker for Reezh, and my counterpart, yes," Hsieh agreed. "Come, Mage-Captain."

She did not, he noted, wait to see if he agreed to leaving his people behind. Kay hadn't had much of an opportunity to dig in to the structures of the Dual Republics, but Dyad Minister Hsieh certainly wasn't used to anyone arguing with her!

Not that Kay was worried. He had yet to see *any* Mages, which meant that he was quite confident in his ability to fight his way back to Chaudhary and his commandos—or even, if necessary, teleport himself back to *Rose*!

He followed Hsieh out into the halls of the parliament building, noting that *she* had a pair of escorts. They wore extremely old-fashioned business suits, a contrast to their charge's bright-white toga, but Kay recognized both their weapons and their low-profile body armor.

The Dyad Ministers, it seemed, armed their guards from *Chimera's* armories. It made sense, but it spoke again to the quiet power of the man who claimed to "merely" be the system Chief Naval Officer.

Hsieh clearly expected the bodyguards to fall in exactly as they did. The escorts and the Dyad Minister knew where they were going, and Kay simply followed along for the moment.

If he *happened* to have dropped a couple of fingernail-sized drones that would map the route and report it back to Chaudhary, well, clearly, they'd just slipped out of his pocket without him realizing!

CHAPTER 14

KAY ASSUMED THAT the top-floor east-side corner office belonged to Minister Hsieh, but the being occupying it when they arrived was a reezh. A floor-to-ceiling window looked out at the back of the east sphinx, and the creature he presumed was Dyad Minister Izhaj Ojak stood looking out at it with their arms crossed behind them.

It was the head and the limbs that made it most obvious that Ojak wasn't human, Kay recognized. The reezh had one more joint in their arms than humans did—strange-looking enough to his eyes—but their doubled elbows were ball-and-socket joints on the same model as a human hip, with far greater flexibility than the human version.

Ojak's arms were crossed *twice*, in a helical manner that would have suggested major injuries on a human. From the back, their head managed to look somewhat less alien—and given the armored frill that surrounded their skull and neck, that was saying something!

"Mage-Captain Riordan," Ojak greeted Kay as he followed Hsieh into the room. "Welcome."

"You *can* sit down, Izhaj," Hsieh told the alien, leading Kay to a small seating area on the opposite side of the office from a massive desk.

The room was about what Kay would expect from a planetary head of state. He hadn't spent much time in such spaces, but he'd seen a lot of footage of various Governors' offices. The desk was positioned against a solid wall, with a view out over the city through windows with a subtly greater tint than the rest to keep screens clear of sunlight.

On the other side of the room, four comfortable chairs were gathered around a small table—and Kay judged that the furniture and the nearby wall could all be moved to create a small conference room with full audio-visual equipment if Hsieh needed a breakout meeting.

For now, though, two trays of cups were waiting on the small table and Karim stood by with a steaming carafe of coffee.

"I presume Mr. Karim has provided for your refreshment, Izhaj?" Hsieh asked as she took a seat and gestured the alien and the Nemesis Mage to other chairs.

"He has." Ojak took a seat in a chair that had been subtly modified to accommodate their physiology more readily. It was only then that Kay realized that the alien wasn't wearing shoes—because they had feet that more closely resembled *hooves* than human feet and would likely have found human-style footwear uncomfortable.

Karim filled two coffee cups, passing one to Hsieh black and then looked questioningly at Kay.

"Black is fine, Mr. Karim," Kay said. He took the cup and watched as the secretary bowed his way out.

"Your hospitality is appreciated, Ministers," he told the two locals. "One is never sure what to expect in circumstances like this. We didn't expect to find anyone out here... Certainly not nonhumans."

"Minister Ojak's people were here before us," Hsieh observed. "Fortunately for my ancestors, as I understand it. We were... rather lost by the time we found Chimera."

"And my ancestors were stewards of a rapidly failing tech base," Ojak said in their impossibly gravelly voice. Whatever mechanism they used in place of vocal cords could pronounce English perfectly intelligibly.

It just sounded very wrong, since it was in tones and at pitches no human could actually duplicate.

"From the records I have read," Ojak observed, "we had no supplies of key components required to maintain our modern technology and... well, half of the planet was using wood-fired steam engines and glaring at the half that was relying on fusion plants that were a few bad days from shutting down completely."

"An interesting situation for everyone," Kay murmured.

"Hence the Dual Republics and our syncretic culture," Hsieh told him. "The Expedition needed food and a place to settle. In exchange, we could offer the reezh a technology base that wasn't dependent on supplies that no longer existed."

Which begged the question of *why* those supplies had ceased to exist. On the other hand, given the state of many of the surrounding star systems, Kay could *guess.*

"The Protectorate was not aware of your Expedition," he reminded Hsieh. "Or of the reezh. Where did your people come from, Ojak?"

"We were a similar group to Minister Hsieh's Founding Expedition," Ojak told him. "In some ways, even less well planned, but you have seen the stars around us, I assume. My people were fighting a brutal civil war, and my ancestors fled it here."

All of which sounded perfect and good, and yet... Ojak was dancing around pieces, Kay suspected. There was only so hard he could push, though. *He* needed different things from the Dyad Ministers than an actual Protectorate Mage-Captain would, after all.

"These are dark and violent stars," Kay said consideringly. "Not ones in which the Protectorate treads lightly, but that same darkness draws our fears as we consider the source of the taint that birthed the so-called Republic of Faith and Reason."

"We... I do not understand," Hsieh admitted.

"I look to the Dyad for answers, for this is a human question," Ojak said, their tone an amused desert.

At some point, Kay might work out if the alien was male or female or just had a preferred English pronoun. No one had given him any clues on that front yet.

"You know what horror lurks at the heart of Admiral Wang's ships," Kay said. It wasn't a question. If they *didn't*, well, he didn't mind driving a wedge between the Republicans and his new home.

"The Prometheus Interface is not, at its heart, a *human* technology," he told them. "We have learned this, in our hunt for the source of the horror. Alien schematics, for a technology never intended for human magic and human Mages, were delivered into the hands of the men and monsters who forged the Interface.

"And no alien known to the Protectorate ever forged such a thing." He leveled his gaze on Izhaj Ojak. "No alien known to us ever traveled the stars at all. And yet here I find an alien colony, one delivered here by some artifice unknown to us. We are in these stars to seek the source of the taint that saw thousands of our children murdered to fuel an alien technology.

"So, I must ask, Dyad Minister, *how* did your people come here?"

"I think you go too far, Captain," Hsieh growled. "You are welcome here, but the Dyad will speak of the future, not of a past that we know nothing—"

Ojak held up a hand, showing two fingers and two opposing thumbs in a gesture that Kay suspected they'd *learned* for communicating with humans.

"If the Mage-Captain speaks true, then his question is not unreasonable," the Minister observed. "I look to the Dyad for answers. Does he speak true?"

There was a long silence.

"I do not know," Hsieh finally conceded. "*We* came here on ships propelled between the stars by Mages trained on Mars, foreswearing the Compact between Mage and Mundane and the castes we already saw it forging. I know nothing of these Prometheans but what Admiral Wang has told us.

"And while Wang speaks of horrors and lies, *he* has no idea of where the true origins of the Interface lie."

"Then I feel the Mage-Captain's fears, while leading him false, do deserve an answer," Ojak murmured. They twisted in a literally inhuman fashion, leveling their lower pair of eyes directly at Kay.

"Nine and nine Guides of the Astral, what you would call Jump Mages, delivered our colonists here," he told Kay. "Their families sustained their knowledge for some time, but by the time the Founding Expedition arrived, no wielders of the Astral remained on Chimera."

"The story is much the same for our own Mages," Hsieh added. "There are no Mages on Chimera, Mage-Captain. Not because they were not welcome, but because their gift has been lost to us."

Kay nodded slowly. The Protectorate had an entire government department—the Royal Testers—whose job it was to make sure that every child of the Protectorate was tested for the Mage Gift in their preteen years.

The vast majority of children of Mage parents were Mages—Mages by Blood—but not all. And random chance saw enough of the Mages by Right, Mages with no prior magic in their families, born to make the Test necessary.

He could see how a small group of Mage families could slowly die out without that addition. He wasn't sure when the Royal Testers had started thoroughly testing *every* child... but he suspected, now at least, that it had been after the Founding Expedition had left.

From the sounds of it, Hsieh's ancestors would have brought a testing apparatus if they could.

"So, your people know nothing of the use of murdered Mages to fuel jump ships?" he demanded.

"I had heard of no such thing until Emerson Wang and his people arrived," Ojak confirmed. "Does that answer your question, Mage-Captain?"

It did... and it didn't. There was something here, Kay knew. With everything else that seemed to have happened to the reezh frontier, this world was the closest outpost of the reezh to human space.

He sincerely doubted they knew *nothing* of what had happened. He was prepared to concede that Dyad Minister Ojak might not... but that only meant he had to dig deeper.

"Come; if that is settled, let us speak of the future," Hsieh told him. "The Dual Republics wish for friendly relations with the Protectorate. Tell me, Mage-Captain, how best you think we can achieve that."

Kay smiled, focused on the deception in front of him and marshaled his best lies.

CHAPTER 15

SIX DAYS SINCE LEAVING the Nemesis System, three since arriving in Chimera and a full day and a half since entering Garuda orbit, Kay wasn't sure he knew any more answers than the long-dead fleet base had given him. The reezh in Chimera were definitely the Reejit, which meant there *had* to be a connection between the seemingly friendly aliens and the manipulative monsters who had created Project Olympus and enabled the Eugenicists.

Still, his meeting with the Dyad Ministers had been... fascinating. While they were chewing on their new reality, they'd invited him to stay in and tour Twin Sphinx. He wasn't sure that playing tourist in an alien capital was going to serve his purposes, but he had found out least *one* thing of interest:

The reason there were no government buildings on top of the hill at the center of Twin Sphinx was because the *entire* hill was a historical-preservation park, with an immense sprawling museum at the center.

Kay didn't expect that the museum was going to have a *lot* of answers, but everything about the system rang ever so slightly false to him. Going back to the beginning and the stories—the *lies*, he suspected—they told about their origins might give him some ideas of where to start poking.

So, he walked across the plateau, hunched against what the locals called a *brisk* hundred-kilometer-per-hour breeze as he approached an entrance that even *he* recognized as a duplicate of the Mycenaean Lion Gate on Earth. The *rest* of the building was a sprawling, low-slung structure, built of a mix of concrete and glass in an odd-looking mix of late twenty-third-century human and what he was now recognizing as similar-era reezh architecture.

The architectural styling of the reezh government buildings was as intentionally archaic as the styling of the human buildings. The two stylized representations of the past were merged surprisingly well in the Joint Museum.

He suspected that, like the Dual Republics' houses of parliament, the east entrance was based on human history and the west on reezh history. The replica Lion Gate, with its two-meter-tall lionesses above the entryway, marked the human side of the museum.

"Come in, come in," a voice urged him from the shadow by the gate. "Some of us are too old for this wind, Mage-Captain!"

Kay could only grin at that.

"Some of us were never young enough for this wind," he replied, finally ducking into the shelter of the walls that marked a wind-free portico in front of the gate. "I have no idea how you handle it."

"Practice," the speaker, an elderly woman with shockingly white hair and a tripod cane, told him as she stepped carefully away from the entrance. "But it does wear. Sadly, there is nowhere on Garuda to escape it. The noise even gets inside."

"So should we, I think," Kay offered. "I am Mage-Captain Caleb Riordan."

"I know who you are, young man," the woman told him. "I am Eastern Dyad Curator Drusa Sciarra."

Kay took a second to process the title, then smirked as he stepped through the sliding doors under the lionesses.

"I take it there is a *Western* Dyad Curator who is reezh?" he asked.

"Of course." Sciarra bowed slightly. "For all that we claim to be two Republics, the *Dyad* is the reality of most of governance, Mage-Captain. One human, one reezh, speaking as one. Dyad Curator Oj will join us later, when we get to his portion of the museum."

"I'm curious about the founding and the original merger of the Republics, I have to admit," Kay told her. "Though I suspect you may find me somewhat overfocused on the reezh component of affairs." He smiled gently. "I know most *human* history, after all."

"And past the point we share, I only truly know the history of one world," Sciarra confirmed. "On the other hand, my grandfather was Captain of *Better Than Columbus*, the Founding Expedition flagship, so I have some attachment to that particular history."

Sciarra was probably into her second century, Kay judged. Even so, her grandfather would have been very old when she was a child if he'd been old enough to command a jump ship fifteen decades earlier.

"Well, tell me about the Founding Expedition, then," he invited her. "I presume there are exhibitions to support the story?"

"My dear Mage-Captain, larger chunks of *Better Than Columbus* herself are *in* the museum," Sciarra said with a chuckle. "How else to honor history but to include it where it can easily be shown?

"Come. As you say, there is a story to be told."

Kay had seen a lot of starship simulacrums in his life. Not as many as a true Jump Mage like the Mage-Captain he was pretending to be would have, but more than the average citizen of the Protectorate. He was familiar with their nature, with the runes that shifted across their surface, the semiliquid, semi-*alive* nature of the model magically bound to the ship around them.

Somehow, that made the *dead* simulacrum in the Joint Museum worse. He half-consciously circled the silver effigy of *Better Than Columbus*, studying the model of the ship.

BTC had been over a kilometer long, with six separate rotating rings mounted on a central keel. A relatively ordinary colony ship, there were a few key features that marked her as part of the second-generation ships built in the twenty-two-seventies. She was longer than the first-generation ships, with six rotating habitat rings instead of two.

"*Better Than Columbus* was a Twenty-Two-Seventy-Three model colony ship," Sciarra told him, as if answering his unspoken question. "She was the newest and biggest ship in the Founding Expedition... and twenty-six years old with four prior colony expeditions under her belt when the Equality Foundation purchased her."

"The Foundation being the organization behind your Founding Expedition?" Kay asked. The death of the simulacrum wasn't as *wrong* as it felt, really. *BTC* had presumably been dismantled to build the city around him, an intended use of her design.

Colony ships weren't built to be single-use—well, *most* weren't—but all of them ended their days as part of their last colony. At a quarter-century old, serving as pieces of Chimera's new capital was the best *BTC* could have hoped for.

Kay just felt like the simulacrum should have been buried gracefully somewhere instead of being left on display with the rest of the starship's bridge.

"The Equality Foundation was born as a political organization opposed to the differential justice systems of the Mage-King's Compact," Sciarra told him. "Frankly, we don't have a lot of information on what the Compact entailed beyond separate justice systems for Mages and non-Mages, but our ancestors found that concept unacceptable.

"When political activism failed, the diaspora still presented an opportunity. While the vast majority of colonies were founded by ships jumped by members of the Mage's Guild and therefore were required to accept the Compact, the Foundation sought out volunteer Mages who would act outside the strictures of Guild and Compact.

"Some Mages, of course, *also* found the differential justice system a concern, so they had more than enough to carry six ships to the far reaches of the galaxy."

"Six million people?"

"Closer to ten," Sciarra said. "Our ancestors had a lot of people who wanted to come and not enough money to buy more ships. They were going far enough that they couldn't do multiple trips, so they packed everyone aboard."

The colony ships were designed to provide relatively comfortable living for a million people for a year or so while initial farms and settlements were set up. Kay had only ever visited them as museum ships, but he had the distinct impression that *relatively comfortable* didn't survive doubling up.

"Come. The story continues."

He chuckled.

"Is the museum set up like that?" he asked.

"This part is," she confirmed. "This is the Hall of the Expedition."

Still chuckling, Kay followed her into the next space. Where the prior room had been *Better Than Columbus*'s simulacrum chamber bridge with a few exhibits, this was a more regular exhibit hall.

Which was, of course, filled with a massive model of a star system.

"Where is this?" he asked.

"According to our records, it's System WKLY-One-Seven-Nine-Five in the Protectorate's records," Sciarra told him. "It had been identified by the Long-Range Exoplanet Survey Project as a viable colonization target in the late twenty-third century. The Foundation paid for the colonization rights, including bribing members of the Project to erase any sign of a liquid-water world from the entry in the Protectorate's databases."

That, Kay suspected, was a lot more common than anybody realized. It was part of why the worlds conquered by the First Legion were completely unknown to the Protectorate—though, admittedly, they had known there were *inhabitable* planets in about half of those systems.

"This isn't Chimera," he observed, looking around the model of the system. It took a moment for him to follow the iconography—it was *designed* to be easy to follow, but he was used to the military style that was designed to be far more information-dense—and he stepped over to the planet in the liquid-water zone.

The *dead* planet.

"No. Depending on who you're talking to, it's either the Zhocha System or Foundation's Folly," Sciarra said quietly. "The Founding Expedition arrived to find that the habitable world they'd been aiming for was *gone*, seared by orbital bombardment by an unknown foe."

"Our scans of the region suggest that is... disturbingly pervasive here," Kay said. "What do you know about it?"

"We know the reezh here were refugees from a civil war," Sciarra told him. "More than that, Mage-Captain, is not my story to tell." She gestured at the models, which he noted included six very-much-not-to-scale representations of twenty-third-century colony ships.

"*This* is humanity's story in the Chimera System, and it is my task to tell it," she continued. "We can move on if you want, but you did ask."

"Not yet," Kay murmured. The more he knew of the stories the Chimerans told themselves, the more he'd be able to find the holes and flaws. Somewhere in the *stories* was the *truth*—and while the truth might not set anyone free, it would show him where he needed to go *next*.

"Arriving to a dead system," he observed, stepping over to look more closely at the model ships. "From what you've described, they had far fewer resources than a colony expedition of that size should have had."

Ten million people should have occupied at least *ten* colony ships, with a similar number of attending freighters. The colony ships carried vast amounts of cargo along with their passengers, but a new diaspora world required even vaster amounts of infrastructure, food and agricultural beginnings.

"They did," Sciarra agreed. "They already knew that, unlike most expeditions, they would need to move most of the colonists onto the planetary surface immediately. Without a planet to move people onto, they were going to run short on fuel, food and even *air* in a matter of weeks.

"But they had a fallback, a second system that they located from Foundation's Folly that also appeared to have a habitable world." She gestured for him to follow her and he did.

The doors opened into a short hallway, flanked by three-meter-tall bronze statues. The man and woman facing each other across the hallway were dressed in the bulkier shipsuits of almost two centuries earlier, but the Mage Medallions they wore hadn't changed much in the last hundred and fifty–odd years.

Each bore a golden coin at the base of their throat marked with three five-pointed stars—the mark of a fully trained civilian Jump Mage since the beginnings of the Mage's Guild and the Protectorate of Mars.

"Mages Yevdokim Lester and Elvira Peura," Sciarra introduced them, gesturing to each statue in turn. "They pushed themselves too hard, delivering the Expedition to Chimera only to die of long-term low-grade thaumic burnout."

Kay considered the two statues and held his tongue. There was no such thing as *long-term low-grade thaumic burnout*. Burnout, especially *fatal* burnout, was an instantaneous thing. Jumping too early was one way to trigger it, but the training and instincts drilled into Jump Mages made it impossible to do by accident.

It took a lot of will and determination to manage to do it intentionally, and just *getting there early* shouldn't have been enough to need it.

So, either the story Sciarra was telling was underselling the degree of difficulties the Founding Expedition had been in... or those two Mages had died for very different reasons.

Taking his silence as understanding or, perhaps, respect for the dead, Sciarra stepped forward and opened the next chamber. This one had a neatly-marked pathway around a life-size diorama of three humans and three reezh standing in an open field. One wall was painted with a mural showing a set of old-fashioned landing craft, and the opposite wall with a very clearly reezh city.

"First Contact," Sciarra intoned, the capitals clear. "Once they knew there was an existing autochthonous population, the commanders of the Expedition despaired. Even if they were prepared to embrace darker options, there were few soldiers and fewer weapons aboard the Founding Expedition.

"But they had no choice, so they approached the reezh and opened discussions. They didn't know it then, but the reezh were in desperate straits of their own, and the presence of outsiders with differing technology was a symbol of hope to their settlers.

"It would take weeks for them to manage enough translation to truly communicate, but luck and surprisingly shared touchstones allowed the initial humanitarian need to be communicated. Food and air were arranged, allowing the Expedition to remain in orbit until initial landing rights were agreed."

"I imagine it took longer than that to sort out the Dual Republics?" Kay asked.

"Four years," a new voice said, the gravelly tones making it clear the speaker was a reezh. Kay and Sciarra both looked up to see a reezh with faded blue-gray skin emerging from a door he suspected led to the reezh equivalent of the pre–First Contact history he'd just walked through for the humans.

"Dyad Curator Oj," Kay presumed, bowing his head slightly in a gesture of respect. It was getting easier to pretend that the reezh didn't make his skin crawl by their mere presence, but a lifetime of practice in concealing his true emotions served him well.

"Four years?" he asked.

"The initial landings Curator Sciarra speaks of were on the eastern continent, where axial tilt and a fluke of weather created a microclimate damp enough and warm enough to be of lesser interest to the limited population of the original Allosch colony," Oj told him. "Our Speakers recognized that the strangers had value to offer and were in a difficult situation, but separating the peoples was necessary at the beginning."

"There were... incidents, nonetheless," Sciarra admitted. "But eventually, an accord was written and Twin Sphinx was founded to serve as a meeting point. Originally, the Dual Republics were quite separate outside of Sphinx."

"One to the east and one to the west, I presume?" Kay said.

"Hence the titles of Eastern and Western Dyad Minister. And Dyad Curator, for that matter," Oj agreed. "We are far more intermingled now, but the form of the Dyads and the Dual Republics endures."

"Fair." Kay looked between the two historians, a small smile playing across his face. If he read it correctly, the bluish tinge to Oj's skin and the faded color of his horns suggested that he was at least as old as Sciarra.

"I will admit, Curator Oj, I am curious," he told the alien. "With the Founding Expedition, I merely needed a little bit of detail on the Expedition itself. I know the history of humanity and the Protectorate, as well as any one man who isn't a historian can.

"But I know nothing of the history of the reezh. How you came here, what your people are like and where you came from."

Oj focused all four of his eyes on Kay, a gesture that sent a shiver of atavistic fear down his spine. The multifaceted upper eyes looked like they *shouldn't* focus like that to him, but it was somehow very clear that he had the curator's full attention.

"Allosch was here before your people were," Oj observed. "We saved less than Sciarra's people did. Necessity was a burden upon us, Mage-Captain, for our entire technology base was failing."

"I don't understand that," Kay admitted. "You must have come from somewhere—Sciarra and the Dyad Ministers clearly knew of the Protectorate before Admiral Wang arrived. Surely, you know much of the source of your people as well?"

Oj made a strange clucking sound that it took Kay a moment to realize might be laughter.

"That the Protectorate existed and endured was important, Mage-Captain," he told Kay. "The leaders of the Expedition had faith that the Protectorate would negotiate with us... as nations, if not perhaps as equals.

"But we still knew the Protectorate existed and would come to Chimera in time. With the Reezh Ida, well..."

The Reezh Ida. Kay caught the sequences, the familiarity of a pair of words he'd *never* heard and that had still shaped his entire life. The Reezh Ida. The Reejit.

The Reejit wasn't the name of the *aliens* who'd built the Olympus Mons Amplifier. It was the name of their *government.*

"Well what?" he asked, prodding as gently as he could as he sensed the edge of what he was seeking.

"Allosch was founded by those seeking to move to the edges of the Ida's control," Oj said slowly. "It seems, in the eyes of history, that they misjudged the center of gravity of our people, but they sought to move beyond that which the Reezh Ida demanded.

"They failed at first, and success had a far greater price than they imagined." Oj's armored frill shifted in a strange gesture that Kay took for discomfort—a gesture of an earlike muscle that equaled a shrug, perhaps?

"So, without the Ida, our ancestors suffered. Our focus was on survival, until the arrival of the Expedition allowed us to build a *new* technology base, anchored on technology we could build ourselves rather than that requiring the goodwill of a distant church."

"I don't understand," Kay admitted. "With all of that, it sounds like this Reezh Ida would be a greater concern than the Protectorate."

"That would be the case, it is true, Mage-Captain," Oj acknowledged. "If the Reezh Ida still existed."

CHAPTER 16

IF THE REEZH IDA *still existed.*

Six words. Six words that tore apart the entire foundation of Kay's presence in the Chimera System, the entire purpose of Nemesis, the entire cause for which he had led, lied, murdered and sacrificed.

If the Reezh Ida *didn't* exist, for what struggle had Nemesis shaped the Protectorate? If the Reezh Ida didn't exist, for what purpose had Kay struggled in the shadows his whole life?

If the Reezh Ida was gone, if Nemesis had seen their own fears in the ghosts of the past... for what had he fought? Nemesis had unleashed blood and fire and atrocity to reforge the Protectorate and the Mage-Queen's Navy into a sword and shield against the enemy they had *known* was coming.

If the Reezh Ida was no more, *what was the point?*

"Surely, Chimera is not the last of your people," Kay said slowly, somehow managing to keep the threat to his entire world out of his voice.

"You may as well show him your Hall, Oj," Sciarra said. "I'll walk with you if you wish."

"I am honored that the Curators of the Joint Museum are prepared to host me themselves," he told them. "I would be delighted to see the history of the reezh side of Chimera. As I said, I know *human* history well enough."

"Very well. Walk with me."

The reezh turned on his heel without another word, striding away with the strange multi-angled gait of his species. Kay set off after him without hesitation.

Not everything that had been said could be true. Not everything that was said was lies. The *stories* were important, but he had studied enough history to know that even the *true* stories were shaped to tell a specific truth.

Even if the Reezh Ida were gone, that hardly meant that the factions that had sought to turn humanity into fuel cells were no more. The fall of an empire did not destroy its people or its legions. The cities might break and the legions might scatter, but wealth and roads and swords remained.

The legacy of the Reezh Ida could easily be as great a threat as the Ida itself!

"As I said, we do not know as much of our history before the arrival of the Founding Expedition as I would desire," Oj told Kay as he flung open a door into a long, open gallery. Where the history of the Expedition had been a series of dioramas and entire sections taken from the old starship, the reezh history appeared to be told in artwork.

Given what Kay knew of reezh artwork in the ruins in and near the Protectorate, that was fascinating in itself. The Keepers had swept five different ruins over the years, but *none* of them had included any representation of people.

"But Allosch was founded some three hundred and fifty of your years ago," Oj continued, "fifty Garudan years before the arrival of the Expedition."

Garuda had a fourteen-hundred-and-thirty-eight standard-day year, Kay recalled. Fifty Garudan years was a bit more than two centuries.

"We know, now, that our ancestors were not *permitted* to go any further than they did," Oj noted. "We were required to be within the Shining Shield of the Nine."

"Which was..." Kay asked.

"The reach of the armed forces of the Reezh Ida," the curator told him. "The Nine were the Lords of the Astral, the ancient gods of our people. I do not know if my people came here to escape the Nine or merely to escape the Ida, the rule of the Nine's Church.

"Certainly, worship of the Nine was forsworn by the time of the Founding Expedition's arrival, but that was not a path that proved simple to walk."

Oj finally stopped at a section close to the far end of the gallery, tapping a wall panel to adjust the lighting.

Kay hadn't had a chance to really *look* at any of the paintings, and now the lighting changed to draw attention to each of the artworks in turn. Oj gestured a two-thumbed, two-fingered hand toward the painting in front of him.

"If my ancestors thought they would be free, the Reezh Ida soon disabused them of that concept," he said calmly.

The painting was extraordinary, in skill, in medium—and in content. Kay knew enough about art to recognize that the paint was something entirely new to him, a mix of some form of oil with flecks of specifically chosen stone.

The artist had used that slightly-different-to-him medium to communicate with skill. He didn't know the concepts and ideas that they were attempting to communicate—art at this scale had to include some level of metaphor, he knew that—but much of the story was clear.

In the distance, a burning ship fell from the sky. In the foreground, nine reezh were kneeling as nine other reezh, these drawn as taller and in what Kay guessed was meant to be modern-ish combat armor, stood before them. Landed ships flanked the kneeling locals.

There were almost certainly subtleties of metaphor he missed, but Kay got the gist. The Allosch colonists had been brought to heel by *force*. And just the presence of reezh in the painting told him of at least *one* cultural difference between the reezh here and the reezh who had visited Mars.

"Like the rest of the Reezh Ida, Allosch paid tribute to the Nine in gold, iron, bodies and minds," Oj continued, stepping over to the next painting. This was something closer to the watercolors Kay was familiar with, similar to Earth's historical Impressionist styles.

It still only took a few seconds of staring at the colors to get the idea. Open-mouthed starships consumed unending lines of reezh and carts full of... well, given the detail level of the painting, all Kay could say was that the carts were full of *something*.

GLYNN STEWART

"Gold, iron, bodies and minds," Oj repeated, studying the painting. "Metaphor, one presumes, for the extraction of young reezh to be soldiers and the vast draw of raw resources."

Kay wondered, though. *Minds.* It had been quite literally brains that were needed for the Prometheus Interface, and if the Reezh Ida had used something similar for even a *portion* of their travel, he could see them having extracted young Mages to be sacrificed to become Prometheus units as tribute.

The next artwork was, at first glance, a stylized night sky. Constellations— presumably those visible from Garuda's surface; Kay wasn't going to go outside and check at that moment—glimmered.

And then he realized that it wasn't a still painting and what he'd taken for the glimmer of metallic paints was *fire.* A chill ran down his spine as he focused on the art and the mix of light and metal pulled his attention to spot after spot, as the long-dead reezh artist had intended.

The sky was burning. It was *just* a night sky, and yet the stars were on fire—and he knew, without even checking, that if he were to match the art to the constellations in the night sky and to the scans his people had made of the region, the burning stars would be worlds that had been swept clean by antimatter fire.

"The Burning," Oj said quietly. "Those who came before us chose to remain as neutral as possible. We needed resources from the Nine that we could not produce ourselves. We lacked the resources, the arms and, perhaps, the courage to stand against church and gods alike.

"So, when our sisters in the Ida rose, we stood aside. When fleets tore the skies, we stood aside. When the Nine unleashed hellfire on the rebel worlds, we stood aside."

Kay joined the old reezh in staring at the constellations.

"For twenty-five of our years, our sisters fought each other, and we stood aside," Oj said quietly. "By the time the Burning came to an end, the supplies from the Nine had grown thin here in Allosch.

"So, too, had the power of the Nine. When a single ship arrived to demand tribute, my ancestors stormed it."

The artwork Oj led Kay to now was a sculpture of plaster and stone, with some form of crystals carved to create the illusion of light and fire.

"From what I have read, they believed the ship would have sufficient resources aboard to sustain Allosch for some time," Oj observed. He gestured to a stone model of the disk-like starship. "They were wrong."

"There was nothing aboard, as I recall," Sciarra added. Kay had almost forgotten the human curator was still with them, his focus solidly on the reezh and the artwork of the reezh artists.

"Barely any soldiers, even, and certainly none of the resources they were supposed to provide in exchange for the tribute," Oj agreed. "They believed they had been tricked and expected revenge. Instead... nothing."

"They realized the horrifying truth: there was nothing left. The ship that had demanded tribute wasn't from the Nine. It wasn't even from the Reezh Ida. There *was no Reezh Ida* for it to be from."

"Surely, they didn't wipe themselves out?" Kay asked.

"We do not know," Oj conceded. "The Reezh Ida was more the colonies than the central systems: the Nine and the Primes. The Ida were no more. We knew that.

"The Nine and the Primes may endure. We had no ships, no Guides of the Astral, with which to learn more."

He led the way to the next painting. The foreground could have been any pastoral scene from about a millennium of paintings on Earth. The background, though, was still an apparently high-tech reezh city.

"The technology our ancestors possessed was intentionally flawed," Oj told Kay. "There were components they could not replicate here. A special alloy used as the filament for the fabrication systems that could not be produced without resources and equipment no colony was allowed to possess. Only the worlds of the Nine and Primes could produce those resources.

"And without those resources, Allosch's technology base could not be sustained. They had limited knowledge of old technology and the tools to build such. They did what they could, but our world had descended into a divided culture: to the west, great farms ran on steam and fire and nothing more, yet in the center, a single citadel of our ancient technologies and sciences.

"A doomed citadel, whether it fell to a failure of engineering or the hatred of those who were blocked away from its lights."

Kay could see how that would have stuck in the throats of the people nearby. He could also hear and *feel* the gaps in the story. There was no mention of brain ships—and while the Reezh Ida might be no more, it sounded like the core empire, the *Nine and Primes*, likely endured.

"What do you know of the Nine and Primes?" he asked. "They seem like something my Queen should be warned of."

"The Nine is our home system, named for the nine Lords of the Astral," the curator explained patiently. "The Primes were the first colonies, those who stood equal in the eyes of the Lords.

"We have heard nothing from any of them in fifty Garudan years," Oj concluded. "Since long before the Founding Expedition came to this system. And..."

The reezh twitched his armored frill in what Kay was now certain was a shrug.

"We do not know much to begin with," he admitted. "The... data-storage devices used by our ancestors lost integrity rapidly without power. Short interruptions were fine, but even a few days would see severe and permanent data loss.

"With the difficulties in sustaining both the power systems and the overall tech base, decisions were made." Oj stared blankly into space. "We only have one intact data core, I believe, and we restrict access to it carefully."

"That seems... strange," Kay said. "I would think you would want that knowledge as widely disseminated as any history."

And it was in what the reezh were *hiding* that he would find his truth.

"It's not a question of desire," the reezh told him. "The data core has power because it is attached to the remaining power supply of a starship. Which... is in a state of perpetual meltdown, such that the halls of the vessel and even the central containment regions are actively dangerous.

"Even my people can only spend minutes in the central containment dome over the ship, with the best of our radiation gear," Oj noted. "It is enough for us to make sure the core retains power and to enable occasional data connections, but any attempt at a permanent link to the core has proven unable to handle the environment in the central dome."

Kay blinked. Just *what* had the ship been *using* for a power source? Light-water graphite-moderated uranium fission?

"Where is this ship?" he asked.

"You're standing on it," Sciarra told him. He glanced back at her in shock.

"What?"

"Seven layers of specialty concrete, covered by dirt each time, makes for a solid barrier to radiation and also for quite a hill," the Eastern Dyad Curator told him. "The entire historical district is built on the burial mound of the last known ship of the non-Chimeran reezh."

"Huh." Kay was going to have to get his people to check the radiation levels. Among other things. Parts of the story were too far-fetched to be true. Others *felt* like lies—but some of the bits that *felt* too out-there to be believed, he had seen proof of with his own eyes.

Humans, he wanted to believe, wouldn't have wiped dozens of worlds clean of *human* life. On the other hand... the Reezh Ida had apparently been a theocracy, and humanity had done some horrible things in the name of religion.

"So, you have heard nothing of the rest of your people in two centuries?" he asked Oj.

"Indeed. While as I said, we believe the Nine and the Primes—the home system and the old core systems—may have survived, the Primes did not all choose the same side in the Burning. The Nine may well have burned the Primes to secure their survival.

"I do not believe the Primes would have burned the Nine. Desperation and war may have changed that, but the Nine and Primes had defenses the Ida lacked."

"Do you know what those were?" Kay asked, then grinned as the reezh gave him an obvious questioning look. "I am a soldier, Curator. Forgive me my professional curiosity."

"We know very little of the Nine and the Primes, Mage-Captain," Oj admitted. "There are days I wonder if those who came before me made *certain* that we did not. But so much was lost it is hard to say."

"Do you know where they are?"

Before Oj could say anything, Curator Sciarra put her hand on Kay's shoulder and made a *tsk*ing sound he swore teachers learned in their training.

"Even if Curator Oj knew where the reezh homeworlds were—and he does not!—I would not permit him to tell you," the human woman told him warmly. "You are still a stranger here, Mage-Captain, and while we will share our history with you, our *secrets* are ours to keep."

Kay nodded and chuckled his acknowledgement.

On the surface, anyway. One way or another, he needed to know those secrets. And if the Dyad Curators wouldn't tell him what he wanted to know, he was *quite* certain they wouldn't be able to stop him from *taking* what he needed.

CHAPTER 17

"UESUGI HAS CONFIRMED. The next jump takes us into that system."

Roslyn nodded and considered the situation.

Thorn was eleven days out of Tau Ceti now, following a course that had taken *Rose* and her Nemesis crew almost fifteen days. She'd worked poor Tracker-Commander Uesugi and her Jump Mages—including herself!—to the bone to get there, but one thing had been clear all along.

Nemesis had known where they were headed.

"So, this was their destination," she observed.

"Should we prepare to jump, sir?" Mage-Commander Tod asked. The ship's Navigator was a soft-spoken woman easily five years older than Roslyn and a full grade junior to her—an ongoing problem for Roslyn, though Tod had taken it with surprising grace.

"Not yet," Roslyn said softly. She surveyed her bridge, then smiled. It seemed she wasn't the only one who'd figured that they had to be at their destination, given that they were only about eleven light-months from the unknown star system Nemesis had aimed for.

That meant she had most of her senior officers on the bridge. It was a good time to reveal one of the secrets of the Protectorate, she supposed. Especially since she *needed* it now.

"Lieutenant Commander Leavitt."

The Tactical Officer didn't quite spring to his feet, but he turned to her and vibrated with enough energy to give about the same impression. Everyone was eager to finally bring *Rose* to bay.

For her own part, Roslyn figured that the Nemesis ship wasn't going to be there. It had been sixteen days since *Rose* would have arrived here. Kent Riley and his traitorous band would have moved on by now.

But she hoped to find answers in what they'd been looking for.

"Please focus your processing systems on sensor cluster E-R-One-Five-Three-D. Mirror protocol, when it asks."

She brought up a concealed control system on her own console, plugging in a series of authentication codes and then several carefully calculated angles.

"We... don't have a sensor cluster by that designation, sir," Leavitt said slowly.

"Put it in, Commander," Roslyn ordered. "Trust me."

Rose didn't have a Mirror. Roslyn wasn't entirely sure why *Thorn* did—except that *she* had always been slated to command *Thorn* and she was *completely* trusted by every adult living Rune Wright.

"I have an input," Leavitt said slowly. "What... What am I looking at, sir?"

"If I've plugged the adjustments in correctly on my end, a window into that star system, Lieutenant Commander," Roslyn told him. "That *Thorn* is equipped with a Star Mirror runic artefact is highly classified, people, but this is *exactly* what it was designed for.

"It doesn't give a lot of information—size is a major limitation—but it should warn us if we're jumping into a trap. So, tell me, Commander Leavitt, what do you see?"

"I'm still sorting out what I'm getting at all," he admitted. "Give me a second."

Roslyn waited. Her bridge crew were all cleared to know about the Star Mirror—assuming *need to know*, anyway, and *that* decision was hers to make. She needed her crew to make full use of the secret tool in their sensor arsenal.

As she waited, she could almost *see* Leavitt and his people wrapping their brains around the tool she'd released to their control. She'd spent time with it herself—there'd been very little documentation and *no* prebuilt tools for integrating the software and hardware aboard *Thorn* with the powerful magical scrying tool they'd been provided.

Leavitt would, hopefully, improve on the tools he'd been given. He might even realize that the only reason he *had* tools was because his Captain had realized there weren't any.

A screen opened on the display surrounding the simulacrum chamber, an overlay expanding out from the glittering star of their destination. A system map first, probably as much drawn from *Thorn*'s main sensors with a light-year delay, then following with more data in a clear sweep as the Mirror changed angles.

If her math was right—and because the Mirror's position was defined by the magic of the Mage preparing it, it had *better* be—the window was positioned about fifteen light-minutes away from the local sun.

Two meters by two meters was a tiny window, but many of *Thorn*'s scanners had smaller receivers than that. The cluster of scanners pointed at the Mirror weren't particularly downsized from the versions on her hull.

As the Mirror slowly rotated back and forth through a sixty-degree arc, it would give them a complete, if sparse, view of their destination—and Roslyn could see it in the data codes and details that began to fill in on the expanding display.

"F-Six star; we can tell that from here," Leavitt observed. "Eleven planets. Asteroid belt. Three gas giants. One planet in the liquid-water zone, but..."

There was a long-enough silence for Roslyn to pull up the information on her repeater screens.

"What... No, I know what," she said, staring at the dead world. "Planetary impactors?"

"Not kinetics," the Tactical Officer said grimly. "I can't be sure, even with the Mirror, but I think we're looking at antimatter strikes."

A horrifying thought struck her.

"How recently?" she demanded.

There was a long-enough pause that she pushed aside the repeater screens and turned to focus directly on Leavitt.

"How. Recently. Lieutenant. Commander."

If Kent Riley had stolen a Martian cruiser and gone on to commit an atrocity of *this* scale, she wasn't sure the stain of that would *ever* be cleansed from the Navy's honor.

"Years," he told her. "I don't think we can estimate through the Mirror, but we're talking years, maybe decades. Plus..."

"Commander?"

"Our missiles can't do that," Leavitt admitted. "There are... over twenty safeguards, between our fire-control systems and the missiles themselves, to keep us from hitting a planet with an antiship missile."

Roslyn, who had the unusual distinction of being one of *very* few officers to order RMN ground-bombardment missiles fired in general—and, she suspected, the *only* one to order them fired at a Protectorate city she was currently standing in!—had forgotten that momentarily.

She exhaled in relief and nodded to the Lieutenant Commander.

"Thank you, Commander. I needed the reminder. The possibilities were..."

"What we're seeing is bad enough, sir," Leavitt admitted. "It looks like there was some massive infrastructure above the fourth planet before it was bombed. The stations were destroyed as well, and I'm seeing multiple major debris clouds suggesting deep-space action.

"None are recent, though, and I'm not seeing any active energy signatures."

"And if *Rose* is using every part of the stealth technology that allows *us* to hide from our enemies?" Roslyn asked.

"I can't guarantee she isn't in the system," the Tactical Officer said levelly. "I can't see why she'd be hiding, and I can't see anyone *else* in the system.

"This... *Star Mirror*, you called it, sir? It's an incredible tool, but it can't give us the resolution and angles necessary to really analyze what looks like absolutely ancient battles."

"It's intended to scout for traps," Roslyn admitted. "Which I suppose we have done."

She gestured Mage-Commander Tod over.

"Do you see anything we need to *avoid*, Commander Leavitt?" she asked.

"No, sir. We should be safe to jump."

"That's what we needed to know," Roslyn allowed. She turned her attention to Tod.

"Ready, Mage-Commander? The simulacrum is yours."

Approaching the fourth planet was worse, in many ways, than looking at it through the narrow window of the Star Mirror. The planet was on the outer side of the liquid-water zone and would have been chilly and dry for human standards, but it *had* been inhabitable.

"Do we have any scan data on this system?" Roslyn asked. "I mean, it would be centuries out of date, but we would be able to say when it had a habitable world."

"No." She looked up sharply to see that Commander Beck had stepped onto the bridge. He shrugged at her look. "No battle stations, no need for a second staff on CIC," he reminded her. "I figured this was going to require a lot of brains in one room to sort out what was going on.

"And while the bridge was staring at the Star Mirror, wondering who put *that* on our ship, I started looking up old astronomy databases."

He shrugged.

"Damien Montgomery," Roslyn said. "To answer the question of who put the Star Mirror on our ship. Or, at least, he *made* it." She wasn't certain if installation of the powerful runic artefact had required a Rune Wright. She knew its *construction* did—the standard Martian Runic language couldn't manage the complexity of the magic involved in the Star Mirror.

"And the databases?" she asked.

"Purged," Beck said flatly, taking the observer seat next to the command chair—the one the Captain used when someone else was jumping the ship. "The *star* exists, sure. The databases even say that exoplanet searches swept the system. I think we've scanned every F- and G-type star we've spotted within four or five hundred light-years of Earth at this point.

"But those surveys report nothing. No planets in the liquid-water zone, no gas giants with useful-looking spectrography. Nothing."

Roslyn nodded, then gestured at the star system around them.

"Nothing, huh? I see a liquid-water-zone planet, even if it's dead now, plus *three* gas giants that would serve handily for fusion fuel."

"Hence, purged," Beck agreed. "Someone bought the data and paid for the survey companies' silence. Probably spent some straight-up bribe money wiping university databases, too."

"Or hacked them," she said. "Nemesis could have done that."

She stared at the dead world.

"Or even before that," she murmured. "Do you have a time frame on when those surveys were done?"

"Twenty-ish years ago," Beck said. "Might be some earlier ones that have been completely wiped, and there's always some that don't make it into the *Protectorate's* databases, but the long-range survey I can see is about two decades old."

"And sanitized."

"And sanitized," he confirmed.

It was one thing to read the files—the Nemesis File deserved its capitals for the amount of work and analysis put into it, to make sure that the core operatives of Mars knew what they were dealing with—and another to consider just how pervasive the organization had to be to make minor survey data disappear.

Though she supposed that hiding the Reejit is what the Keepers had *done*, prior to Nemesis breaking them into pieces.

"Then what *do* we know?" she asked Beck.

"That *Rose* was here sixteen days ago. We don't know when she left— I'm sure the Tracker-Commander will have that information for us soon enough, but right now, we only know when she arrived.

"We know that this system was heavily industrialized and occupied at one point and saw at least one major fleet action."

"And we know that there is no way that fleet action involved *us*," Roslyn concluded, looking at the data. Her Tactical Department was continuing to update the displays and the background information as they spoke, and Leavitt had left his console to stand by one of his Chiefs and carry on a quietly urgent conversation as they dug in to the scans.

"Not least because the low end of our estimates puts the battle a hundred and eighty years ago," she noted. "A hundred and eighty years ago... That would be, what, twenty-two-eightyish?"

"Late twenty-third century, that's for sure," Beck agreed. He was looking at the data on his own repeaters now, digging for the same answers she was. "The Protectorate *existed*, I suppose, but the farthest explorations on record were only about eighty light-years from Sol.

"Not almost two hundred and thirty–odd," Roslyn murmured. Two hundred and thirty-three, in fact, she noted absently. It wasn't a straight line between Sol, Tau Ceti and the alien system.

There was a pattern to the debris, she realized. Not just the battle—the course of *that* was quite clear, even with centuries of drift in play. Roslyn, like every cadet of the Royal Martian Navy, had served several weeks on the Solar System's Ghost Guard, the informally named branch of the High Guard tasked with tracking and mapping the wreckage of the long-ago battles of the Eugenicist Wars.

Every weapon left a trace. Every lost ship endured. Space lacked the scavengers and natural processes that would often render a planetside battlefield little more than memory in a generation. The traces of even a small space battle could be seen years later.

Large battles, like those that had marked the Eugenicist Wars' limited hot zones, or those that had torn through this star system, left active *danger* zones for decades and centuries. There were debris clouds in Sol that were flagged as still having a risk of active munitions—though the Eugenicist Wars, thankfully, had been fought without antimatter.

This battle hadn't been. They knew that from the crater patterns on the dead world they were decelerating toward. Gigaton-range antimatter warheads, weapons the RMN had only been comfortable building and deploying in the last thirty or forty years, had been deployed *centuries* earlier.

That... was worrying.

"This was a fleet base, wasn't it?" she murmured to Beck.

"Major defensive formations, much of them almost certainly FTL-capable," he said slowly. "I'm seeing what looks like cloudscoop debris at the gas giants, so they were drawing fuel from there.

"Big space stations, but scans are already suggesting the volume was greater than the mass, so... Shipyards, yeah. And, of course, someone threw a fucking *fleet* at it and burned the planet beneath."

He met her gaze and nodded.

"I would agree, sir," he said. "This was a major fleet position, like... Nia Kriti before the Secession."

"Seems bigger," Roslyn noted. "And Nia Kriti wasn't exactly *small* before the Republic rolled over it."

She'd spent her Mage-Ensign "work experience" cruise aboard a destroyer doing anti-piracy patrols out of the Nia Kriti fleet base. The station had been intended to provide an anchor for security around a chunk of the Fringe, and had been upgraded after the Secession but before the war.

None of that had saved it when the RIN had deployed their fleet carriers in the best imitation of Pearl Harbor since the twentieth century. Nia Kriti had been overrun in the opening hours of the war.

Prior to that, though, it had served as home base to a squadron of cruisers and fifteen destroyers. A major force by the standards of the time—though the Protectorate had learned harsh lessons about the need for heavier ships than cruisers along the way.

"More in terms of purpose than size, I was thinking," Beck admitted. "I would think if they had any significant installations closer to us, we'd know about them and Nemesis would have gone *there*. So, this was the closest big base to humanity and probably served as watch on the frontier—much as Nia Kriti did for us, until suddenly we had a *border* as well as a *frontier*."

He had a point.

"Thinking about some of the stuff in the Nemesis Files," Roslyn said slowly. "We *know* there were several small outposts belonging to the Reejit in what is now Protectorate space. The Keepers and Nemesis cleaned them up, but they were abandoned anyway. Little more than fuel depots for scouting ships, as I understand it.

"But this, I suppose, would have been where the supplies and resources to build those depots came from."

"And the backup they were expecting if they needed it." Beck was silent for a few seconds, looking at it.

"Until it became a battlefield." Roslyn focused on the scans of one of the debris clouds. There was nothing definitive attached to it yet. It would take a while for the teams to pull together enough analysis to tell her anything about those ships.

"We don't even know who the sides were," Beck said. "We presume, based on the Nemesis Files and that Nemesis came here, that this place belonged to the Reejit. But all we really know about *them* is a name."

"Well, we now know one more thing," she replied. "*Someone* hated them so much they burned a world to ash with antimatter fire. And that, Commander Beck, worries me."

CHAPTER 18

THERE WERE a lot of reasons for Kay to be pleased to be back aboard *Rose*. Every moment he was on the surface, he was pretending to be someone else. That was a skill he was good at, that didn't take as much out of him as it might have, but it was still an active exercise.

That Kamilla O'Shea had effectively dragged him straight to his quarters once the initial business of his return was complete was a definite bonus, though.

Bringing drinks back to bed after the initial round of exercise, he passed her a glass of wine and spent a moment drinking in the naked form of his chief engineer.

Immediately post-sex wasn't a time when anyone was going to engage in a balanced and fair assessment of their partner's attractiveness, but he certainly had nothing to complain about! Beyond that, though, there was no question in his mind—regardless of whether they'd recently had sex—that O'Shea was unquestionably the single smartest person aboard *Rose*.

No one aboard the stolen cruiser was stupid, especially not amongst Kay's key leadership cadre, but the engineer put them all to shame.

"It's good to be back aboard," he murmured. "The pretending to be something I'm not wears after a while."

She chuckled at him, crossing her arms under her breasts and smiling up at him in a way that he should have *known* was a warning.

"When are you ever *not* pretending, Kay?" she murmured. "On the planet, you're pretending to be a Martian officer. Aboard *Rose*, you're pretending to have all the answers and be utterly sure of yourself.

"Even in here, you're pretending you're in love with me."

Kay winced and took a sip of his wine.

"Beyond the degree to which any man does that with a beautiful woman who just bedded him, I wasn't aware I was doing that," he pointed out delicately. "But perhaps a bit less psychoanalysis when you have me naked?"

She laughed at him, intentionally jiggling her chest to draw his attention, and then took a deep swallow of her wine. She wasn't meeting his gaze—but then, Kay knew how much she *hated* eye contact, and didn't read it the same way from her as he might from someone else.

"I might need my favorite of your attributes," he murmured, taking a seat on the bed.

O'Shea arched a playful eyebrow at him, then giggled.

"Why is it that I think you're the only man who actually *means* my brain when they say that?" she asked.

"Because I do," Kay told her. "And I imagine I'm not the only man you've had in bed who did, either."

"You'd be surprised how many *thought* they did until they got my clothes off." She ran a hand along his thigh. "What are you thinking, Kay?"

"There are a lot of gaps in the history the locals are giving us," he said, covering her hand with his own and enjoying the warmth of her skin against him. "Some, I think are... real. There are things that at least the people *talking* to us don't know."

"In four days, you've already dissected their culture and found the lies they tell themselves, have you?" she asked. She shifted on the bed to lean her head against him. The weight and the warmth relaxed part of the tension in his shoulders.

Kay didn't pretend he loved O'Shea. He was reasonably sure he didn't. But he also suspected he came closer than he had with anyone else in a long time. They'd only grown close with the planning and execution of the takeover of the *Thorns*; he really hadn't spent much time in her company prior to that.

He wasn't entirely sure, looking back, whose idea sex had been. There certainly hadn't been anything he could call a *date*; they'd just gone from a briefing to his hotel room at one point.

It was odd and strange and not quite emotional, but it worked for them both. And given their position at the heart of a conspiracy that was currently being hunted across the breadth of the Protectorate and their flight *beyond* the Protectorate with a stolen cruiser, *working* was a pretty damn high call for a relationship of any kind.

"I think... I'm looking for gaps in specific places, Kamilla," he finally told her. "And they're there. Not just in what they're not saying but in what they don't know they're not saying.

"The fact that there's apparently a melting-down nuclear plant in the middle of one of their major cities bothers me."

"Does it help if I tell you that part's true?" she said. "Getting the deep-scan data without drawing attention wasn't easy, but our people are good at *that* kind of sensor sweep."

"Oh?"

"Pretty much exactly what they told you. Seven layers of concrete, with dirt in between each of them, over a disk-shaped ship about two hundred meters across. Though..."

She trailed off, squeezing his leg to tell him she was thinking.

He waited. He knew it was generally worth it.

"Did they say what ship was under there?" she asked.

"They didn't," he said slowly. "I figure it was a colony ship, like the pieces of *Better Than Columbus* in the surface museum."

"It's not." O'Shea moved suddenly, the absence of her skin on his resulting in a sudden chill as she grabbed her wrist-comp and set up a small hologram.

The ship rotating above the computer was strange to him, looking more like a refugee of science fiction than anything he'd ever seen built. It had the same standard hundred-meter radius as the ships they'd reviewed in the Nemesis System, though, and was the same two hundred meters high that it was wide.

"We got some pretty decent information on her and she's a *warship*, Kay," O'Shea told him. "If I had to guess, a specialty-design assault ship."

Kay exhaled a soft whistle.

"The tribute ship," he told her. "The ship from the Nine that the locals stormed, hoping to find parts and supplies."

"I'm guessing the thing wasn't built to run on a bunch of uranium fission piles," she pointed out. "Because they might have had better control systems or containment methods if it was. I can't say for sure what went wrong, not least because their containment dome is doing its job *very* well.

"But what deep scans I have suggest an ongoing meltdown, exactly as they said. How they're getting enough power out of that meltdown to run a data core, I don't know. But..."

"But if it's not a colonial core, it might contain some information on the state of the core Reezh Empire, whatever they called it, at the end of the civil war."

Kay considered the situation.

"The Nine and Primes almost certainly still exist," he noted. "And it's quite possible that the people behind Project Olympus reported back in. If they're still in a state of cold war, they might see the ability to source jump drives from humanity as just the weapon they need to tip the tide."

"We don't know enough to say," O'Shea admitted. "But if there are any answers..." She stabbed a finger into the hologram. "They're in the data cores of that ship, it sounds like.

"Assuming that the locals aren't lying about the lack of backups and copies."

Kay chuckled.

"Oh, they're lying," he told her. "About a lot. I suspect that there are layers upon layers of deception, some of them so ingrained almost *no one* realizes the truth.

"But I think Chimera exists to allow the reezh to examine humans without anyone knowing. It's a dual-purpose experiment: it provides a shield if the Protectorate comes looking, a barrier where we might be inclined to stop, and it lets them prepare for the real war.

"Human Mages aren't much use to them if they don't have the infrastructure to process us."

"You think they're using Chimera as a shield to distract anyone who comes looking while they... what? Prepare for an invasion-and-kidnapping scheme?"

"I think it's a threat we can't ignore," Kay said. A threat, the back of his mind told him, that would justify everything Nemesis had done. And one that could very much exist.

"Do you think you can rig up something to keep that data core powered, contained if irradiated, and pull data from it?"

"Yes, yes, maybe eventually," O'Shea said briskly. "It might take a day or two to set up the gear to keep it contained—it *will* be irradiated."

"That's fine. Chaudhary and I will need to put together a plan to get into that ship without being killed by the radiation—and to get ourselves and the data core out!"

"Later," she told him with a wicked grin, tossing her wrist-comp back onto the pile of clothes as her other hand suddenly slid back onto his leg. "First, you need to find that lube again."

CHAPTER 19

WITH OVER EIGHTEEN hundred people aboard, commanding *Thorn* was akin to being mayor of a decent-sized village as well as being the military commander of a powerful combat unit expected to show the flag and hold the line for the Protectorate of the Mage-Queen of Mars.

Roslyn didn't *quite* roll out of bed and get to work. She only checked her wrist-comp for absolutely critical messages before she showered.

The essentials managed, she checked the time to confirm she had neither meetings nor a watch for a couple of hours and took her seat in her office.

She'd barely touched the adjusting surface of her office chair before the door to Baars' tiny attached kitchen popped open, her steward bustling through the door with a steaming tray in hand.

"Do *not* turn that on," Baars said firmly, nodding toward the console. Roslyn *could* access all of her files through her wrist-comp's holographic screen, but it was easier to handle paperwork on the full-size screen.

"Not until you've eaten. I was warned, you know. *You think destroyer captains are bad*, I was told. *But they've nothing on cruiser captains. Buggers don't sleep unless you sit* on *them!*"

Roslyn's keeper shook her head firmly.

"You'll work faster and better if you stop and eat first," she declared, laying the tray—holding a steaming cup of coffee and a plate of waffles— on the desk.

"So eat."

Roslyn couldn't help but laugh.

"There are urgent tasks, you know," she pointed out—while taking the cup of coffee, at least.

"And we both know you checked your wrist-comp for them ten minutes ago," Baars replied. "Anything urgent that isn't on your wrist-comp would—"

The office admittance chime sounded.

"Would involve Kovalyow arriving at your door the moment she thought you were awake," the steward finished with a long-suffering sigh.

"Enter," Roslyn ordered. Neither she nor the steward were surprised to see the graying Master Chief step through the door, a concerned expression on her face.

"Tajana?" Roslyn asked.

"Second coffee, coming right up," the steward replied.

"Make it three," Roslyn ordered. Something in the Chief of the Ship's face told her this was going to be a thing. "I get the feeling I need the kitchen council."

"Probably," Kovalyow admitted, pulling a chair up without waiting for an instruction. "You should eat those waffles. They're better warm, and I can talk while you eat."

Baars returned with two cups of coffee, hooking a chair of her own over so the two senior NCOs faced Roslyn across the desk as the Captain took her first bite of the waffles. Baars had, unless Roslyn was mistaken, baked white chocolate chips *into* the pastries.

It was probably calorie-rich enough to make up for the fact that she'd forgotten lunch the previous day. Probably.

"Part of the job the pair of you share is to make sure I *don't* work myself into an early grave," Roslyn murmured. "So, I know you're not in here, as close to off the record as the ship's Captain can manage, because it's something simple or easy."

"We're in the zone where you need to not take official notice yet," Kovalyow warned. "Because you might need to officially *not* take notice, if you catch my drift?"

Roslyn took a long moment—and another bite of white-chocolate waffle—to process that.

"There aren't many things even the Captain can make disappear," she said slowly.

"Cross-signatures from the Captain and the Ship's Doctor can erase things that should end a career," the Master Chief said bluntly. "Dr. McConnell can *seal* a record, but it takes both of you to *delete* it.

"Especially something that should be a Captain's Mast, minimum, if not straight to dishonorable discharge and a Fleet Penitentiary."

Roslyn swallowed that with the last of the first waffle, then pointed her fork at the Chief of the Ship.

"Precious Kovalyow," she said slowly. "I trust you. A lot. But I think I need to know what the hell is going on."

"Senior Chief Petty Officer Aurelija Vasiliauskas is our senior transfer from Tau Ceti, right?" Kovalyow said—and while Roslyn could tell the Master Chief was drawing out the explanation, she let her for now.

"Yes. They sent a pile of PO-Twos who needed to be bumped grades but that they didn't have senior slots for," Roslyn confirmed. "Vasiliauskas was a tactical noncom, served in the Second Heavy Squadron of the Tau Ceti Security Fleet at the Battle of Ardennes."

The Tau Ceti Security Fleet was like the Ghost Guard of the Solar High Guard. The name wasn't *official*, but everyone knew what it meant. In the case of the TCSF, it meant Tau Ceti System Defense Force squadrons—*not* individual ships, but entire squadron-level formations—deployed outside the Tau Ceti System.

At any given moment, the Security Fleet was generally four squadrons or less. Mostly destroyers, with at most a single cruiser squadron showing the flag somewhere important. When the UnArcana War had started, something like three-quarters of the TCSDF had become Tau Ceti Security Fleet—and most of those officers, Mages and spacers, like Aurelija Vasiliauskas, had served with distinction.

"Decades of experience, combat decorations for bravery, in every sense deserving of the bump to Senior Chief," Kovalyow agreed, then paused again.

"What happened, Precious?" Roslyn asked.

"She punched out Lieutenant Commander Leavitt. Knocked him clean unconscious. Beat down two other Chiefs who tried to restrain her. Took four Marines to pin her down long enough to get her into sickbay and sedated."

"That seems..." Roslyn sighed. "I'm not sure that's something I can pretend not to have noticed, let alone something I can make disappear, Chief."

"Depends on what happened, doesn't it?" Baars suggested. "I doubt the Master Chief is suggesting we bury it without a reason."

"Nobody—and I mean *nobody*—seems to be clear on what the fuck went down," Kovalyow said grimly. "Leavitt is in sickbay under medical supervision. McConnell is reasonably concerned about him being knocked unconscious!

"The rest of Tactical is in an uproar. Both Leavitt and Vasiliauskas are popular in their own way, though Leavitt would like to *pretend* he's an ironclad dictator. No one saw quite what went down, and even the Chiefs Vasiliauskas laid out are unsure what the Chief and the Commander said to each other—but it wasn't much."

"You think she... snapped," Roslyn said, slowly. "Which suggests she found something in her analysis. Striking a superior officer is a hell of a thing, Chief. A *hell* of a thing. What was she even *looking* at?"

"I don't think Leavitt deserved it, no," Kovalyow told her. "And I tried to pull the records of the data analysis Vasiliauskas was working on from her console, Captain. They're gone. She wiped them."

"That... stretches my presumption of innocence, Chief," Roslyn warned. She glanced down at her empty plate and the inactive console. "You said Leavitt's awake, right?"

"Yeah, he was only out for a few minutes. McConnell just isn't letting him out of sickbay until she's a lot surer how much damage the blow did."

"Being punched unconscious isn't taking a gentle nap; that's for sure." Roslyn considered the situation grimly and swallowed a curse.

"Okay. You want me to withhold judgment for now, I take it?"

"I'm withholding my own damn judgment, skipper," Kovalyow told her. "Something about this has a very particular odor. One that tells me we need to know what Vasiliauskas saw."

"Not what Leavitt said to her?" Roslyn asked.

"The tone and the odor... No, I think Leavitt just had shitty timing," the Chief said. "I think Vasiliauskas saw something in her data analysis that she couldn't handle. Unfortunately, her first panic reaction was to delete it and her second panic reaction was to punch the person who asked why she'd deleted it.

"We can reconstruct it—I borrowed a pair of systems specialists from Todorov's team to do just that—but the best person to tell us what happened is... well..."

"Senior Chief Vasiliauskas," Roslyn concluded. She nodded. "All right, Kovalyow. You've bought about a couple of hours before we either need a medical report or a scheduled Mast."

"I need you to talk to Leavitt, sir," Kovalyow admitted. "I don't know the LC well enough to go outside rank like that. And while most of his iron skin is an act, I don't think now is the time to call him on it."

"All right. Let's get to sickbay before I have to start taking official notice of things, shall we?"

Normally, there were no Marine guards on sickbay. The single corporal standing at the main entrance didn't say a word to slow Roslyn and Kovalyow, but her presence alone was a warning sign that things weren't right.

Despite the presence of the guard, the infirmary was surprisingly quiet. Even in normal day-to-day operations, Roslyn would expect the ship's sickbay to have at least a few patients under treatment. Somewhere in the paperwork she hadn't got to would have been a list of who was currently under care.

At that moment, the number was apparently low enough to put everyone in private cubicles, leaving the main space open for potential emergencies.

"Sir." Surgeon-Lieutenant Anabella McConnell probably shouldn't have been manning the triage desk. That was supposed to be one of her nurses' jobs, Roslyn knew.

"If you're trying to pretend nothing is going on, you should probably keep things more normal," Roslyn murmured as she took a seat, gesturing Kovalyow to do the same. "We can have this chat in your office if you want."

"I doubt our portion of this chat is going to be very long," McConnell observed. "My head nurse is briefing the juniors on the... issue of the day. I had my piece to say, and now I'm watching the door while he backstops a bunch of panicked kids who were trained to deal with battle crises and *not*, apparently, small-town fist-fight drama."

Roslyn had to swallow a chuckle at that description. She suspected McConnell was correct—the nurses would have had a great deal of training in managing the crisis of being in sickbay during a battle, including what Roslyn knew to be terrifyingly realistic simulations.

They had less training on how to deal with *a popular chief punched a popular officer and you can't tell anyone anything about what you know*. A blind spot, she supposed.

"And said drama?" Roslyn asked. "This is... Anabella and Roslyn, to be clear, not the Ship's Doctor and the Captain. Mage-Captain Chambers isn't taking official notice yet."

"That doesn't help with the feeling that this is an ugly mess, you know," the doctor replied. "When the captain is in the room but the *Captain* isn't, that's usually a bad sign."

"It's always a bad sign," Roslyn agreed. "So, how about you tell me the state of our *popular chief* and our *popular officer*?"

"Leavitt is fine," McConnell said, inverting the order. "Or, at least, as fine as anyone who actually got cold-cocked unconscious ever is. I'm going to keep him under supervision for another couple of hours, then run one final scan. So long as it doesn't show any intracranial bleeding or bruising that we missed earlier, he'll be cleared for release then. Most likely, he can return to duty tomorrow.

"No harm, no foul, in a lot of ways."

"Except that a Senior CPO cold-cocked her department head," Roslyn murmured. "So, how is Chief Vasiliauskas?"

"That is a lot harder to judge," the doctor admitted. "By the time the Marines got her here, she'd collapsed. No need for sedatives or restraints, but she's still in a secured room with another guard."

Roslyn glanced around and realized she couldn't even see the guard. McConnell clearly followed her look and smiled sadly.

"Our secured cubicles are intentionally positioned to be invisible from the entrance, Skipper," she observed. "Otherwise, people walk in, see a Marine, and get worried for some reason."

"Fair. So, what happens now?" Roslyn asked.

McConnell checked something on her desk.

"Vasiliauskas is asleep at the moment. She didn't *move* after we put her in the room, but she was still awake for two hours. I hesitate to let anyone wake her up," the doctor said warningly. "My *guess* is that we're looking at a psychiatric incident, which means I have an obligation to dig in to what and why and how before I make any recommendation at all."

"She punched a superior officer," Roslyn murmured. "Hard to make that disappear."

"I can sure as hell make sure it doesn't go in front of a Mast, though," McConnell replied. "Yang's Sergeant-at-Arms has interviewed everyone who was in the room already and, I suspect, made blood-curdling threats to slow the rumor spread.

"I need to review those interviews and talk to Vasiliauskas myself when she wakes up. Everything I have seen so far suggests rapid-onset situational trauma."

"There's nothing new in this star system to *cause* that," Roslyn noted. "The system itself is a shock to the psyche, but we've been watching that on everyone."

The Royal Martian Navy did not really expect to end up orbiting dead worlds seared by antimatter fire. They'd managed to keep *their* wars away from that level of massacre.

Whoever had owned this system hadn't, which made just *being* there hard on the crew.

"I don't know what she was working on," McConnell agreed. "That's why I need to review those interviews and talk to her. What I *can* tell you is that she was not in her right mind when she was brought in.

"That's enough, in my mind, to activate the initial phases of Article Nine."

Article Nine of the Navy Foundation Act, the fundamental law and code of the RMN, covered the responsibilities of the Royal Martian Navy with regards to its injured personnel. Including mental, moral and emotional injuries.

"It's your call," Roslyn agreed. "My job—and Chief Kovalyow's job, for that matter—is to make certain this ship is a functioning warship of Her Majesty's Navy. That may well never include returning Chief Vasiliauskas to duty."

"Of course." McConnell shrugged. "The most likely scenario *I* see, sir, is a medical leave of absence that sees her restricted to sickbay and her quarters until we can return to base and hand her over to a more-complete medical facility.

"That may or may not follow up with a full Article Nine discharge."

"Which will be a hell of a day for all of us," Roslyn said. "Her seniority transferred, but she's been an RMN noncom for less than a month."

"I..." McConnell considered her words. "I have the suspicion, sir, that it didn't matter *who* the senior noncom running analysis in tactical last night was. Nothing in Senior Chief Vasiliauskas's medical records makes me think that she was more vulnerable to this than anyone else. If the senior had been a long-service RMN NCO, I think the odds are something similar might have happened."

"And that, Anabella, is why I want to know what the hell happened."

The doctor sighed, glancing behind her as four uniformed nurses emerged from the room they'd been closeted in.

"You can talk to Leavitt, if you want," she allowed. "No one is talking to Vasiliauskas until she wakes up on her own. I would strongly prefer to interview her *before* anyone, officially the Captain or not, talks to her."

"We'll see," Roslyn said noncommittally. "That depends on what Vladislav says. Article Nine gives you and me a great deal of authority to make things... go away, let's say. But Leavitt can make that a giant pain in the ass."

"That would require an extraordinary action on your part, sir," McConnell warned.

"We do not know what happened in Chief Vasiliauskas's mind," Roslyn said. "But I am prepared to consider that as an option, *if* I believe that it will be in the best interests of the ship."

McConnell nodded. The doctor understood. Both Roslyn and Dr. McConnell would have to sign off on returning the Chief to duty. It was McConnell's job to think about the best case for Chief Vasiliauskas.

And despite her best intentions, what was best for the Chief was at most third on *Roslyn's* list of priorities.

CHAPTER 20

LEAVITT WAS sitting up when Roslyn stepped into his cubicle, leaning back against the wall and regarding the door with a baleful glare that she suspected worked wonders when he was pretending to be a tyrant to his staff.

The visible bruise on his forehead didn't hurt the intimidation factor, she judged, but Roslyn had been glared at by the Lord Protector of the Republic of Faith and Reason. And while that man had *preferred* to give off an air of bemused befuddlement, he'd also had a glare to make ice shiver.

"Captain," he greeted her. "I take it you're not here to inform me I'm being released."

"Not yet, Commander. May I sit?"

"It's your ship."

"It's your sickbay room," Roslyn said. "I don't want to put too much pressure on you."

Leavitt half-chuckled, half-groaned.

"As I have assured Dr. McConnell and her all-too-attentive nurses, I am *fine*," he told her.

"You don't look fine, Lieutenant Commander," she pointed out.

He poked at the bruise with two fingers and winced.

"Fair; I'll have to adjust my hair to hide this," he said calmly. "Can't quite grow the beard *up* to cover it, can I?"

"Not really," Roslyn agreed. "But you're okay?"

"I don't like to think of myself as a one-punch man, but other than my pride, I'm pretty sure I'm okay," Leavitt told her. "How's the Chief?"

His tone was fascinating to her. It was a practiced thing, a cadence and pitch that managed to both suggest that he didn't care and yet very clearly communicated that his words were sincere and heartfelt.

"Which one?"

"Vasiliauskas, of course," he said. "The doctor has been very... circumspect about what she'll tell me. It's almost enough to make a man worry about someone who punched him!"

"Reading between the lines of Dr. McConnell's... *circumspection*, she was basically catatonic by the time the Marines brought her in, and is currently asleep," Roslyn said slowly. "You seem less worried about being punched than I expected."

There was a long silence and Leavitt seemed to look right through her.

"I... am not *certain* what Chief Vasiliauskas saw," he finally said. "I know what she was looking at, though, and some of the numbers..."

"Commander?" Roslyn prodded in the silence.

"To be perfectly honest, Captain, my emotional brain is doing some rather spectacular shying away from the conclusions *logic* says I should draw," Leavitt admitted. "I..."

This time, she waited him out. It was a good minute before he looked down at his hands, and he hadn't seen *her* for any of that time.

"My assessment was that we were looking at a frontier fleet base," he said quietly. "Chief Vasiliauskas was tasked with scanning the surrounding area for the systems said fleet base was positioned to cover.

"I didn't see the final conclusions of her analysis pass on our sensor data before she deleted them. But I know one thing: there are no fucking inhabited planets around here. Not enough to justify a fleet base capable of hosting dozens of warships.

"So, either this fleet base was dozens of light-years from any system it was supposed to protect—which raises questions I don't like—or *something happened to those worlds.*"

He fell silent again, staring down at his hands. Like Roslyn, Leavitt had learned the mask of command. *Unlike* Roslyn, it was not yet a permanent part of his exterior, forged by the fire of battle.

There, in a quiet sickbay room with just his Captain, it was fragmenting into pieces.

"You think she learned what happened," Roslyn murmured.

"Or enough to guess." He finally looked up at her. "And I, being an idiot who pretends not to care, made a stupid fucking joke about her having lost a few dozen alien colonies."

Roslyn nodded slowly.

"I need to talk to Vasiliauskas," she told him. "Dr. McConnell has already activated Article Nine protections around the Chief, but we both know that you can make that damn difficult on us."

Psych assessment or not, it was still within Lieutenant Commander Leavitt's purview to press charges. That would leave Roslyn in the unfortunate situation of deciding what was better for the ship: to hold a formal Captain's Mast and have the Article Nine shield put fully on the record, or to *informally* step on one of her key officers.

"I... I think I also need to talk to the Chief," Leavitt said softly. "And it might be the head injury talking, but at this moment, I am inclined to say I don't remember enough to press charges."

"She's awake."

"I need to talk to her," Roslyn told McConnell. "I am fine with you being in the room and continuing your interview, Doctor, but I have to talk to Chief Vasiliauskas right now."

The doctor looked like she was going to argue for a few seconds, but Roslyn simply met her gaze and waited. McConnell *could* fight her on this, but Roslyn would win.

Not because the doctor didn't have the authority to override her—McConnell most definitely *did*—but because Roslyn would only make the demand she was making if it was critical to the ship and the mission.

McConnell might not know Roslyn well enough to trust that yet. But the doctor was going to *have* to trust her, sooner or later.

There was no better time to start than the present.

"We'll talk to her together, and if I kick you out, you *stay* kicked out, that clear, sir?"

"As crystal, Doctor. Let's go."

McConnell still looked hesitant for a moment, then sighed and nodded. Gesturing for Roslyn to follow her, she led the way into the back of the sickbay, turning around a corner that the angles helped conceal from the door.

Around that corner, a pair of Marines in light body armor equipped with SmartDart stunguns waited. They flanked a door that looked the same as the other cubicle entryways except for a telltale thicker framing.

"The Captain and I will speak to the Chief," McConnell told the Marines. It wasn't a request. "No one else goes in or out."

"Yes, sir."

The senior Marine tapped his wrist-comp against the door frame. There was a barely audible sequence of clicks as several locks released, and the other Marine pushed the door open.

While practice and training meant that one of them was always a step away from the door, with hands clear for a weapon, Roslyn could see the slight difference between them expecting an escape attempt versus, well, expecting Chief Vasiliauskas to cooperate.

If only because she'd been on the other side of a cell door once. And while she'd never *say* so to any Marine, it had been very clear where the Republic Space Assault Force had taken their doctrine from.

"Chief, the Captain and I are coming in," McConnell warned Vasiliauskas. She didn't wait for a response, stepping through the door the Marine had opened and entering the small room.

The space, thankfully, was intended to be large enough for emergency surgery. There was enough space for McConnell to have two chairs positioned by the bed before Roslyn joined her.

"I'm surprised you don't have me restrained," the Chief said quietly, the soft accent of a native Hindi speaker blurring her words slightly.

"That depends, I suppose," Roslyn told Vasiliauskas. "Do *you* think that's necessary?"

"No."

"Do you remember what happened?" McConnell asked.

"Does it matter?"

"Yes."

There was a long silence, and Vasiliauskas stared at the ceiling.

"I feel like I should be asking for a lawyer," she finally said.

"That's an option," Roslyn told her. "We have a legal department under Lieutenant Todorov. I can have counsel here in about ten minutes."

She hadn't thought of that, and she should have.

"Right now, though, this isn't a Captain's Mast and everything you say in this room will be covered under patient-doctor confidentiality."

"With the Captain in the room?" Vasiliauskas asked drily.

"I am here, Chief, because you deleted information from our scan analysis that I am afraid I need to know," Roslyn told her. "The aftermath of that... There are enough questions in there to keep you and Dr. McConnell busy sorting out whether or not you do need a lawyer.

"But for the *ship* and the *mission*, I need to know what you deleted. And why."

The Chief turned away from them, looking blankly at the far wall.

"There was no *why*," she whispered. "Didn't think. Couldn't... couldn't... It *can't be right*. But... all those systems. All those radiation signs."

"Chief," Roslyn said gently. "I have to know. We're already working on reconstructing what you saw. But if you tell me what you saw..."

"Death."

The single word hung in the sickbay room.

"Okay. That's... ominous," Roslyn said with a forced chuckle. "But—"

"Does *genocide* sound better?" Vasiliauskas demanded. "The killing of worlds and the death of a *civilization*. No living worlds, only corpses. No *planets*, only debris and the radiation of antimatter fire."

Each word was a tombstone, and Roslyn understood how poorly the joke of *lost a few dozen alien worlds, have you?* had landed.

"That's..." She swallowed, corralling words like panicked horses. "That's what I needed to know, Chief."

"Commander Leavitt is... okay?" Vasiliauskas asked quietly.

"His pride is more bruised than his skull," Roslyn reassured her. "There will be some unfun conversations, Chief. Next time you and I talk, I will make sure we have a legal officer present."

She rose.

"For now, I leave you with Dr. McConnell."

Roslyn needed to go find the people reconstructing the data. They'd already lost time they couldn't afford... and, hopefully, forewarning of what they might find would prove a shield against shock and trauma for the *next* team of her people who discovered they'd walked into the valley of death.

CHAPTER 21

"SO." KAY LOOKED around his leadership council and smiled. It wasn't a pleasant expression, and it was one every person there had seen before.

"According to the Chimerans, the Reezh Ida is and never has been a threat to the Protectorate," he told them. "According to them, the Ida never had anything like the Prometheus Interface, never even investigated human space and were only a danger to themselves."

He looked around his people, his smile never wavering.

"In *the Burning*, as they call it, they know of over forty worlds that the Reezh destroyed," he continued. "*Forty* worlds. They didn't have population numbers that they were willing to share, but estimates we were able to track from the system datanet and similar... put it somewhere in the region of sixty billion sentient beings.

"*This* is the empire the locals want us to believe is no longer a threat," Kay said. "I... can do no such thing."

"So, what are you thinking?" Chaudhary asked. "They've seemed welcoming enough, thinking that we're from the Protectorate, but if they haven't told us the truth..."

"We *know* they haven't," Koskinen growled. "I haven't been down there with you and the boss, but I've read your summaries. There's a lot of gaps, a lot of missing pieces."

"More than anything else, we *know* there were reezh on Mars," Kay reminded everyone. "We *know* the Prometheus Interface was based on alien schematics and *could not have worked* for humans without Dr. Finley's modifications.

"It took one of the most powerful Mages of our generation, with a gift for magic unmatched outside the Royal Family itself, to forge that alien technology into a weapon the Republic could use. We allowed that to happen because we *needed* the warning to our people."

If there was a piece of any of this mess that Kay actually felt guilty for, it was enabling Finley to do that. He'd worked with the man and his child... but he'd be damned if he didn't think working with Samuel Finley had been Winton's greatest mistake.

"So, we know they're lying to us," Tomas agreed. "So... what do we do?"

"We find the truth," Kay snapped. "O'Shea?"

The engineer gave him a calm nod and opened a holographic projection of the dome at the heart of Twin Sphinx.

"Thanks to our discussions with the locals, we know that the 'hill' at the center of their capital is actually a giant radiation-containment dome," O'Shea told the others. "Seven layers deep and extremely effective; they still appear to trust the containment more than I would."

"On the other hand, they didn't put the capital there until *after* the Equality Foundation arrived," Kay pointed out. "It was a useful landmark close to where the Foundation landed and where the one still-high-tech city the reezh had was.

"Assuming they're telling the truth about all of that, at least, it lines up with the story they told about the Last Ship."

"The *Last Ship*?" Tomas asked, the Mage sounding out the clear capitals.

"The last time they *say* they saw other reezh was when a ship arrived demanding tribute, about forty years before the Equality Foundation landed," Kay explained. "Instead of delivering the tribute, they stormed the ship, hoping to steal the supplies they needed to run their tech base."

He shrugged.

"As it turned out, the people on the Last Ship were pirates. Or, at the very least, if they *did* answer to the central government, the central government wasn't planning on paying up either! There were key components necessary to produce, maintain and operate the Reezh Ida technology base—and none of those resources were aboard the Last Ship

"Without them, they were in a permanent decline. One only halted and reversed by the arrival of the Equality Foundation with a late-twenty-third-century *human* tech base."

"One thing I feel I need to make clear is that the Foundation's tech *sucked* to the reezh," O'Shea said quietly. "I'm in their system datanet, and, engineers being engineers regardless of species it seems, there is an entire subculture of breaking down and trying to reactivate old reezh tech.

"Two hundred years ago, give or take, reezh tech was more advanced than ours today. The primary constraints on their tech? A supply of complex organic carbon molecules requiring *atomic-scale manufacture.*

"We're barely at reasonable mass production of nanotech robotics. Atom-scale production? Precision artificial molecules?" O'Shea shook her head. "The stuff the re-engineering community is talking about is from the extreme cutting edge of the most delicate and uncertain experimentation.

"With the twenty-third-century tech base of the Foundation, they couldn't duplicate it."

"Then why use our tech?" Chaudhary asked.

"Because their tech base was intentionally crippled so that they couldn't function without supply from the Nine and Primes," the engineer said. "From what I can tell—and what Kay was told—they had one functioning city left when the Foundation arrived. The rest of the planet was basically an agricultural state running on steam and water power."

"And they still managed the containment dome," Kay said. "I'm impressed."

"Which is part of why Chimera's tech base is a heterogenous mess even now," O'Shea told him. "They have the tech base from the Equality Foundation, which was *good* for the time. They have fragments of the reezh tech base, the bits they've managed to either keep operating or replicate—which are *still* their most advanced tech—with, of course, a hundred and fifty–odd years of development on the Foundation's tech... all reinforced, a few years ago, with a supply of military technology and schematics from the Republic."

"But why is this dome important?" Tomas asked. "Because of the Last Ship?"

"Because of the Last Ship," Kay confirmed. "Or, more accurately, because the Last Ship's *computers* are still online and represent, if nothing else, the only complete and unmodified reezh database they've told me about."

His smile sharpened as he saw that sink in.

"Our answers, my friends, are in that ship. The situation inside the dome makes it highly unlikely that they have modified that data the way other databases clearly have been."

"Are we really going to find anything, though?" Tomas asked softly. "At every turn, we have found more and more evidence that the reezh are not the threat we thought they were. That, quite possibly, the faction on Mars was operating on their own and has been long-since lost."

"I do not believe that everything we have done has been for nothing," Chaudhary snapped. "There has to be a point, Tomas. And everything here in Chimera *stinks*. There are too many lies, too many evasions—too many things the Foundation humans have hidden from Admiral Wang, too many things the reezh hid from the Foundation humans.

"This system is lies built on deception, and while I don't think it was aimed at *us*, we are the ones currently being lied to."

"There are answers in this system," the commando declared. "I'm not certain that even the people here today know that they're hiding them, but they are."

"If nothing else, Tomas, my suspicion is that the scientists on Mars came from the reezh home system," Kay told her. "From the Nine. Somewhere, far beyond where Mars ever looked, lurks the heart of an empire. A dark heart, one whose leaders are so lost to what we would call reason that they burned forty worlds to regain control.

"An imperial center that, when their colonies could not be brought back into line, *wiped them out*."

Kay met each of his people's gazes in turn—well, except O'Shea, but he spent a moment gazing at the top of her head anyway.

"That was the Burning," he reminded them. "Not the rebellion. Not the civil war, even. No. The Burning was the result, when the Nine and

Primes realized they could not bring their equivalent of the MidWorlds and Fringe back into the fold.

"They burned them all. Chimera survived because they were obedient, at least on the surface, to the very end. Until the empire had lost contact with them and forgot they existed."

He focused his gaze on Tomas.

"Those are the people whose minions built Olympus Mons," he said quietly. "Who came to their own colonies and demanded *tribute* of Mages to feed their jump drives—and there is *something* there we're still missing, I think, something hidden behind the veil of lies the Chimeran reezh have told themselves.

"In humanity, they might have seen the solution to their problem," he reminded Tomas, specifically. She was the only other Mage at the table, the only other person who truly understood the depths of the danger they faced. "They fought a civil war and burned their empire over supplying minds for their jump drives.

"An external source for those would take away the cause of that war. Too late to prevent it but still an answer, a solution, to prevent a future war." He shook his head. "It is the Nine and the church-empire they forged that are the threat to humanity.

"And as O'Shea warned, their technology was beyond ours two hundred years ago," he reminded them. "We need to know *everything*. And that, my friends, means we have to *go* to the Nine.

"And if the reezh on Chimera even *know* where the Nine and Primes are, now, they will not tell us. That's not information they would share prior to forging full diplomatic relations and alliances with Mars." He snorted. "Relations and alliances that *we* cannot arrange. If nothing else, despite everything we have done, sooner or later? The RMN *will* follow us.

"I do not know how much time we have. Thanks to countermeasures we put in place, it should be months—long enough that no Tracker could follow the trail—but I will not put it past Montgomery and his protégés to tear down the infrastructure we left behind and find the Nemesis System.

"Eventually. But *eventually* is not long enough for us to run an entirely fake diplomatic negotiation and forge a false alliance with the Dual Republics. We need our answers *now*."

He gestured at the hologram of the containment dome.

"And if nothing else, that ship's computers *will* contain the location of the Nine. So. Are you with me or do we have a problem?"

Tomas snorted.

"I'm with you, Kay, you know that," she told him. "We've come too far and done too much not to go to the end of the line. So long as any of us continues this quest, we're all going to be dragged along.

"So, let's finish what we started. How are we going to steal an ancient computer from inside a radioactive hellzone in the center of a fortified capital city under the guns of an entire RIN carrier battle group?"

Kay chuckled, letting his smile brighten and soften.

"I'd thought you'd never ask."

Kay took over control of the hologram from O'Shea with a grateful nod, expanding it slightly and highlighting several key components of the structure.

"The Joint Museum has significant underground storage houses and, presumably, administrative spaces," he explained. "We haven't been given access to them, but between scans and the system datanet, we have a decent idea of their layout and locations, here."

The underground levels flashed.

"Most importantly, the *only* access to the containment dome's airlock system—that we can find, at least—is concealed in the lowest subbasement of the Joint Museum," he noted. The airlock flashed. "Each of the airlocks is a lead-lined elevator that descends ten meters, accessing the limited open space inside the next level."

"The various levels of the containment domes do appear to be used for storing lower-risk radioactive waste and byproducts," O'Shea observed.

"Because of this, there is an industrial lift connecting the exterior loading docks to the access floor.

"That isn't on the official plans," she noted. "We found it on the deep radar scans. I..." She shrugged. "I am not certain those scans went undetected, but no one has said anything."

"There are seven domes and six outer layers before we reach the inner core," Kay reminded his people. "The most complex structures are in domes six and seven, the outermost regions. Two through five appear to be little more than monitoring stations, with space for maintenance on the sensors and elevators.

"The central dome contains the Last Ship, and everything I have heard from the locals suggests that the entire central dome is a high-radiation zone. Which, yes, raises some *fascinating* questions about the Last Ship and what the *hell* happened to it!"

"Unfortunately, we have very little information on the layout of the ship in question," O'Shea observed. "Otherwise, as I understand it, our Jump Mages could just... jump in and jump out."

"Because of the lack of data, we need to go in on the ground, via the elevator airlock system," Kay confirmed. "Tomas, our real joker in the deck here is that *we* have a fully functional amplifier and fully trained Jump Mages. Getting us out is going to be on you."

The Ship's Mage was silent for a few seconds, studying the map.

"Along with the computers, I presume?" she asked.

"Exactly. O'Shea?"

"That is what I was researching reezh reconstructionist technology for," the engineer said. "We have rigged up a containment zone in one of the antimatter-missile magazines that should have plenty of space and will handle *any* level of radiation. I also have an interface set up that should be able to provide power to the system once we have it here."

"The problem is that if the core loses power for more than a few hours, the data starts degrading," Kay warned. "We have limited leeway there."

"I have already set up *three* different possible power interfaces and have a team working on a fourth," O'Shea said drily. "The first attempt will almost certainly fail. I do not expect it to take more than an hour to get power flowing to the data cells.

"*Accessing* those systems will take longer," she warned. "I have acquired as much information as is available on interfacing with reezh legacy computer tech, but it is quite limited. And that *includes* having hacked several Dyad Ministry Systems.

"I have enough information that I believe I will be able to access the systems in time, and even decrypt and translate as necessary, but do not expect this to be a fast process," she warned. "We are talking days, maybe even weeks, before we have useful information."

"I'm concerned about us commandeering a missile magazine for this," Chaudhary said. "What did we do with the missiles?!"

"We didn't have them in the first place," Koskinen growled. "If we'd been able to do everything on plan and on time, *Rose* and *Thorn* would have been fully loaded. But since Kron and Aloysius decided to charge off on a half-cocked plan to *kidnap the fucking Mage-Queen*, we've got the munitions load for a test cruise."

"More than that," Kay said. "We did move more munitions aboard both ships while we were taking over. We had quite a bit of control at the time, until everything went to pieces."

He sighed.

"That said, Koskinen is basically correct. We only have half the missiles aboard we should have, which gives us lots of space for things like radiation-shielded storage for computer cores."

"I'm a touch concerned about the plan being for *me* to get the computer out," Tomas noted. "Teleporting things aboard the ship is something I've trained for but rarely done. It needs *extremely* accurate and up-to-date information."

"Chaudhary, myself and a squad of the commandos will infiltrate the inner dome," Kay told her. "The need for radiation protection limits how subtle we can be. The best option would be full-up exosuits, but if we drop in heavy combat armor, well..."

"They're going to know we're there no matter what," Chaudhary noted. "*Infiltrating* may not take us very far."

"Lightweight rad gear gives us options," Kay replied. "Right now, the plan is that we'll attach ourselves to a cargo-pickup flight that's scheduled in about six hours.

"The flight comes low and slow over the central hill, so we should be able to drop without issue. We'll break in through the loading dock and commandeer that industrial elevator.

"If we can get into the domes without detection, we're basically home free," he reminded them with a chuckle. "The infiltration team will be carrying eight encrypted radio beacons. Once we turn *those* on, it will draw attention, but that should shape a cube that you can pull up.

"Right, Tomas?"

She looked pained but nodded.

"In theory," she emphasized. "The calculations will not be quick. I can pre-run a bunch of the numbers and keep updating them as we orbit, but until you have the beacons up, I'm just guessing on a lot of details."

"I've met Mages who could do it," Kay said. There was no real heat to the statement—if nothing else, the Mages he'd met who could do it had been *Hands*. And, well, Damien Montgomery, who was terrifying for a *lot* of reasons. One of them being that he was probably among the two or three greatest experts on non-starship teleportation in the Protectorate.

Given that Montgomery was also the Protectorate's *head of government*, Kay was potentially more terrified by the fact he'd found the *time* to become and stay that much of an expert than anything else.

"I can *do* it," Tomas insisted. "But I need *time*. Once those beacons go up, we're looking at five, maybe even as much as *ten*, minutes before I can move anything.

"And I'm moving *everything* in that cube."

"I'm counting on that," Kay told her. "Because that, Mage Tomas, is how *I'm* planning on getting out of there myself!"

"So, they'll know something is going down by the time we turn on the beacons at the latest," Koskinen observed. "What do we do when they start asking questions and our friend Admiral Wang starts charging lasers and loading missiles?"

Kay gave Koskinen a cold level look.

"We are Nemesis," he reminded the other man. "Acting on the orders of the First Mage-King of Mars, to prepare His Protectorate for the war against the Reejit by any means necessary.

"The names and the details may have changed. We know, now, that the Reejit were the Reezh Ida—and that the locals believe the Reezh Ida is no more. But unquestionably, the core worlds of the Ida remain, and they will bring fire and death to the Protectorate if we do not act.

"I will not see Mages sacrificed to fuel the power of an alien imperium. That is the danger we were assembled to prevent. A nightmare we must pay *any* price to avoid."

He had never stopped smiling, but he *knew* how cold his eyes were.

"Does that answer your question, Commander Koskinen?" he said softly. "I have every faith in you and Mage Tomas to control the situation outside the Joint Museum while Chaudhary and I deal with the situation *inside* it.

"I leave the necessary decisions in your hands. But I remind you. We are tasked to preserve humanity *by. Any. Means. Necessary.*"

Koskinen nodded calmly, his expression level. Message received.

It was time to get to work.

CHAPTER 22

"TS FLIGHT CONTROL, this is supply shuttle *Rose*-Three. We are on the designated approach and air lane. Estimating touchdown in four minutes, thirty seconds."

The pilot's voice echoed through Kay's helmet, a key but background piece of information as he finished triple-checking Chaudhary's gear.

"Altitude at drop will be two hundred fifteen meters, plus/minus five," one of the commandos reported. "Drop in sixty seconds. Stand by."

It was a dangerous height. The equipment and wingsuits they were using *should* put them down safely, but in many ways, they'd have been safer jumping from a higher altitude.

They also would have been a lot more noticeable.

"Remember, avoiding detection as long as possible is critical," Kay told them. "Do not hesitate. Shoot first, shoot to kill. We're not likely to see many humans in this mess."

There were two pieces to that: one, that he didn't have SmartDart programming for reezh, so they weren't even bothering. His people were going in with the Royal Martian Marines Corps' favorite "Death Parrot": the MACCAW-9. Officially the Martian Armaments Caseless Close Assault Weapon, Nine Millimeter, the Death Parrot was a surprisingly controllable bullet hose.

The second piece, of course, was that he was a *lot* less worried about killing reezh than he was humans. Especially any reezh inside the containment dome, which was where he expected to find the people who actually knew about the Prometheus Interface's precursors and the reality of what had happened to the Reezh Ida.

A lot of people were going to die today. If the Chimerans had just told him the truth from the beginning, that wouldn't have been necessary, but Kay had a duty and a mission.

No horn-faced aliens were going to get in his way.

"Drop in twenty seconds," the commando announced. "Popping the hatch."

Now was the first of many moments of truth. The shuttle could maintain airspeed with the hatch open, but it required a noticeably higher level of energy and a clearly changed airflow profile. If the locals were paying enough attention, things would be getting dicey *fast*.

"Ten seconds. Five. Four. Three. Two. One. GO!"

Chaudhary was third out. Kay was sixth. Two more commandos came after him, and he had a momentary glimpse of the shuttle's ramp retracting before the low-profile parachute snapped open.

Training kicked into gear at the same time as the automated systems. Everything about their gear was meant to avoid attention and reduce radar profile, but that also meant it required more active control.

Not that a two-hundred-meter drop could be done on automatic, anyway—especially since he needed to hit a very specific target zone.

Fortunately, RMMC training had covered everything from High Altitude Low Open jumps to rappelling down from an aircraft in motion.

This was *not* the most terrifying part of his training, and he remembered it with surprising ease. His commandos had taken the same training—some privately, from other Nemesis commandos, but mostly through either the RMMC or the Republic Space Assault Force—and within moments, they had themselves sorted out into a descending wing.

And moments later, they were on the ground. Two hundred–odd meters was a matter of seconds, even using wingsuits and parachutes to reduce terminal velocity.

"Clear!"

"Clear!"

"Clear!"

Commandos were sweeping the loading dock. It was late evening by Twin Sphinx time, which bought them some leeway.

"This way," Kay ordered, projecting the map on his helmet. He made it about four steps before Chaudhary tapped his shoulder to hold him up.

"Gear, boss. Ditch it. We've got eyes on a dump bin; we'll drop it all in with a timed igniter."

"Good. Thank you."

He'd disconnected the parachute, but he'd still been about to charge underground in a complete wingsuit. And whatever happened next, he wasn't planning on making any more base jumps!

The access to the big freight elevator—large enough for a full transport truck, Kay realized, hence O'Shea's description of it as an industrial elevator—was exactly where his engineer had predicted it would be.

It took his commandos less than twenty seconds to breach its basically nonexistent security and open the door. There actually *was* a transport truck parked in the elevator, currently turned off and presumably left there overnight until its driver came back for it.

"Anyone read that logo?" Kay asked as he glanced at the vehicle. It *looked* like some sort of government vehicle, but the text was in the strangely familiar interconnected loops of the reezh script.

No one volunteered a translation, so he shrugged and crossed to the control panel.

"According to O'Shea, we're looking for sub-level five and this *should* go all the way down," he observed on the channel. "And, like industrial gear everywhere, this is set up to be as simple as possible."

The control was a physical lever, currently at the highest of six notches. Kay couldn't read the labels—everything about this elevator was labeled in the reezh language. That was telling in itself.

Most places he'd seen so far in the Dual Republics were labeled in both languages. As he understood it, most of the locals of either species could at least understand basic English and the main reezh language, even if they couldn't necessarily *speak* the one they weren't fluent in.

That this setup was only labeled in reezh script told him that he was exactly where he needed to be, and he yanked the lever to the lowest setting.

"Sub-level five, here we come," he told the commandos. "Watch for contact. The place *should* be quiet, but we can't count on that!"

Despite the old-fashioned nature of the elevator control, the platform itself moved smoothly and quietly, descending into the ground without Kay even noticing it start to move.

"Take positions," Chaudhary ordered. "Use the truck for cover. We don't know what's down there."

Kay moved with his commandos, summoning a shield of magic to protect himself from stray bullets as he watched the levels move past.

The elevator came to a halt as silently as it reached the bottom. There wasn't even a door at this level, with the elevator opening out into a large cargo-handling area. It was mostly empty, with a single shipping container off to one side and a few crates piled up by one of the exits.

"They do a poor job of pretending this is just a museum," Chaudhary muttered, the commando's gaze sweeping the room and coming up empty for threats.

"Have you *been* in the back storage areas of a museum?" Kay replied. "Five levels of storage are probably too *little*."

His subordinate chuckled and shook his head.

"Alpha, Bravo, move, sweep," he barked. "Charlie, Delta, secure the boss. Echo, Fox, with me."

Two commandos moved out to check the open cargo area, while two shifted to flank Kay, and the last two followed Chaudhary toward the north door.

The commando leader, Kay guessed, had the same map up that he did. The north door led to the working areas of the museum's sub-levels. If there was anyone down there to trigger an alarm, they'd be in there.

"Flagging security systems," Delta reported. The commandos could probably use their names here, Kay figured, but the practice of never operating with even distinctive code names if they could avoid it was ingrained now.

"I have them," Kay confirmed as they flickered into existence on his helmet screen.

It wasn't much. A dozen cameras, already marked with icons telling him that his people had control of them.

"Their firewalls suck," Delta observed. "Better than the Foundation arrived with, I hope, but still awful compared to anything we're used to."

"We trained you to breach the Mountain," Kay pointed out. "*Any* museum's security should suck compared to that."

The commando chuckled and fell into step behind Kay as Nemesis's leader strode forward into the vault. Chaudhary—"Lead," in the deployment parlance—was checking the access to the museum to make sure they weren't interrupted.

Kay's task was to find the next step forward. There, in that moment, the answer lay on the western wall of the storage space. Even more than the cargo elevator, there was no sign that *anything* was there. The elevator, after all, was part of the museum's structure even if it was clearly mostly for the reezh half.

The complex lead-lined airlock leading into the containment dome wasn't supposed to be there at all. Kay had the sneaking suspicion that the *entire* Joint Museum had been built to cover the entrance to the Last Ship.

The reezh were hiding a *lot* there on Garuda, and all of the secrecy and subterfuge told him he was getting close to the truth. The Western Republic might pretend that they were innocent and unknowing, but their every action seemed dedicated to concealing what remained of the Reezh Ida and the Church of the Nine.

Unfortunately for their plans of secrecy, O'Shea had put ground-penetrating scanners on every shuttle they'd flown over the city of Twin Sphinx in the last week. He didn't have a perfect map of the complex underneath the hill, but he knew where the access through dome seven was.

"We have the security under control, yes?" he asked, surveying the seemingly blank concrete wall.

"All the cameras and alarms we've found are routed through central consoles on each floor, relaying to primary and secondary control centers on the second surface level and the first underground level.

"We have worms into sub-level five's central console. All alarms on this level are shut down, but it is possible a manual alarm can be triggered, and, well, we can't stop someone just placing a com call."

Kay grinned inside his helmet.

"Fair enough. Do we have any idea of the controls for this wall?"

There had to *be* controls, he knew that. Somewhere in the twists of cables and computers that dominated *any* modern installation were the controls that would open the solid concrete block. He presumed it was on wheels or something else—there was no point in having a cargo-sized elevator facing into a cargo-handling space if no one could get cargo from one to the other.

"We can find them," Delta assured him. "But it'll take time."

"Does anyone here think we *have* time?" Kay asked drily. "This city is going to become very dangerous to us very quickly."

He stepped closer to the wall, placing his hand on the concrete to feel the cool surface through his gloves.

"Needs must," he told them. "Stand back."

His commandos were *very* used to working with Mages and caught his intention immediately. Everyone fell back, moving well away from the concrete barrier between them and their next step.

Kay drew in a breath and power with it. Magic rippled through him, and he drew his hand back for a moment—and then struck, slamming his palm into the concrete.

The entire wall trembled under the impact of his hand, shivering in the darkness for a few moments as his magic spread out.

And then a ten-meter-by-five-meter section of the wall disintegrated into dust, a sharp wind scattering the wreckage of the wall across the vault as his magic tore mere concrete to pieces.

Behind the "wall" there was a wide corridor that led to a massive door that looked like the blast bulkheads of a starship. If he was looking at the elevator, that wasn't even a bad description—though starship bulkheads usually only had a few millimeters of lead for radiation management.

According to the specifications O'Shea had found, these elevators had three *centimeters* of lead.

"Any alarms so far?" he asked aloud, striding forward into the gap he'd opened.

"Nothing we're seeing. That may have set off seismographs in the city," Chaudhary warned, the senior commando leading his people up to join Kay. "But so far, no one seems to have realized we're here."

"It won't last," Kay warned. "Let's get this door open." He smirked. "It might be a bit harder."

If nothing else, concrete was a lot easier to reduce to dust than lead was.

CHAPTER 23

SECURITY ON THE DOOR WAS, as Kay had expected, completely detached from the security for the Joint Museum. The containment dome over the Last Ship predated the human arrival, as did whatever archives and secret facilities were inside the dome.

They'd only found records of the domes being used for storing radio-active byproducts, but the scans showed relatively large complexes in the outer two domes, around the connecting columns where the airlocks cut through the domes themselves.

"So, security on this is still trash," Chaudhary told Kay, watching two of his people argue back and forth over a half-dismantled control panel. "Except that it isn't *human* security, where the security for the Museum is derived from Protectorate tech."

"And this is pure reezh tech," Kay concluded. "O'Shea warned it might be even more advanced than our current gear?"

"If it is, Charlie and Delta aren't admitting it," the commando told him. "But it takes time when you're working through completely alien hardware architecture. On the other hand, electrons only flow one way, as I under-stand it, and most of the actual *mechanics* are the same, so..."

A shout of pride cut through the two officers' conversation, and the big lead-lined elevator door slowly slid apart. As it moved, it was clear that it was made of eight pieces, each sliding inward and then sideways until the two doors had compressed into a quarter of their original width.

In doing so, the doors had become almost three meters thick, and Kay whistled silently as Chaudhary led the way into the airlock elevator.

"Seventy-five-centimeter doors," he observed. "And this is the *outer* dome."

"Well, why would you build seven different elevators when you could build seven of the same type?" Chaudhary asked. "Looking at the scans, the domes themselves are fifteen meters thick."

"With twenty-five-meter dirt layers between them," Kay agreed. "There's a reason they were fine with building their capital city around this pit. Whereas *we* need to find what's at the bottom of it."

"Everybody in the lift," Chaudhary ordered. "There's only going to be one way out of here, folks, and anyone who isn't in the box when upstairs picks it up gets to argue innocence with the locals!"

"You mean with the rhino-faces?" Echo asked drily.

Somehow, Kay was *not* surprised that the commandos had come up with an ugly nickname for the reezh. Any of his commandos that *hadn't* been Royal Martian Marines had been Republic Space Assault Troopers... or had been trained by people from the first two groups.

They might not be soldiers for a nation these days, but they were soldiers. And in some ways, soldiers never changed.

"Everyone's in," Chaudhary said as Kay walked over to the controls inside the elevator.

It was smaller than the industrial elevator outside, but it would still have fit the truck they'd ridden down with. The Nemesis team would have needed to be *inside* the truck to fit with it, but the truck could have made the trip.

"Delta, the controls?" the commando leader asked as Kay examined them.

"Security was apparently all on the outside," Kay replied. "In here, well... all they really have is a giant button."

Kay pressed said giant button as he spoke. It lit up softly under his hand and the doors started unfolding again. It was somehow even *more* intimidating to watch from inside.

If nothing else, getting caught inside those massive blocks of steel and lead would be very quickly *fatal* to any poor bastard carried along with them.

The elevator down from the surface had been quiet. *This* was not. Machinery audibly clanked to life around them as the doors finished unfolding, seam lines *vanishing* as they fit together far more perfectly than Kay would have expected.

"Down we go. Next stop, dome seven," Kay said aloud. "What are we expecting, Lead? Men's clothing, secrets and radioactive waste?"

"Pretty sure the radioactive waste is on level four and the secrets on level zero," Chaudhary replied with a chuckle. "So, I guess my guess is men's clothing?"

The airlock elevator didn't move quickly. It was a twenty-meter descent, Kay judged, and it paused to allow doors to open underneath it at least four times. The sequential airlocked domes were *probably* overkill—but then, he had no idea just what disaster had befallen the Last Ship.

It was possible that even with all of this, they *still* should have built the city on the other side of the planet.

"There's no cover in here," Chaudhary warned. "Be ready to advance immediately. No holding back."

The commandos knew their work and Kay knew *his* part. He had *been* one of the commandos once, and he knew that *they* wouldn't realize or accept that he was deadlier than any of them.

He would let them lead the way, while standing ready to shield them from fire if he could.

"Doors opening," Alpha snapped. "Ready!"

MACCAWs up, the team waited for the grinding seconds as the door panels slid inward. As soon as the first gap opened, the first team was moving. The second team was moments after them, with everyone except Kay and Chaudhary in motion by the time the second set of panels started moving.

The gunfire started at the same time as the two leaders moved. Kay wasn't sure what local security would be armed with, but he was relatively sure it wouldn't be pistol-sized nine-millimeter caseless rounds.

The MACCAW, even in single-shot mode, had a distinct sound to anyone who knew their guns. The only shooting was from Kay's people, and he charged out after them to see what they were shooting *at*.

The department-store joke in the elevator felt truer than it had probably deserved. The elevator opened onto a passageway that could easily have been a surface road if not for the five-meter-high vaulted ceiling, but on each side of it was a series of cubicles, storage spaces, and displays clearly organized to *someone's* logic.

Everything from offices to what might actually *be* a men's clothing store was visible along the underground "street." The only people Kay could see, outside his own team at least, were reezh—but where he'd been expecting everything to be shut down at the beginning of local night, there'd clearly been several dozen reezh working at various tasks in the underground complex.

And he'd ordered his people to leave no witnesses. There'd been no need to check for a threat—the *presence* of people, presumably with coms, was all the threat they needed.

The reezh workers bolted for cover and Kay added his fire to his people's. *No witnesses. No survivors.*

He didn't know who the people working in the secret archive were, and at this point, he didn't have time to find out. He shot down a trio wearing what he thought was body armor—and then realized was probably radiation gear, on reezh who were about to go even deeper into the dome.

It was over in seconds, with at least thirty people dead in the space.

"Alpha, Bravo, sweep and clear," Chaudhary ordered grimly. "Charlie, tell me you're jamming local civilian frequencies."

"Since the boss dusted the wall," Charlie—the team's electronics expert—confirmed. "But these guys are working in a top-secret bunker that doesn't officially exist."

"Hence Alpha and Bravo are destroying coms," Chaudhary ground out.

And killing anyone who was merely wounded, Kay knew—a single gunshot rang out from the searching pair, as if in confirmation of his thought.

"There might be something of use here," the commando leader murmured. "I see archives, boss."

"We *definitely* don't have time to search the fucking indexes at this point," Kay pointed out. "And while Tomas definitely *can* do the pickup, the less volume she needs to teleport, the better. If we try to include this in the zone, she'll be trying to move a block at least two hundred meters tall. She can't."

"Fair." Chaudhary nodded, looking around. "If nothing else, there isn't enough space in that magazine the crew cleared to *fit* that much crap."

"And we'd leave a giant hole through the radiation-containment dome," Delta said. "And there are actual *people* on the surface."

Kay knew exactly what the commando meant. Unlike the commando, *he* was only slightly less willing to sacrifice humans for the mission than reezh, but the thought had weight for all of that.

"We keep moving," Kay ordered. "Charlie, get on the next elevator. Everyone else, sweep, then cover.

"We're on a countdown now until someone tries to call one of these guys, if nothing else."

"This main concourse is only about a fifth of the dome-seven complex," Chaudhary noted. "There's quite possibly more reezh in this layer."

"Then our time is even shorter, isn't it?" Kay asked. "Because we can't afford the time to sweep for them. Let's move."

There was a clear path from the first airlock elevator to the second, one they could have driven a truck down. That was very clearly its purpose, in fact.

The security was no lighter, Kay noted, watching as Charlie and Delta worked through the hardware. The two commandos clearly had a better idea of what they were doing this time, but it was still a slow process of basically hot-wiring the elevator door.

"Clear!" Delta finally declared, moments before the panels on the airlock door started sliding inward.

"I take it we still have no idea how the control panel actually *works*?" Kay asked drily, following the commandos into the airlock.

"Oh, we know how it *works*," Charlie said cheerfully. "But why bother linking the computer to an interface that can read it and breaking the security firewalls, et cetera, when all we need is to feed power to the motors?"

She... had a point, Kay had to acknowledge, and gave the commando a nod as he stepped into the elevator.

"Two down, five to go," Chaudhary muttered. "No real trouble so far."

Kay hit the button and the door started to close behind them.

"And *why* did we decide to taunt Murphy this evening?" he asked.

"Because it's only a question of *when* are we fucked, not *are* we fucked," Chaudhary replied. "We'll get your damn computers, boss, but this is already going *far* more smoothly than I dared hope."

"What are you expecting, elite warrior Mages backed by tanks?" Kay said. "Because I never really expected this place to be *defended*. It's the security that comes in after us when an alarm gets sounded that I'm worried about."

"I'm more worried about the damn radiation," his subordinate noted. "From what O'Shea said, we have no idea *what* is so damn radioactive down there."

"Locals say it's a meltdown." Kay shrugged. "While I can't see anyone having been so foolish as to put a fission plant *capable* of melting down on a starship, I suppose I *can* see a starship-scale fission plant managing to continue to melt down for several hundred years."

The other man grunted, checking the count on his magazine, and then swapping it for a full one.

"Check your bullets," Chaudhary ordered the team. "Reload now, not when you're under fire."

Kay followed suit, swapping a two-thirds-full magazine for a full one and tucking the old mag into his harness. While the gear they wore was primarily radiation gear, it was *Marine Corps* radiation gear.

Which meant that while it was rated for walking into the beating heart of an operating fission plant, it was designed to do so while carrying guns and ammo. There were pouches and bandoliers for magazines and grenades.

Kay had less of both than any of the commandos, but he was still more than well-enough equipped for the task ahead. He hoped.

His momentary distraction meant he lost count of the airlock doors opening through the dome and misjudged their arrival time. The commandos didn't, moving forward as the door started unfolding open again—and a momentary spark in his mind was the only warning they had that they were *not* alone.

A gout of white fire blasted through the narrow opening, hammering into the lead commandos in the half-second it took Kay to fling up his own defenses against hostile magic. Alpha and Bravo never even had time to scream before they were incinerated by the attacking Mage.

Kay caught the incoming fire in his shield spell and flung it back outward, buying the surviving commandos time to rush out the door. This time, they were definitely *not* the only people firing.

Several other weapons, deeper-sounding and slower-firing than the MACCAWs, echoed in the cavern as Kay's people advanced under the shield of his magic. The staccato crash of the caseless assault guns replied, and Kay stepped out into the newest cavern on the tail of his people, his magic shielding them from bullets and hostile magic alike.

The main connection was much the same as the one in dome seven, though shorter, with a road linking the two airlock elevators and an open area divided off into various sections. The people down there had clearly had *some* link to the higher level, as they'd thrown together impromptu barricades and dug up firearms while Kay's commandos had broken through the airlock.

"Take *cover*, sir," Chaudhary snapped—age-old habit overcoming his usual title of *boss* for Kay.

"Not this time," Kay replied absently as he walked forward into the hail of fire. The defenders, he noted, were using carbines of decent quality. High-velocity, heavy-caliber—and hence high-*energy*, but his shield could handle bullets readily enough.

His concern was the reezh in the center of the defender formation, her own magic guarding her people as his guarded the commandos.

"You should not have come here," she told him, her voice carrying the same gravelly tones as *every* reezh speaking English. "I do not know what you seek, but you will not find it here. The way is barred to you and yours."

"I am the sword of humanity, the inquisitor who will breach your lies and find the truth," Kay told her. His magic wove into her shield, layering pieces of air sharpened to blades through her barrier of force, and then *pulled*, shattering her shield for a critical few moments.

The Mage saved herself. She didn't save the hastily assembled militia of archivists and historians armed with weapons they barely knew how to use. His spell tore through the room and left the Mage as the last defender standing.

Ignoring his companions now, Kay advanced on her.

"First among the lies, I suppose, was that there were no more reezh Mages on Chimera," he murmured. She was strong but poorly trained, he judged as he overwhelmed her next attempt to attack him.

"I am the Warden of the Astral, trained to guard our world from the night," she snarled. "And you, it seems, are the very night I was warned of."

She hurled power at him, shoving him back a step.

"We have come a long damn way," Kay told her. "And if your people had only told me the truth, none of this would have needed to happen. So, tell me now, *Warden of the Astral*, where is the Nine? Where does the knife lurk that your people have prepared for the back of humanity?

"Where do the lies end and the truth begin?"

She snarled at him, summoning more power as she battered him with flames from several directions—and he lashed out with a precise strike. The reezh mage, the Warden, attacked with wide gouts of flame, half-directed billows that flared in half a dozen directions as she tried to hit one target.

He unleashed a thin line, barely the width of his finger, that superheated and hardened air into a lance that struck across the air between them. The Warden's shield failed, and his power pierced her flesh, driving her back and shattering her oddly jointed leg.

She didn't even fall, summoning power around herself to stay upright as she faced him.

"This place was never for your kind," she spat. "Your delusions buy you no rights. I have triggered the alarms. More are coming."

"Unless you have dozens of Wardens where I was told you had none, it will not matter," Kay told her, yanking her toward him and off her own supporting magic. He suspended her in the air in front of him, studying her and looking for signs of weakness.

"I know what it means to be tasked to guard secrets that cannot be forgotten but cannot be known to all," he murmured. "But I need the secrets you guard to save my people. It didn't have to come to this."

She found his weakness before he found hers. He'd missed the blade she'd carried, and her power was enough to push through his for a few seconds.

Long enough to strike.

Gunfire crashed in the underground vault and fire seared across Kay's side as the blade scored his armor—but did not reach skin, Chaudhary's bullets flinging the reezh woman aside before she could truly plant her blow.

There was a long silence as Kay looked down at the dead Warden of the Astral—a woman, he suspected, who shared much the same mission as the Keepers of Secrets and Oaths he'd once served.

"Thank you, Lead," Kay said quietly. "I was foolish."

"Your suit is damaged," Chaudhary said, wise enough not to allow judgment into his voice. "You should patch it."

"Get Charlie and Delta on the next door," Kay ordered. "I'll patch my suit as they work."

"She wasn't lying about triggering broader alarms. I suspect we will see security from the people these bunkers belong to first, but they will recognize their limits soon enough."

Chaudhary snorted.

"And what does that mean, boss?"

"It means Assault Troopers from Wang's fleet," Kay said flatly. "It means exosuits and guns that will make the armor in these radsuits irrelevant.

"So, let's get moving before the men in armor show up."

CHAPTER 24

BY THE TIME the Nemesis team had reached dome two, it was clear that only the top two layers had seen regular occupation and real use. Once they were through seven and six, they didn't see another living being as they overrode each elevator in turn, leaving the moving airlocks wrecked and disabled behind them.

Domes three and two both held radioactive waste, compressed cubes of the byproducts of fission-power production that even modern technology couldn't salvage. While, at first glance, the quantity of waste seemed relatively low, Kay knew roughly how much waste a modern fission plant left behind.

"Either they were running some seriously wonky fission reactors, or they were running a *lot* of them," Kay told Chaudhary as Charlie and Delta worked on the last elevator airlock.

The commando grunted, looking over at the stacked cubes.

"Each of those cubes is, what, a decade of running a power plant?" he finally guessed.

"They're about a meter on a side, so yeah." Kay studied the waste— from a safe distance. His suit's built-in Geiger counter was quite clear that *this* containment dome had notable levels of radiation. He assumed most of it was from the waste blocks rather than the ongoing meltdown... but not all.

"There are a few places that use them," Kay continued. "They run about a cubic meter of waste per gigawatt-decade, so this is..."

"A hundred plants run for a century, given what we saw in the last dome," Chaudhary murmured. "You want to know what that means, ask your girlfriend. I can do the math, but I don't get it."

Kay blinked.

"I..."

"What, you thought *anyone* on the ship had missed you and the Chief?" the commando asked. "She tears *strips* off people without ever looking at them, but she sure as hell looks at *you*." He snorted. "Don't worry. Probably makes us trust you more. Both of you need the humanizing."

Kay snorted softly.

"Hadn't thought of it that way," he admitted. "Not like we were actually trying to keep it secret. I just..." He chuckled. "I may have assumed that the criminal conspiracy to guide the galaxy in the right direction didn't suffer from *gossip*."

His subordinate echoed his chuckle.

"Boss, Nemesis crew's still human. Hell, still soldiers, mostly. We might serve all humanity now, not the Mage-Queen, but we're still human. It helps to know that you and the Chief are human."

Before Kay could respond to *that* particular comment, Charlie turned to give them a thumbs-up, the mighty airlock doors unfolding as had the six sets before them.

"Last one," Kay said. "Time to see what's hiding at the bottom of the pit."

"I'm watching my Geiger counters and my guess is *hell*." Chaudhary snorted. "Isn't the first hell I've walked into for humanity, so let's get moving."

The first six airlock elevators each had identical traversal distances. They'd descended through the fifteen meters of the dome itself and then twenty meters to a flat area above the next dome.

Including their own height, each elevator had moved forty meters.

The last moved that forty and kept going. This time, Kay judged, they were descending to the floor of the original dome—which was, according to the scans O'Shea had taken, actually inside a pit. The Last Ship was two hundred meters wide and equally tall, but the pit meant that the main dome was a "mere" quarter-kilometer tall.

His estimate put the descent of the final elevator at around three hundred meters when it finally came to a halt. The moment the doors slid open, his helmet's Geiger counter immediately spiked, and he whistled softly.

"What the actual *fuck* did they do to that power plant?" Charlie asked, putting the thoughts of the entire surviving commando team into words. "It's been melting down for a hundred and fifty years and we're still getting that many rads here?"

"The good news is that we don't need to check on the plant itself," Kay told his people. "From what the Dyad Curator told me, the only reason they ever come down here is to access the very computer system we're looking for.

"That should make it easier to find, at least."

None of the commandos responded to his reassurance as they moved out of the elevator. This dome, Kay swiftly realized, had never been filled with dirt. His suit's sensors were telling him the air wasn't particularly *safe*, but there was air.

His assessment of the depth of the pit looked about right, too. He wasn't sure of the original source—potentially the ship had blasted a midsized crater as it landed, or possibly the reezh had excavated around it to lower it into the ground before they'd put the dome over it.

Possibly it had even settled before its reactor had gone into meltdown. Without knowing the full sequence of events that had put the Last Ship in its current state, he could only guess.

The ship itself was impressive, filling the vast majority of the concrete cavern. The disk towered as high as it was wide, and there was no visible damage to the exterior. Even the effects of age and time had been muted by being covered by the containment dome, Kay judged.

Looking directly at the ship, he could tell that it wasn't truly a warship. There were visible weapons on its exterior, but the ones he could identify resembled the RMMC's railgun turrets—intended to cover a landing, not fight other starships.

It probably had lasers and missiles as well, but it was obviously an armed transport—the *tribute ship*, the museum had named it.

"I think I see the path," Chaudhary told him, gesturing toward a line of lights that woke up as they approached. "I'd call those solar lights except..."

"Drawing power from the radiation," Kay guessed. "Clever use in a space like this. Marks the path, provides light."

There was more light in the space than he would have expected, he realized. His suit had powerful light-gathering optics, but even they shouldn't have let him get a decent look at the ship. Larger-scale versions of the radiation-powered lights were mounted on the exterior of the dome, bringing the whole place into an ominous dim twilight.

"We know where we're going, I suppose," Kay said grimly.

"And we know the most likely place pursuit is coming from," Chaudhary replied. "Charlie, Delta. Pass Echo and Fox your demolitions and your extra ammo. We need you two for technical.

"Echo and Fox, I want you to wire up the elevator shaft," the commando leader continued. "If you think you can demo it such that nobody can come down ever again, do it. Otherwise, set it to blow when the first wave arrives.

"Once you're done, follow the glowing path and catch up. You'll see when the beacons go up. At that point, you are out of time. Tomas is only going to take a couple of minutes to prep her spell, and *she's* not going to know if you're not in the pickup zone.

"Get me?"

Kay left organizing the commandos and their gear to his subordinate. Wrapping magic around himself as an additional shield against radiation—he didn't *need* it with the suits they'd brought, not yet, but it made him feel better—he started along the single pathway marked out by the lights.

At best, the commandos' efforts would seal off one entrance to the central dome. Kay would eat *Rose*'s port thruster if the elevator airlock was the only way in there.

By the time he'd crossed half of the distance to the ship, Chaudhary had caught up with him.

"No one should go anywhere alone down here, boss," the commando told him. "It *might* be the uncountable tons of dirt and concrete above us, or the shitty lighting, or the creepy alien ship built for mass kidnapping... I'm not sure, but *something* tells me this place is bad news."

Kay shook his head, but he held up while Chaudhary moved up beside him. The commando officer held his MACCAW at the ready.

"Charlie and Delta will only be a minute," Chaudhary continued. "I don't like leaving Echo and Fox behind, but... I didn't like leaving Alpha and Bravo behind, either."

There hadn't been enough left of Alpha or Bravo to bring *with* them, Kay knew. And while he wasn't going to point it out, all of the commandos—including Chaudhary—had suicide implants in the base of their skulls to make sure there wasn't enough left to identify them if they fell into Protectorate hands.

Chaudhary could detonate his people's charges. *Kay* could detonate Chaudhary's. He wouldn't without reason, but Nemesis didn't have the resources, especially this far out into the dark, to *leave no man behind.*

If he was very lucky, though, they'd made the right assessment of the lit path and it would take them where he needed to go. He didn't think there was anything *else* down there that the locals would be regularly accessing, anyway!

The lights led up to a ramp that had clearly rusted into place. It was probably, Kay judged, meant to automatically retract and extend, allowing access to what he'd *guess* was the highest non-rotating deck of the ship.

He also judged, from the dirt, tracks, wear and outright rust, that the ramp hadn't been retracted since before humans had set foot on Garuda. It wasn't the massive open cargo space he'd seen in the artwork above them but more of a secondary personnel entrance.

It was also a clear source of the irradiated air that was making the entire inner dome dangerous. Thanks to biology he didn't pretend to understand, the reezh enjoyed a higher radiation tolerance than humans, but even *they* worked in radsuits down there.

And, given the levels he saw as he stepped into the ship, with serious time limits.

"Our suits are better than the locals have been using, but we cannot spend very long down here," Chaudhary warned, clearly following Kay's thoughts as he entered the old alien transport.

"We're already halfway to the maximum daily exposure for people working in antimatter-manufacturing facilities," the commando continued. "And the levels are rising. We're going to hit monthly or even annual allowances for working in high-rad facilities before we're done."

"We knew that coming in," Kay replied. "Let's find these damn computers."

There were more lights inside the ship, though the wavelengths were all wrong for humans. These, he supposed, were the lights reezh who never knew non-reezh existed used for their own comfort.

Thankfully, while reezh were shorter than humans on average, it wasn't by enough to make the ship uncomfortable to move through. And, well, physics lent itself to basic similarities, no matter how differently the brains of the people designing the ship were wired.

The corridors weren't *quite* the right height and the angles weren't *quite* right angles—the reezh seemed to think in flattened hexagons rather than squares when designing corridors. That might have been a consequence of the extra joints in their arms and legs, but Kay didn't know.

He'd picked up a lot of skills over the years, working in and then leading a galactic conspiracy, but xenosociology hadn't been one of them.

"Thankfully, nobody has bothered to dust in the last century or so," he told Chaudhary drily, kneeling to inspect the dust—irradiated to dangerous levels, his scanners informed him—on the floor as they reached the first intersection. "There are a few places they've been going, but it looks like most of the traffic is going *that* way."

"And so are we?" Charlie asked, the commando tech finally catching up.

"And so are we," Kay confirmed.

If O'Shea hadn't sourced images of what Reezh Ida–era computing technology looked like, Kay would never have guessed he'd found his target. A human central computer core consisted of racks upon racks of black boxes with blinking status lights, a structure that hadn't changed much in four or five hundred years.

The *contents* of those boxes had changed—a single server unit aboard *Rose* possessed roughly the processing power and storage capacity of the entire early twenty-first-century internet, for example—but the basic layout and concept were the same.

The reezh did not even *begin* to share that layout and concept. At first glance, Kay would have thought he was in a munitions depot that had been rotated ninety degrees. A ten-meter-high space was filled, from floor to ceiling, with meter-wide cylinders he would have figured were attack missiles.

On closer examination, he could see that each pillar consisted of meter-wide, meter-high disks stacked on top of each other. The links between them carried data and power, sustaining and accessing complex multi-dimensional holographic storage that stored even more data than the pico-scale components of modern human computers.

"This is it," he said. He eyed the room. Hopefully, it was the only computer core—or at least the right one! From the paths in the dust, it was the one that the reezh had been regularly accessing, at least, which was the only clue he really had to go on.

He judged that it was ten meters high and twenty meters square. He *thought* it was designed to rotate—for a ship that supposedly had run on rotational pseudogravity, very little of what he'd seen had suggested it.

Kay's *guess*—he'd run it by O'Shea later—was that the ship was built on circular corridors and that the rooms off those corridors could rotate around them to align with either rotation or thrust gravity.

It sounded complex as all hell, and he again *guessed*—this was outside his skillset!—that only part of the ship was laid out like that. It had to be wasteful of space, though there might be ways to align the individual compartments to minimize that waste.

"So, we set up the beacons?" Charlie asked. "We haven't heard anything from the locals sin—"

Even *inside* the Last Ship, they heard the detonation as Echo and Fox set off the charges on the elevator.

"Get on those beacons," Kay ordered. "If they were blowing the shaft to block it, they'd have detonated it already. This late in the game, they held until they saw someone coming."

Which *hadn't* been Chaudhary's orders. They'd been supposed to rig a trap.

But Kay had done Chaudhary's job before his current commando leader had, which meant he could put the pieces together between the orders and what he'd heard. Echo and Fox had chosen to hold off and trigger the trap manually—they'd probably planned to head for the ship when the beacons went up, but the landing team had arrived first.

"Echo, Fox, report," Chaudhary snapped on a short-range channel.

"Bunch of armored radsuits dropped a thermite cutting charge on the roof of the elevator car," Echo replied. The commando sounded slightly out of breath. "Not sure if it was people or reezh in them; didn't wait to ask before hitting the button."

"We're on our way," Fox added. "Demo will have collapsed the bottom of the column in on itself, but there's just too much exposed elevator inside the inner dome for a full blockage.

"Give them five minutes and someone is going to put those cutting charges on the side of the shaft, and then they'll have their own lovely doorway into the dome."

"Get here now," Kay ordered. "Charlie, Delta. Up! You have the top four beacons. Lead, you're with me. We have the bottom four."

CHAPTER 25

THE NEMESIS COMMANDOS had *expected* to need to plant beacons on the roof, which meant that Charlie and Delta went up the walls with gecko gloves. If they'd had more time, they had launchable bolts and ropes to climb more safely, but they very clearly did *not* have time.

Kay and Chaudhary had the easy part, laying the four lower beacons at the corner of the room. As they worked, Kay's helmet started to draw in the cube marked by the beacons as he made sure all of the computer columns were covered.

"How are these things even still getting power?" Charlie asked, locking her second beacon into place. "I'm not seeing any cables or anything?"

"According to the Chief, old reezh tech goes for solid connections. So, the power linkages are in the floor and the ceiling, and we're probably going to partially cut them off," Kay told her. "I'm still twitching over the fact that they still have functional thermopiles in the power core drawing electricity out of an ongoing *meltdown*."

It wouldn't have been the primary power-extraction method for the power core. That had almost certainly been something at least resembling the age-old turbine-and-steam arrangement, on some level. But there had been enough thermopiles set up to convert heat to energy to keep the ship's basic systems and computers online, even with the main reactor in full meltdown.

And they were still working after almost two hundred years. There was a *reason* to everything Kay had done, and the level of advancement and capability of the tech the Reezh Ida had possessed two centuries ago only reinforced it.

The Chimerans might want to pretend they weren't a threat, but their refusal to direct him to the real enemy told him everything he really needed to know. The Chimeran reezh were a smokescreen, potentially even allowing an experiment on a captive human population—and they were protecting the true enemy.

"Echo, Fox, where are you?" Chaudhary snapped. "All beacons in place."

"Sixty seconds," Echo replied. "Just setting up a camera on the door."

As the commando spoke, the feed popped into the tactical network. Like the helmets, the camera was set up with impressive optics that made the dim twilight of the dome clear enough to see the enemy coming.

And the timing was horribly perfect. The camera came online, giving all of them a view of the massive concrete pillar the elevator ran through just as explosives ripped a massive hole in it a hundred meters from the ground.

"Activating the beacons," Kay said flatly. "If you're not here when Tomas picks us up, you're *walking* home, Echo and Fox."

The reality, everybody knew, was that Kay would detonate the suicide charges of anyone not in the bucket when Tomas teleported them up. He didn't even need to *tell* them that.

They couldn't leave prisoners behind to be handed over to the Protectorate when they finally arrived.

"We'll be there," Echo promised.

The translucent cube his helmet was showing flickered as the beacons came online. Much more powerful than the communicator in his suit helmet, those beacons would penetrate the multiple concrete domes and their dirt fill, reaching all of the way to orbit where Tomas awaited.

They *also*, as a minor side effect, could be used as a carrier channel for communication with *Rose*.

"Koskinen, report," Kay said flatly. "Tomas, you better be running your numbers."

"She's nose-down in a silence bubble," the tactical officer confirmed. "The locals were getting suspicious, but I don't think they'd definitely decided the raid was us until now."

"Something changed, did it?" Kay asked.

"We had a cruiser drifting more toward us than was really necessary, but no one had *said* anything," Koskinen said. "They just went to full active on sensors and locked us up. My discretion, sir?"

"I'm not there until Tomas finishes her spell," Kay replied. "Make sure I still have a ship to come home to, Commander. We have a mission to complete and this is just the latest stop.

"Whatever it takes."

"Whatever it takes," Koskinen agreed.

He sounded... disturbingly more enthused with the prospect than Kay preferred.

Kay left the channel to *Rose* open in the back of his network, his own microphone muted, as he turned his attention to the immediate situation. Without the elevator cabs that his people had left useless behind them, the locals had both been limited in what they could move into the radiation dome and also, in some ways, *less* limited.

As was made clear when the first helicopter gunship ever so carefully edged its way out of the hole the demo experts had blown. Autocannon tracked across the open space around the Last Ship, scanning for threats as the aircraft delicately lowered itself to the level where it could deploy rappelling ropes.

More helicopters followed. They were small aircraft, smaller than the gunship—and the gunship was an urban-security model that Kay recognized, built by the Republic to deal with riots inside skyscraper-filled downtowns.

It was lightly armed as combat aircraft went, but it was also small enough to fit in the elevator shafts. How they'd got it down to the layer above the main dome, he *had* no idea, but there it was.

Only four troopers in armored radsuits dropped from it, their initial sweep looking for the commandos who, thankfully, were inside the ship.

"I've got six helicopters inside the dome," Chaudhary reported. "Two are gunships; four are police transports. A dozen sets of boots on the ground and more coming in.

"We need to move."

"I got that," Kay admitted. "Is everyone in?"

"Yes, sir," Echo confirmed. He glanced up to see the two remaining commandos *skid* around the entrance to enter the beacon-marked zone.

"In a minute or two, they're going to have a full platoon on the ground, and our only saving grace is that I *think* we're mostly looking at Army troops from before Wang arrived," Kay told his people. "Anyone who comes down that corridor *dies*. Am I clear?"

"Crystal, sir."

The four commandos picked their positions carefully, making sure they both had clear lines of fire to where attackers needed to emerge *and* were inside the block of space Tomas would teleport into space.

For his own part, Kay was starting on a triple-check of the beacons when a gentle ping from Koskinen told him that *something* was happening in orbit.

"Where is your commanding officer?" Emerson Wang's voice echoed in Kay's head. A couple of commands put the video feed from *Rose*'s bridge on his helmet, next to the feed from the exterior camera.

"I'm afraid Mage-Captain Riordan isn't available at the moment," Koskinen said cheerfully. "But if your cruiser doesn't back off, Admiral, things are still going to get ugly."

"Treacherous Martian *fucks*," Wang snarled. "Your people are murdering innocents on the surface as we speak, and you want to talk about *getting* ugly? Stand down your thugs or we will blow your cruiser into the next millennium."

"No. You won't."

Kay knew the tone Koskinen was using. He knew it because the tactical officer was mirroring *him*, the calmly flat tone he used when he *knew* he was going to say something the other person wasn't expecting.

Usually because *most* people believed there were limits that couldn't be crossed. Kay had decided, long before, that humanity's survival was more important than any limits anyone could try to put on him.

"You are outgunned, outclassed and trapped," Wang told Koskinen. "You will order your people on the surface to stand down and *you* will prepare to be boarded."

"No. I won't." Koskinen's tone was unchanged. "*You* will pull your people back and order your cruisers to stand the hell off. You will turn your targeting arrays away from my ship and you will open the range."

"Or what?"

"This ship has an amplifier, Admiral Wang, and any of your ships that are still targeting *Rose* in thirty seconds *will* be destroyed," Koskinen said calmly. "More important to you, I suspect, is that I have dialed in the reezh secondary capital and both cities of the Duchy of the Blue River as targets for our Talon Ten ground-attack munitions."

Kay's subordinate spoke in the exact same level tones that Kay would use, the kind that made people take a second to realize you'd just promised mass murder... and made it so much harder to *disbelieve* that you'd actually do it.

"I only have five missile tubes reallocated for ground munitions," Koskinen continued, "so I will *only* destroy those three cities in the first salvo. If you continue to threaten my ship, I will proceed to additional targets in decreasing order of population.

"Of course, if you *fire* on *Rose* herself, those first munitions will launch automatically. How many people are you prepared to see die today, Admiral Wang? Because to me and my superiors, our mission is more important than your entire planet."

"You cannot be..."

"Why would I lie? You have fifteen seconds to break off your targeting, Admiral Wang, or we start destroying ships and cities.

"*Choose swiftly.*"

"Hang on," Tomas told them five minutes later, her voice hoarse in a way that made it very clear that she'd been listening to Koskinen's threats when he'd convinced Wang to back off. "This should work, but I don't promise it's going to be *pleasant*."

The warnings from on high had apparently been enough to keep the locals from trying to storm the Last Ship, as they'd enjoyed several minutes of peace—though Kay would bet a planet or three that the troops outside were trying to work out if they could get in and take *him*, specifically, prisoner before Koskinen did anything rash.

They didn't realize that Koskinen would sacrifice Kay, too, in pursuit of the mission. That was what Kay would *want* him to do—though completing the mission without the computer cores they'd set to teleport might be difficult.

"Do it," he ordered Tomas.

The world promptly tore around him. He could *see* the air slip as untold millions of molecules were suddenly told they were wrong about where they thought they were. They *thought* they were down on the surface, inside the Last Ship.

They were *actually* in orbit, inside *Rose*'s missile magazine delta.

Since those molecules included the ones making up Kay himself, the momentary confusion of quantum reality *hurt*. He'd made long-distance solo teleports, but he'd never been moved by an amplified Mage that wasn't *part* of what was being teleported.

He closed his eyes against the sudden pain and nausea—and when he opened them, he was looking at a very different set of walls—and a full dozen radsuited people standing carefully outside the zone.

One of them was next to him in moments, her hand tucking under his shoulder in a way that prevented anyone else from realizing he'd almost fallen.

"Chief," he greeted O'Shea, surprised at both her consideration and his own spike of relief and pleasure to see her.

"Your suit is irradiated enough to be an active hazard all on its own," she told him in clipped tones. "All of you need immediate decontamination."

"You've got the computers?" he asked.

"Of course." O'Shea gestured behind her, where her people were moving forward with what looked like oversized baseball base mats full of parts and wires. "First try might not work, like I said, but we've got options.

"We'll be fine."

"Thank you." He tapped her hand, both a sign that he no longer needed her support and a half-concealed gesture of affection.

She released him, turning to bark orders to her people as he focused his attention on the bridge.

"Tomas, is Császár there?" he growled. Császár, unlike Kay or Tomas, was a Navy Mage. While he trusted Tomas to do a complex trick like pulling a building-sized chunk of space up from the surface, he knew *Császár* was trained to jump a starship out of orbit.

And he suspected yanking the computers up had taken as much out of Tomas as a full jump would have.

"Yeah. You?"

"All aboard. Have Császár get us the fuck out of here."

He wasn't going to stick around to see how long it took Wang to realize no one was left on the surface!

CHAPTER 26

"CAPTAIN ON DECK!"

"At ease, everyone," Roslyn ordered.

Chief Kovalyow, who'd made the announcement of her arrival, followed Roslyn to the conference table and took her seat at the Mage-Captain's right hand.

"Thank you, everyone," Roslyn told her officers. Baars emerged from the steward's hatch with a carafe of coffee, refilling everyone else's drink as she delivered Roslyn's. "I apologize for my own delay; we received a transmission from Mars that I wanted to check on before arriving."

It hadn't been important, thankfully, but like orders from an Admiral, transmissions from the Mountain carried a high priority regardless of their *official* headers.

Glancing around the room, Roslyn concealed a smile as she realized that this was the first time Tracker-Commander Uesugi had joined the rest of her senior officers for a command meeting. While their abilities meant that they were almost as junior for their rank as Roslyn had been when *she'd* been promoted to Commander, Uesugi was still one of the four most senior officers aboard the cruiser.

Mage-Commander Tod and Commander Beck, the Navigator and XO, were the only other Commanders on the ship. Major Yang, the senior Marine, was considered equal to the various Lieutenant Commanders—like Chief Engineer Waldfogel and Tactical Officer Leavitt in this meeting.

The two Lieutenants filling out the room—Lieutenant Todorov, running admin and logistics, and Surgeon-Lieutenant McConnell—brought the number of other officers in the room to eight. Kovalyow, as Chief of the Ship, was included—as was Master Sergeant Femie Krastev, Yang's top Marine NCO.

Including Roslyn, there were eleven officers and noncommissioned officers of the Navy and Marines of the Mage-Queen of Mars in the room. She only knew Yang and Kovalyow as well as she'd like, but none of them had disappointed her yet.

"We have spent three days here in the DIO-Nine-Seven-Five System," she reminded them all, using the catalog number to give them *any* kind of context for the system they'd found the ruined fleet base in.

"Part of the reason we've done this is because we know, thanks to Tracker-Commander Uesugi, that *Rose* spent *seven* days here," Roslyn told them, nodding to the Tracker. "I wanted to know what Kent Riley found."

"Plus, frankly, we needed to understand some degree of what happened here and what happened *around* here," she concluded. "Commander Beck, if you'd care to brief everyone on what we have learned."

Her XO nodded wearily and rose to his feet. He picked up a tablet from the table and activated the room's holographic projectors.

"Commander Leavitt and I have gone over all of the data his people have been able to gather and analyze, and we have a... rough concept of what happened and when," Beck told everyone.

Seemingly unconsciously, his hand crept up to touch the scar where Roslyn had shot him with a SmartDart. "We know this system was Nemesis's destination," he continued after a moment. "We needed to learn as much as we could, and unlike *Rose*, we have the full designed crew, skills and knowledge to use this ship's sensors and systems to their maximum capability."

He smirked.

"I suspect we have learned more in three days than they learned in seven. I warn you, though, very little of this is pleasant. Distance and time buy us some shield, but I strongly recommend that no one try to fully... internalize what we are about to discuss.

"It is both unnecessary and unwise."

Not everyone in the room quite followed that, Roslyn knew. If nothing else, the details of Chief Vasiliauskas's situation *had* been purged, and the rumor mill had proven surprisingly willing to forget what the Captain needed them to forget.

That was a sign, to her and Kovalyow at least, that the crew fundamentally agreed with her course of action.

The *problem* was that Vasiliauskas wasn't alone in psychiatric observation now. Two specialists, sensor analysts who'd worked on the same information at different stages, and one of the freshly promoted Ensigns were now all on medical leave.

For all that the Secession War loomed large in people's memories and the RMN was a dedicated, competent military force, there was a level of violence and destruction that even Roslyn's crew found hard to swallow without breaking.

"The exact timelines of the fate of the DIO System are unclear," Beck warned. "It very much looks like all of the telescope data and similar from the Protectorate has been acquired and cleaned by Nemesis and the Keepers in the past.

"But based on the star system *itself*, a minimum of two hundred and fifty years ago, this was a flourishing system with a major fleet base positioned to cover the outer frontier of a large interstellar polity.

"In or around the twenty-two-twenties, roughly in the middle of the Eugenicist Wars for us, a series of space battles were fought over the system, ending in the catastrophic bombardment of the planet and orbital shipyards approximately two hundred and forty years ago.

"I cannot even begin to estimate the loss of life," Beck said calmly. "But the planet was hit with a clearly intentional ecosphere-killing antimatter strike. Some of the orbital stations remained intact after that and were abandoned and scuttled at a later date—we estimate within a year of the destruction of the planet."

"This system is not without relevance to us," Roslyn warned. "This base served as the anchor for a series of outposts that reached out beyond their territory, culminating from our perspective in the refueling outpost in the Andala System.

"We *know*," she said quietly, "that the Andala System served as a support base for what we believe was a *research team* on Mars, working with Project Olympus."

She smiled thinly, looking over at Mage-Commander Tod.

"We know," she repeated, "that it was Reejit engineers and Mages that provided the schematics and rune matrices for the Olympus Mons Amplifier. It was not intended to—and should *not*—have worked for humans beyond its use as a detection tool."

Everyone in this room was cleared for that. They weren't necessarily cleared for what that *meant* in consequences—the fact that only the Rune Wrights, among all human Mages, could see the true magic of the amplifier well enough to control the planetary-scale amplifier on Mars.

"The question the Keepers and Nemesis have always asked, the question that drove them into their... *choices*," Roslyn said, "was *when are they coming back?*"

"We now can answer that question," Beck said grimly. "The destruction of this system could, barely, be justified under even some concepts of limited war. It was primarily a military base, one capable of repairing or even constructing vessels on par with our own dreadnoughts.

"But here in DIO-Nine-Seven-Five we see... the edge of the true nightmare." He entered commands on his tablet and the display zoomed out, reducing the DIO-975 System to a single star on the map.

It flashed red.

"DIO-Nine-Seven-Five was destroyed, as I said, in the late twenty-two-twenties," Beck noted. "The timelines of the systems around it are harder to judge, but I would guess it was not the first system to share that fate."

More stars flashed red.

"Every red-highlighted star system contains a planet that sits in the liquid-water zone with a high likelihood of habitability," the XO noted. "None of the planets in the red systems appear to have breathable atmospheres.

"In multiple cases, while it is difficult to be certain at this range, the planets appear to have been physically destroyed to a material level, though I imagine shared centers of gravity and such will result in re-formation of even disrupted planetary crusts over enough time."

Beck's words were calm, clinical. Roslyn had seen most of the data herself and *knew* just what he was saying. She also knew that he was doing everything he could to soften the reality of what they were looking at.

"We cannot be certain how many of these systems actually possessed inhabited worlds," he noted. "We *have* detected remnant antimatter from disruption-scale strikes in multiple star systems."

A number—twenty-two, Roslyn knew from the data she'd seen—of the red star systems flashed a brighter red, closer to the tone of fresh blood.

"Somewhere between twenty-three—including DIO-Nine-Seven-Five—and *eighty-six* inhabited planets were annihilated between three hundred and two hundred years ago," Beck said softly.

"Commander Leavitt's and my analysis of the... astrography of the destruction, well..." A highlight washed over the three-dimensional display, making the sphere of the known swathe of dead worlds clear.

If the shape was consistent throughout the entire Reejit polity, that swathe of destruction was about a third of the alien race's territory—and about the central quarter of the sphere was still beyond their ability to extract useful data.

"I would guess that we are looking at the equivalent of our MidWorlds and Fringe," Beck said quietly. "As part of an overall larger interstellar state, roughly twice the size of the modern Protectorate, but using Mid and Fringe world populations as a basis..."

He swallowed.

"Over the course of about a hundred years, we are estimating a minimum of eighty billion dead," Leavitt concluded into Beck's silence.

The sick quiet that covered the entire room spoke volumes as to why three of the key people who'd put together this analysis were in sickbay.

"What's *left*?" Yang finally asked, the Marine pushing to the heart of the matter.

"Firstly, the highlight I drew around our identified problem stars tells me that we're only looking at about a third of the Reejit territory," Beck observed. "This may have been a relatively localized conflict that left most of the rest of their state intact—the sheer level of devastation certainly implies that this was a region they felt they could lose.

"But we can only really assess enough details to detect habitable planets within a limited distance." Beck shrugged. "Inside that distance, we do have four points of interest."

Three stars lit up blue.

"These three star systems contain planets that appear to be habitable," he observed. "All appeared to be on the warm and wet side, on the inner edge of the habitable zone, with high water content in their spectrographs.

"They'd be habitable to humans, but we'd probably find them unpleasant without careful site selection on the surface. I would *guess* that the people who settled this region of space preferred a drier and colder climate than we would, meaning those worlds were effectively uninhabitable for them."

"So, they colonized every world that was of use to them and then wiped them all out?" Tod asked, sounding nauseous.

"Basically," Beck agreed. One last system lit up in green. "We have located *one* planet in what we assume was this base's area of responsibility that is still intact."

Every eye in the room focused on the floating green orb.

"Scans suggest the third planet is habitable, though cold and dry. There's a degree of separation between them and the other systems that may have been key to their survival—they were a newer colony, one that I would guess tried to remain neutral in whatever conflict led to... this."

Beck's gesture took in the markers of dozens of definitely and merely *potentially* destroyed planets.

"Wait, you mean it's not just habitable but *inhabited*?" Waldfogel asked. Roslyn suspected the engineer was focusing on anything except the historical atrocity blazoned across the table.

"Yes," Beck confirmed. "It's forty-two light-years away, at roughly the same distance from Protectorate space as DIO-Nine-Seven-Five.

"Forty-two years ago, we had clear signs of high-energy radio transmission and similar evidence of high-tech habitation. Leavitt?"

"I *did* send some information to your department for review," the Tactical Officer gently told the Chief Engineer, but he then shrugged. "There's not a lot that we can really pick out other than basic wavelengths at this distance. Actually *interpreting* the signals is impossible from more than a dozen light-years or so.

"But as the XO says, forty-two years ago, the system in question was home to a high-energy civilization equivalent to a system on the vague line between MidWorld and the Fringe."

That was the problem with informal classifications that were half-economic and half-geographic. There was a MidWorld, Panterra, that by geography and age should have been a Core World. There were Fringe Worlds that, by wealth and industrial power, should have been MidWorlds—but their location and relative youth left them classed as Fringe Systems.

Time sorted out the categories, Roslyn knew, but it left the zone between MidWorld and Fringe very vague, with a number of systems classed as one or the other based as much on their *neighbors* as anything about themselves.

"While the presence of a technic civilization in the DRQ-Four-Six-One System is of definite long-term interest to the Protectorate, it is not necessarily relevant to our immediate mission," Roslyn reminded her people, nodded to Beck to sit back down.

"Tracker-Commander Uesugi has confirmed that, twelve days ago, *Rose* left this system on a course to DRQ-Four-Six-One," she said calmly. "Which makes that system of the utmost interest to us.

"It provides us with the opportunity to catch up further to our foe. Rather than tracking *Rose* on a jump-by-jump basis, we will head *directly* to DRQ-Four-Six-One."

No one argued. Everyone was staring at the color-coded star systems floating above the table, a bland and simple iconography to mark mass murder on a scale the Protectorate had never truly believed could happen.

"I guess there is one question we have to ask."

Roslyn looked over at Lieutenant Todorov. By any metric, the admin officer was the most junior officer in the room—and he was smart enough to know that, regardless of what any table of organization said, he *wasn't* really senior to the Chief of the Ship and the Gunny—but he wore the widest variety of hats.

Part of that was the expectation that the admin officer acted more as a deputy to the XO, who held *true* final responsibility for all of those hats—and that all of the pieces the Logistics Officer was responsible for interfaced with other departments, giving him a lot of seniors to lean on in managing his flock of Ensigns.

"And what question is that, Lieutenant?" she asked.

"What did Nemesis think they were going to find here... and what are they looking for in DRQ?"

Roslyn gave him a grateful nod. One of the hats Todorov wore—more shared with the XO than most—was *intelligence*. By *her* choice, she'd have had a more-senior officer in his role. But they'd had limited options in Tau Ceti regarding who could be pulled aboard in the two weeks they'd had.

"I'm not sure," she admitted. "But I think the answer is in the very name of Kent Riley's organization: *Nemesis*. They were looking for an enemy, people.

"An enemy they believe has been lurking in the shadows, preparing a campaign to *harvest* humanity's Mages for a very long time." She gestured to the display.

"Commander Beck said he could answer the question of *when were the Reejit coming back*," she reminded them. "Nemesis has spent decades—longer, maybe, since we don't know when that particular group began operating independently of the Keepers—trying to prepare humanity for that war.

"The Secession was created to upgrade our forces so that we could fight the Reejit." She snorted. "Hardly the most efficient method, I suspect, though I can see the outline of their logic. But here, today, we look at the reality of the enemy they feared."

Dead worlds. Burned ships. Memories and atrocities and death. She didn't say the words, but she knew her people were reading the icons as she spoke.

"They were never coming back to our stars," Roslyn whispered. "While I doubt we are looking at the complete death of their species, we *are* looking at the devastation of their interstellar empire.

"The Reejit have not been a threat to humanity for two hundred years."

"So... what is Nemesis looking for *now*, then?" Todorov asked.

Roslyn grimaced.

"An excuse," Kovalyow said flatly, the Senior Chief's voice deathly cold. "Their *reason* is a lie, but they are fanatics who committed or enabled horrific atrocities. They need to find an *end* to justify their *means*—or they must face that they became monsters for *nothing*."

CHAPTER 27

"JUMP COMPLETE."

Mage-Ensign Leela Jain was not, at least, the young woman who'd been jumped past her entire last year of training to serve aboard *Thorn*.

She was only about eighteen months *older* than Mage-Ensign Sigourney, though, and Roslyn couldn't help feeling that the twenty-one-year-old junior officer shouldn't have looked *quite* so young to her eyes.

It wasn't really the age difference, Roslyn knew. She was only seven years older than the Ensign. Even including Uesugi, Roslyn's presence *lowered* the average age of officers Commander and up aboard *Thorn*.

But then, Roslyn had been on her first *cadet* cruise when the war had broken out and she'd found herself an Acting Ensign. She'd made up her formal training in correspondence courses since, but she'd started her active-duty career far earlier than she should have.

She had a full *decade* of experience—much of it *combat* experience, even if she'd served on an Admiral's staff in parts of said combat—on her youngest officers.

Sometimes, it felt like a century.

"Go rest, Leela," Roslyn ordered. "I have the con."

Not that the junior Jump Mage had ever *truly* had the con. She'd had the *simulacrum*, which was close enough most of the time, but there was a reason that at least one of the three older Jump Mages was present whenever one of their four Ensigns jumped.

"Leavitt, report," Roslyn said, activating the controls to slide her chair over by the simulacrum. She was rested enough that she could theoretically take the cruiser into the DRQ-461 System immediately, though caution and doctrine alike suggested that she give it the hour-ish wait the plan called for.

"Well, a light-year away gets us the geography and some general information that we're working on. Unless..."

Roslyn snorted at the Tactical Officer's half-hinted question.

"At this point, Commander, you have full access to the Star Mirror," she told him. "Do *tell* us Mages that you're using it—like the gravity runes, it requires recharging—but I am not going to blind us to keep a secret I've already given away!"

"Understood, sir. Bringing up cluster E-R-One-Five-Three-D and aligning on the DRQ-Four-Six-One System."

The Star Mirror gave the Martian warship eyes the renegade they were chasing would never have had. She supposed that Nemesis *had*, at one point, had access to a Rune Wright—but if Samuel Finley had created a Star Mirror or equivalent for Nemesis, it would likely have failed by now.

Having babied the runic artefact this far, Roslyn had an unpleasant opinion of the device's longevity in actual use.

"Um, sir... I think you need to see this," Leavitt said, cutting into her reflection on her secret weapon's weaknesses.

She turned to the junior officer and raised an eyebrow.

"That's your job to decide, yes," she said drily. "What am I looking at?"

An overlay screen turned nearly transparent, allowing Leavitt to put the feed from the ER153D Cluster up, clearly visible to everyone.

"We have a Republic carrier battle group in the target system, sir," Leavitt told her. "We're checking IDs, but..."

"It's *Chimera*," Roslyn said instantly. "We knew she was out here somewhere, making the Legion nervous."

The rogue Republic fleet anchored on *Chimera* had fled during the war, well before the collapse of the Republic. The latter had seen the ships that claimed the name First Legion flee into the outer regions and invade half a dozen off-record colonies.

RMN Intelligence figured that *Chimera* and her fellow deserters had found a similar off-record colony. They *knew* that two cruisers from that group had collided with a Legion scout group in a system that was, now Roslyn checked, on basically a straight line between Mackenzie and DRQ-461.

"We don't have a solid ID on her," Leavitt repeated. "Because she's got full combat ECM up and multiple gunship squadrons on active patrol through the system.

"*Chimera* and a battleship are in orbit of the planet we assessed as inhabited," he continued. "But I'm picking up at least four cruisers positioned through the star system, each accompanied by gunship forces, with additional gunships all over the place.

"I'd say someone just poked the hornet's nest, sir, and the RIN battle group is *pissed.*"

"Rotate the Mirror as best as you can and get me an idea of what's going on, Lieutenant Commander," Roslyn ordered. "You've seen six ships, but we know *Chimera* fled Legatus with *fourteen.*

"I'm not betting that they've still got them all, but I'm also not going to assume they only have six, either."

"And *Rose*, sir?" Leavitt asked.

"I am unfortunately quite certain that our Nemesis friends are why the Republic is up in arms," Roslyn told him. "But if she's still in the system, I need to know. I want to know *everything* we can find out before we make the jump, Commander."

Not least, she needed an idea of where to arrive where she'd get a chance to *talk* before the locals assumed she was *Rose* and started shooting.

Assuming, of course, that *not* being the Nemesis ship was going to make her any *more* welcome.

Roslyn had only looked at the information on the Reejit in passing as part of her review of the Nemesis File. Her focus had been on the conspirators and traitors themselves, rather than on the long-missing aliens that drew the focus of madmen and murderers.

Still, she'd seen enough of the visuals in the File and again in the DIO-975 System to recognize the general shapes and patterns—spheres and hexagons where humans would use cylinders, rings and squares.

The space stations above their target world were a mix of both, but thanks to the Star Mirror, they had to do very little guessing.

"We're still having difficulty breaking down a lot of the civilian communication," Beck told her from the Combat Information Center, his battle station. "It's definitely our tech, but it's had a few decades of divergent evolution with some *interesting* parameters applied.

"That said, well..."

The repeater screen showing her link to CIC split, with a second image appearing next to Beck. The framing was shockingly normal, very clearly a political spokesperson giving an update of some kind, but the person *behind* the lectern was something else.

A round, armored frill protected the neck from above and would deflect blows heading toward the large insect-like eyes at the top of the skull. Horns and a protruding bony ridge protected a second, smaller set of eyes, positioned above a nose and mouth almost laughable in how closely they matched human appearances.

"This, Mage-Captain, is a reezh," Beck said calmly.

"Not a reejit?" she asked, studying the alien. The odds of there being *two* alien species in the same area of space was low, and while they had limited visuals of the reejit, the reezh could have fit in the suits she'd seen.

"I can see some similarities in the naming, obviously, but the name *reejit* doesn't show anywhere in the English data feeds."

"What are they saying?" she asked—and as she asked, she realized she both recognized the symbol on the lectern's seal *and could read the text*.

It was a single gold chimera on a red bend sinister surrounded by a gold rim. Every aspect of the heraldry was not merely human but *European*—and while the *top* version of the text was in an oddly familiar script she didn't recognize, the lower text was in plain English.

The Dual Republics of Chimera.

"I am basically certain our horned friend is speaking English, honestly," Beck admitted. "But while we're managing to extract individual still images from the data stream, we're not actually getting video or audio yet.

"Give our teams a couple of hours and we might manage it," he told her. "On the other hand, the situation there is sufficiently riled, I wouldn't be surprised to learn that *Rose* just left."

"In which case we need to learn what's going on as quickly as possible," Roslyn agreed. She studied their rapidly filling map of the unknown star system—Chimera, apparently?

She doubted the star system had been named for the Republic fleet carrier now guarding it, which raised all kinds of questions she was going to need answers to.

"Leavitt, Tod," she said, pulling the attention of those two officers. "I'm looking at the system and where it appears the locals have sent their ships—and it *looks* like we can split the difference and jump in about halfway between Planets Two and Three without being directly in anyone's line of fire.

"Can you confirm that for me?"

A couple of light-minutes was the usual minimum safety margin around a planet, with a larger factor for the star itself. The third planet was far enough out from the star that she wasn't worrying about its safety zone.

For that matter, with the Star Mirror to help her identify *current* locations for things, she had faith in her ability to jump directly into *orbit* of the third planet.

She was also quite certain that doing so would get her ship blown to pieces before she could even say *hello*. It wasn't a thing you did in friendly systems that weren't expecting you, let alone potentially unfriendly systems that looked like someone in a very similar ship to yours had just pissed everyone off.

"If we come in three light-minutes starward of planet three, there's civilian traffic but nothing armed, I don't think," Leavitt told her. "I think we want to give the civilians a good berth, too. The last thing we want is to imply a threat we don't mean."

"Agreed." Roslyn dropped an icon on the map. "I make this at least five million kilometers from the nearest civilian shipping and three light-minutes from planet three. Almost ten light-minutes from planet two."

The entire system was drawn on a ridiculous scale, one derived by the burning furnace of its F7 central star.

"We definitely *don't* know where all of the gunships are, sir," Leavitt warned. "Even assuming that they haven't built any beyond the ones *Chimera* carries, we *see* a hundred and fifty.

"Which means there's at least a hundred more floating around somewhere."

There was the argument, Roslyn supposed, that *Chimera* might have lost some of her two hundred and fifty parasite warships somewhere in the last seven years. But it was *more* likely, in her opinion, that the Republican deserters had set up a gunship yard as their first order of business upon having somewhere to protect.

"And if they jump us, we will defend ourselves," she told Leavitt. "And we will *only* defend ourselves; is that clear? We're not here to start a war.

"Quite the damn opposite."

CHAPTER 28

KNOWING THAT there was a potential threat on the other side, even if Roslyn's orders and plans called for a diplomatic interaction, she waited for one of the juniors—the forever-youngest Mage-Ensign Sigourney, in fact—to be ready to make the jump.

"I have the con," she declared at the same moment as the tiny Black woman declared, "Jump complete."

For all that Sigourney looked like a stiff breeze would carry her away normally, she appeared surprisingly unexhausted by the jump procedure as she saluted Roslyn and rose from the jump seat.

Roslyn had her suspicions about how long Sigourney would maintain that composure after she exited the bridge, but she wasn't going to poke at the teenager's projected illusion. Sigourney might be unusually powerful for a Mage by Right—one of the Mages detected in preteen testing without any prior Mage family—but she was also barely twenty.

If she was forcing herself to appear chipper after jumping a starship so everyone thought she was strong and ready for the job she was doing, *Roslyn* sure as hell wasn't going to undermine that.

"Status report, people," Roslyn ordered, turning her attention to the displays around her. As planned, there was nothing close to *Thorn*. The closest civilian ship was a solar clipper, a barbell-shaped ship with a multi-kilometer-wide array of sail fabric pushing her slowly out toward the third world.

"Closest contact is at eight million kilometers," Leavitt reported. "Closer than I'd like, but even *that* much accuracy is handy."

Normally, Roslyn would have been limited to picking her emergence point compared to the *planets*. She'd have had *no* idea where the military and civilian ships were—and even less idea of how the locals were currently behaving.

Thanks to the Star Mirror, they had made sure they had emerged outside laser range of any unknown spaceships. That had minimized both their own danger and, hopefully, their apparent threat level to the locals.

"Lieutenant Kinley, set a course for planet three," Roslyn ordered the junior non-Mage Navigator at the helm. "One gravity. We'll be nice and slow and non-threatening until someone gives us permission to move at speed.

"Lieutenant Strange, get our identify beacon and diplomatic codes blazing at maximum power," she continued, turning her attention to Lieutenant Tumaini Strange, her Coms Officer. Strange, like Sigourney, was a petite Black officer who could have passed for Sigourney's cousin physically. Unlike Sigourney, who had lived at the Academy with access to civilian hairdressers recently and still had *very* fashionable long hair, Strange's head was shaven down to about half a centimeter of dark fuzz.

"All beacons and codes transmitting as of completion of the jump," Strange reported crisply. "I took the liberty of pulling files on *Republic* coms protocols and am also transmitting our identity and diplomatic codes on those protocols and frequencies."

"Well done, Lieutenant Strange," Roslyn told them. "Thank you."

It was one thing, she reflected, to see the level of traffic between the belt and the hot Jupiter in the innermost orbit via the Star Mirror. It was quite another to watch that stream of civilian traffic file past on short-range scanners.

She'd grown up in Tau Ceti and served in both Legatus and Sol. She knew what the Protectorate's Core Worlds looked like, which made this level of traffic look almost quaint. On the other hand, she'd spent a *lot* of her service in the Protectorate's Fringe, where system governments and local corporations would have killed to have *half* this much in-system shipping.

The Dual Republics of Chimera, it seemed, were doing quite well for themselves.

"Sir! Contact alert!" Leavitt barked. "We have twenty gunships that were ballistic along the civilian shipping route. Range is nine million kilometers; engines just went fully active at ten gees."

Roslyn swallowed a curse. She'd *needed* to be close enough to the civilian traffic for her beacons to be picked up by nonmilitary ships. The more people saw her transmissions of goodwill, the more likely it was that the military would feel they had to talk to her, regardless of whatever had poked the hornet's nest before she'd arrived.

The risk, of course, was that the locals were being careful and had patrols along the shipping lanes. The capital ships were in orbit around the planets, but that was what sublight corvettes and gunships were *for* in most systems' service.

"Hail them," Roslyn ordered. "Diplomatic codes."

"Already transmitting," Strange reported. "Full pulse of everything on the beacons."

They paused and then shook their head.

"No response, sir. No acknowledgement of our transmission at all."

"VAMPIRE!"

Leavitt's shout of the standard code for *missile launch detected* froze Roslyn's spine in place, even as her fingers automatically laid in the commands to bring up the full information.

"Full launch from all gunships," Leavitt continued after half a second. "One hundred twenty missiles in space. Antimatter engines; appear to be Excalibur Fives."

"Understood," Roslyn said levelly. "Commander Leavitt, RFLAMs free. Lieutenant Kinley, maximum thrust and full evasion, if you please."

She turned her gaze on Leavitt before he could even ask and smiled gently.

"Permission to return fire denied."

The Rapid-Fire Laser Anti-Missile turrets were her ship's primary defense against incoming missiles. *Thorn* carried over two hundred of them, positioned across her hull so that almost any approach vector faced at least a hundred five-hundred-megawatt beams capable of firing every few seconds.

"Sir, they have opened fire on us," Leavitt pointed out softly. The missiles were still well out of range of their defenses, though Kinley had them burning away at fifteen gravities.

Versus the ten *thousand* gravities the missiles were generating, their retreat wasn't going to buy them much time—but even fractions of a second could count.

"Yes. They have," Roslyn conceded. "And I am not entirely sure why. We are still not going to *give* them a reason to have fired."

"Understood, sir. I think."

She nodded calmly to him and placed her hands on the simulacrum, sinking into her ship and its defenses through her magic. The link into the rune matrix wouldn't let her activate or control any of the ship's systems, but that was why the simulacrum chamber had the specialist displays it did.

With the light hitting her relayed directly from the outside, it was enough for her to have a sense of the universe *through* the ship. Her Rune of Power shivered as she sent a trickle of energy through it to the amplifier matrix and judged the missiles' approach.

They were as far beyond her ability to reach them with magic as they were beyond Leavitt's ability to reach them with RFLAMs, and she withdrew from the simulacrum after a moment.

"Strange, record for direct transmission to the gunships," she ordered, adjusting her position to bring the simulacrum out of the camera's view.

"You're on."

Roslyn focused on the camera pickup.

"Republic gunships, this is Mage-Captain Roslyn Chambers of the Royal Martian Navy warship *Thorn*. We are not—I repeat, *not*—hostile! Hostilities between the Republic and the Protectorate of Mars ceased almost *seven years ago*."

It was possible that they didn't know. Unlikely, but possible. It was also possible that these were First Legion holdouts, but that didn't sound right to her, either. They'd detected *Chimera*, which suggested these were the ships that had deserted the RIN at the Siege of Legatus, when the truth of the Prometheus Interface had come out.

"We are not your enemies. Stand down your missiles and I will refrain from returning fire!"

Twenty gunships didn't count as an existential threat to *Thorn*. They could rough her up if it came down to it, but their *best*-case scenario was to launch all three of their missile salvos before Roslyn's ship destroyed them.

"Message sent," Strange confirmed.

"They have not fired a second salvo, but their first one is still incoming," Leavitt replied. "Range is five million kilometers and dropping."

The other option was to get the hell out of Dodge. That was, after all, why Roslyn had waited for Sigourney to make the jump. *She* was still able to jump the cruiser to safety, and her palms itched back toward the simulacrum.

"Strange, do we have *Chimera* dialed in sufficiently for a direct transmission?" Roslyn asked.

"We do, but it's a four-minute round-trip," the coms officer warned.

And they didn't have four minutes *left* before the missiles hit. *Chimera* would, *probably*, get a message before the missiles arrived—but she doubted the rogue Republic ships still had FTL coms.

Their Links, after all, had relayed through the base systems in the Republic. Systems that the RIN would have used to track them—and systems the RMN would have seen them use by now if they had.

So, unless the gunships—thirty light-seconds and a sixty-second com loop away—decided to find their brains, *Thorn* was going to have to deal with the first salvo no matter what.

"Record for *Chimera*," Roslyn ordered. Strange gave her the nod and she focused her attention on the camera again.

"This message is for the commander of the defense forces of the Dual Republics of Chimera," she said swiftly, hoping that the use of the name they'd picked up from the local transmissions would buy them a moment of thought.

"I am Mage-Captain Roslyn Chambers, commanding officer of the Royal Martian Navy cruiser *Thorn*. We are under fire from ships of your forces in what I hope is a case of mistaken identity.

"We have no conflict with the Dual Republics and no desire to exchange fire with your fleet, but if your vessels continue their attack, I will have no choice but to defend my ship with all necessary force.

"My orders from my Queen are for peace. I am here to speak for Mars. Will you listen?"

She tapped her fingers for a second she knew she couldn't spare, then nodded to Strange.

"Send it."

"Sent." The Lieutenant grinned. "I *may* have sent it on a wide-enough beam that the gunships will get the fringe of it. It might help."

"It might," she agreed. The missiles were at twelve light-seconds and closing. At ten, she'd be able to reach them with the amplifier. Or, of course, she could simply get the hell out of the gunship's neighborhood. They were close enough in to everything to make a microjump risky, but she *could* just flick a light-year away and come back in a few hours.

"Do we have the time?" she muttered. Then, more decisively, she opened a channel to CIC.

"Beck. We can jump out and return in about two hours, avoid their fire entirely," she told him. "I don't know if we can afford the *time*. Your assessment of the threat?"

Her XO was silent for a few seconds, seconds in which the missiles continued their ten-thousand-gravity journey toward *Thorn*.

"There is always a threat, sir," he told her. "We should be able to get them all, but the crew isn't as smooth as I'd like, and a hundred and twenty missiles is a lot of fire for one ship to handle."

They were almost in range for the amplifier, and Roslyn hesitated. *Time* was *everything*. Every hour she delayed being able to search for and track *Rose*'s jump was an hour Nemesis could use to get away from her.

But if she stayed, she was risking her ship and her people. Her ship's armor could handle a hit from a gigaton-range antimatter warhead. *A* hit. Two would probably cripple her, unless they were perfectly spaced.

"There are days to spend lives for time," she said, very softly, on the channel to Beck. "I don't think today is one of those days. XO?"

"I..." He paused, then the tiny image of him on her repeaters nodded. "We can be back in, what, two hours? Why take the risk? We can kill the gunships, but it won't take much luck for them to get a missile through our beams."

Roslyn nodded sharply, the decision made as she tapped the command to move her chair into the simulacrum.

"All hands, prepare for jump," she barked. There wasn't enough time left to calculate a microjump, but a canned one-light-year jump took mere seconds to put together.

"Sir!" She blinked, almost glaring at Leavitt as he interrupted her prep for the missile launch. "I have warhead detonation, multiple self-destructs in the incoming salvo!"

It wasn't all of them initially, Roslyn observed, which was probably going to lead to some *fascinating* conversations once the gunships were back home. About a third of the missiles went up over the course of ten seconds or so, crippling or destroying another third with the collateral damage of their detonations.

The rest detonated as one as either the commander went along with the fait accompli his people had handed him—or the last ships fell into line. There was no way for Roslyn to tell which.

"Keep the defenses online and scanning those gunships," she ordered swiftly. "Lieutenant Kinley, keep opening the range for us. Lieutenant Strange, do we have any incoming coms?"

"*Chimera* will have *just* received the message," they replied. "No transmission from the gunship force."

"Gunships are maneuvering to shed velocity and keep with us," Leavitt reported. "Estimated five gees acceleration."

The bullet-shaped *Accelerator*-class gunships didn't have magical gravity, which meant that five gravities of acceleration would *suck* for the crews. Still, *Thorn* had three times their acceleration and the squadrons had an opposing vector. They'd be a problem for a while yet—the velocities and accelerations of spaceships were nothing compared to the accelerations of their missiles—but they were moving *away*.

"Holy mother of—"

The exclamation wasn't a *useful* report, but it drew attention to the main displays as the world rippled and empty space suddenly *wasn't* empty.

"Multiple contacts, multiple contacts!" one of the Tactical chiefs chanted.

"Two ships, estimate fifty megatons each, at six million kilometers," Leavitt reported after a second. "CIC identifies as *Courageous*-class carrier *Chimera* and *Combination*-class battleship *Scharnhorst*."

The core of the Republic battle group that had been in orbit, Roslyn recognized. They'd made a *perfect* jump from high orbit of the third planet to precisely twenty light-seconds from her ship.

Too perfect. Only the most experienced and careful of Mages, with lots of time to do the calculations, could make a jump that precise. Regular Prometheus Drives couldn't.

All of which meant...

"Their Prometheans are awake," Roslyn said softly. "That's... a good sign, I think."

Awakened Prometheans were far more dangerous than the Republic of Faith and Reason had ever realized. The only thing stopping them from being gods inside the reach of their ships' sensors was that the Republic had only been able to conceal regular jump matrices in their starships.

While the nature of a Promethean's existence meant none of them would ever be able to sustain the "Navy rate" of a jump every six hours, their direct access to their ships' computers gave them a precise control no unaltered human Mage could match.

There was a long silence as *Thorn*'s bridge crew stared at the two immense warships. For all of the Martian ship's advantages over the ex-RIN vessels, she was utterly outgunned and outclassed. Twenty gunships were a threat *Thorn* could handle. Two RIN capital ships were not.

As if to add to the point, a scramble launch put another *sixty* gunships in space around *Chimera*, and Roslyn concealed a snort of amusement.

"Lieutenant Strange?" she asked.

"Incoming coms, sir," they confirmed a second later. "Recorded transmission."

"Still a forty-second turnaround, but we want to stay outside of each other's close weapons range," Roslyn said. "Play it."

She blinked as she recognized the man on her screen. She'd never met Admiral Emerson Wang herself, but she'd heard about him from Damien Montgomery. Wang had been in command in the Korma System at the start of the war, when the then–First Hand had coordinated a humanitarian relief expedition to save the system from an unexpected famine.

He had, so far as Montgomery could tell, *allowed* himself to be forced into a catch-22 situation where he could stand down, despite his orders, and allow the Protectorate to feed the people under his protection.

"Mage-Captain Roslyn Chambers," Wang said flatly. "Your near-suicidal refusal to engage in confrontation serves you well, I suppose. It is sufficient for me to believe *your* lack of ill intent, at least.

"But after the actions of the *last* ship your Queen sent to this system, no Protectorate vessel is welcome in the Chimera System. Given my understanding of your likely jump limitations, you have one hour to withdraw.

"If you do not withdraw in that time or if you begin maneuvering toward any of the planets, we will destroy you."

CHAPTER 29

ROSLYN EYED the two heavy warships silently for a long few seconds, then sighed.

"Lieutenant Kinley, cut our thrust," she ordered. "What's our vector without acceleration?"

"Roughly right angle to the course between planet two and planet three in the ecliptic," the helm officer confirmed.

"Thank you." She'd wanted to be sure.

"Anyone have anything I should know before I start trying to explain our exact nightmare to Admiral Wang?" she asked drily.

"Who?" Beck asked from CIC.

"Admiral Emerson Wang," she explained. "We didn't know he was *Chimera*'s Admiral when they defected, but we knew who he was." She shook her head. "Strange, send a request to Mars for Wang's full file. Given that I think he's officially *dead*, I doubt he's in our onboard files."

Fortunately, with the Link, accessing the full RMN Intelligence archives on Mars was a matter of minutes at worst.

"Sir, I think there is something you want to know," Leavitt warned. "We've been interweaving our live data now that we're here with our scans through the Star Mirror, and what was a suspicion before is a certainty now."

"And is..." she prodded.

Her Tactical Officer flicked her a focused view of the innermost planet, the hot Jupiter that their scans suggested Chimera relied on for hydrogen fuel.

"There's an accelerator ring going up around the gas giant, sir," Leavitt told her, highlighting the construct in the shared screen. "I'd say it's about two-thirds complete—the keel structure of the ring is in place, but the accelerator and support structures are incomplete."

Roslyn whistled silently.

For the Protectorate, antimatter production simply required a Mage. Almost *any* Mage. A fully trained and qualified transmuter worked more efficiently, but a period of work in a transmutation facility was the standard punishment for Mages guilty of moderate-to-severe crimes.

For the UnArcana Worlds, antimatter was a *lot* harder to come by. It required massive amounts of power and specialized particle accelerators. An accelerator ring wrapped around a gas giant, though, combined tidal power, ready access to hydrogen and helium for fusion plants and enough sheer *scale* to produce major quantities of antimatter.

Almost enough to feed a Core World's and a Navy's demand for the substance.

The fact that the Republic had built a second accelerator ring in secret had very nearly tipped the war back against the Protectorate at one point. It seemed that *Chimera* had arrived with enough of the schematics to start building one there.

It wasn't complete, but it would be a huge boost to the system. Whether or not that was a *problem*, well... That depended on the next few hours and days, Roslyn suspected.

"Okay," she told Leavitt. "So, Chimera could be a valuable ally or a dangerous enemy. We all know which one Her Majesty would prefer. It seems I need to talk to the Admiral."

The files she'd asked for appeared on her display as Strange received them from Mars, and she flicked through key pages. There wasn't much she saw that could change anything.

Wang had been a gunship officer in the Legatus Self-Defense Force until the Republic had been born, his thirty years of experience in the LSDF pushing him to the heights of the RIN as one of their first carrier group commanders.

RMN Intelligence had lost track of him around the same time as the Siege of Legatus, but they hadn't had any information that had placed him *at* Legatus. On the other hand, they hadn't known who *Chimera*'s carrier group Admiral had been.

"Strange, record for transmission," Roslyn ordered as she faced her pickups once more.

"Admiral Emerson Wang," she greeted the Chimeran officer. "I assure you, on the honor of the Mage-Queen of Mars, that no Royal Martian Navy ship has entered this system prior to our arrival.

"Thanks to our operation of a modernized Link network, I have *confirmed* that in the last few minutes," she continued. She supposed that was a piece of intelligence she was giving up, but she didn't want to fight Wang. She was prepared to give up quite a lot of information to avoid that, in fact.

"Unfortunately, that leaves me quite certain of what *has* happened here," she admitted. "My ship is in active pursuit of her sister vessel, the *Thorn*-class exploratory cruiser *Rose*. *Rose* was stolen by a rogue faction of covert operatives from inside the Protectorate."

She spread her hands, palm upward.

"These operatives believe that the Reejit—who I believe are the people you know as the reezh—are preparing to invade the Protectorate to use all of our Mages to feed Prometheus Interfaces like the ones aboard your ship," she told Wang. "I... fear that they have reacted poorly to the continued evidence of their own eyes that their beliefs are false.

"I *must* track this ship, Admiral Wang. If they have committed crimes here in Chimera, I am prepared to add the weight of those actions to the justice that already awaits them. I have neither the desire nor the intent to cause conflict with Chimera, but my impression is that we *both* want *Rose* and her crew brought to justice."

She paused to think, then mentally shrugged and continued. In for a penny, in for a pound.

"While all I *need* is a chance to survey the location they left this system, any information you can provide on what they did while they were here would be of value."

Roslyn tapped a command, sending the message winging its way toward *Chimera*, and considered her options. While everything she said was true, she suspected it would take more than her earnest argument to buy herself a chance to pursue *Rose* through this system.

Without any idea when or where the other cruiser had left from or where they'd been going, her trail ended here. Uesugi couldn't track a jump through the Star Mirror. If she was going to bring Riley and *Rose* down, she needed the locals to help.

"Strange, I need a link to Mars," she told her Communications Officer. "I need to speak to the Prince-Chancellor."

"I met Admiral Wang *once*," Montgomery pointed out. The Protectorate's head of state was alone in a room that Roslyn guessed to be a private office off his quarters. It wasn't the big formal office she was used to seeing him in these days, and there were two different cats visible in the feed.

The night-black cat sitting on his lap Roslyn recognized—no one who interacted regularly with the Prince-Chancellor could avoid knowing Persephone, the kitten the Mage-Queen had acquired as therapy for the Chancellor's damaged hands. The sprawling black beast on Montgomery's lap was no kitten anymore, but she was still a known presence.

The other, small and dust-gray, cat curled up at his elbow on his desk was new to Roslyn. She suspected the cat's presence meant the Princesses McLaughlin, the Prince-Chancellor's twin daughters, were in residence at Mars at the moment.

"I suspect you left an impression, my lord," Roslyn told him. "Certainly, Nemesis has done *something* to leave him and his utterly furious at us. I need someone whose words he'll believe, without question, to tell him the story.

"Because while my words may be true, the last person who introduced themself to him as a Mage-Captain was lying about *everything*."

Montgomery sighed, carefully petting the cat on his lap, then looked up and nodded.

"I don't have long," he warned her. "You *know* how little time I get with my wife and daughters already. If I am drawn away too long, there will be *four* extraordinarily powerful and brilliant women angry at me."

The fourth being the Mage-Queen of Mars, who Roslyn *knew* felt guilty for the separation of her Prince-Chancellor from his family. Admiral Grace McLaughlin was the commanding officer of the Sherwood Interstellar Patrol and was only barely more capable of being away from Sherwood than Montgomery was of being away from Mars.

"Thank you, Damien," she said quietly.

"Just have Lieutenant Strange link up a relay," Montgomery instructed. "I hope the Admiral doesn't mind cats, because Persephone isn't going, anyway—and Ash is sick, so I don't want to let her out of my sight. The Princesses are good girls, but the best of intentions aren't going to let a pair of children handle a sick cat the way she needs."

There was no visible sign of illness on the gray cat, but Roslyn wasn't going to argue. She deactivated the privacy screen around her command seat and turned her gaze on Strange.

"Lieutenant Strange, set up a direct relay from the Link to Mars and the Prince-Chancellor to *Chimera*," she ordered. "Live, if they'll accept it. Twenty seconds isn't much over two hundred and fifty light-years!"

Seconds ticked away as Strange worked through the procedure of ping-and-response to set up a live call with Admiral Wang. The Chimeran officer hadn't replied to her own message yet, and she wasn't even sure if he *would* take the call—but Strange flashed her a thumbs-up as the forty-second mark came up.

Wang reappeared on the main display, looking less angry and more exhausted than he had before.

"Mage-Captain Chambers, your words have bought you a discussion in the chamber of second thoughts," he said drily. "I have passed some of your claims on to the Dyad Ministers of Chimera, but *I* am not wholly convinced of..."

She *saw* the moment the return image of Damien Montgomery reached him and he trailed off. It was a three-way call, with one participant linked in from Mars and the other two separated by twenty light-seconds.

"Emerson Wang," Montgomery greeted him. "It's been a long time, and you're *still* causing trouble as my people are trying to help yours."

The time lag meant that Roslyn and Montgomery alike had to wait forty seconds for Wang's response, but it felt necessary *to* wait.

"This is not Korma, Lord Montgomery," Wang said slowly. "I don't know what title you are currently holding, but I suspect neither of us is who we once were. In Korma, I was bound by the orders of higher authority. A higher authority we *both* know now to have been lost to anything I would accept as honor, justice, or even pragmatism.

"Here, I serve as the highest military authority for a civil government I respect and honor. And the actions of *Rose* and Mage-Captain Caleb Riordan leave both me and that civil government with little willingness to extend trust to Mars.

"Your Mage-Captain Chambers has made interesting arguments, but it is not up to me if I trust her."

Montgomery leaned into the camera, picking up Persephone and putting her on the desk next to Ash. Roslyn knew enough about cats to realize that the older cat's approach to and nuzzle of Ash was a solid confirmation of the statement that the gray cat was ill.

"Captain Chambers has kept me well briefed on what has happened," he told Wang. "I can tell you two things, Admiral Wang, that I hope help. Firstly, that *Rose* is no longer a warship of the Royal Martian Navy. She has been stolen by a rogue faction, and Captain Chambers' orders are, in fact, to bring her home or destroy it.

"Secondly... there is no Mage-Captain Caleb Riordan in the RMN." An image joined Roslyn and Montgomery on the feed, presumably set up by the Prince-Chancellor while they had waited on the link.

She recognized Kent Riley now. She *hadn't* known the name or the face when he'd pretended to be Angus Killough, an MISS agent on Sorprendidas. Under that false identity, he'd helped her take down the secret lab creating the Orpheus weapon... and had stolen all of the information on the weapon itself while she'd been dealing with its creators.

"If this is the man who introduced himself as Riordan," Montgomery continued, "you need to know that he is part of an organization that is directly responsible for, at a minimum, the creation of the Prometheus Interface as well as a long list of other charges.

"He is a criminal and a traitor—and Mage-Captain Chambers is tasked to bring him in to face the justice of Mars."

And then, again, the forty-second wait before Wang spoke. It was a strange, stilted conversation—and yet having the near-live conversation helped in some ways, Roslyn judged.

"That is the man who claimed to be Caleb Riordan," Wang confirmed slowly. "And under that name, he broke into a radiation-containment dome in the Dual Republic's capital, killed several dozen people and stole an irreplicable and irreplaceable component of a reezh starship in that dome *while creating a radiation risk to the city.*"

The Admiral paused, swallowing a clear spike of rage.

"When challenged, his people threatened to bombard Twin Sphinx, the city in question, along with other reezh centers of population if we intervened. He fled the system without executing on that threat but is directly guilty of dozens of murders and creating a major crisis in the capital city."

Roslyn shivered. It was impossible to be aware of everything Nemesis had done without knowing they were ruthless, but threatening to bombard cities—not just *a* city, which would be bad enough!—to protect Riley?

"I understand," Montgomery said before she said a word. "I wish I didn't have to, but I understand. You have the Word of the Mountain and the Mage-Queen of Mars, Emerson Wang, that Kent Riley—or Caleb Riordan, whatever name matters—did none of this under our orders."

There was a formality to his tone that Roslyn had only heard on occasion. This wasn't even the Prince-Chancellor speaking. This was the Hand of the Mage-Queen of Mars, speaking in Her Voice and in Her Name.

She could see in her bridge crew's postures that they heard it as well, as spines stiffened and ratings whose posture had been acceptably military suddenly snapped to full parade-ground.

"But our intention and our orders do not matter," Montgomery continued, his tone still formal despite the two cats curled up at his left elbow. "Crimes were committed, and the people of the Dual Republics suffered for the trust they extended to a crew and a man they believed to speak for Mars.

"The honor of the Protectorate has been stained and your trust abused. That you hesitate to extend that trust again is rational and reasonable,

Admiral Wang. Were you closer to the Protectorate, I could commit ships and hands to support your people in handling the damage done.

"I will offer any and all services that Mage-Captain Chambers can provide to your people, but I believe the best service that she and *Thorn* can do for either of our nations is to chase *Rose* down.

"I ask—I *beg*, Emerson Wang—that you allow her to do so. Any and all aid that the Dual Republics require to deal with the aftermath of Kent Riley's treachery is yours for the asking. Be it engineers to repair the damaged dome or simply monetary compensation for your losses, we offer it freely.

"But please. Let Captain Chambers chase them down."

Seconds ticked away once more, and Roslyn had to consciously *not* hold her breath for the full forty seconds.

"You always were a silver-tongued bastard, weren't you, Montgomery?" Wang finally said. "My people have confirmed this is a legitimate Link transmission from Mars, too. I believe it is you. I believe that you and Mage-Captain Chambers speak the truth."

He sighed.

"I will speak to the Dyad Ministers," he promised. "I suspect Mage-Captain Chambers' own words might have been enough, but we will be well served to go one step further. I will confirm with my civilian government... but I believe that you and I, Mage-Captain, will shortly be speaking in person."

CHAPTER 30

ROSLYN HOPED that Admiral Emerson Wang picked up the dual message of her arriving aboard his ship accompanied only by Commander Matthias Beck. The two officers stepped out of the shuttle onto the carrier's flight deck without a single Marine or even a visible weapon, returning the salutes of the Dual Republic Marines waiting for them.

The first half of the message was a sign of trust and willingness to compromise. Wang hadn't *asked* her to come unescorted, but she'd heard enough about Riley's visit to the system now that she figured not bringing a squad with her wouldn't hurt. The hidden layer even in *that* part of the message, though, was that Beck was her Executive Officer, the other person expected to command *Thorn* in action.

The second half of the message was a warning. The gold medallion at her throat didn't have the symbols a civilian's Mage Medallion would, but that was a warning in itself. Even *without* the Rune of Power, Roslyn had enough personal magical power to thwart any open attack and escape back to their shuttle.

She didn't *need* an escort.

Both naval officers' magnetic boots clicked on the deck as they walked down a clearly laid-out path. The central flight deck between the carrier's hulls couldn't have centrifugal pseudogravity, and the Dual Republics didn't have the Mages to maintain gravity runes.

Reaching Wang, Roslyn braced to attention and gave the astronomically senior officer an Academy-perfect salute—beating him by about a quarter-second.

"Mage-Captain Chambers," he greeted her, holding his salute a second longer than she did. "I *can* read Royal Martian Navy award ribbons, I have to note. *Three* Medals of Valor?"

"One for surviving the Nia Kriti attack that came with a battlespace commission to Lieutenant, one for being kidnapped alongside and rescuing Mage-Admiral Crown Princess Jane Alexander, and the third for saving over a *hundred thousand people* from First Legion slavery," Beck reeled off before Roslyn could say a word.

She wouldn't have actually *given* the list, but she supposed she could allow her XO to stroke her ego in this circumstance.

"I forget, sometimes, how out of date on news from home I am," Wang admitted. "What information I have after the Fall of Legatus is limited to what we *acquired* from the First Legion."

"And while they had their links into the Protectorate, they were working in the shadows after the defeat of the Republic," Roslyn said. "I imagine you didn't get full downloads from them, either. I understand you had one ugly clash with them—though I did see your ships at Exeter."

"That was you, was it?" Wang asked. "I remember the reports of that battle. We had a pretty good idea of who was involved, though there were some questions about how you'd ended up at the fleet base being assembled to watch *us.*"

"Base Deveraux now serves as a frontier outpost for Mars, but we aren't watching Chimera from there," Roslyn told him. In fact, Base Deveraux—named for the Promethean who'd died saving the kidnapped workers she'd been forced to deliver to the star system—had been intended to act as the base of operations for the *Thorns'* exploration mission.

A mission that had been *planned* to be far slower and more methodical than this.

"We have not scouted it since," Wang admitted. "Thanks to our accidental involvement, we were quite certain it had fallen to the Protectorate and..."

"You didn't want to draw our attention. A desire that, regretfully, Nemesis has made seem even more justified in hindsight," Roslyn said quietly.

"That they did. Walk with me, Mage-Captain, Commander?"

Wang hadn't introduced his officers. A tall blonde woman, as broad and Germanic as her Admiral was stout and Mongolian, stood at his right side in a Commodore's uniform. A slimly Slavic woman walked at Wang's left side, with a smaller redheaded man trailing one step behind the Commodore Roslyn presumed to be *Chimera*'s Captain.

"We have a great deal to discuss, I fear," Roslyn murmured. "But if you could spare me the time, I would be delighted to hear how a Republic battle group became the core of the Dual Republics' fleet!"

The history lesson carried them to a conference room inside the rotating hull, a space sufficiently convenient to the flight deck that it was clearly designed for this purpose. Roslyn suspected it was the same place Wang had brought Riley when the Nemesis leader had come aboard, but she could only guess at that.

"I have to be very clear, Mage-Captain," Wang finally told her as he took a seat, gesturing her and Beck to chairs of their own. "I have minimal emotional attachment to the former Republic, but it *was* my nation. My enthusiasm for Mars and the Protectorate remains limited. I put aside that judgment once and my people suffered for it."

"I understand," Roslyn told him. A steward put a glass of ice water in front of her, and she nodded her thanks to the woman before taking a measured sip.

Poison was the one trick Wang could pull that would actually threaten her, and they both knew it. Drinking the provided water without hesitation was another tiny part of the game they were playing.

"We did not know any of the details of Chimera," Roslyn noted. "We knew, thanks to the First Legion and your presence at the Battle of Exeter, that there was at least one more unrecorded colony beyond our frontiers with access to Republic ships.

"All we truly knew beyond that was that you and the First Legion didn't get along. And *that*, Admiral Wang, was frankly a *recommendation* in our books."

"I understand you had the pleasure of interacting with Admiral Muhammad's little empire," Wang said drily. "At Exeter, from what you said, which I suspect was the worst example of his issues."

"I was at Exeter, yes," Roslyn allowed slowly. She hadn't seen the rest of the First Legion's conquered worlds, but she'd read the reports. "And, unfortunately, it was *not* the worst of the First Legion's crimes. A hundred and fifty thousand forcibly transported and effectively enslaved workers... and it was only... third on the list?"

There was a long, frozen silence in the room.

"We didn't know," Wang said softly.

"Neither did we," Roslyn agreed. "And we, Admiral Wang, had a far greater ability to *do* anything about it. In fact, Muhammad's little empire didn't last long after we found him. Those worlds have now either chosen to join the Protectorate or are in the final stages of organizing plebiscites on the decision."

"Forgive me for asking, Captain, but what happens if they *decline* membership?" the unnamed Commodore asked, leaning forward slightly.

"Then, like the Independent UnArcana Worlds that remain of the Republic, they will go their own way as they choose," Roslyn told the woman. "As with the IUW, we will offer a security agreement if they wish it, but Her Majesty is as clear as her father was before her: no world, no people, will be forced into the Protectorate."

The *nation*, at least. Roslyn knew Kiera Alexander's opinion on the distinction between the Protectorate of the Mage-Queen of Mars, the *nation*, and what her title *Protector of Humanity* required of her.

The Royal Martian Navy was the Mage-Queen's left hand, the shield to the sword of Her Hands. Where the Mage-Queen commanded, they would go—and where humans, regardless of nation, were in danger, Kiera Alexander would send them.

"That aligns with what we were told by Riordan, but you will understand that we now question everything that man said," Wang observed.

"I don't know what *Rose*'s crew told you," Roslyn noted. "As a Captain in Her Majesty's Navy, I carry a certain degree of plenipotentiary authority, but the details of Chimera's relationship with Mars are an affair to be hashed out between diplomats over time.

"Prince-Chancellor Montgomery already committed us to any assistance or compensation required to resolve the damage Nemesis left behind," she reminded them. "For my own part, I would provide any assistance my ship can offer regardless.

"My mission, however, means I cannot stay long in Chimera. I am here to bring down *Rose* and the Nemesis traitors who stole her." She shrugged. "The information you've given us should suffice for my Tracker to establish her course, but the more I know about what they might have stolen, the better."

"Riordan stole what could not be given," Wang said grimly. "The Dual Republics are... just that. Two separate nations. Heavily intermingled in many ways, but reezh and human operate under different structures and keep different secrets."

He considered her levelly.

"The human half of the Dual Republics doesn't actually *have* very many secrets," he admitted. "I would have been delighted, if we're being honest, to conceal the existence of the Prometheans, but that wouldn't have been fair to anyone."

"We'd have been fine," a voice said from a speaker somewhere in the room.

Roslyn, who had both spent time aboard a ship with an Awakened Promethean as its *Captain* and helped kick off the Protectorate's research-and-rehabilitation program for the Prometheans they'd retrieved from the First Legion, raised an eyebrow at the air.

"I presume you are *Chimera*'s Promethean?" she asked the air. "May I have your name?"

"I am Cam," the voice replied, sounding surprised and pleased. "*Chimera*'s senior Promethean. Ty, my counterpart, dislikes strangers. Her opinion has not been improved by Kent Riley's treachery."

The Promethean, Roslyn noted, had switched over to using Riley's actual name rather than the assumed one he'd used in Chimera. A Promethean's intimate integration with the ship's computers went well beyond even an augmented human's computer hardware, which might make it difficult not to use the most updated facts.

Or so she guessed. She might even ask one of them one day.

"Thank you, Cam," Roslyn told the voice, turning her attention and a small smile back on Emerson Wang—who appeared pleasantly surprised by her reaction.

"I should perhaps note that Base Deveraux, our fleet base in the Exeter System, is named for the Promethean Sharon Deveraux, who helped us find the system and liberate its prisoners at the price of her own life.

"I have worked with several Prometheans, but Sharon Deveraux was the first and has left me with a deep debt of gratitude and honor I owe to any of her siblings-in-kind."

"I... did not know Deveraux," Cam observed slowly. "But I am pleased to know that others of our fellow victims found some level of peace and power. Choosing to remain in this form was difficult, but I have grown used to it now. And there is much to be said for having the body of a supercarrier."

"I don't think the RMN is going to be putting Prometheans on our ships anytime soon," Roslyn replied. "But as time separates us some from the original atrocity, and the necessity of caring for the remaining Prometheans forces us to become familiar with the technology, we are beginning to see some positive uses for the technology."

She wasn't convinced herself, but some of the doctors working with the Prometheans were talking to disability advocates about whether there was a value for the technology in the care of people paralyzed beyond Protectorate medicine's ability to fix.

So long as the removal of the brain was required, Roslyn suspected the answer would be *no*—but she suspected that as they found ways to create the deep neural connection with the brain still in its owner's head, the usefulness of the technology would expand dramatically.

"You are not, perhaps, what I expected of an RMN officer," Wang conceded, studying her. "Riordan—Riley, I suppose—was closer. But then, I think he was as aware of what I would expect as I was."

"Riley once convinced me that he was an agent for the Martian Interstellar Security Service and an ally against Nemesis," Roslyn pointed out. "The man is exceptionally deceptive, I believe. I cannot blame Chimera for falling for an all-too-believable lie."

"But I need to know what he learned here."

Wang sighed and nodded slowly.

"I can give you the basics," he told her. "Rior—Riley was very focused on the Reezh Ida, the old empire our reezh citizens broke away from.

"About a quarter-millennium ago, all of the space around here belonged to the Ida. Then they had a nasty civil war, which..." Wang paused for a few seconds considering. "I am not sure if the *civil war* was what the reezh call the Burning or if it *led* to the Burning, but the two are inextricable."

"The Burning." Roslyn rolled the two words around her mind and grimaced. "The destruction of every inhabited world in this region of space."

"So far as I can tell, the destruction of basically *every* reezh world equivalent to our MidWorlds and Fringe," Wang said softly. "The Nine and the Primes—their Core Worlds equivalent—are believed to have survived, but the reezh haven't even told *me* where they are."

He snorted.

"We can guess, of course, at least enough to keep a scout ship on the most likely approach to watch for trouble. But the Reezh Ida is no more. The Nine and Primes appear to remain, but they have been focused on each other for as long as there have been humans in the Chimera System."

That lined up with what Roslyn had seen—and the *Reezh Ida* sounded vaguely familiar.

"The Reejit," she murmured.

"The what?" Wang asked.

"The Reejit, Admiral," Roslyn told him. "I suspect a mistranscription or other error of recording of the Reezh Ida. A group of nonhumans who were on Mars in the first half of the twenty-second century.

"Aliens who helped build the Olympus Mons Amplifier and left behind schematics that would eventually form the basis for the Prometheus Interface."

The room was deathly silent.

"My god," Wang whispered. "Riordan... said there were aliens involved, but not that you had a *name*. The reezh *here* were horrified when they realized what drove my ships between the stars, Captain. They had no concept of any such thing. They knew magic, yes, but their Mages were mostly gone by the time any humans arrived here.

"To my knowledge, there were no Mages in the Chimera System prior to Riley's arrival. No one here knew about any intervention on Mars, Mage-Captain. I do not know if I disbelieve you, but..."

"I doubt anyone here knew anything," Roslyn agreed. "Certainly, my impression is that the scientists and Mages who intervened on Mars operated at the limits of reezh capability and authority... and the fact that humanity has *never* seen reezh since makes me wonder if they even managed to report home."

That sank in as she smiled grimly.

"Kent Riley and the rest of Nemesis believe that everything, from Project Olympus to today, is one coherent plan, lining the Protectorate and humanity up for harvest," she explained quietly. "The destruction of the fleet base they knew of would have fragmented that belief.

"Now they find themselves faced with the reality that all of their crimes, all of their atrocities and murders and violence, were in service to a *mistake*. An error."

"The type of people who would do what we saw Riley and his people do would not accept that," Wang said grimly.

"No. They will burn the galaxy, trying to find proof of the enemy they are looking for. But unless I am severely mistaken, the Nine do not even know humanity exists," Roslyn said. "Which means, Admiral, that the man I am hunting is about to find a monster that doesn't even know we exist and *wake it up*."

She met each Republic officers' gaze in turn, watching that sink in.

"That is why I need to know what he learned and where he may be going, Admiral," Roslyn told Wang. "Because a stern chase is a long chase, and if I don't catch *Rose* and Kent Riley, he might just kick off the war his entire organization was *supposed* to be about preventing!"

CHAPTER 31

"SO, NOW WE KNOW our enemy."

Kay's words hung in the conference room like a falling sword, and he smiled brilliantly at his people.

Between continuing to jump the ship away from Chimera to avoid any clever ideas on the part of Admiral Wang and the delicate, multifaceted process of interfacing with, decrypting and translating an alien computer core... every one of his people had been run off their feet.

But they *had* escaped Chimera without pursuit. They *had* interfaced with the computer core. They *had* decrypted and translated the data.

And it had taken Kay and Koskinen two full days to pull enough information out of that data for him to have a damn clue what he was looking at. Six days, all told, for him to be standing in front of his exhausted officers in triumph.

"People. The Nine."

Holographic images of nine reezh appeared above the central table as if conjured by his words instead of the command entered on his tablet. All were exactly the same height, a uniformity that spoke more to the art style than anything else, Kay presumed.

"The Mother, the Father, the Builder, the Smith, the Warrior, the Brother, the Sister, the Child and the Night. The nine core deities of the Reezh Ida's state religion, the *theocracy* that rules the star system of the Nine," he explained.

Only clothing and the tools they held really distinguished the nine reezh divinities from each other. Kay could list the portfolios and suchlike for the deities, but it wasn't really relevant to the discussion at hand.

"The core reezh government has been a theocracy ruled by the Church of the Nine—the Kazh—for over two thousand years," he continued. "Imagine if Rome had, instead of converting to Christianity and slowly declining, somehow tripled down on its polytheism and, in so doing, found the will to resume their military expansion."

"Would have taken more than that," O'Shea pointed out.

"Of course. Remember that we are currently basically at summaries of high-school textbooks for ancient history," Kay told his people wryly. "None of us can read *that* quickly.

"Important for *our* purposes, however, is the recognition that ancient tradition says that *all* Mages *must* join the Kazh. No exceptions. Presuming the genetics and inheritance around magic are much the same for reezh as humans, that likely means that most reezh Mages were born inside the Kazh, to the Priest-Mages of the last generation."

He shrugged.

"There is no mention in any of the documents of any equivalent to our Mages by Right or the Royal Testers," he noted. "I suspect that sustaining a working Mage population drove much of the perquisites and requirements of the priesthood.

"But, as we move forward into slightly *less*-ancient history, they mastered an equivalent to our jump matrix in the late nineteenth century. By the time we were struggling to colonize Mars, they had built the Ida, a holy empire spanning a large number of worlds."

It wasn't entirely clear how many. They had, after all, stolen a *pirate ship's* computers. They didn't exactly include the most recent full updates on historical research—and the Last Ship postdated the Burning. Her crew probably hadn't known the full extent of the Reezh Ida themselves.

"Without the ability to identify Mages, the priesthood was strictly limited to the Nine, the home system," Kay continued. "That appears to have eventually expanded to the Primes, the original colonies as they grew more powerful, but that was part of the restrictions on the later colonies.

"The colonies' technology was heavily dependent on parts from the Nine and Primes—*and* they required the Priest-Mages to move anything anywhere."

"How does *that* lead to putting Mage brains in jars?" Tomas asked grimly.

"Simple, if horrifying." Kay told her. "They didn't know they were putting Mage brains in the jump drives."

"That needs some explaining," O'Shea told him after a moment.

"When they developed their version of the Prometheus Interface, in the early twenty-first century, it was based off the discovery that certain *non-Mage* minds *could* channel magical energy. Using the Interface to guide that channeling, they could feed the jump matrix, and their Engine of Sacred Sacrifice was born."

He could see the question forming in Tomas's eyes, but it was actually O'Shea who asked it first.

"I'm no Mage," the engineer said slowly. "But my understanding was that *anyone* who can do anything I would call *channeling magical energy* is a Mage."

"Yes." Kay and Tomas spoke simultaneously, and the Ship's Mage looked sick.

"From what I can tell, no one in the Kazh or the Ida *ever* realized that," Kay told them. "They identified *channelers*, and they became the Sacred Sacrifices that fueled the Engines.

"According to the historians, the Reezh Ida *paid tribute to the Nine in gold, iron, bodies and minds*," Kay quoted. "Literally, I believe, in the case of minds. From the information we have, I think the tribute ships carried the systems for identifying channelers. The answer to their Mage shortage was in their hands all along, but instead, they turned to murder. To the Sacred Sacrifice."

"And in so doing, kicked off the civil war that nearly ended their species," Koskinen concluded grimly.

"That was my read of what the historians on Garuda said, yes," Kay agreed. "There may be details or counterarguments in the Last Ship's files, but I haven't seen them yet. On the other hand, I was looking for something quite specific."

The divine statuary vanished from the hologram, replaced by a star system. Nine planets and an asteroid belt orbiting a warm Go-type yellow dwarf, very similar to Earth's Sun.

Much like Chimera, there was a hot Jupiter-type gas giant inside the liquid-water zone. In this case, it was the second planet—creating a shield against solar radiation and debris that had likely helped the third planet evolve life.

The third world was chilly and moonless, but it had breathable air and liquid water and shared its name with the Builder god of the Nine. It was the reezh homeworld, the true center of the Reezh Ida and the civilization that threatened humanity.

Six more rocky worlds, the asteroid belt and a second gas giant orbited the star, all of which would have been visible from the Builder's skies.

"And this is the *other* Nine," Kay said drily. "Each world named for a reezh god. Utterly under the control of the reezh Kazh, even after the Burning. There are notes in the files that suggest the Primes were divided against each other and the Nine, but that even *they* hesitated to raise a hand against the mother system."

"Our enemy," Chaudhary said grimly. "The source of Project Olympus and the Prometheus Interface alike."

"Exactly," Kay confirmed. "Someone from this star system came to Mars and taught the Eugenicists to detect potential *channelers*. What happened to take it from that to the birth of the modern Mage, we don't know. There is no reference in the Last Ship's files to such a mission—but neither the pirate ship she became nor the tribute ship she began as would have had that information.

"The only place we can be certain those records remain is here." He pointed at the star system. "In the hands of the reezh Kazh, who could have buried the information for a thousand reasons—but I have my guesses."

"If they're trapped in a cold war with the Primes, they may hesitate to act rashly," Koskinen said slowly. "They would need enough force to guarantee their own security while they raid us for channelers and confirm that our Mages *could* be used for the Engines of Sacred Sacrifice."

"They have one advantage on that front," Kay admitted. "One that will require us to be *very* careful."

A new icon appeared on Builder, a red-gold pyramid that threatened doom to all of Kay's carefully laid plans.

"Priest-Mages from the reezh Kazh built the Olympus Mons Amplifier," he reminded his people. "And the files from the Last Ship are clear: there is a planetary amplifier on the Builder."

"While such an amplifier has limited use without a Rune Wright, it is still a dangerous tool."

He chuckled softly.

"We are lucky, I think, that the reezh had no concept of what a Rune Wright like the first Mage-King could do with the Olympus Amplifier. While I have seen nothing in the files to suggest that the reezh have any Rune Wrights like the Royal Family, the amplifier remains a threat we must move carefully around."

"Fortunately, we are aboard the most stealthy warship the Protectorate ever built," Tomas murmured. "If anything in the galaxy can sneak around the Nine without being spotted, it's this ship."

"Which raises the question, of course, of just where *is* the Nine?" O'Shea asked.

Kay poked at his tablet, bringing up the astrographic map.

"Interestingly, Chimera is basically on the direct line from Sol to the Nine," he told them. "Following that line, they are one hundred and eighty light-years away from Chimera."

He smiled thinly.

"Roughly one hundred and sixty-five light-years from our current position. We can be there in eleven days."

His command staff were silent, all of them studying the map. They'd come a literally incomprehensible distance to reach their current location. To reach the Nine, they'd be traveling a similar distance again—only three-quarters of the distance from Tau Ceti to Nemesis, but still an immense gap of space and time.

"Chimera was the outer limit of the colonies of the Reezh Ida," Kay reminded them all. "That is part of how they survived the Burning. I suspect they still function as an outer scout post, a relay the Kazh is using to keep an eye on humanity."

"And a handy shield, presenting a lovely face of a group of reezh who *aren't* theocratic fanatics," Chaudhary observed. "I don't suppose there's any sign in the Last Ship's files that the core empire of the Kazh is any... calmer than it was?"

"When the Last Ship came to Chimera—Allosch, then—the Burning was less than ten years prior," Kay noted. "The files *suggest* that some of the inner worlds outside the Nine and Primes remained but were finding themselves caught in the conflict between the Kazh and the rebel factions.

"Proxy wars." He shook his head. "Proxy wars that we have every reason to believe ended much as the Burning did. I would not expect to find anything left of the reezh but the Nine and the Primes."

He highlighted the Primes on the map.

"We *could* go to one of the Primes," he noted. "Those are eleven star systems in a rough globe around the Nine. Those colonies were established before humanity had even reached *orbit*, people. They are very old, densely populated and technologically advanced.

"It seems unlikely that two centuries of cold war has left the Nine and Primes technologically degraded from the Reezh Ida at its height. *Smaller*, yes. There is little evidence that they have expanded since burning their own outer colonies to the ground, but I doubt their technology has held still.

"And that, my friends, is what we need to bring back to the Protectorate," he told them. "The Kazh in the Nine has to know about the Protectorate. They are almost certainly planning to use our resources—at the very least, the minds of our Mages!—to turn the tide of their cold war.

"That means they *will* have a fleet of jump ships, some with traditional jump matrices but many with the Engine of Sacred Sacrifice, prepared for the invasion. We must locate that fleet. Learn what it is armed with. Bring all of that intelligence home."

Armed with the proof of the threat and the intelligence needed to save the Protectorate, Kay hoped they would be able to argue their case. Even if they failed in the end, they would still have fulfilled their duty.

Everything Kay had done, after all, had been to serve the Protectorate. In the reezh Kazh, he saw the enemy he had spent his life fighting—the *Nemesis* that would doom Mars and all humanity if he didn't finish his mission.

"What happens if their scanners are able to locate us?" O'Shea asked. "This is not an MISS stealth ship. Even with magic and the amplifier, we cannot become a true hole in space at background temperature.

"If their tech is that much better than ours, it is possible we will be found."

"It is possible," Kay agreed. "We have to take that chance. We will be as careful as we can be, but we will not enter the system until we have Mages ready to both sustain the invisibility spell *and* jump us out.

"We serve no one dead—or, worse, as prisoners of the Kazh!"

Kay hadn't realized O'Shea was following him until she slid her foot in the door to his quarters and followed him in. He *should* have—decades of trained instinct made him hard to follow, especially in the confined environment of a starship.

Before he could interrogate that thought too much, the Chief Engineer dropped herself onto his couch and looked up at him, resting her chin on steepled hands.

"What?" he asked.

"You do realize there are a thousand possibilities other than the ones you're focusing on, right?" she replied. She patted the space next to her on the couch, then recombined her hands.

"Maybe," Kay allowed. He half-sat, half-perched on the couch as he studied the gorgeous woman in his living room. "I'm not sure what you're pushing for."

"It's possible no one left in the Nine and Primes knows *shit* about humanity," she told him. "They burned two-thirds of their fucking empire to the ground, Kay. Killed *billions*. I have to wonder what the *hell* would keep them from coming after us for easy resources in the last two centuries."

"For the first of those centuries, the fact that they were busy burning their own empire," he said drily. "Nothing I have seen out here, Kamilla, makes me think these are people I want anywhere near humanity.

"Whatever is happening, we need to know what resources the Kazh commands. The Protectorate is in danger and they don't even want to admit it."

"Not arguing that," she conceded. "But... I mean... if they lost the information on us, that would also explain what we've seen. They've been focused on each other for hundreds of years because they forgot we existed."

"There are risks to poking this, Kay."

"Except Chimera already knows we exist, Kamilla," he said, shaking his head. "And they know Chimera exists. Even if the Kazh has somehow lost the reports and documents, and even if Chimera is as innocent as they appear... the Kazh will come for Chimera, and from there, they will come for the Protectorate.

"Thanks to us, humanity is almost ready. Now we need to make sure they get enough information to be *entirely* ready."

She chuckled, reaching out to pull his leg into her lap and force him to sit more thoroughly.

"We have achieved that much," she conceded. "Today's fleet is not the one they would have fought twenty years ago." She started rubbing his leg, half a massage and half an invitation for something more.

"Do you think we're pushing too far?" he asked.

"I think that the moment we *stop* pushing, too many people on this ship are going to start asking questions we don't want to answer," O'Shea admitted. "So long as we can tell them that there is an enemy in the Nine and Primes and we are leading them in that direction, Nemesis will follow you.

"If we start trying to tell them we were wrong somewhere along the way?" She shook her head. "It won't be pretty, Kay."

"I don't think we were wrong," he said. But her prodding made him stop and examine the statement. *Was* he certain? Or was he... well, looking for a reason to justify everything he'd done?

Did it matter?

"It doesn't matter," O'Shea told him, and he wondered if she'd somehow read his mind. "It *doesn't matter* if we were wrong, Kay. If you and I and the rest of the leaders want to survive, we have to keep going. We have to find something to prove to our people that we were right."

She chuckled as her fingers drifted far enough to make him shiver.

"And I agree with you, to be clear: everything about Chimera and Garuda stinks. There were too many secrets there. The questions raised there can only be answered in the Nine. I'm with you to the end."

"For the answers?" he murmured, reaching down to take her hand, pulling them closer together.

"Answers. Promises. Other things," she replied. "I don't plan on surrendering and letting Mars shoot me, to be clear. I recognize that *you* might regard that as duty fulfilled, but I plan on living."

She kissed him, sharply. Fiercely. *Desperately.*

"I'd rather prefer you lived too," she admitted.

CHAPTER 32

"I SEE THAT MAGIC, for all of its great power, can not convince bureaucracy to accelerate to meet even their own needs."

Roslyn looked up from her desk to see Beck standing in the door of her day office. The door was open, allowing his unheard approach, though *most* people would have announced themselves or been announced by the Marines.

The Executive Officer of any starship was a law unto themselves, of course.

"You were expecting something different?" she asked, gesturing for him to come in.

"It took us most of a day just to make orbit after everyone had agreed to stop *shooting* at each other," Beck pointed out as he took a seat. He made a questioning gesture toward the carafe of coffee on the corner of her desk.

She nodded her permission and took a sip of her own coffee. The beverage was edging toward too cool to drink, but it was still okay. Mostly.

"Three days since we made orbit, and we've had one meeting with Admiral Wang, and Uesugi has been able to run their little trick," he continued. "We *know* where *Rose* went, skipper. Shouldn't we be after her?"

"There's an argument," Roslyn agreed. "And it's possible that if we set off now, we might find them before they move on. Except... well, it appears that Mr. Riley is more paranoid than you might think."

One tapped command closed her office door. Another threw the imagery she'd spent the last few hours glaring at up onto the main wallscreen.

Beck studied the imagery of the antimatter explosion with scant favor.

"Delayed-detonation warhead to cover their tracks?" he asked after a few seconds. "Picked up through the Star Mirror?"

"Leavitt and Uesugi confirmed it two hours ago," she agreed. "Uesugi says they can *probably* track through it, but it will take them longer. A lot longer."

"Forgive me, sir, but wouldn't that mean we should get going faster?" Beck asked.

Roslyn sighed, wiping away the explosion with a touch on the desk controls. She looked past her XO to the light sculptures on the shelf behind him. They weren't the ones she'd acquired aboard her first command, *Voice of the Forgotten*, but that was actually fine by her.

All of them were from the same artist, a young woman who had been in the Tau Ceti Landing City Juvenile Detention Center alongside Roslyn. The other ex-delinquent had done decently by herself, but Roslyn was perfectly happy to spend her entire office-decorating budget with an old friend each time.

Navy service paid both better and more reliably than being an independent sculptor, after all.

"Chasing a thing is rarely the right way to catch it," she finally told Beck. "Look at the light sculptures. You could follow the light, couldn't you? Find the emitter. Find all of the lasers, work out how the piece was created.

"But could you duplicate it? Even with all of the *technical* knowledge of how it's built?"

Beck shifted the chair, his coffee in hand as he turned to study the pieces. He was silent for half a minute, then chuckled.

"I can see how the visual is created," he said slowly. "I *can't* see how that piece on the end, for example, both shows me a fox *and* makes me feel generally calmer. I might be able to duplicate it—the technical knowledge, as you say—but I'm not convinced I could repeat that effect.

"And I know I couldn't make a *different* version of it—and I see three foxes, a badger and what I think is an RMN destroyer on that shelf alone."

"It is a destroyer," Roslyn confirmed. "Alexis and I were teenagers together, long ago. I bought art from her for *Voice of the Forgotten*'s Captain's office, but that didn't survive *Voice*'s loss."

Voice hadn't been *destroyed* in action, but she'd been battered into a useless wreck the Navy had scrapped rather than repair. The Captain's office had been lost in the process, vaporized in its entirety by a First Legion battle laser.

"Alexis made the piece of *Voice of the Forgotten* as a gift and would not take a penny from me for it," Roslyn concluded. "I'm sure the cost was lost in her margin on what I *did* pay for, but I was still touched."

Beck chuckled, eyeing the destroyer.

"It's *supposed* to make me fierce and energized, isn't it?" he asked.

"Yes," she confirmed. "Like any art, the effect depends on the viewer, but that's the *intent*."

"I'm still not sure I follow your point with *Rose*, though," he admitted.

"We can follow her," Roslyn said. "We can duplicate everything she does—and, in the main, we can move faster than she does and *probably* catch up. But I don't know if we can catch up before she reaches what's left of the Reezh Ida."

"But if we know the *goal*, we can beat her there?" Beck asked.

"Exactly. Unfortunately, the longer I wait for them to decide to *tell* me what I want to know, the more it looks like we *should* have gone with the slow and ugly tracking method." She sighed. "But there is more in play than just catching *Rose*, too. That's the main mission, but they did a lot of damage here in Chimera.

"Every hour we are here and quiet and friendly buys a small but measurable amount of trust with the Dual Republics. I am *hoping* that trust will get us the information we need to chase *Rose* and bring Riley to bay.

"But earning that trust is a worthy endeavor in itself."

"And if the effort costs us *Rose*?"

"It won't." She smiled sadly. "Uesugi and I are going to sit down and confirm numbers in an hour or so, but we still have time to track her. We *will* go after her before we run out that clock.

"I just... have the feeling that there are more secrets here than the ones we've asked about, and the more of them we *know*, the better off we'll be when we go after Riley. Nemesis is operating on assumptions and fanaticism.

"*We* will operate on truth and fact."

"What happens if we don't intercept *Rose* in time?" Beck asked softly.

"Best-case scenario, they do a perfect stealth scouting of the Nine and learn everything they want to know about the reezh," Roslyn said. "They bring that back, we thank them prettily for their intelligence and then arrest them all for their crimes."

Beck looked... uncomfortable at the thought, but it *was* the best result.

"From everything I have seen and read, I suspect they have no idea how to fully operate the stealth systems of their ship," he pointed out. "And we know very little of what the Nine will have for defenses and security.

"What does the *worst* case look like?"

"Kent Riley and *Rose* awaken a sleeping giant and fill it with a terrible hunger."

Baars was replacing the coffee carafe when the coms staff told Roslyn she had a live transmission from *Chimera*.

Hoping for good news, Roslyn waved her steward out of the view of the pickup and accepted Wang's call.

"Mage-Captain Chambers."

"Admiral Wang. How may I assist?"

Wang chuckled.

"Said so helpfully, as if you hadn't spent the last three days yelling at a wall for my politicians to make up their minds," he said.

"Politicians are politicians, Admiral," Roslyn replied. "And your people are in a strange situation, one aggravated by a man that I can *say* wasn't one of us but wore our uniform and commanded one of our ships."

She shrugged.

"The situation is not simple. There are limits on how long I can wait, but your people have the right to make up their own minds."

"Would I be correct, Mage-Captain, in assuming that you've spent some time in the company of Damien Montgomery beyond our conversation the other day?" Wang asked.

"I entered the RMN Academy on his direct personal recommendation, sir, so yes, you can say that," Roslyn told him. "I hope that's a *good* thing."

"Maybe. You just sounded rather disturbingly familiar," Wang said drily. "Regardless, I hope your patience will stretch a few more hours. I have been asked to invite you and a senior officer of your choice—feel free to bring Commander Beck again—back aboard *Chimera* for dinner this evening.

"Eighteen hundred Twin Sphinx time."

"And dinner will answer my questions?" Roslyn asked, her tone equally desert-like.

"I am merely providing the dining room and cook," the Admiral told her. "Your *hosts*, Mage-Captain Chambers, will be the Dyad Ministers of the Dual Republics of Chimera. The leaders of my new government are inviting you to dinner on my ship."

"I see," she allowed. She supposed she couldn't blame the locals for not wanting to let anyone *else* in the uniform of an RMN Mage-Captain down to the surface after what Riley had done. "I would lean toward accepting your invitation anyway, Admiral, but I appreciate the context."

"Good. I dislike having control of even small parts of my ships taken away from me, Captain Chambers, and all I have been informed about the guest list *beyond* the obvious is that the *Ministers are bringing guests.*"

That... struck her as a security risk, though she supposed heads of state could get away with giving those instructions to mere military commanders in chief.

If it was important.

"You and your Ministers have piqued my curiosity," she admitted. "Is eighteen hundred the time of the meal or when I should have myself and Commander Beck delivered?"

"The latter, Mage-Captain. I look forward to having you aboard *Chimera* again—and, I hope, to making certain that you and I remain on the same side in any future... difficulties."

CHAPTER 33

WHILE ROSLYN HAD SEEN multiple reezh on video feeds and even seen a handful in person the first time she'd been aboard *Chimera*, Dyad Minister Izhaj Ojak was the first reezh she'd actually *met*.

Ojak was slightly taller than she was, with strange double-jointed limbs that swung into angles utterly impossible for a human. His head resembled a guitar pick to her, with a broad armored frill at the top narrowing down to his shoulders. A pair of horns guarded the Minister's large upper eyes, with a smaller lower pair shielded by a seemingly armored brow ridge.

He had rough gray skin with an almost pebbled texture, but his *smile* was close enough to human to reassure Roslyn as the reezh politician bowed to her.

"We appreciate your patience," Ojak told her. "Minister Hsieh, for one, was far less tolerant of our discussions than you were."

"I am an outsider," Roslyn said, glancing over at the towering Asian woman. While Roslyn tried not to be *vain* about her appearance, she knew she was a very attractive woman.

But Hsieh Ai Ling made her feel dowdy and dull in her plain black-and-gold uniform. Expertly done near-black makeup drew attention to the Minister's blue-black hair and deep, soulful eyes.

Eyes that *Roslyn*, at least, realized were spending noticeably longer on Emerson Wang than on anyone else. It might have been her generally over-tuned hormones—the solitude and celibacy required of a starship captain were physically *painful* for Roslyn at times—but it seemed the Dyad Minister appreciated their Chief Naval Officer for more than his ships.

"I am not an outsider, so discovering the depths of the secrets my counterpart was concealing was a rather unpleasant surprise," Hsieh observed. "I knew there were *some* things that the reezh hadn't been transparent about, but this has been a week of rude awakenings for all of us."

"The decisions around what was hidden and from whom were never mine," Ojak noted, his English precise despite his voice sounding like he was gargling gravel. "In truth, even *I* was unaware of much of what has been dragged into the light by Riley's attack."

"Forgive me, Ministers, but I believe I am missing much of this conversation," Roslyn told them. "I suspect that a briefing is planned? If so, then I don't believe any recriminations are necessary.

"If the weight of history here is anything like what hangs over Mars, I doubt the decision to share it was easy. It has taken what it has taken—let us move forward."

"Well spoken, Mage-Captain," Wang agreed. "If we have decided to give Captain Chambers what she needs, that is enough. I hope.

"Shall we go find our meal?"

The dinner guests were sparser than Roslyn had expected. She had brought Beck, as instructed. Wang had brought Commodore Falkenrath, *Chimera*'s commander. Roslyn assumed that Cam and Ty, the ship's Prometheans, were eavesdropping.

But that was it for the military part of the dinner. Four visible and two invisible members of the party. The civilian side was only *five*—the two Dyad Ministers, a human and a reezh that both radiated *historian*—and a third reezh whose gray skin had faded to the shades of white marble.

Unless Roslyn was misreading the signs, that reezh was *ancient*.

All of them were brought into a small formal dining room in what Roslyn figured were the diplomatic sections of the ship. Like most capital ships, RIN carriers were designed to show the flag and carry out all kinds of secondary duties—such as formal state dinners.

The decorations had clearly been swapped out since *Chimera* had been a Republic of Faith and Reason warship. The table was standard military-issue beneath its delicate white tablecloth, and whatever the original decorations had been, they'd been replaced with a large seal of the Dual Republics on each wall, flanked by heavy blue curtains that helped conceal the stewards' entrance.

"Introductions are in order," Hsieh announced as the doors closed behind the stewards. "I assume Mage-Captain Chambers knows of myself and Minister Ojak, but the Dyad Curators and our... other guest are less well known."

"Myself and Commander Matthias Beck are known to you in turn," Roslyn agreed. "The Curators?"

"Much of the Dual Republics is anchored on the system of the Dyad," Minister Ojak told her. He and the other two reezh had seats that resembled more stools with a supporting pole than chairs to Roslyn's eyes, with the Minister between the two older reezh.

"Where the Republics act as one, it serves us well that one of each species is involved in the decision. There are an Eastern and a Western Dyad Minister to serve as heads of state." The reezh half of that Dyad gestured to the two historians.

"There are an Eastern and a Western Dyad Curator to manage the Joint Museum, the central archive and historical education facility of our entire world," Ojak concluded. "Eastern Dyad Curator Drusa Sciarra manages the part of the Museum that covers human history. Western Dyad Curator Oj manages the reezh portion of the Museum."

"A portion that apparently includes secret archives inside the radiation dome the Museum was built on," Hsieh said, her tone acidic.

"Forgive me, Minister," Sciarra said quietly, the old woman sounding tired. "I and the Eastern Dyad Curators before me have *always* been aware of the archives in the containment dome of the Last Ship.

"While I was never fully privy to their contents, I agreed—as did my predecessors—that the reezh were entitled to decide what of their history was shared with us."

The Dyad Minister sighed and nodded, glancing over at Chambers as if to apologize with her eyes.

"This is fair, I suppose, until that history comes back to bite us all in sensitive places," Hsieh pointed out.

"And that is why I am here," the last reezh, the one with skin faded to white marble, said in the softest voice Roslyn had heard from a reezh yet. Even in the recordings and video she'd reviewed, reezh tended to sound like they had a throatful of gravel.

The old reezh still sounded distorted, but much of the sharpness seemed to have been ground away.

"The Dyad Curators, of course, are known to all the Chimeran members of this party," the stranger continued. "I... am not."

She turned her head slightly to focus on Roslyn, the gesture confusing for a moment until Roslyn realized that the stranger's left upper eye was dull and clouded. It was hard to tell with the gem-like multifaceted upper eyes, but she had the distinct impression the stranger was blind in at least one of their four eyes.

"I am the Reezh Ida Lachai," the reezh intoned. "My *name* is Razhkah and I am a Warden of the Astral."

Roslyn could *guess* what that meant, though she didn't know for sure. What she *did* know was that she could see Emerson Wang, and the Admiral looked absolutely stunned.

"We were told there were no Mages left on Garuda," he murmured.

"We lied," Razhkah said flatly. "To be clear, Admiral Wang, we lied to many people. When you arrived, I was the last and we *knew* I would be the last. Except..."

She raised a strange four-digited hand before Wang could continue.

"What followed from your arrival, I suppose, is relevant to why I am here," she said quietly. "The Reezh Ida Lachai is the Historian of the Empire of the True People."

Roslyn couldn't read the reezh expressions, but Sciarra's face suggested that was a *far* more precise and impolitic translation than the Dyad Curator would prefer.

"It was my duty—the duty of my predecessors and of the apprentices I have trained—to preserve the history of the Reezh Ida," Razhkah told them all. "To keep the secrets of the shadows and horrors we could not even admit to ourselves. To *remember*, so that when the time came, we could *warn*."

Roslyn leaned back, studying the ancient reezh.

"We had a similar group on Mars," she noted. "You will forgive my hesitancy, I hope, if I note that *Nemesis* was born of that group—and that Kent Riley, specifically, was a member of our Keepers of Oaths and Secrets."

"It is an issue," the Lachai confirmed. "But if a secret is never to be needed, it does not need to be preserved. We are tasked not only to keep our secrets *safe* but to judge when they must *cease* to be secrets.

"Do you understand, Mage-Captain?" She looked around at her own government, clearly tracking with her one working upper eye. "My Ministers?"

"I was... displeased to discover the depths of the reezh's secrecy," Hsieh admitted. "We accepted that there were secrets that each of us would keep, but it is easy to believe that you feared our ancestors would never work with you if the truth was told."

"That is exactly what our ancestors feared," Razhkah replied. "And so, the secrets were kept, even from many of our own people." She gestured at Oj, the museum curator's body language almost readable even across the species barrier.

Roslyn wasn't sure, but she suspected Oj was *pissed*.

"Curator Oj will need to rewrite several key theses of their career, I am afraid, and I apologize for the deceptions," Razhkah told them. "But we are here, and the data cores of the Last Ship have been stolen by someone who will seek the Kazh—the Church of the Nine.

"The time to give up our secrets is now. I beg your patience and I hope the food is pleasant. This may well resemble a lecture."

CHAPTER 34

IT WASN'T ENTIRELY clear to Roslyn how much of all of this Wang had known about in advance. It seemed that Lachai Razhkah was as much bringing many of her own people—human and reezh alike, for that matter!—up to speed as she was briefing Roslyn.

However much Wang had known, the dinner was well set up for Razhkah to present while her audience was fed by the stewards. The reezh waited for the appetizers to be served and then stepped up to the head of the table.

The spring rolls might *look* the same on both sides of the table, but Roslyn suspected she didn't want to try the ones served to the reezh. Presumably, there were enough food compatibilities for two species to live off the same crops, but she wasn't going to assume they had the same *taste buds*.

"I will begin near the end," Razhkah told them, gesturing vaguely with a half-eaten spring roll of her own. "The arrival of Admiral Wang's ships and their Prometheans. Everyone was *told* we had no concept of any such thing.

"This, as Riley guessed and I imagine Mage-Captain Chambers suspects, was a lie."

Roslyn could see Wang's thunderous expression out of the corner of her eye. She doubted there would be much in terms of *consequences* for the deception, but the Admiral was clearly unhappy.

"We knew it as the Engine of Sacred Sacrifice," the secret keeper explained. "It was both the key to the wave of expansion that created the outer worlds of the Reezh Ida and the fracture point that destroyed it.

"The Kazh controlled all Mages of our people. All Wardens of the Astral, Guides of the Astral... All with the Gifts of the Astral were required to be members of the priesthood and to have children.

"This sustained our Gifted population, but it limited the Kazh in how widely we could spread and how much we could achieve. Until they discovered that they could detect the ability to *channel* the Astral in non-Mage portions of the population."

Razhkah was silent for a few moments. Roslyn held her tongue—she could guess where this was going, and it *terrified* her.

"Admiral Wang and his people, of course, knew that their Prometheans were murdered Mages," Razhkah said softly. "*We did not*. With a limited number of Astrally Gifted, all of them serving as a religious caste, expanding our interstellar travel seemed... worthy of sacrifice."

"So, the Ida looked for these *channelers* and made them into Sacrifices?" Wang asked, his voice sounding vaguely ill.

"Yes. And the demand for this tribute spawned the civil war and the Burning of Worlds," Razhkah confirmed. "Thankfully, the capacity to *duplicate* the Engines of Sacred Sacrifice was not available to Allosch prior to humanity's arrival and the transition to Chimera.

"We *did* possess the ability to detect channelers, but like the Reezh Ida, we did not know we were finding Mages.

"The arrival of Admiral Wang and the truth of his Promethean Interfaces laid bare the tragedy of the Reezh Ida. The *mistake* that damned our people, destroyed the Reezh Ida itself, and led to the Burning.

"The Reezh Ida could detect Mages, but either by error or sheer elitist blindness, they did not *realize* that was what they were doing."

"The Mages were... a closed caste, basically?" Roslyn asked. "The concept of a Mage *not* being of the priesthoods and the associated families wouldn't even occur to them."

That was *exactly* the fear that had spawned the UnArcana Worlds among humanity, she knew. The Compact, established at the end of the Eugenics Wars by a *very* traumatized bunch of Mages who'd just broken free of being basically *breeding stock*, guaranteed a great deal of protection and power in exchange for the Mages providing interstellar travel.

Large parts of that had been rolled back in the new Constitution. Even before that, much of it had been kept under control by *fear* of a closed caste—but also by the regular infusions of Mages by Right, the Mages found by the regular Royal Tests.

An infusion the Astrally Gifted of the Reezh Ida had never even accepted was possible.

"And in their blindness, they destroyed everything our people had built," Razhkah agreed. "When I learned about the Prometheus Interface, I arranged for the one scanner we had to be dug up. A volunteer class of university students were put through it—I will confess to deceiving them. They had no concept of the blood that soaked the arcane artifice they were subjected to.

"Two of those students registered as Channelers of the Astral. One, when I told her everything, very nearly called the police on me," Razhkah said with a sound of rattling rocks Roslyn took for a chuckle.

"The other became my student. She was trained and armed as a Warden of the Astral... and your Kent Riley murdered her when she sought to protect the Last Ship."

Roslyn exhaled sharply.

"Kent Riley is an unusually powerful Mage," she murmured. "Fully trained in every form of mundane and magical combat, he was an elite special forces Marine officer *before* he became the leader of Nemesis.

"I am not certain many of our own combat Mages could stand against him."

That was, after all, one of the reasons Roslyn had a Rune of Power. They'd known they were going to come up against Kent Riley, and they had *no idea* what the man had for magical augmentation at this point.

"My apprentice, who had not yet completed the training I—who was never fully trained—could give her... stood no chance," Razhkah said stonily.

Roslyn looked down at her empty plate, crumbs of the spring rolls still visible but offering no alternative for meeting the old reezh Mage's gaze.

"Do you know what Riley was able to steal?" she finally asked.

"We had maintained the central quantum data core of the Last Ship," Oj explained. "Ida-era quantum cores required continuous power for proper data storage. Through the nature of the ship's power draw and careful effort on our part, we kept that power up for the time the ship has been down there.

"Riley and his people teleported the entire data core aboard their ship." The Dyad Curator snapped his teeth together in an unpleasant sound. "I presume that they spent time researching the technological-reconstruction hobbyists and had a receptacle waiting that would allow them to power and access the core."

"Access to the Last Ship's core was restricted to the Lachai and people approved by them," Razhkah added. "It would have given them the details of what I have just explained. They would now understand the tragedy of the Reezh Ida." She hesitated.

"Would that turn them aside from a course of danger?"

"No," Roslyn told the Lachai softly. "It would only make them more determined. What is this *Last Ship* and why would its data core be important?"

"It is... roughly what the name implies," Oj told her. "The last ship to ever visit Allosch from the Reezh Ida. It is physically an Ida tribute ship, but it was in the hands of pirates when it arrived here.

"Our ancestors refused to yield the gold, iron, bodies and minds they demanded." The curator repeated the snapping sound. "From Razhkah's secrets, I presume they wanted channelers to fuel Engines of Sacred Sacrifice aboard their ships—but they didn't serve the Nine."

"The scanner I used to find my apprentice was from the Last Ship," Razhkah explained. "So yes, it had all the tools of a tribute ship. It also, I must note, did *not* have an Engine of Sacred Sacrifice. It was brought to Allosch—Chimera—by a Guide of the Astral."

"But a tribute ship would have been expected to deliver certain key supplies and technological components to allow our tech base to continue functioning," Oj observed. "Our ancestors stormed the ship to steal those supplies, only to find them missing."

"And to find that the ship was running an unusual power array," Razhkah noted. "A phased uranium oxide fission sequence system, quite effective but also quite unstable."

"Our ancestors had no idea how to operate the system properly, which resulted in an uncontained meltdown within a Garudan year of seizing the ship," the museum curator concluded. "Hence the containment domes and the difficulty reaching and using the Last Ship's data core."

"The radiation leakage from Riley's attack has been secured now?" Roslyn asked quietly. "I know Lord Montgomery promised any aid we could provide, but I have not received any requests."

"At this moment, Mage-Captain, our *request* is that your people do not set foot on our planet," Hsieh said quietly. "We do not require the Protectorate's assistance at this time, and our previous visitor has left our trust... strained."

"Fair, I suppose," Roslyn allowed. The main course arrived before she could say anything else, and she waited for the plates of a strange-looking pasta to be laid on the table before she continued.

"Beyond *what happened to the Reezh Ida*, what is Riley likely to have learned?" she asked. "He will be looking for a threat he can use to justify his actions. I don't know what logic chain he is proceeding down, but the man is a criminal who helped trigger a civil war in the Protectorate because of fear of the reezh."

That, it seemed, was a step further than anyone had put together there.

"Riley's faction created the Prometheus Interfaces, Admiral Wang," she told the Republic officer. "They supplied the technology to the conspiracies and system militaries that became the Republic."

There'd been a Rune Wright involved, too, but *that* was a complicating factor she wasn't revealing just yet.

"Their goal was to prepare humanity for the war with the Reejit—the reezh—that they believed was coming," she continued. "But as Kent Riley has run ahead of us, each step will have shown him that the reezh are no threat. That everything he has done has been for nothing."

Oj and Razhkah exchanged a long look, one that she would have taken for a silent conversation in humans. With reezh... she *still* took it for the two historians and secret keepers silently exchanging opinions.

"He will find the Kazh—the church that ruled the Ida—the Nine and the Primes," Razhkah said quietly. "In them he will find his threat and he will not be wrong."

"The Nine and the Primes are...?" Roslyn prodded.

"The Nine is our home system," Razhkah told her. "Nine worlds, each named for one of our ancient gods. Ruled by the Kazh, the Church of the Nine, and their holy Workers of the Astral. They had not changed in a thousand of your years, Mage-Captain, and I doubt they have changed much in the last two hundred.

"But they will have spent those two hundred years pointing spears at the Primes and the reverse. *Those* are the eleven closest colonies, systems inhabited by the reezh for over a hundred and twenty Garudan years."

Roslyn did the math. Five hundred years, give or take a few decades. Those colonies had existed since before humanity had *any* kind of space travel.

"I have seen what was the Ida," she said slowly. "Wouldn't the Nine and Primes have suffered a similar fate?"

"No. None of our kind would raise that kind of blade against the Nine," Razhkah told her. "Even if we could—and the Primes will have been unable to, just as the Nine would be unable to rain fire upon them.

"The Nine and Primes are all guarded by the Mountains of Astral Might."

Roslyn swallowed hard as she processed what *that* meant.

"Planetary amplifiers," she said slowly. "Like those on a starship, but on a vastly greater scale?"

"I am not entirely familiar with those terms," Razhkah admitted. "But it sounds likely. The Mountains of Astral Might are fortifications from which the High Chosen can unleash magic across their entire star system.

"So long as one of the Nine and Primes has a *single* Mage able to stand in the Chosen's place, no mundane armada will challenge that power."

Roslyn wasn't sure about the full capabilities of the Olympus Mons Amplifier. What humanity *knew* about it was classified to a level she didn't have access to—and she knew enough to know that humanity's knowledge of it was patchy at best.

"So, regardless of where he is going, he is going to sail his ship into a system with a planetary amplifier," she observed softly. "I don't suppose we can hope that the Kazh, for example, is likely to be unable or unwilling to respond to that provocation?"

"I have never, in any of the records I have seen here on Chimera or aboard the Last Ship, seen any reference to your species prior to the Founding Expedition's arrival here," Razhkah noted. "I do not believe the Kazh know you exist."

"Something that Riley is about to fix," Roslyn said grimly.

"It is impossible for us to predict the status of the Nine and Primes at this point," the reezh historian told her. "It has been over fifty Garudan years since the Last Ship arrived, and we can hardly regard a *pirate* ship as a useful source of information on the status of the core governments of the reezh.

"At that time, it appeared that the Nine and Primes had fractured into three factions," Razhkah continued. "The Kazh itself continued to control the Nine and roughly a third of the Primes. A second faction remained aligned to the concepts, at least, of the rebellion that led to the Burning. The third, at least two systems from what I can tell, just wanted the fighting and the violence to *end*. Given their control of a Mountain of Astral Might, they were in a position to declare neutrality and protect it.

"While I cannot see a way for the situation to have changed significantly, we are talking about almost two hundred of your years," the reezh concluded. "We cannot predict the situation now."

"Fair. But... that doesn't actually answer my question," Roslyn noted. "Will they be able to do anything upon learning of our existence... and *what* are they likely to do?"

"It is likely that the Kazh maintains a fleet sufficient to take any of the Primes by storm if they cease to be able to operate their Mountain of Astral Might," Razhkah said quietly. "Their largest limitation, of course, will be the Guides of the Astral and their ability to source channelers for the Engines of Sacred Sacrifice.

"It is... possible they may see your people as a solution to the latter problem."

Roslyn didn't bother to conceal her distaste at that concept.

"Which is exactly what my people believe led to the reezh presence in human space to begin with," she warned. "If they have that much firepower, we need to make sure Riley doesn't find them."

She laid her fork aside and leaned forward to focus on Razhkah.

"Which means I need you to give me the information Riley stole," she told the reezh equivalent of the Keepers. "He will, by nature, go for the most certain target. He will go for the Nine, and I need to beat him there."

Ojak started to open his mouth but stopped as Razhkah held up her hand again.

"It was my duty and my oath to *preserve* all of this information," she told them. "To keep these secrets until the time where they must be revealed.

"This is that time."

The four words hung in the air.

"I ask, Mage-Captain Chambers, that you share all you have learned tonight with your Queen and your government," Razhkah said. "Unless the Dyad Ministers see some barrier I do not, I will provide all of the maps and other information I have on the Nine and Primes, that you may proceed intentionally instead of making errors as Kent Riley has."

"I do not see a *barrier,* but I do feel that perhaps some trade should be made," Ojak said slowly. "What can the Protectorate offer that is of value to Chimera?"

"That is obvious, Minister, is it not?" Razhkah said, making the harsh snapping noise Oj had made before. "You can detect Mages, yes? Our device for detecting Channelers is old, failing and... well, quite large. We also have no one capable of *training* Mages.

"Send us teachers. Let the students I never knew I could have learn from Mages who know better than I ever did. Share your knowledge, as we have shared ours."

Roslyn smiled and inclined her head.

"I have a limited authority to commit the Protectorate," she said. "It is more than sufficient to promise that, Ministers, Curators, Lachai, Admiral. If Chimera wishes us to send the Royal Testers and a team of Mage-teachers, it may take some time to arrange... but I have no worries committing the word of the Mage-Queen of Mars that it *will* happen."

It meant something *very* specific for an officer of the Royal Martian Navy to commit the word of the Mage-Queen. She saw in his body language that Admiral *Wang* certainly knew that.

Roslyn's word as an officer was one thing. That was an oath *she* could not break.

But committing the word of the Mage-Queen of Mars meant exactly what it sounded like. She was binding *Kiera Alexander* to keep that promise—an oath an officer would only swear if they were either very desperate or *very* certain that what they were offering was in the best interests of Mars.

It was not a promise lightly made—because the Mage-Queen *would* keep it.

CHAPTER 35

ONE OF THE ADVANTAGES of the Royal Martian Navy using Olympus Mons Standard Time was that Roslyn knew it was just as late in the day for Kiera Alexander as it was for her. Still, the Mountain's communication staff had managed to make a connection with the Mage-Queen on short notice.

Alexander was still in her office, the massive wood-paneled room that opened out onto the upper slopes of Olympus Mons. Roslyn wasn't entirely sure on the *security* of that, though she suspected the Royal Guard had their eyes on all aspects of it... and the fact that the upper slopes of Olympus Mons didn't have *air* probably helped.

"I also asked to link in the Prince-Chancellor," Roslyn told Kiera when she realized it was just the two of them. "This seemed like an affair that required you both."

"Damien is currently on the most romantic tropical island I could find in the star system with his wife—with his communications kept under lock and key by the Royal Guard," Alexander said brightly. "*I am the only person who gets to decide if his vacation time is being interrupted, and I don't see a hostile fleet in the Solar System.*"

"I... see," Roslyn allowed. She certainly wasn't going to argue with the Mage-Queen imposing vacation time on the Protectorate's head of state. She had a... rather distinct impression of Damien Montgomery's willingness to take vacation unless sat on by his wife.

It was somewhere *below* zero.

"Unfortunately, while my news isn't of a hostile fleet in the Solar System, it may be attached to a *risk* of that," she continued grimly. "Thanks to the situation Kent Riley has created, the Chimeran equivalent of our Keepers apparently decided to do the part of the job *our* Keepers never did:

"Come clean and tell everyone what they know."

Kiera's expression swung between pleased, surprised and sad for a few seconds before settling on grief.

"God, so many people would be alive now if the *idiots* had done that twenty years ago," she half-whispered.

"I know." Roslyn sighed. "Or, I guess? I can only estimate, looking at what I know. Your *aunt* might actually be the best equipped to judge that."

Admiral Crown Princess Jane Alexander had spent said twenty years as a senior naval officer *with* full Royal Family security clearances. Roslyn didn't think there was anyone else who had as much high-level information combined with personal experience of the last twenty years of the Protectorate's military buildup against, shadow war with and *real* war with the Republic.

"I assume there's a report, but you also think this is important. High level?" Alexander asked.

That was, after all, why Roslyn had arranged a live connection across two hundred and fifty light-years to have this conversation.

"Basically, as we suspected, the reezh used a form of the Prometheus Interface," Roslyn said. "But they never officially recognized that the people they were putting in it were Mages."

"Officially?" Alexander prodded.

"The historians I spoke to here in Chimera said they'd never realized," Roslyn replied. "One of them put the pieces together reading the reports on the Prometheus Interface and called it *the Tragedy of the Reezh Ida*. But the structure of the Ida and the Kazh—its central governing body—looks like *exactly* the kind of ugly caste system that might just decide that Mages outside it are better turned into fuel cells than brought inside the ruling caste."

The Queen's expression grew colder and colder, suggesting she *very* much followed Roslyn's thoughts.

"Like we might have become, without the Royal Testers and without having the UnArcana Worlds warning about the price of going too far," she said grimly.

"Exactly." Roslyn shook her head. "The fundamental issue we face right now is that the priests and Mages of the Kazh remain in control of the Nine. Or, at least, they did two hundred years ago... and they had a planetary amplifier to make *sure* they stayed in control."

"So did every one of the major reezh colonies they call the Primes."

The channel was quiet for long enough that Roslyn worried there'd been some kind of technical glitch, before Kiera Alexander finally just swore in an absolutely exhausted tone.

"Okay." The Mage-Queen of Mars raised her head to meet her Captain's eyes, then waved a finger at her in a vague imitation of a knighting ceremony.

"Congratulations; you now have Titan Clearance. Make sure to talk to my staff before you end the call and have them send you the Tartarus File. It's everything we *know* about the Mountain.

"You're already cleared for the biggest part: we need a Rune Wright to use the Mountain. The rest is... uglier, given this context."

"Your Majesty?" Roslyn asked.

"The reason we need a Rune Wright is because the amplifier wasn't built for humans, Roslyn. *Any* reezh Mage could walk into the throne room of Olympus Mons and do what I can do, because the damn thing is built for them.

"So, wherever Riley is going, he's going to arrive in a system with a local omnipotent deity that is *not* going to tolerate peeking around the corners, Kiera. We can't even *duplicate* the damn thing—personally, I think the reezh intentionally buried some chunks of the matrix inside collapsed tunnels so that we would never have a full schematic to work from."

"I don't suppose we can hope this *Kazh* has mellowed over the last two centuries?"

"The locals don't think it's likely," Roslyn warned. "Their estimate is that the Kazh has spent the time since their last contact with them in a cold war with at least half of the Primes. All of them have planetary amplifiers, all of them have the ability to produce Prometheus Interface equivalents and all of them have Mages.

"They are basically waiting for one of the star systems to run out of Mages to run the amplifiers. Building their fleets. Preparing for war with each other. And Riley is about to sail into that. The only hope I really see is that *Rose* is a stealth ship."

Alexander's grim expression told Roslyn the problem even before the Mage-Queen shook her head.

"We've tested it. The Amplifier allows me to track any ship in this star system, Roslyn. Including the MISS stealth ships, which are both *smaller* and somewhat more invisible than the *Thorns*."

Everything the cruisers had for stealth had been built and tested for the MISS ships—but *those* ships had been the size of couriers or fast packets. Less than a million tons' displacement, a couple hundred meters long.

Compared to *Thorn's* fifteen million tons and half-kilometer height, the MISS ships were toys. It wasn't practical to put the same density of stealth systems on the cruisers as the stealth ships had carried—and even if it *had* been, the sheer size would have made them harder to hide.

"My belief is that Riley is going to go for the heart," Roslyn told her Queen. "He *needs* to find something to prove that everything Nemesis did was justified. He's going to head to the Nine—one hundred eighty-two light-years and eleven days' travel for *Thorn* from here.

"He has fewer Mages but a head start of unknown size. He had to decrypt and translate the maps, where we were handed versions already transferred into measures and iconography we know.

"Unless you have different orders for me, Your Majesty, I intend to take *Thorn* to the Nine and use the Star Mirror to watch for *Rose's* arrival. I will do everything in my power to prevent him from provoking the Kazh or even, if possible, revealing our existence to them."

"Those were your orders," Alexander confirmed. "I see no reason to change them now, Mage-Captain. Make sure you get the Tartarus File from my people and make sure you send us all of the information the locals provide you on the Kazh and the Reezh Ida.

"Whatever happens in the Nine, I do not think the Protectorate will be able to ignore the Kazh. In Chimera, I hope to find a friend for our nation—and I *hope* we can at least talk the Kazh to neutrality."

"And if the Kazh and their enemies alike both see us as a resource to be exploited?" Roslyn asked quietly.

"I am the Protector of Humanity, and the Royal Martian Navy is my shield," Kiera Alexander said calmly. "They may try. They will not succeed."

CHAPTER 36

"THIS IS IT, PEOPLE," Kay told the gathering. The clock was ticking, and all of his key people had gathered for what would be the last time before they entered the reezh home system.

"We've gone over *Rose*'s weapons system as best as we can," Koskinen told them all. "I don't know what we'll be facing—none of us do—but we'll have all of our weapons.

"At least to start." He grimaced. "I don't have enough people to man every launcher and laser. We can fire everything from the bridge, but the moment there are problems, someone needs to be there to fix them."

"I thought we were hoping *not* to fight?" Tomas asked, the Ship's Mage looking concerned. "I have spent a great deal of time studying the magic used to augment *Rose*'s stealth systems. I do believe we can hide her."

"That is the plan, yes," Kay agreed. "But we know far too little about the capabilities of the Kazh. The Nine is their home system, and they've been space travelers for far longer than humanity.

"It is possible they can pierce our cloak of invisibility. We will be ready to fight and I will be ready to carry us to safety." He smiled. "We're going to be fine, people. We're going to pull this off."

"Császár is ready to jump us on your order," Tomas conceded, her tone grim. "I will have the invisibility spell ready to go. I may be able to jump us out, even having held that, but..."

"We won't take the risk unless we have to," Kay told her. "That is why we have waited this long, so that every Mage on the ship is ready to jump and we have *options*."

Császár would jump them into the Nine. Tomas would run the invisibility spell while Kay commanded the ship—but if the reezh spotted them, Kay would take over to teleport them to safety.

"I have people positioned at key spots throughout the ship," Chaudhary told them. "I'm expecting to serve more as relays and scouts for damage control than anything else, but we're trained for that."

Kay nodded to the commando. His people weren't *as* well trained for that as Royal Marines would be—or, at least, as freshly trained. The Marines stayed on top of that training, where his commandos had different focuses.

"What about the rest of *Rose*'s systems? O'Shea?"

He glanced over at his lover. He had to suppress a smile just at the *sight* of the woman—what was *wrong* with him? O'Shea, for her part, was studying her wrist-comp projection as she always did.

"I have gone through every component of the stealth systems aboard this cruiser," she said carefully. "While I am comfortable that I understand each of them and how they work, I have to warn that I don't believe my *people* are as comfortable.

"This system is complex and fragile—and is managing immense amounts of heat and energy to prevent our detection. As with Commander Koskinen's weaponry, I can guarantee that it will work to start.

"I cannot promise that it will continue to function at full efficiency for long. I will keep it *operating*, but even with perfect crews and perfect understanding, the effectiveness of the system would degrade over time.

"It will degrade faster for us."

"If we stay at a minimum light-minute distance from any sensors, how long will we have?" Kay asked her.

"I can't make guarantees," O'Shea warned. "It depends on how well the magic works and how good their sensors are. I would *estimate* that, at that kind of distance, we are probably safe for several hours."

"So, for the Nine, we'll stay on the safe side," Kay decided aloud. "We'll start with one hour, entering the system one light-minute above the ecliptic plane aligned with the Smith's orbit."

The Smith was the fourth planet, providing them horizontal as well as vertical separation from everywhere he was expecting activity.

"What are we seeing at this distance?" Tomas asked. "I feel like the science team must be busy."

"I'm not sure any of them have slept in the last two days," Koskinen said drily. "Which, given that most of them do double duty as my tactical analysis team, was an issue. I ordered them all to rest four hours ago. We'll wake them back up when we jump.

"But we've got a decent survey of the area around the Nine and the Nine itself. That's how the boss picked the Smith as our destination."

"Show them," Kay ordered. He'd seen the survey of the Nine and some of the high level of the rest.

"All right."

Koskinen didn't have his wrist-comp hooked up to the breakout room's systems, and grabbed a tablet to give instructions to the holographic projectors.

A moment after Kay gave the order, *Rose*'s current location—roughly nine trillion kilometers from the Nine's core star, whose name appeared to have been completely superseded by the description of the planets—appeared on an astrographic display.

"We are a touch over eleven light-months from the Nine," Koskinen observed. "Everything we are seeing of the reezh home system is eleven months out of date. Our information on the Primes ranges from about three to sixteen years out of date, depending on our closest approach, but that still lets us get *some* idea of what we're looking at."

The Nine was highlighted in a red-gold color that managed to be both ornate and ominous to Kay's eyes. Ten of the Primes were the regular red of "hostile systems"—and the eleventh was a red so dark as to be black.

"Most important, I suppose, is that there are no longer eleven Primes," Koskinen noted. "We haven't had time to go back over our data and establish the exact point where the final conflict happened, but our data on what should have been the Chozhar System is about eleven years old.

"Eleven years ago, there was no major technic civilization in Chozhar, nor did our scans suggest any inhabitable planets in the system. At some point between the records we acquired from Chimera and eleven years ago, the system was burned clean of life."

The silence that followed Koskinen's calm statement was predictable and cold. Again and again, the reezh had stretched to levels of genocide and massacre that humanity had, so far at least, avoided.

They *couldn't* let these monsters come upon an unprepared humanity.

"Outside of the missing Prime, the other ten are about what we expected," Koskinen eventually continued, gesturing to the red-highlighted stars. "Massive infrastructure and populations supporting immense fleets.

"We don't know enough to definitely estimate populations, but using the metrics for *humans*, we would estimate an average of about eleven *billion* reezh in each system. Exact strengths of fleets are difficult to assess— let alone the distinction between sublight and jump-capable ships—but..."

The former RMN officer shrugged.

"There are individual ships that can be clearly recognized at ranges of a dozen light-years," he concluded. "Their energy signatures are off the scale. I expected to be able to identify and estimate the strength of formations based off what we know of our ships and the wrecks in the Nemesis System.

"We were able to do that. But we also detected multiple vessels I can only call *megaships*. My guess is mobile asteroids refitted with antimatter engines, likely several kilometers long and carrying enough firepower to devastate a *fleet*."

"The good news is that I don't see *any* way one of those ships can jump," Kay reminded his people. "Tomas... you're the expert here. How large can a jump matrix be expanded?"

"So far as I know, the RMN's dreadnoughts actually represent the largest amplifier or jump matrices we have ever built," the Ship's Mage replied. "I've even heard rumors suggesting that they *aren't* a single amplifier and require perfectly synchronized jumps by two Mages."

"They don't," Kay said with a grim chuckle. "I know *that* much about them. So, the largest matrices *we've* built are a kilometer long and half a kilometer at their widest, carrying roughly a hundred million tons.

"These megaships vastly exceed that size and mass. I find it unlikely they can jump under their own power. They are more... monitors, massive system-defense ships for people who expect real war to be brought to their stars."

As opposed to the corvettes and gunships that tended to make up the *Protectorate*'s in-system sublight fleets, cheap ships more suited for high guard duties than actual war.

"They're all ready for war, is my guess," Koskinen warned. "I am seeing multiple major deployed formations throughout each star system. Civilian ships don't get lined up in groups *that* big with *that* much power generation.

"Only military formations on guard or ready to deploy do that."

A small expanded view of each of the Primes appeared, allowing Kay and the others to see the marked formations. Kay knew, better than the others, he suspected, just *how* immense a formation of ships had to be for it to be visible at this range, and the number of flagged formations was... concerning.

There were Prime Systems they hadn't passed close enough to for a really good look, but based off the ones they'd passed within five or six light-years of, *each* of the Prime Systems mustered a fleet of hundreds of warships.

It was possible—likely, even, given the information they had—that the majority of those ships lacked either Mages or Prometheans to move them between the stars.

But Kay suspected that the only system that had *no* ships capable of interstellar travel had been literally wiped out. Whatever the last couple of hundred years had looked like for the reezh, *peace* and *compromise* didn't seem to be on the agenda.

And these were the people who had intentionally bred up humans to be a new source of brains for their "Engines of Sacred Sacrifice." They'd waited for the numbers of humanity's Mages to expand, but the numbers were terrifying.

It would take the Mages from several star systems to provide enough brains to empower the entirety of one of the Primes' fleets. But the entire Royal Martian Navy was less than four hundred star ships—a force that *each* Prime system could match.

"The Nine, of course, are as far ahead of the Primes as Sol is ahead of our Core Systems," Koskinen said quietly. "We have a more solid concept of what we're looking at in the Nine, though even from eleven light-months, the resolution is limited."

The regional starmap vanished, replaced by a single nine-world star system.

"There is a major formation, accompanied by megaships and even less-mobile orbital fortresses, above the Builder. I have *confirmed* one hundred and twenty ships, each a minimum of a quarter of *Rose*'s size, in orbit of the Builder. My estimate is that we are looking at a similar number of smaller vessels as well, given the energy signatures."

The second planet flashed.

"Planet two, the Father, is an in-system hot Jupiter the Kazh uses as a source of hydrogen fuel and, I suspect, their primary military infrastructure and shipyards," Koskinen continued.

"That suspicion being based on the fact that the fleet orbiting the Father is just as large as the fleet orbiting the Builder," Kay explained drily.

"The second gas giant—planet seven, the Sister—also has significant infrastructure but the defense fleet is much smaller," Koskinen agreed. "The planets between the Builder and the Sister—the Smith, the Warrior, and the Brother—are all terrestrial planets with varying degrees of exploitation.

"The Smith appears to have undergone magical terraforming similar to Mars," the tactical officer noted. "Even with solar mirroring and an artificial greenhouse effect, the Smith must be *freezing*, but it is habitable and inhabited by the reezh.

"At least one moon of the Father has also undergone magical terraforming, but it doesn't appear to have fully taken."

"Or it took perfectly but wasn't enough to make the place inhabitable to reezh," Tomas suggested. "Anything orbiting the Father would have... average temperatures in the mid-hundreds Celsius. Artificial installations have ways to manage that, but they're hard to implement on a planetary scale.

"You might be able to get it down to merely *inhospitable* to humans, but the reezh need it even colder and drier than we do."

"Exactly," Kay agreed. "They tried, but even magic can't change physics forever. Even so, that's two inhabited planets and two majorly built-up gas giants, with a minimum of four hundred warships across the four worlds."

"Four hundred confirmed frigate-sized or larger ships," Koskinen clarified. "Five megatons or bigger. Anything smaller is just background heat at this distance—and there is enough of that to suggest significant numbers of ships equivalent to RMN destroyers."

"More capital ships than the RMN has *ships*, basically," Kay concluded. "This, my friends, is why we have done everything we have done."

"I suppose the question is whether we know enough already to go back," Chaudhary asked. "We know... enough, don't we?"

Enough to help the Protectorate but not enough to buy them clemency. Kay wasn't going to say that out loud, though he suspected all of his key people were thinking it.

"We need to prove to the Protectorate that the reezh are not only a threat but are *coming*," he told them all. "We know, from all we have seen, all we have learned, that the Kazh are behind Project Olympus and are merely waiting for the right moment to *harvest* humanity to fuel their own damn war.

"But we all know the Mountain won't accept that. Even if the *Queen* does, the bureaucracy and government won't. Not without hard proof. We need to learn the full extent of the threat. If possible, we need to use what we've learned of their computers to hack their system remotely."

He gave O'Shea a hopeful look.

"It is..." She paused carefully. "It is possible we will be able to access their system datanet infrastructure. I would not expect to be able to breach their government or military computers, but generally available information should be accessible."

"That may be enough," he said. "Either way, our first test is as much of our invisibility as anything else."

Kay smiled grimly.

"We're all agreed, I think, that the laws of physics still apply to these bastards. So, we'll sit at a distance under our best stealth and see if they see us. Either way, we'll have plenty of time to get clear.

"And we will learn the things they don't want humanity to know along the way!"

CHAPTER 37

THE CRUISER'S BRIDGE was very, *very* quiet.

It was a meaningless silence by any measure. Just the video link to the main engineering control center consumed more energy and produced more heat than any sound or single action anyone on the bridge could take.

Sound, after all, didn't carry in space. Sound wouldn't betray them to the enemy whose *extraordinarily* heavily fortified home system Kay and his people had just entered.

Heat was the issue. Even a full light-minute above the ecliptic and well away from any of the inhabited planets, Kay knew that the Nine would have sensors that could pick up *Rose* from the background chill of the universe.

Three Kelvin. Barely above the absolute zero of the universe, shaped by the near-complete lack of *anything* in space.

Rose could capture over ninety-nine percent of the heat she produced and dump it into short-term heat sinks, but even with that, she was far warmer than the rest of the empty void around her. And those heat sinks could only hold a few hours of *gentle* operations' worth of heat before they needed to be vented.

They could directionally radiate heat away from the ship, limiting the zone that could see them to a roughly twenty-five-degree by twenty-five-degree cone, but even that had limited effectiveness.

Technology could make *Rose* hard to see. Someone who wasn't *looking* for her would almost certainly ping her as a sensor ghost at worst, or even completely pass her over. But even the best technology available to the Royal Martian Navy couldn't make a ship invisible.

For that, they needed magic and a starship-scale amplifier. Fortunately for Kay and his people, they had both. At that moment, Tomas's magic wrapped the cruiser in a veil of power that would render *any* technological vision of her impossible.

But physics was physics, which meant that the lower the ship's external temperature, the easier it was to tell the universe it wasn't there. So, all of the technological systems were online, buying them time.

"We've confirmed the presence of the four major fleet positions we'd identified before," Koskinen reported. "Our estimate on lighter ships appears to be bang-on. My people are arguing xenosophistry as they work, but the basics are this:

"They're running five classes of ships. Numbers ratio one to one-point-five all the way down. Mass ratio... varies. Biggest ships appear to be around seventy megatons. Smallest are a megaton. Each fleet appears to be anchored on sixteen of the big bastards."

He paused for a moment, then shrugged.

"We lowballed the numbers by about ten percent in our estimate," he admitted. "So, with the one-megatonners, three hundred–ish for each of the two big fleets. Two smaller fleets appear to be exactly *half* of the big ones.

"There's about another 'fleet's' worth of the three smaller sizes scattered around the system, including playing escort to the big asteroid monitors."

Kay nodded grimly. A thousand starships—twelve hundred, in fact, if Koskinen's "about another fleet" of the lesser ships was accurate.

Each of those fleets could probably take on the entire Royal Martian Navy. They had done horrific things to prepare Mars for war, and they hadn't even come *close* to the reality of the enemy in front of them.

"Any analysis yet on their armament?" he asked. "O'Shea? Assessment of their tech?"

"Their big ships aren't moving," the engineer pointed out. "We've got eyes on a bunch of the one-megaton ships moving, and it looks like a bloody *Republic* fleet.

"If, of course, the Republic's fusion rockets were twice as efficient as Mars has."

It took Kay a few seconds to parse that. The Royal Martian Navy, with access to Transmuter Mages and an effectively infinite supply of antimatter, used antimatter engines exclusively. The Republic, with a far more limited supply of antimatter, had built fusion engines capable of an antimatter-fed "boost" mode for their capital ships.

Their missiles had used antimatter drives, though. The RIN had just prioritized their antimatter supply—and they already knew perfectly well that the reezh had a *lot* of antimatter.

They'd used it to end worlds, after all.

"So, they're, what, using less reaction mass to achieve the same thrust?" he asked.

"More energized reaction mass with less waste heat, so... both less reaction mass *and* more efficient energy use in expelling that mass," O'Shea told him. "Antimatter is a sufficiently more-energy-dense fuel that *Rose's* engines could dance rings around them, but, well... the limitation on our maneuverability is magic and the squishy bits, not our engines."

The *squishy bits*, of course, being *Rose's* crew. Engineers were... not normally Kay's favorite people.

"Okay. We know they have better fusion thrusters. Presumably fusion reactors, too. Anything else we have enough details on to be worth noting?" He hesitated for a moment, glancing over to where Tomas was hanging on to the simulacrum to sustain the cloak of invisibility over their ship.

"Any sign of the planetary amplifier?"

"It's almost certainly on the Builder," Koskinen told him. "But you knew that. There isn't anything that's going to show up on our scanners to mark it out."

"We're nineteen light-minutes from the Builder," Kay murmured. "That gives us some leeway, even if things are going sideways. Any sign the fleet at the Smith has seen us?"

The Smith looked less populated than the Builder, but the estimates on his displays weren't promising. Seven to eight billion on the Smith. *Twice that* on the Builder.

The Solar System had about twelve billion human beings, total. The population and industrial level of the Nine put humanity's home to shame.

"Well, their belt certainly looks... interesting," O'Shea said. "Take a look here and here."

Two sections of the asteroid belt, hundreds of millions of kilometers farther out from the star, were highlighted, and Kay zoomed in on them. They looked... spotty. The asteroids he could see looked odd and the patterns were all wrong.

"What am I looking at, Chief?" Kay asked.

"Slag," O'Shea replied. "That's what's *left* after you process an asteroid for useful metals. And those are entire *clusters* of slag rock, billions of tons' worth. An asteroid belt is an immense amount of resources, but I would take bets that they've melted down anything *easy* to process.

"They've been doing high-intensity resource extraction on this system for a thousand years. All of this industry is being fed from *somewhere*, but I don't think it's the asteroid belt in the Nine."

"Some of it is being extracted from the Warrior and the Brother, plus the moons of the Father and the Sister," Koskinen said. "That's why there are warships throughout the system. They're trying to protect *everything* here."

"They're prepared for raids," Kay guessed. "They have several layers of fleets and magic to stand off a major attack, but small raids on resource-extraction facilities and materials convoys are probably an ongoing risk."

"Also, there are almost certainly out-system resource-extraction sites," O'Shea told him. "We don't have the names of the surrounding systems, but only eleven of them were the Primes. There are other star systems within a dozen jumps. Big-enough ships could move a lot of resources even with limited jump capability."

Kay nodded silently, his eyes still on the displays as the analysis team dropped more information on the display. The industrial complexes above the Father and the Builder were the largest—much as Jupiter and Earth were the main focuses of industry in Sol, even with the political and magical importance of Mars.

The vast majority of the nonmilitary ships they were seeing had to be sublight, restricted to this system—but then, from what he understood of the nature of the Kazh and the Nine, they wouldn't have many places for people to *go*.

Some of the Primes were probably aligned with the Kazh still, but that wasn't guaranteed. It was entirely possible that the whole mess had disintegrated into an eleven-way standoff, with *no* functioning alliances.

Yet, through all of this, the evidence he had was that the central reezh government *had* to know what had been done on Mars.

"Are any of the fleets positioned as if they're preparing for offensive operations?" he asked. The only hope he could see for humanity at this point was that the Kazh wasn't keeping up to date on developments in the Protectorate and wasn't planning on moving just yet.

They had a timeline in mind, he supposed. The more information Nemesis found, the better off the Protectorate would be.

"Not currently," Koskinen said after a few moments of analysis. "They seem to be anchored on eight-ship squadrons of dreadnoughts. Two squadrons above the Builder and the Father, one squadron apiece above the Smith and the Sister.

"With attendant escorts, as noted. Still... all of those forces are quite close to their gravity anchors. Those are defensive positions—but I'm not seeing anything suggesting they *couldn't* move out without an—"

The universe tore.

One moment, Kay was listening to his ex-Navy tactical officer's analysis of the disposition of the enemy fleets, all of them confident in their cloak of invisibility.

The next, both of them were on their knees as nausea ripped through them. The sounds of vomit and distress filled the bridge for long enough that it took Kay multiple seconds to understand just what had happened.

Rose was no longer in deep space above the ecliptic plane, well away from the eyes and guns of the reezh and their defenders. They'd been spotted. They'd been marked.

And then they'd been teleported into high orbit of the Builder, under the guns of sixteen reezh dreadnoughts—with at least *fifty* escorts between them and the Builder in case they decided to take the planet out in a sui-cidal blaze of glory.

Kay had no idea how their stealth had failed. He wasn't even sure how they'd been moved to their new location—though he knew the planetary amplifier had to be involved.

That was how his predecessor as the leader of Nemesis had died, after all. Teleported into a trap by the Mage-Queen of Mars, seated upon her throne and wielding the full power of the Olympus Mons Amplifier.

Now the reezh had turned their own amplifier on him and pulled him into the same kind of trap.

"We're surrounded," Koskinen shouted. "Why aren't they *firing?*"

"I don't care—*shoot them!*" Kay bellowed—but the answer to Koskinen's question was clear a moment later, as a swarm of dozens of white-painted shuttles lit up their engines and suddenly became *very* obvious.

He shoved Tomas out of the way, the Ship's Mage gasping in shock as she fell to the floor. Kay's hands slapped onto the simulacrum in the same place Tomas's had been, and he funneled power.

Each of the dreadnoughts outmassed *Rose* five to one—and they were merely the *largest* of the reezh order of battle. Even the lesser ships mostly outmassed the fifteen-megaton cruiser—but they had committed the car-dinal sin of fighting the Royal Martian Navy.

They were inside the reach of *Rose's* amplifier.

The shuttles were the immediate threat, and Kay reached out to wipe them away. Destroying a flotilla of shuttles was more complicated than attacking a ship, but the power needed for each craft was smaller, and he leaned in to the spells he'd learned with certainty.

Only for them to do nothing. Kay stared at the void around him, half seeing the simulacrum chamber displays with his own eyes and half per-ceiving the space around *Rose* through his magic.

He'd unleashed magic that should have wiped the boarding flotilla from the universe, only for it to be smothered before it had reached its targets. His magic was *there*; he'd channeled energy and released it, only for it to be... erased.

By the amplifier.

He'd assumed that the reezh using their amplifiers were more limited than the Rune Wrights using the amplifier on Mars. *Now* he realized he'd got it the wrong way around.

There was only one way out. He channeled magic differently, summoning the standard emergency jump spell. Six light-months straight forward wasn't going to get him anywhere except *not here*—but *not here* was where he needed to be.

Except that the jump spell was smothered before he even completed it. A stronger magic settled over the entirety of *Rose*, a stifling blanket of power that held the ship physically in place and muffled the amplifier.

The ship's amplifier was *useless* in the presence of a *planetary* amplifier. Kay's attempt to summon magical power alongside the blaze of energy from *Rose's* lasers failed again, and he released the amplifier, turning his gaze to the video link to the bridge.

He could already tell that Koskinen wasn't going to stop the boarding shuttles. They were fast and maneuverable ships, with comparable accelerations to their Martian counterparts but even *more* maneuverability—backed by decoys and jammers unlike anything they'd ever seen.

Kay looked Kamilla O'Shea in the eyes through their video link and *knew* the order he needed to give... and for the first time in his life, knew he couldn't give it.

Not because it wouldn't serve Mars.

Not because it would kill him.

But because it would kill *her*.

"Kamilla," he whispered. The chaos of the bridge, the snapped orders as the RFLAMs and battle lasers crashed out uselessly. All of it was secondary. Unimportant.

"Kay."

"I need... We need..." He stopped. He couldn't say it. He saw the understanding grow in her eyes—not just of what she needed to do but of *why* he couldn't say it.

"I'm sorry." His words hung. There should have been a silence to hold them, but instead there was a cacophony of alarms. "The reactor is... *humanity's* only hope."

"I know. I lo—"

Her words were cut off by a wide-bladed sword erupting from her chest—and so was any chance she could overload the reactor core.

Kay stared in horror as Kamilla O'Shea fell, barely registering the dozen white-armored reezh who had just *teleported* aboard his ship as they massacred the rest of the Engineering crew.

Rose had self-destruct charges, but Kay and his people didn't have the codes to arm them. Overloading the core had been their only chance of vaporizing the ship before the reezh took it.

Kay had no illusions about the commandos' ability to *stop* the hundreds of armored soldiers now tearing through the cruiser's hull.

CHAPTER 38

"SKIPPER, A MOMENT OF YOUR TIME?"

Roslyn looked up at Leavitt's words. They were coming up quickly on the last jump before things got *really* interesting. Their next jump would put them exactly one light-year from the Nine, allowing them to use the Star Mirror to see if they could find *Rose.*

"Of course, Commander," she told her Tactical Officer. She minimized the scan data she was looking at—the assessment of the Primes made for depressing reading when one wasn't sure if they were friend or foe, after all—and turned to face her subordinate.

She realized he wasn't alone. A step to the right and behind, failing to hide behind the Slavic Tactical Officer, was Senior Chief Vasiliauskas. Vasiliauskas looked a lot better than she had when Roslyn had seen her in the infirmary bed, though there was a haunted look to her eyes that Roslyn recognized.

For all that it had been hundreds of years before, the Kazh's Burning of Worlds had left its mark on the psyches and souls of Roslyn's people.

"Chief, Commander. What's up?" Roslyn asked.

"The Chief had an idea I thought you should hear," Leavitt said, showing no sign of the fact that Vasiliauskas had cold-cocked him unconscious not that long past.

Vasiliauskas was *definitely* aware of that and looked like she wanted to sink into the deck plating rather than answer questions.

"Well, Chief?" Roslyn prodded gently. If Leavitt had brought Vasiliauskas to speak to the Captain, he both thought the information was critical *and* that it might help rehabilitate the noncom for the incident that had officially never happened.

"I don't know as much about the Star Mirror as I'd like, sir," the Chief said slowly. "But I *do* know our new stealth doctrine. And... well, *Rose's* crew were *ours* once, right? That's the one useful piece of dealing with traitors?"

"We don't know if any of them were Navy, but it seems highly likely," Roslyn confirmed. "What are you thinking, Chief?"

"They'll follow the same doctrine and logic we would," Vasiliauskas said. "And... they don't know the Star Mirror exists. So, they'll put their ship above the ecliptic, with their directional heat radiation going even farther from the ecliptic.

"So, if we can position the Star Mirror above the star, looking 'down' into the system, *we'll* be able to spot *Rose* even while they're hiding from the locals."

Roslyn considered the concept in silence for a moment. It wasn't a bad plan at all, but...

"Your thoughts, Commander?" she addressed Leavitt.

"So far as I know, the Star Mirror is basically giving us a window that's *exactly* one light-year ahead of us, aligned with the spine of the ship," the Tactical Officer admitted. "So, while the Chief's idea is, in my opinion, brilliant... it would require significant adjustments to our last pre-Nine jump."

"That's my assessment as well," Roslyn agreed, then turned her best Captain's Smile on Chief Vasiliauskas. "Including, I should note, that the idea is brilliant. As I understand it, there has been an average of *two* Star Mirrors at a time aboard RMN warships over the last thirty years. They are normally only present aboard warships that serve as the support vessels for Her Majesty's Hands."

The strange part was that, so far as Roslyn knew, there had never been a *plan* to give her a Rune of Power—making her a strange not-quite-Hand—but *Thorn* had always been intended to have a Mirror under her command.

"The advantage of that is that even if Nemesis knows the Star Mirrors exist, they have no reason to believe we have one. The disadvantage is that we are barely beginning to feel out the best uses of the system.

"So, as Commander Leavitt has noted, the Star Mirror is currently in a very fixed orientation. That's because any adjustment to the orientation beyond a brute-force rotation of the Mirror itself requires careful work by... well, me."

She wasn't a Rune Wright, but she'd been given the briefing on how to manage orienting the Mirror. There were only so many changes a non–Rune Wright *could* make, but she knew how to do that.

"So, I will need to take a few minutes with Mage-Commander Tod and then spend some time in a secure sensor chamber... but yes, we can arrange to put the Star Mirror above the ecliptic."

Roslyn's smile widened.

"And my assessment of our doctrine agrees with you, Chief. That *will* allow us to see *Rose* even while she's hiding from the reezh. An important note—and one we'll want to pass back to the High Command.

"Putting some sensor platforms above and below the ecliptic may help us counter the risk of stealth technology falling into hostile hands!"

The Star Mirror did not, if Roslyn was being honest, look much like a mirror. It consisted of a two-meter-wide square of glass—glass that, in its current form, looked like a window into open space—surrounded by a fifty-centimeter steel panel inlaid with extremely precise silver carvings.

Only about half of those carvings even *resembled* the runes of the standard Martian Runic script Roslyn had learned to work with. The rest were the art of a Rune Wright, a complex and unfollowable pattern drawn along the exact courses of magic rather than a language *almost* matched to the energy's course.

Even knowing exactly what she was looking at, though, Roslyn had a moment of panic when she saw the core mirror. Years of training sent her looking for an emergency seal patch before self-control re-exerted itself, and she shook her head at her own reactions.

She'd entered the secured chamber—concealed in the water-storage tanks for the officer quarters—three times before. Neither the Star Mirror nor the sensor cluster aimed at it required much in terms of maintenance.

The Mirror needed recharging like any runic construct, though it took very little energy, considering its power. Roslyn hadn't changed its settings or arrangements since locking it in at, as Leavitt had noted, one light-year ahead of the ship's bow.

Now, though... adjusting the jump would get them to a better position, but they'd need to angle the Mirror itself to get the angles and view they needed.

She needed to change *that* piece of the framing. Slide this—easily movable!—set of runes to link in to a different piece of the matrix. A control on the side of the device allowed her to rotate the entire construct—including the sensor cluster, thankfully—so that it was pointing at almost ninety degrees from *Thorn's* keel.

By the time she felt the jump ripple around her, her work was almost done. A few last adjustments, and the Star Mirror, instead of creating a window a light-year away and pointing straight ahead, was creating a window a light-year away about fifteen degrees above the line of *Thorn's* keel that was pointed "down" toward the same line.

And if Tod had managed the jump as planned...

Roslyn tapped her wrist-comp.

"Bridge, Captain Chambers. How's the Mirror looking?"

"We're still resolving, but we appear to have a view point roughly three light-minutes up and out from the star, looking down on the Nine," Leavitt told her. "It's... a damn busy system. We'll need some time to build enough of a background to be sure we pick up *Rose*."

He paused.

"Do you think we made it into position ahead of her?" he asked softly.

"We don't know how long it took them to translate the data," Roslyn replied. "Time is almost certainly *not* our friend, but do you see any sign that the Kazh is stirred up?"

"Beyond the system looking like their fleet deployments were put together by a professional paranoid? Not yet. There's a *lot* going on, though. Just nothing that looks like a firefight."

"All right. I'll be back on the bridge in a few. Don't turn Mage-Ensign Jain's hair white before I get there, please."

With everything going on, Roslyn was making sure there was a Mage who could jump the ship on the bridge at all times. *She* was probably recovered from her last jump, but Jain was next up on the rotation.

And was a good kid. Even if said "kid" wasn't as much younger than the cruiser's Captain as said Captain would *prefer*.

Roslyn didn't make it back to the bridge before everything went to hell. While she'd been authorized to reveal the Star Mirror to her crew—and had promptly proceeded to do so once they were in deep space—the installation *had* been intended for concealment, which meant it wasn't convenient to the bridge.

She was about halfway back before her wrist-comp lit up with a priority alert, and she slammed the Accept key.

"Chambers. Report!"

"We picked up *Rose*," Leavitt told her in clipped tones. "Except we picked up *Rose* in two places. We've got her hiding above the ecliptic *and* we have her in orbit of the Builder."

"Wait. That's..." Roslyn froze mid-step as her brain overtook her words. She'd read the full Tartarus File, including the notes on using the Olympus Mons Amplifier to teleport ships around the star system—and Kiera had *warned* her that the Amplifier could breach the stealth ship's invisibility.

"The reezh grabbed her with the amplifier and dumped her into the Builder's orbit," Roslyn told Leavitt. "She'll vanish from her hiding spot in a couple of minutes, because she *is* in orbit of the Builder."

And they were out of time. Without access to the full displays, she couldn't see how far away *Rose* had been from their window in the Nine.

But she *did* know that their window was about six light-minutes from the Builder.

Six minutes before, Nemesis had been seized by the Kazh. Roslyn didn't necessarily *want* to declare the Kazh the enemy, but she doubted that Kay and his people were going to just *surrender* to the aliens.

And she wasn't on the bridge.

"Take the ship to battle stations," she ordered. "Have Jain calculate a jump into Builder orbit and lay in a firing plan. I'll be there ASAP—but when we jump, you need to be ready to destroy *Rose.*

"*Completely*, Lieutenant Commander. We need to vaporize that ship and then get the hell out of the Nine!"

CHAPTER 39

SIX MINUTES WAS enough time for the universe to change—and everything Roslyn was seeing was six minutes out of date.

To narrow the time gap, she'd have needed to keep manipulating the Star Mirror while coordinating with Leavitt's team... and they didn't have *time* for that.

Not when assault shuttles had been swarming *Rose* six minutes before.

Thorn's scans were still showing two copies of the other cruiser when Roslyn arrived on the bridge, and the general quarters alarm faded into silence behind her. She made an effort to appear composed as she swiftly took her seat, exchanging a nod with Mage-Ensign Jain before she turned her attention to Leavitt.

"Ready, Commander?" she asked.

"All missile launchers are armed and loaded. All laser capacitors are fully charged. We are ready," Leavitt reported.

"XO?" Roslyn asked, the link to CIC coming alive as she spoke.

"Engines are green. Armor is green. DamCon teams are moving to position, and all hands are in combat positions," Beck ran through the list at speed. "I wouldn't mind another ten minutes to clear for action, but I'm looking at the same scan data you are.

"*Thorn* is ready for combat, Captain!"

"Good." The question now was *could they get into combat*, and Roslyn turned to the young woman seated at the simulacrum running through her calculations.

"Mage-Ensign Jain?" she said softly. She didn't even ask the question. *Everyone* knew the question, including the most junior officer on the bridge. The cycle meant that there were *two* Mages aboard the ship who could safely jump—Jain and Roslyn herself.

And they couldn't afford for Roslyn to be disabled when they were jumping into combat.

"I'm ready, sir. On your order."

The tremor in the Mage-Ensign's voice took a great deal away from the certainty of her words, but Roslyn had been supervising her fledgling officers, Mages and non-Mages alike, since leaving Tau Ceti.

She brought up Jain's calculations anyway. She needed to both trust the Ensign and be *seen* to trust the Ensign, but even *Jain* needed her to review *this* jump.

Almost exactly a light-year. Angle and energy levels adjusted for the impact of jumping directly into orbit. They would emerge fifty thousand kilometers from *Rose*'s position as of six minutes earlier.

Roslyn suspected there were a dozen places she could improve Jain's calculations if she took the time... but there *was* no time and the Ensign's calculations would *work*.

Nothing else was important.

"All hands, stand by for jump," Roslyn declared, then leveled her most supportive-yet-commanding gaze on Mage-Ensign Leela Jain.

"Jump the ship, Ensign."

The jump was utterly anticlimactic. Jain focused her energy into the amplifier, and then *Thorn* was there, tearing through reality with a *pop* only barely perceptible to human senses.

The *arrival* was anything but. From the explosion of energy across the forward armor, Roslyn judged they'd arrived occupying the *same space* as one of the shuttles swarming *Rose*.

"Locate that impact," she barked as an alert flashed across the display. "Alert Marines to possible boarders! Commander Leavitt!"

"Establishing target lock; multiple contacts in close," the tactical officer barked. "As we all knew, there's a goddamn *fleet* around us! *Rose* at forty thousand kilometers and closing!"

They'd carried more velocity through the jump than Roslyn had expected. While they had *appeared* to be motionless in deep space, they'd unavoidably been moving relative to the star system.

And that was the velocity Jain had forgotten. The piece of the calculation Roslyn might have done differently—but at that moment, a hundred-plus kilometers per second of velocity toward *Rose* was useful.

"Lock established. Missiles away. Beams firing!"

Rose was doing neither of those. Whatever fight the Nemesis crew had in them was long gone. The cruiser was in the hands of the enemy—and a hundred antimatter-tipped missiles blazed out to give her and her people the only mercy Roslyn could provide now.

"Captain, multiple shuttles are on courses *away* from *Rose*," Beck warned from CIC. "Flagging them in the system."

"Leavitt. Take them out," Roslyn ordered. There were a hundred arguments that destroying *Rose* was a hot-pursuit situation, an action that was *hostile* but not *an act of war*.

Firing on those assault shuttles was an act of war. It wasn't a distinction that was going to matter much—except perhaps at Roslyn's court-martial.

"Evasive maneuvers," she ordered the helm. "We have surprise, but they are going to start—"

The screens around them darkened as automatic eye-protection systems engaged. Multiple torrents of energy—not lasers, something more *physical*—crashed through space around *Thorn*, missing only because Lieutenant Kinley had started maneuvering somewhere around the *v* in *evasive maneuvers*. Possibly before.

"I don't know what those are, but *do not* let them hit us," Roslyn ordered. She finally completed her movement to take over the simulacrum from Jain, sliding her runed hands into their places.

Fire filled the skies around *Thorn*, far closer to any planet than Roslyn could possibly be comfortable. A solid echelon of smaller warships blocked the two human warships from firing on the Builder, and at least two dozen ships—the smallest twice the size of *Thorn!*—were close in to the seemingly captured Martian ship.

But it appeared they hadn't realized *Thorn* was going to fire on her sister ship. Twenty-gigawatt battle lasers connected the two ships, aimed at data-processing cores and navigation systems rather than the reactors.

Leavitt's gunners weren't trying to kill the ship with the lasers. They were trying to make certain the reezh didn't get any information *off* the ship before the missiles arrived. For the same reason, the RFLAMs lashed out at the shuttles Beck had flagged as leaving the ship.

Roslyn didn't *want* to make official first contact between the Protectorate and the Kazh a battle, but she didn't have much choice. *Rose* had been trapped and attacked. She couldn't save the Nemesis ship if she *wanted* to, which meant she needed to destroy *Rose* and any intelligence the reezh might have acquired.

"Target destroyed."

Leavitt's softly spoken report took Roslyn a moment to process—her attention yanked away from the dozens of immense starships now turning to unleash more hell-beams in the direction of her command. Where *Rose* had rested a moment before, there was only a rapidly expanding ball of fire.

The reezh might have taken out a few missiles, but they hadn't stopped *enough* of the antimatter weapons to save the cruiser. Roslyn ground her distaste at what she'd just done underfoot and focused on the moment.

"Locals are launching missiles," Leavitt reported. "Scans suggest fusion engines, but they are burning at *ten thousand gravities.*"

The RMN was at most two generations from their *antimatter*-fueled missiles only making that level of acceleration. Fusion-drive missiles were generally a tool for private security and the cheaper system militias, rarely exceeding *four* thousand gravities of acceleration.

"We need to get out of here, sir," Beck said grimly in her ear. "Mission accomplished."

Roslyn nodded silently and focused her mind onto the amplifier. There was a moment where the bridge shifted away and the universe around her ship was as clear to her as if she was standing outside the cruiser.

The closest reezh ships were thirty thousand kilometers away, but their velocity toward *Rose* was also a velocity toward the thirty-megaton heavy warships that had been trapping the Nemesis cruiser.

The next-closest ships were the megaton-range escorts that had been in place to stop Nemesis doing anything genocidal. After *them*, though, were four seventy-megaton dreadnoughts sweeping in from a high orbit position.

Just behind those dreadnoughts was a mobile asteroid that outmassed every other ship in the situation *combined*. By an order of magnitude or so.

They weren't *all* launching missiles, she noted absently. Only the battleships between her and *Rose* had fired. With thirty-plus starships in that formation, the bigger ships didn't *need* to fire. The missiles heading *Thorn*'s way were already beyond counting.

The hellfire of their beam weapons had cooled as well—and Roslyn put together the warnings of *that* just before the alert rang out across the bridge.

"Boarders!" Beck snapped. "We have multiple intrusion situations—*teleporters*."

"Bad choice," she said aloud. "We are *gone*."

Roslyn threw her power into the simulacrum, summoning the jump spell with the ease of long practice and training. There was no careful calculation, but the escape jump didn't need it. She *knew* this magic.

And she could tell when it broke. When another magic, like a hand from on high, pressed down on hers and smothered it before it was even fully born.

"My god," she whispered. "That's why they didn't run."

"Sir? Those missiles are coming *real fucking fast*," Leavitt barked. "All turrets are free and I'm launching in defense mode, but I can't stop that."

The reezh probably could. They wouldn't have sent boarders onto *Thorn* if they couldn't—there wouldn't be enough *time* for the boarders to do anything useful if they were teleporting back out before the missiles hit.

Normally, Roslyn could lend her own power to missile defense—but against this type of fire, it was a wasted effort. She needed to get them out.

She guessed, *now*, that Kent Riley had also tried to jump out and failed. They had every reason to believe the former Marine had been trained as a Jump Mage—and even if he hadn't, the ship had Jump Mages aboard. They had tried and *failed* to escape.

Half-unconsciously, Roslyn tore her left sleeve open, shivering as the inlaid silver in her forearm was exposed to the chill of the bridge. Compared to the multiplicative effect of *Thorn*'s amplifier, the Rune of Power was a rounding error. She'd tested the combination and she *knew* it wouldn't let her jump farther.

But it would let her put more power into the same spell, to go the same distance with more... push.

"Sir? Ten seconds to impact!"

"They will abort," Roslyn told Beck softly. "And between their boarders and their guns, it doesn't matter, anyway."

She met her XO's horrified gaze for an eternity that couldn't be more than half a second, and then plunged her hands back onto the simulacrum.

Roslyn summoned every scrap of power one of the strongest scions of Tau Ceti's First Families could muster. She summoned every *fraction* of multiplicative effect that the Rune of Power Damien Montgomery had given her could unleash.

And she powered all of it into the simulacrum. *Thorn* thrummed with power around her as she channeled it into the amplifier matrix and *held* it there. She felt the incoming missiles. She *felt* the boarders inside her hull.

She felt the stifling blanket of magic laid upon her ship by the power of the amplifier on the planet below, and then she formed *all* of her power, all of that amplification and focus and strength, into an intangible blade of strength and *cut* that blanket in two.

Through the chaos of the unleashed power of their broken spell, she thought she *heard* the gasp of astonishment and strange curse words of the reezh in the Mountain of Astral Might—and it didn't matter.

The muffling lifted... for a moment... for a breath.

And then *Thorn* was gone, torn away from the trap by her Captain's will and nothing more.

Victorious... but leaving behind an awakened giant.

CHAPTER 40

EXHAUSTION HAD taken Roslyn the moment the jump was complete. When she awoke, she was in her quarters—with Baars visibly seated at the entrance to her bedroom, a shotgun visible in the steward's lap.

"Is the shotgun for me or something outside?" Roslyn croaked, surprised at how awful her voice sounded.

"Hopefully, merely for my paranoia," Baars replied. She laid the gun aside and brought Roslyn a tray with a pitcher of water and a glass. "*You*, sir, are not allowed out of bed until Dr. McConnell makes it down here."

"What?" Roslyn asked. That seemed... a touch out of line, but the sharp cracking in her voice and the pain in her throat suggested part of the reasoning.

"I wasn't on the bridge when you jumped us out," Baars said slowly. "But the description I was given was *started bleeding from one eyeball and convulsing like she was being electrocuted*. Thaumic overload, I presume?"

"That's... probably right," Roslyn agreed. Now that her steward had described the reaction, she could *feel* the soreness around her right eye. "I didn't think I'd gone... that far."

"You also have the equivalent of a nasty scald around your runes," Baars noted. "Your palms look like you put them on a heating element. I'm not quite sure *what* that Rune of Power did to you."

"Much the same," the doctor's voice said calmly. Roslyn looked up to see the main doors to her quarters close behind Anabella McConnell. "There's basically a *platoon* of Marines outside the door, so we're safe here."

"What is going *on?*" Roslyn demanded.

"That part is probably for Beck and Yang to brief you on," the Surgeon-Lieutenant said drily. "But we *did* jump out of the Nine with reezh boarders throughout the ship. The situation is controlled, but the Marines have been keeping me busy.

"Though not busy enough to not have a digital eye on the Mage-Captain. So." McConnell laid a portable medical checkup kit on the bed by Roslyn's feet. "I'm going to start with lights in your eyes, and I suspect that is going to suck."

McConnell did not undersell the unpleasantness of the examination. When she finally closed the kit and met Roslyn's gaze, she looked... displeased.

"Well, given the medical literature I was provided on that *thing*"—she gestured toward the Rune of Power—"I can safely assume that whatever the fuck you did either would have been impossible for a lesser Mage, killed a lesser Mage or possibly *both.*"

"I'm going for *both,*" Roslyn admitted. "I'm not sure of... a lot. I need to talk to the Mountain; I don't think anyone anywhere else is going to have the information I need."

And by *the Mountain* she meant the Mage-Queen. The Tartarus File contained everything humanity had *recorded* about the planetary amplifiers, but Roslyn suspected there were things that the Royal Family hadn't shared.

They could no longer afford that secrecy. In the face of an enemy hiding with an amplifier of their own, the Royal Martian Navy needed to know just how bad things were going to get.

"Can I get up and get dressed?" Roslyn asked the doctor drily after a moment. The advantage of having a personal steward was that she at least *knew* who had stripped her to her underwear to put her unconscious body to bed.

"Yes." McConnell considered her for a long moment. "Light duty, Mage-Captain, for at least three days. You are *off* the jump roster for a week. If I thought I could tell you to completely avoid magic for that week, I would, but I've known too many Mages like you."

Roslyn chuckled. *Some* Mages kept their abilities under wraps, pretending to be ordinary humans except when using their powers to serve a purpose. She, however, was from the Tau Ceti First Families, whose attitude was summed up by *We are empowered so that we can serve, but we're not going to not use our magic for our own convenience.*

"I will refrain from grand acts of power for a few days," she promised. "At least until my face stops hurting."

"Pay attention to your right arm and your hands," McConnell warned. "I *have* read the literature on what Montgomery did to himself, and you were closer to it than you think. Your palms and forearm have been sprayed with a sealant that contains a painkiller. It will wear off. Baars has more."

"Thank you, Doctor," Roslyn told McConnell. "Should you be checking on the Marines?"

"Given that Yang is waiting outside the door for you to get dressed so he can report, I think we might be okay," Baars told her. "I presumed you'd rather the Major not see you undressed. Your physique is... Well, frankly it distracts many straight men, and you have work to do."

Roslyn, who was well aware of the benefits and distractions of her *physique*—and that said effect wasn't limited to *straight men*, either—just shook her head at her steward.

"You have a uniform ready, I presume?"

Yang was in full combat gear, his exosuited form looming ominously in the living room of Roslyn's quarters. He'd at least taken the helmet off, making it easier for him to salute her.

She returned the gesture and then chuckled tiredly as she studied her room.

"I'd ask you to sit, but I think the armor would break my couch," she told her Marine CO. "What's our status?"

"Six boarding teams, each of eight reezh, teleported aboard the ship prior to our escape," Yang told her. "We can now, with some certainty, say that they were made up of four-reezh teams anchored on a single Mage per team.

"All have been neutralized." He paused. "We have seven prisoners, all wounded. The rest were killed. We took eleven fatal casualties and twenty-two wounded ourselves."

Roslyn winced. She'd hoped that she'd managed to get everyone out, but as soon as she'd known there were boarders...

"There may be one or two boarders still loose on the ship," Yang warned. "We're isolating sections with the ship's scanners and the Marine counter-boarding parties and securing deck by deck. All critical systems are secure, but I want to be sure there are no stragglers."

Forty-one reezh had died *aboard her ship*. Let alone however many had died aboard *Rose* or the shuttles they'd destroyed to hopefully keep intelligence on humanity out of the reezh's hands.

"Unfortunately, the presence of teleporting boarders means they may have succeeded in getting information off of *Rose*," Roslyn told Yang. "That's a problem, but not one we can do anything about now.

"Is the ship secure enough for me to get to the bridge?"

McConnell cleared her throat.

"I am not on the jump rotation," Roslyn assured the doctor. "But I do still command this ship."

"Of course, sir."

For a woman barely out of med school and holding the lowest rank a full doctor *could* hold in the RMN, McConnell managed to get a great deal of authority and condescension into three words.

It must be part of the training.

"Baars—have Kovalyow and Beck meet me on the bridge," Roslyn told her steward. "The situation may be under control, but that doesn't mean we don't have work to do."

The bridge was a tense quiet as Roslyn walked into it. The ship was still at readiness one, barely half a step down from full battle stations, and with the potential for infiltrators still being active, Roslyn wasn't *expecting* a scene of calm and relaxation.

Matthias Beck was in the command chair and rose as she came in, saluting her crisply. Mage-Ensign Sigourney held down the simulacrum next to him and made it about halfway out of her seat before Roslyn waved the young woman back down.

"At ease, everyone; we have better things to do right now than jump to attention," she told them.

Beck remained standing as she crossed the room to stand next to him.

"Leavitt and Kovalyow are on their way up," she murmured to him. "Good call on sending Leavitt to rest."

"I wasn't expecting to end up so suddenly in command," Beck told her. "I had a direct video link to you, in case you forgot."

"And?" Roslyn said, as cheerfully as she could.

"Please. Don't ever do that again," the XO said very quietly, shaking his head. "I might even stop poking you about shooting me if you promise not to... well..."

"Bleed from one eye and convulse like I'm electrocuted?" she asked.

From the way he physically *winced* at the description, McConnell had been understating just how terrifying that had been for the bridge crew. Roslyn suddenly suspected the only reason she'd woken up in *her* bed instead of sickbay had been due to the active combat operation *on the ship*.

"What did I miss?" she asked her XO.

"You got us about six light-months out of the Nine," Beck told her. "No one else on the damn ship could jump at that point, so we had a *very* uncomfortable forty-five minutes, with a firefight mostly around Engineering, until Mage-Lieutenant Tolliver could get in here and move us another light-year.

"You were out for four hours," he observed. "Thanks to Mage-Commander Tod organizing the kids"—to Roslyn's amusement, Mage-Ensign Sigourney didn't even *object* to the description of the five Ensigns and Lieutenants making up the junior Jump Mages as *the kids*—we managed to jump three more times.

"We are now four and a half light-years from the Nine in what, so far as I can tell, is a completely random direction," the XO concluded. "Unless they have Trackers, we're fine."

"And even if they have Trackers, I arranged for us to leave behind timed charges," Tracker-Commander Uesugi interrupted, joining them at the command seat. "We have swept the last three jumps with antimatter explosions. It will buy us time, if nothing else."

"Let's keep doing that," Roslyn ordered. "We're down a Jump Mage for now—after getting us out of the Nine, McConnell has taken me off the jump roster."

"What *happened*?" Beck asked.

"Waiting on—"

"We're here," Kovalyow told her, the Master Chief seeming to materialize out of nowhere, with Leavitt and Tod in tow.

The senior Ship's Mage looked like the Chief had literally pulled her from her bed and not even given her time to find a hairbrush.

"Commanders, Chief," Roslyn greeted them all. The space around the command seat was getting crowded, but she needed to be seen.

"The Kazh, as expected, had a planetary amplifier on the Builder. It turns out that you can use one of those to stop a ship jumping," she explained swiftly. That had *not* been in the Tartarus File and she hadn't considered the possibility. An error that had very nearly killed them all.

"Hence *Rose* still being there despite being yanked into orbit by the amplifier," Leavitt said grimly. "I'd wondered. Not that I really had much *time* to consider the situation."

"No. Our visit to the Nine was very short and very busy," Roslyn agreed. "It took all of my power, augmented by the Rune Prince-Chancellor Montgomery gave me to help retake *Thorn*, to breach their nullification long enough to jump."

"Which turned out to be more than a merely human body could handle," Mage-Commander Tod said grimly. "I don't see a way to stack Mages for that stunt, but I don't think having one Mage both break the barrier and jump was a good plan, sir."

"Good or not, it's the only plan. There are less than two dozen Runes of Power in the entire Protectorate," Roslyn pointed out. "We need to find an answer to a planetary amplifier that doesn't leave a Rune-equipped Mage wrecked."

"Don't go near it?" Leavitt suggested.

"That's my first choice," Roslyn agreed. "We cannot, however, assume they didn't get anything off of *Rose*. We need to report in, and we need to get back to friendly territory."

"I have the kids in order," Tod promised. "Even without you, we're jumping twenty-four times a day. Where do you want us to go?"

"Chimera," she said flatly. "Whatever else they learn from *Rose*, they know where Chimera is, and they know it had their people in it. If they investigate, they'll find the Dual Republics, and the Dual Republics can lead them to the Protectorate."

There was a long silence before anyone spoke.

"I looked at the scans and positions," Leavitt finally said. "There wasn't anything in the Nine that was prepared for offensive operations. Any of their fleets *could* be moved to offensive ops, depending on how many Jump Mages or Prometheus-equivalents they have, but those formations were defensive.

"They were ready for war with their neighbors, not an invasion across four hundred light-years."

"They didn't know we existed," Roslyn agreed. "Whatever happened at Olympus Mons, whatever the reezh who created Project Olympus did and whoever they were, I don't think the Kazh knew about it.

"It's *possible* that one or more of the Primes knows about us, but from what the Chimerans told us, it's the Kazh—the original empire—that we need to worry about."

"And thanks to Nemesis, they now know we exist," Kovalyow said grimly. "What happens now?"

"I don't know," Roslyn admitted. "For us, we check in with High Command and we get moving back to Chimera.

"Nemesis is effectively gone now. What's left shouldn't cause any *more* trouble... but I fear they may have already caused *enough*."

CHAPTER 41

"OFFICERS AND MINISTERS, Her Majesty, Kiera Alexander, the
Mage-Queen of Mars."

The announcement made it *sound* like Kiera Alexander had just joined
a meeting where Roslyn and the other attendees were waiting. Instead, the
entire meeting had connected and interlinked everyone in the moment
before the Mage-Queen's secretary had announced her.

Roslyn was... *very* junior compared to everyone else in the virtual conference. Ministers of the Protectorate Cabinet, drawn from the Parliament
of the Protectorate, lined one "side" of the virtual table. The other side was
the Admirals and Generals of the Protectorate High Command.

Thorn's Mage-Captain was at one end of the table, facing the Mage-
Queen of Mars and the Prince-Chancellor across its length.

All of this was illusory, of course. Roslyn would be surprised if any two
members of the conference were in the same room. She *knew*, for example,
that Damien Montgomery was on Earth and Kiera Alexander was on Mars.

If nothing else, Montgomery's clearly visible sunburn suggested both
that he didn't spend enough time outside the Mountain normally and that
he'd managed to spend too much time outside recently.

"Thank you for joining Us, Mage-Captain Chambers," Alexander said
calmly, though her tone and the royal *We* made it clear that it was Roslyn's
Queen, not Roslyn's *friend*, who was speaking. "We believe you are familiar with everyone present. Please, speak up if you're not and your system
doesn't carry enough information.

"We don't believe any of us have time to spare for significant introductions."

Roslyn nodded her understanding, glancing around the room. She didn't know anyone except the Queen and Montgomery well. She'd hoped that the Crown Princess, her former boss Mage-Admiral Jane Alexander, would be present, but there was no sign of the eldest Alexander.

"If you would, Mage-Captain, please summarize the incident in the Nine as briefly as you can," Alexander ordered.

Roslyn nodded again, swallowing a breath as she considered everything.

"*Thorn* was ordered in pursuit of the cruiser *Rose* after its theft by the organization known as Nemesis," she said briskly. "We followed them to the Chimera System, where we first encountered the aliens known as the reezh.

"They are remnants of a multistellar empire that dominated that region of space up to about two hundred years ago. Nemesis *stole* the location of their original homeworld—and recognizing our shared needs, the government of Chimera gave us the same information.

"We used... classified imaging systems to survey the system at a distance and discovered that *Rose* had beaten us there by at least a few minutes, if not hours," Roslyn continued. "They were fully stealthed but we positioned our imaging to pick up on their directional heat radiation.

"We then found ourselves looking at *two* copies of *Rose* due to lightspeed delays. The reezh of the Kazh, the church that we believe still rules their old empire, possesses a planetary amplifier and used it to capture *Rose*."

Roslyn considered her next few words carefully, then mentally shrugged and sent a holographic visual along with her video feed. The Link had the bandwidth, and someone on Alexander's side swiftly turned the hologram—a not entirely artificial reconstruction from *Thorn*'s sensor data—into a visual at the center of the virtual table.

"It was very clear that the reezh were boarding *Rose* without any attempt at communication or negotiation," she warned. "Given what we knew of the Reejit—what we now know to be the Reezh Ida, the empire ruled by the Kazh in times past—my orders were to prevent major intelligence on the Protectorate from falling into potentially hostile hands.

"We jumped into orbit of the central planet and opened fire on *Rose* with antimatter missiles," she continued. The entire sequence of events had lasted less than two minutes from there, and she let it play out as she spoke.

"We were successful in destroying *Rose*," she noted. "We also engaged multiple assault shuttles that were leaving the cruiser, carrying, we believe, intelligence and prisoners taken aboard the ship."

She'd almost certainly ordered the deaths of a *lot* of humans and reezh in the last few days. But that was the ugly part of her job.

"When missiles were fired and reezh boarders teleported aboard *Thorn*, we attempted to leave the system." Recreations of the hellfire beams of the reezh warships were tearing through space around the virtual *Thorn*, and she had *no* idea how Kinley had forced the misses he had.

"We failed. The reezh used the planetary amplifier to pin us down in the system." Roslyn glanced around the table before meeting her Mage-Queen's eyes. She was *reasonably* sure everyone there was cleared to know about the Runes of Power—but Kiera's tiny headshake suggested they didn't know about *Roslyn's* Rune.

"Thanks to... additional classified equipment installed on *Thorn*, we were able to breach the jump blockade and escape the system at the price of thaumic burnout and personal injury to the jumping Mage," she concluded. No need to specify that Mage had been *her*. Alexander and Montgomery knew—and so, she knew, did the Admirals it mattered for.

"So, we are now at war with this Kazh? Because of *your* choices?" Minister San Ash was a stranger to Roslyn. She knew of the Arabic-extraction Minister for Interstellar Trade by reputation as a successful in-dustrialist, but that was all she knew about the Procyon man.

"I do not know if we are at war with the Kazh," Roslyn noted. "Certainly, at no point did the Kazh attempt to communicate with my ship or with *Rose*. Certainly, given the use of Prometheus Interface–equivalent drive systems, I am not convinced we would *want* to negotiate with the Kazh.

"The destruction of *Rose* was in line with my orders. The destruction of reezh vessels that had boarded her was an extension of those orders." She shrugged visibly. "I think we can safely say that everything *beyond* that was self-defense, yes?"

"I do not believe anyone here has any real questions around the appropriateness of Mage-Captain Chambers' actions, do we?" Mage-Admiral James Medici said calmly. The current Chair of the Protectorate High Command had commanded Seventh Fleet's cruisers when Roslyn had been Jane Alexander's flag lieutenant.

The nods that followed his firm statement relaxed much of the stress building between Roslyn's shoulder blades, and she took a careful sip of her coffee, using the familiar scent of cinnamon and cardamon to calm her nerves further.

"The question, I suppose, is what happens now," Ash said. "The numbers I have seen in the summary reports are concerning. This one system musters more ships than the entire Royal Martian Navy."

"And that is why we were aiming for the four-hundred-ship Navy," the Mage-Queen reminded her Minister. "I'll admit, I feel like just *telling us* about what they knew twenty years ago would have been more productive than what Nemesis *did* get up to.

"Now that we know, well..."

"Now we know even more," Admiral Amanda Caliver said flatly. She'd been the first Chair of the Protectorate High Command and still served as its voice on Cabinet, as Roslyn understood, though the junior officer wasn't entirely sure what Caliver's official role was beyond "member of the High Command."

"We know that there are eleven systems approximately four hundred light-years from Sol—barely three hundred light-years from the relevant borders of the Protectorate—that have been locked in a cold war with each other for almost as long as our nation has existed.

"A cold war fought, effectively, over the power of Mages and the use of Mage-*gifted* individuals as fuel for jump ships. A familiar story for us, I'm afraid."

"And, thanks to Nemesis, a not-*incidental* mirror," the Queen observed.

"I am concerned, as Minister Ash said, with the military balance," Caliver admitted. "Mage-Captain Chambers, your assessment of the reezh's military technology, please. For example, *what* was that beam they fired at you?"

"I have forwarded all of the scan data we have to BuTech," Roslyn reported. The RMN Bureau of Technology would, hopefully, be able to devise countermeasures or even duplicate the things. "They will have a more-definite analysis in the future, I hope, but my people's preliminary analysis suggests a near-cee particle cannon firing a beam of high-energy protons. It would combine both the high-energy-transfer effects of our own combat lasers with a significant kinetic impact from the relativistic velocity.

"As for the rest of their technology..." Roslyn shivered, looking at the frozen hologram in the middle of the room. "Overall, they appear to anchor much of their military technology on fusion engines and reactors significantly more advanced and efficient than our own versions. While review of the scan data suggests that the missiles fired at us carried anti-matter warheads, that is the *only* use of antimatter we detected.

"That said, their scanners, electronic-warfare systems, beam weapons, fusion systems... everything we have scan data on suggests higher levels of power and efficiency than our current-generation systems," she told them. "Between the numbers of vessels present in the Nine and their high overall average mass compared to the RMN..."

She couldn't finish the assessment.

"Mage-Captain?" Medici asked gently. He was both her current ultimate boss *and* an officer she'd worked with and liked. That was enough for her to inhale sharply and face him squarely.

"Ton for ton, I believe our apparent readier access to antimatter balances out the greater efficiency of their fusion systems," she noted. "Their weapons are more effective. The missiles they fired at *Thorn* are smaller than our own capital-ship missiles, with scans suggesting equally powerful warheads and guided by superior sensors.

"I would not want to fight a ship of theirs of comparable mass to my own," Roslyn admitted. "In a fleet action, I would say we would need a twenty-to-twenty-five percent tonnage advantage to safely regard the situation as even... and the Kazh alone clearly possess a far superior fleet to ours.

"However." She swallowed, focusing on the one sliver of hope she saw. "We *know* that the Burning of Worlds and the destruction of the Reezh Ida were in a conflict over their Prometheus-style jump drives. We *know* that maintaining their Mage populations was a struggle two hundred–plus years ago.

"It is likely—though by no means guaranteed—" she warned, "that only a portion of the ships we saw in the Builder are capable of jump travel. While they can clearly build amplifiers like Olympus Mons, I saw no evidence suggesting such amplifiers were mounted on starships.

"While we have no capacity to attack the Nine and Primes, I was not under the impression that was an acceptable course under our desired policies *anyway*."

"That may change," Kiera Alexander warned grimly. "For now, however, We must play for time and data. The more We know about the Kazh and their weapons, the more We can be ready for a true conflict.

"If possible, We would be *delighted* to negotiate with them. But Our first order of business is to get the *hell out of their way*. Admiral Medici!"

"Mage-Captain Chambers, your orders are to return to the Chimera System and stand watch there for movements by the Kazh," the Admiral told her simply.

"While you are there, you will be given plenipotentiary authority to negotiate on behalf of the Protectorate," Montgomery added. "Regardless of what any of us would *like*, Chimera is now our tripwire against the Nine and the Primes.

"A formal agreement allowing us to base ships there would serve all of us well, I think. Certainly, we are *not* sending a fleet to Chimera without their permission."

"They won't give it," Roslyn warned. "Nemesis burned any goodwill we might have had there. The trust that would have been extended to us was extended to them... and they betrayed it."

"It will fall to you to rebuild that trust, Mage-Captain Chambers," Alexander told her. "We will support you in every way We can, but even Chimera is over two hundred and fifty light-years from Sol. Everything will take time.

"But know that the Protectorate walks with you and that We have faith in you."

Roslyn nodded, swallowing back a renewed spike of fear.

"What about Nemesis?" Ash growled. "All of this was their creation... their horror."

"*Rose* was destroyed," Chambers reported. "While I don't want to dismiss the possibility that any of them were captured and removed by teleporter Mages, we *believe* we took out every shuttle leaving her as well.

"From what I understand of our cleanup operations there in the Protectorate..." She sighed.

"I believe we can finally say that Nemesis is truly dead."

CHAPTER 42

KAY WOKE UP.

For the first few seconds, he remembered nothing. Then he tried to open his eyes and couldn't. He couldn't tell just what had crusted over so he couldn't open them, but when he tried to raise his hands to wipe his eyes clean, he realized his *arms* were restrained.

So were his legs. He was chained to something, with all four limbs tightly manacled in what felt like cold steel.

Still blurry, he called up his magic—and when only a tiny spark answered before vanishing, the memories came crashing back in.

O'Shea—*Kamilla*—dying in front of his eyes, murdered even as the realization of his true feelings left him hesitating for the first time in years.

White-armored reezh had stormed the bridge only moments later, the lead assault elements boarding via magic.

He'd fought. But for the first time in a long time, he'd been emotionally compromised.

He'd fallen. A *sword*, of all things, to the head. And the next thing he knew, was waking up in darkness.

And then Kay realized it was his own blood caked over his eyes. Squinting and struggling, he managed to get the crust to crack enough for him to get a sliver of vision.

The spike of pain from the light didn't help, but he forced himself to focus. The light was dimmer than it initially felt, but the space didn't look like any hospital room he'd ever been in. More like the stone version of the inside of a termite mound, with layers of shaped—not cut—stone rising up curved walls.

A hexagonal room, he swiftly realized, without right angles. As if he'd needed more evidence to recognize that he was a prisoner of the reezh.

Someone spoke. Kay recognized neither the voice nor the language. For a moment, he was tempted to ignore the speaker—but then someone roughly took a cloth to his face, and he found himself staring up into the glint-black lower eyes of a reezh.

The alien spoke again, and he glared at them. He had seen the language on Chimera *written*, but even if this was the *same* language as the Chimeran reezh, he hadn't learned to understand it.

The reezh studied him in silence for a moment, then took the cloth roughly to his face again.

The next few seconds reminded Kay *very* thoroughly that the reezh had much tougher skin than humans. The creature produced a vessel with a straw attached and offered it to him.

Kay almost leaned forward to take a sip, but then some of the brain fog seemed to clear.

He was a prisoner of the Kazh. He could *hope* that they couldn't access *Rose*'s computers, but he knew that there was a limit to the ability of a human body and mind to withstand torture and deprivation.

There was only one way out of this, and the degree of restraint the reezh had imposed suggested *they* knew that too. The possible nurse held the vessel steadily in his face for a good thirty seconds before taking it away with a clicking noise.

As the alien walked away from him, Kay took advantage of his improved vision to survey the rest of the room. There were no windows. One door. A white-armored reezh, armed only with a sword, stood just inside that door.

Guard and nurse exchanged a conversation Kay couldn't follow, and then the nurse left. The guard stepped outside a moment later, leaving Kay alone in the room with his thoughts and his chains.

It was only then that he realized that he'd made at least one key mis-assessment. Only *three* of his limbs were restrained. He'd mirrored the sensations he felt in his right leg onto his left.

Because his *left* leg was gone. That brought another spike of memory—gunfire and magic on *Rose*'s bridge. A blow that had crushed his leg, pinning him against his command chair even as he'd continued to unleash magic.

He'd wanted to either stop them or make them kill him.

He'd failed at both.

Kay couldn't see where the phantom limb ended and the remaining flesh began, but it looked... high. His captors had saved his life, but they'd erred on the side of his life over his leg.

His magic was probably nullified by the cuffs, but he wasn't going to get them off without tools or help. And with only one leg, he wasn't getting anywhere on his own!

The return of the nurse was at least a distraction—though hardly a relief, especially not when he realized what the alien was bringing. A lot of components were different, but the basic concept of a saline drip was easy to recognize across culture and tech barriers.

He dared to hope, as the nurse roughly inserted the IV, that they'd got the ratios wrong and that the IV would kill him rather than preventing him from dying of dehydration. It... didn't feel like it, though.

Even aside from the blood and mess, Kay knew he had a head wound. He wasn't thinking clearly—not *helped* by the rest of his situation.

The reezh weren't going to let him die. He'd refuse food when they offered it, too, but he suspected they had a solution for that.

The door opened a third time, and the reezh that entered looked... strange. He knew he hadn't met all possible variations of the species, but this one had skin that was smooth, white and *gleaming* like white marble.

Over that marble-like skin they wore cloth-of-gold garments. A vaguely robe-like garment, clearly more formal than the nurse's garb, even to Kay's alien eyes.

If he hadn't guessed this was a very important alien, the four white-armored guards who followed them in would have been another clue.

The robed reezh spoke. Kay looked at them silently. He didn't understand their language, and *that* wasn't going to change.

The stranger stepped closer, focusing all four of their eyes on Kay, and spoke again.

"Fuck you," Kay hissed.

The reezh made a strange snorting sound, then stepped backward. Gesturing for their guards to follow them, they turned and left the room.

Somehow, he doubted that was the end of it. He needed to look for opportunities.

Opportunities to end his own life. Even the language barrier, he was afraid, might not prove an insurmountable obstacle for the people who'd invented the Engines of Sacred Sacrifice...

JOIN THE MAILING LIST

Love Glynn Stewart's books? Join the mailing list at:
GlynnStewart.com/mailing-list
Be the first to find out when new books are released and for special
announcements.

ABOUT THE AUTHOR

© Art and Soul Photography

GLYNN STEWART is the author of Starship's Mage, a bestselling science fiction and fantasy series where faster-than-light travel is possible–but only because of magic. His other works include science fiction series Duchy of Terra, Castle Federation and Vigilante, as well as the urban fantasy series ONSET and Changeling Blood.

Writing managed to liberate Glynn from a bleak future as an accountant. With his personality and hope for a high-tech future intact, he lives in Canada with his partner, their cats, and an unstoppable writing habit.

CREDITS

The following people were involved in making this book:
Copyeditor: Richard Shealy
Proofreader: M Parker Editing
Cover art: Roman Chalyi
Layout and typesetting: Red Cape Production, Berlin
Typo Hunter Team
Faolan's Pen Publishing team: Jack and Robin.

OTHER BOOKS
BY GLYNN STEWART

For release announcements join the mailing list
or visit GlynnStewart.com

EXILE
Exile
Refuge
Crusade
Ashen Stars: An Exile Novella

CASTLE FEDERATION
Space Carrier Avalon
Stellar Fox
Battle Group Avalon
Q-Ship Chameleon
Rimward Stars
Operation Medusa
A Question of Faith: A Castle Federation Novella

Dakotan Confederacy
Admiral's Oath
To Stand Defiant
Unbroken Faith

AETHER SPHERES
Nine Sailed Star
Void Spheres (*upcoming*)

VIGILANTE
(WITH TERRY MIXON))
Heart of Vengeance
Oath of Vengeance

**Bound By Stars: A Vigilante Series
(With Terry Mixon)**
Bound By Law
Bound by Honor
Bound by Blood

Manufactured by Amazon.ca
Bolton, ON

37371091R00201